HONOR BOUND: BOOK TWO

ANGEL PAYNE

HONOR BOUND: BOOK TWO

ANGEL PAYNE

WATERHOUSE PRESS

For Thomas...
Who makes it possible for me to fly free every day.
I love you so much.

Special love, always,
to the men and women serving our country in uniform.
You are real-life heroes and heroines.

CHAPTER ONE

A woman screamed.

Normally, that sound got the Dominant in Zeke Hayes's blood pumping in all the right ways. Into all the right body parts.

Tonight, the wail reached into his chest and gave a terrifying twist. It grabbed his legs next, hauling them into a sprint up the front walk to Rayna Chestain's Tacoma bungalow. Past his thundering heartbeat, he muttered, "Hang on, little bird. I'm here."

Little bird? Fuck. He'd given her a nickname. When had that happened? *Why* had that happened? He'd known the woman for all of three months, the last two happening via web chats and texts from over five thousand miles away thanks to a "little day job" called the First Special Forces Group.

Even if that wasn't the case, they weren't supposed to be in nickname territory. He didn't go to that domain with *any* woman.

Especially this woman.

The admission slid him to a stop. He cracked his neck, trying to knock his thoughts back into their proper peg holes. All right, Rayna was special. All right, she was different. All right, she was the first woman in years he hadn't instantly slotted into one of his three preferred categories—all-kink-no-strings, flogger wench, or horny-and-flexi rope bunny. He had no illusions about the reason why. On the night they'd met, a shithead madman had done the honors of tying Rayna up already. The bastard had left nothing to the imagination, and not in *any* of the good ways. Zeke would never forget the sight of her, head sagging and shoulders slumped, her knees bloodied by the packed dirt floor of a Quonset hut in a remote jungle. She'd accepted her fate that she'd soon be someone's new slave, a conviction that didn't disappear even when he'd gotten to her. She'd kept her wrists pressed together even after he'd cut the zip ties from them, and shook like a leaf when he'd pulled her close.

Finally, she'd gazed up at him. Tears had pooled in the dark green depths of her eyes, like he'd pulled down a star from heaven just for her. And what had *he* done? Cracked a stupid-ass grin as if she'd just done the same. It had been one of the best moments of his life.

Which still doesn't earn her a pedestal in your brain, jackass.

The second car in her driveway had a parking sticker for the courthouse, meaning whatever brother was here on guard duty had some heat and knew how to use it. That would buy him a few seconds—if Rayna was screaming at anything other than a bug or a nightmare. Goddamn, he prayed it was just a bug. He could squash the fucker, make sure all the doors were secured, and then get the hell out before said broheim made with the Ward Cleaver foot tap, waiting for him to ask if he could take her to the movies and hold her hand. He didn't do the handholding thing. Life had yanked that circuitry from his brain over twenty years ago.

Rayna needed to have her hand held. She deserved it.

Yeah, he'd be in and out. Assess the situation and then beat feet for the exfil. He'd text her tomorrow to check in.

That'd be good. Maybe they could meet for coffee sometime. Someplace public and safe, no handholding required. No mess. No nicknames.

Another shriek ripped through the air, longer and louder than the first. Z broke into a new sprint. The mist seemed to part for him as he neared the bungalow's door. The action wasn't necessary. A man yanked back the portal, clearly having heard his approach. The guy's dark auburn hair was disheveled, and his scowl fell just an inch short of meeting Zeke eye to eye, meaning he could turn himself into a six-foot-five big-brother blockade if he wanted to.

Despite that recognition, Z was in no mood to play diplomat with Trevor Chestain tonight. Yippee. He'd drawn the short straw and gotten lawyer brother tonight, along with an empty living room and an otherwise peaceful house.

"Sergeant Hayes. What a pleasure. Long time, no see."

"Trevor." He kept the tone civil as he dropped his car keys on the table inside the front door. Damn, he wished for a robber instead of the guy who rocked back on a pair of classy cowboy boots. The shoes were a weird but perfect match with his staid threads, giving Z an opening for a smartass quip, but he stayed his tongue. Rayna was proud of her brother, despite how his overprotectiveness danced on the edge of asshole. For her sake, he'd zip up the wisecracks.

Didn't matter the next moment, anyhow. Another whimper filled the air, shooting from the hallway that branched to the bedrooms.

Zeke grimaced. "She's gotten worse, hasn't she?"

"A lot worse."

"Fuck."

Trevor let him squirm through a silence thicker than the

fog outside. Finally, the guy said, "You were gone longer than she expected."

The comment fit Trev's m.o. Simple statement transformed to instant accusation. The man never left the courtroom, did he?

"Sorry about that. Next time I'm undercover in a South Pacific rogue state, I'll stroll in with a Bundt cake, tell 'em I'm on a time schedule, and ask if they can help out with a few nukes in return."

"Or you can delete my sister from your contacts list."

So much for lawyerly subtlety. Zeke spun a glance around the room, wishing a jury and judge really would spring out of nowhere. Judges came with gavels. Gavels could do serious damage to a jerk brother's head, never mind that said brother was soon going to get his way about the issue. Not that he was going to spill that nugget for the asshat.

He just had to see her one more time. Especially now. He couldn't leave when she was in torment. Not when he knew he could ease her pain and chaos. Not when he could help her, even in this little way, once again.

He crossed Rayna's living room without a backward glance at Trevor.

She cried out again as he got to her bedroom door.

He blinked for a second, letting his vision adjust to the dim room. Everything was the same as he remembered, decorated in soft shades of cream and blue, except for a small lamp on her vanity table. That was new. The bottles of medications at the lamp's base? Not so new. Zeke scowled at the containers on his way to the bed. All of them were still close to full. She wasn't sticking to her plan. No wonder she was worse.

Two more steps got him to the bed. To her side at last.

He was grateful for the excuse to let his knees give way, plummeting him to the mattress next to her. He couldn't account for why the rest of his body felt like C-4, mush with the capacity to create craters, only needing the fire in his chest to detonate.

Wait. Of course he could explain what was happening. Absence made the heart grow fonder, but when the real estate in a guy's heart was limited, fondness found a home elsewhere, like the rest of his body. Suddenly, all sixty days of their separation weighed on his muscles like bricks of the explosive—and damn if he didn't yearn for a few to go off, too. God, please, only a few. To let her get to him...just a little. To know what it was like for the simple nearness of a woman to heat his blood, to storm his senses, to flood his cock with need...

But that was impossible. He only got that rush in one way. It was a fact, plain and simple, another default setting on the Zeke Hayes rewire project. His body's explosives only got discharged by one thing.

Control.

A *hell* of a lot of control.

That was another zip code he'd filed into no-man's-land with Rayna.

Her tears pulled him back to the real reason he was here. Hell. Huge drops soaked her copper eyelashes, still closed in sleep. They flowed over her high cheekbones and across the slender plateau of her nose but never made it to the tip of her heart-shaped chin because she backhanded them away. All this, and she didn't wake up once. Zeke watched in amazement—and anger.

"You shouldn't be wiping your own tears, Ray-bird."

His whisper was only heard by the shadows. Rayna cried

out again. She flailed, fighting off an attacker only she could see. Her hand whacked the heavy oak headboard, but her nightmare had her mind trapped tight. She whimpered and thrashed the other direction.

Her arm headed toward the nightstand and the large glass of water on it. Zeke caught her wrist half an inch before it would've collided with the container and sliced up her hand. He got in a breath of relief before realizing, too late, that he'd probably just intensified the torment of her subconscious.

"Noooo!"

Sure enough, she started fighting his hold.

"Fuck," Zeke muttered. "Rayna." He jerked her hand to his chest, crushing her knuckles against his sternum. "Sshhh, bird. It's going to be—"

"You're dead! You're—you're supposed to be dead!"

He kept her hand locked to his chest as he forced in a breath. Her words, twisted with her despairing tone, painted a searing picture of what was happening behind her twitching eyelids. She was ranting about the cocksucker who'd been part of the human-trafficking network she'd run from for over a year. Once she'd been recaptured, King transferred her to Thailand and then had been ready to sell her as a sex slave without a flicker of hesitation. That was when the squad had stepped in, busting up the bastard's party to rescue Rayna, her best friend Sage, and five more American women. It had been damn satisfying to lock King away in a Bangkok prison—until they'd learned the feds had extradited King's sorry ass back *here*. Inside a day, King pulled a fucking Criss Angel on them all, his backside never seeing a second of time inside FDC SeaTac, thanks to switching places with a secret twin brother he had waiting on the back burner.

"I'm…I'm going to kill him. I need to kill him. Wh-Where's the gun? Where's the gun?"

Despite his tension, he kicked up a proud grin. The angels knew what they were doing when making her hair the color of fire. "That's it, honey," he murmured. "Fight back."

He was pretty certain where her flashback went now. King hadn't been happy to slink back into the gutter from which he'd slithered. The monster had the goddamn nerve to take Rayna and Sage again, along with Josie Hawkins, Sage's pregnant houseguest. King had gleefully enjoyed the triumph until he realized the stateside "clients" who showed up to buy his booty were actually trained Special Forces operatives. Correction. Trained and *pissed* operatives. Sage's fiancé, Garrett, was one of those men. Josie's husband, Wyatt, specially reactivated for the off-the-books mission, was the second. Zeke was the third.

Once the jig was up and the women were safe, King had been taken out—but the bullet hadn't been fired by him, Garrett, Wyatt, or any of the FBI agents stationed outside the target house. The finger on the trigger had been Rayna's.

To the day he died, he wouldn't forget that moment. Tiny redhead. Tiny blue latex fetish dress. Trembling arms. Shaking lips. Complete resolve. Total bravery. Incredible. Beautiful. She'd taken his breath away. What breath he had left, anyway. Having just taken a knife in the gut from King himself, staying conscious had required a deep tap into the determination reserves. It hadn't stopped him from dreaming about kissing her, though. Oh yeah, that would've been good. It wouldn't have been like the chaste lip brushes he'd indulged with her until then, either. He'd yearned to open her wide, filling her mouth, tasting every corner of her. Taking her fear and replacing it with his adoration.

Exactly like he longed to kiss her now.

Rayna moaned and flinched again. She kicked at the covers. Her hand wrenched in his. Z's chest felt like cracking ice. His thoughts of passion were demolished by fantasies of fury. He'd never thought of exhuming a guy just to kill him again, but putting a few more bullets in King's carcass sounded really fucking good right now.

"Ssshh." He ran his other hand gently up her other arm. She was breathing fast, gripped tight by the dream. Breaking her out of it at this point would be worse for her psyche than letting her process the memories. "Rayna, it's all over. You got the gun. You killed the bad guy. You got him, honey."

"No. He's...he's coming." She sobbed and kicked. "Bringing guards this time. Th-They've got the woman with the n-needle. Don't. Please don't. Not down there!"

Z's muscles went to sludge a second time. Relief had liquefied him the first time. Rage was the villain now. He forced his way through it, wrapping her hand tighter in his.

"Needle?" he demanded. "What needle, Rayna?"

He prayed this was some strange glitch of her nightmare and not a remembered reality. If it was, so help him God—

"Not there. Why there?" Her whole body seized. The only part of her that moved was her face, flinching and twisting with strains of horror. "Don't. Oh God. *Donnn't!*"

He pulled her up, cradling her against him. He needed to help her fight off the demons, even if they were only in her mind. "I won't let them do it." He pressed his lips to her temple. "I won't, okay?"

She whimpered and struggled against him. "Zeke!"

"Here," he assured her. "Right here, Rayna."

"Zeke!"

He frowned. She'd started to blink her eyes, but her gaze swept the room without seeing it. Shit. She was still dreaming—and pleading for *him* from that misty mental realm. His reaction was a double-edged blade. Hearing his name on her lips brought a jolt of elation. The panic in it yanked him back to earth. Painfully.

Fuck it.

"Time to wake up, Sleeping Beauty." He gave her a gentle shake. A second one, harder and longer. She flailed at him again.

"Zeke!"

"Honey, I'm *here*."

Her breath hitched in her throat. She blinked with slow confusion. Her free hand curled into his tan T-shirt. "You really are," she whispered.

Her lips parted on a slow, sweet smile. The expression fascinated him so much, Zeke wrestled with his reaction. He liked to smile, right? Then why couldn't he remember how to do it now? Why couldn't he think of *anything* to do right now?

He finally forced his mouth around one syllable. "Hi."

Her smile became a full grin. "Hi." Jolt of elation, the sequel. "How was the mission?"

Was she kidding?

He already knew the answer to that. Nope, she wasn't kidding. The question was typical Rayna, filled with concern for everyone else despite how the tears from a posttraumatic nightmare still gleamed on her cheeks. "Time of my fucking life," he cracked. He wouldn't be able to reveal anything beyond his cynical tone, so he squeezed her shoulder to indicate he was changing the subject whether she liked it or not. "You were having a pretty shitty episode, honey."

Rayna pulled her hand from his top in order to swipe her cheeks. "Yeah. Probably."

He still held her other hand. If she thought she was getting that one back, she could also think it snowed in hell. He squeezed those fingers harder. "The episodes weren't this bad before I left."

"I know."

"You were also staying on your meds before I left."

"Zeke—"

"You don't have to be on them forever, Rayna."

"I *know*, okay?"

"Apparently, you don't."

"Stop it." She tried to jerk free again. Zeke gripped her tighter. "I don't want to talk about it. About any of it."

He treated that statement like a badly hung door on a drug lord's hut and kicked it into nonexistence. "You went on about King for a while."

She sighed. "Yep. Sounds right."

Strands of her brilliant hair fell into her eyes. Zeke let her hand go so he could brush them back. Change of tactic. There were occasions for busting down doors, and there were moments made for silken ropes—especially when they came before the questions he asked next.

"Have you ever dreamed about the bastard's guards, too?"

Her shoulders wiggled in a semishrug. "Of course."

"What about them using needles on you?"

She tensed again. He'd anticipated that and made sure he had her tucked in tight, but his bird dropped a shiz of shock on his precautions, turning him inside out by grimacing through fresh tears. But one thing about her expression dug at him the most. The tremor of her chin. It said everything. That valiant, determined wobble...fighting back images that weren't dreams at all.

His gut writhed in a bath of acid. "Holy shit."

She slammed a hand on his chest. "No. Don't. Don't go 'holy shitting' me, Zeke. It's done. It's in the past. I'm leaving it there."

"Right," he countered. "And that's why you're still having screaming nightmares about it."

He watched her wrestle with that before she pushed at him again. This time, Zeke let her roll back to her pillow. A time and a place for everything—including the silence he allowed to build into uncomfortable stillness.

Rayna squirmed and huffed. Her chin didn't tremble anymore. She was too busy glowering at him. "You going to sit there and gawk at me until they ship you out again, Sergeant Hayes?"

He let her stew as he got back to his feet in one precision move. He unzipped his jacket, unlaced his boots, and then placed both on the floor near her little reading chaise. On his way back across the room, he shut the door with a quiet click. "I'm respecting your request not to talk about it."

Her eyebrows high-fived her forehead. "You are?"

"Yep."

She pushed herself up until she leaned against the headboard. "Thank you."

He joined her again on the bed. "Hmm," he finally said, stroking the top of one of her feet through a cute bootie sock. "That may be premature."

Her foot flinched. He maintained his grip on it. "Premature?" The syllables were laced with suspicion. "Why?"

Zeke carefully schooled his features before looking up

from her ankles. He'd honed the talent since the age of ten. When he was a teen on the streets, his facial wall saved his hide countless times. As a sensual and sexual Dominant, it had submissives taking numbers for sessions with him. As a Special Forces mission leader, it came in handy so many times, the team gave him a new call sign—Zsycho.

Right now, it bought him a much-needed ten seconds. He used them well. By the time he issued his reply, he'd swung all the way up on the mattress and gotten both her feet beneath his hands. He leaned closer, his jaw hovering over her knees, in order to let her see two truths in his gaze. One, for the sake of her well-being alone, he wouldn't accept her refusal again. Two, he was more than ready to back that assertion up, even if it meant waiting her out all night.

"Because you're not going to like what you'll do in place of talking, Ray-bird."

Comprehension began to shimmer against the forest depths of her eyes. Her lips pursed, and she flattened harder against the headboard. "Wh-What do you mean?"

Zeke didn't move. He kept his hands atop her feet in a gentle but firm embrace. He barely blinked as he willed her stare toward him with equal command. She curled in her arms, surely sensing what he was about to say. And dreading it. And probably hating him a little for it. Like that was going to change one word of what he ordered.

"Show me, Rayna. I need to see what they did to you."

CHAPTER TWO

Rayna didn't know whether to laugh or cry.

She would've taken the laughter option in an instant if she thought Zeke was joking about this. No way. He would have been sweating drops of pure serious—if he were sweating. Instead, every pore in *her* body erupted in flows that battled in hot and cold rushes beneath the stare of the man who occupied every inch of her vision. Her breaths escaped her in ragged increments.

She wrote off part of that effect to sheer shock. She still barely believed he was here, living and breathing, a few feet away from her. When his in-and-out mission to Korea had turned into more than that, she'd forced herself to get over it and reset her mind to expect him back well after Christmas. But his towering presence and his radiating warmth confirmed the truth. He touched only her feet, but the rays of heat from that contact spread up well past her knees. Damn, it was really him. Damn, she really couldn't see the rest of the room past him.

Damn, she was really scared.

Okay, it wasn't all him. She needed perspective when it came to Zeke Hayes. A *ton* of perspective. She'd known that from the moment he'd carried her out of King's lair in Thailand, sheltering her in his strength, making her feel safe as a sparrow cuddled by a grizzly. The mountain-sized man with the ocean-wide smile fast became her rock and her friend, clicking into place in her life as if it was always meant to be. When they'd gotten back home, he'd rescued her from King a second time, even taking the man's knife to his gut in doing so.

During Z's recovery from that episode, Rayna had gazed at him one night from his hospital bedside and realized she wanted to expand that *friend* definition. Again, so natural. Again, so right. Those thoughts picked up speed through the weeks after that—until the moment she'd learned how a man like Zeke defined *more*.

Her stomach clenched with the not-so-subtle reminder. Sage had innocently spilled the truth to her over lunch one day, throwing it into the conversation as if Rayna already knew about Zeke's not-so-secret identity. *Master Z.* Not just a lifestyle Dominant but a damn Master at it. A name in the Seattle scene, with submissives wait-listing themselves for sessions with him and standing-room-only status when he gave training sessions for other Doms. Sage's fiancé and Dom, Garrett, was going to such a lesson that week.

Rope Bondage as Foreplay.

Rope bondage? Foreplay? So they also liked playing with oxymorons at those Dominance/submission dungeons, huh?

Thanks to sipping a lot of iced tea, Rayna had cloaked her astonishment from her friend. Turned out it was easy to keep up the ruse for Zeke, too. It wasn't like she avoided the subject. She just needed the right chance, she'd assured herself. Time to find the right moment. Time to find the right words.

Time hadn't been on her side. The text had come from Zeke's CO, Captain Franzen. The orders were clear. Get his ass back to the base double-time with his gun cleaned, his pack in order, and a shitload of mosquito wipes. They were bugging out right away.

The perfect moment had never come.

Rayna admitted her relief to no one but herself. For the next two months, she pretended the lunch with Sage had never happened. Instead, she clung to the impression Zeke gave her over sporadic texts and satellite phone calls. He was always tired but stalwart, happy to make contact, promising he was thinking of her. She refused to feel anything but grateful for the connections. Guys like him didn't get the chance to call home often, and he always used his opportunities to reach out to her. Not the waiting list. *Her.*

She didn't feel like crowing in triumph anymore. Time to feel exposed as a sparrow again—only, Zeke didn't look like he wanted to be protective papa bear anymore. With his chestnut hair longer due to the deployment, his beard grown to a rough scruff, and his eyes glittering even in the dim room, he was definitely giving in to the instincts of another creature inside his psyche tonight. A creature called puma.

Hungry, assessing puma.

"Rayna Eleanor?" Both of his dark brows raised expectantly, another expression she'd never seen before tonight. "Did you hear what I said?"

A glower burned its way out before she could stop it. "Really? Five minutes in the door and you're using the middle name on me, Hayes? What the hell?"

He slipped his hands up beneath her sweats, locking on the backs of her calves. She didn't want to admit how wonderful his long fingers felt on her skin. She didn't want to admit how this new version of him was affecting her, period. Her heartbeat stuttered. Her skin went clammy and then steamy. Her thoughts broke apart like peanuts in a blender. In just a couple of minutes, he'd wrenched her far, far out of her comfort zone.

She yearned for the Zeke who'd cracked a thousand jokes a minute after the hell of Thailand, who firmly held her through all the nightmares. She yearned for the friend who understood about her lapses into the painful memories yet welcomed her back to reality with an easy grin and a tight hug. She wanted the Zeke she'd had in sunshine and summer, not this sinewy shadow of October night, swallowing her with his gaze and overpowering her with his presence.

Did he use that look with anyone on the list, too?

"You're stalling." The words were low but dripped with command. He leaned even closer.

Rayna tried to look away. Like *that* was going to be possible. "No, I'm not." She swallowed. "I'm just refusing you, period."

"Not an option."

"The hell it isn't."

"*Not* an option, Rayna."

She pushed out a grunt. "Says you and that invisible army behind you?"

His whiskers undulated as he clenched his jaw. "Says the friend who's worried about your piercing being infected."

Dread twisted her chest. How did he know? How *much* did he know? A deeper stare into his eyes gave her the answers. Those hazel depths had a new tint to them, flecks of brilliant green that always told her he understood way more than he ever said. Damn it. He knew enough, didn't he? The realization burned awkward heat up her neck and into her face.

"Shit," she muttered.

"That's better than 'no,'" he drawled.

She grimaced. "I spilled the beans in my sleep?"

Zeke didn't answer that one, though his grip on her calves gentled. He grazed the back of her knees with the tips of his fingers. *Hell*, that felt good. Such a deceiving prelude for what he was asking—demanding—she do.

"God." She pressed her hands over her cheeks and slammed her eyes closed. "How much of it *did* I spill?"

"Enough." Though his voice still rumbled with its subwoofer of command, he reined back on the imperious edge. "Enough that I'm concerned, bird. If those assholes didn't disinfect their needle or know exactly what part they had to aim for—"

"Stop." She flung her hand to his mouth. The scrape of his whiskers on her fingers was oddly soothing compared to the images that laid siege to her brain. She was back in King's warehouse in Thailand again. The concrete floor was cold on her back as the bastard's guards held her down, getting ready to spread her legs before they bade the little woman forward, the needle gleaming in her gloved hands.

"Stop. *Stop*. I can't, Zeke. I won't!"

She tried again to kick him away, but damn it, the man was nearly twice her size. He impaled her with a determined stare.

"Rayna," he ordered evenly, "look at me. Come back to me. You're not there anymore. You're right here. *I'm* right here." His gaze intensified, the green hues dissolving beneath a flood of deep gold command. "I know this isn't easy. I just need to make sure..." His jaw stiffened. "If they gave you an infection, we need to know about it now."

Her reaction was surprising, even to her. She actually rolled her eyes while reaching to the dog tags on her nightstand. "Medical corps, Sergeant, remember? I think I'd know if I had an infection."

Zeke barely flinched. "So you've been checking the piercing site every day?" he countered. "Examining it closely for any redness, swelling, discharge?"

She dropped the tags and grimaced. "Thank you. That officially killed my appetite for the next two days."

"You're stalling again."

She closed her eyes. It was the only way to close him out. Even then, it wasn't completely possible. He'd shifted even closer, turning his closeness into damn near an embrace. She breathed in his oaky, earthy scent; her inner calves brushed the ridges of his rib cage. "I'll check it later, okay? I...I promise."

"And the sun'll come out tomorrow, Little Orphan Annie?" His grunt wasn't so gentle this time.

"Yeah. You wanna be my sidekick mutt?"

The softness fled his gaze. "Damn it, Rayna. I'm not messing around."

"And I'm not one of your submissives!"

She longed to yank the words back the second they left her lips. She hated the remorse they brought to Zeke's eyes, the dark resignation sweeping across the rest of his face. This wasn't how she'd wanted to broach this subject with him. From the new dip to his shoulders, she guessed it wasn't his preferred scenario, either.

"I expected you'd get to that page sooner or later."

"It was sooner. I just didn't know how to..." More heat washed her face. "Or *what* to..." When she lifted her gaze, his was waiting for her. Searching her. He'd studied her like that a hundred times before, so why was her heartbeat faltering now? "It wasn't like it changed anything for me, Zeke. You're one of my best friends now." She added a smile, trying to help the sad edge of her tone. "Actually, other than Sage, you're my best friend."

He gave her a lopsided smile in return. Though the look turned his bold features into an irresistible sight, it hardly revealed what he was thinking. His puma side again stomped on the grizzly when he was like this, making her guess at what he'd say or do next. She hoped her confession would yield her one of his engulfing hugs along with an invitation to go downstairs for some Baileys and cocoa and no more talk about the illicit souvenir she'd brought home from Thailand between her thighs.

"Best friend," he finally murmured. "Thanks, Ray-bird. That makes me feel good."

Her taste buds tingled in anticipation of the cocoa. She smiled a little wider. "I'm glad."

"You know what they say about best friends, don't you?"

"What?"

"They're the perfect person to share a new piercing with."

She rammed her knee into his shoulder. "Asshat."

The blow didn't stop him by a single inch. He leaned ever closer, cocking a dark brow with unnerving confidence. "Okay, then. If you don't want to be friends anymore, I'm sure Trevor will want to hang. I think I just heard him open some chips. Fuck, I miss chips. I'll bet they're those good salty ones you keep around too, huh? They'll go so good with him hearing about how his sister might have a piercing infection from her overseas captivity, not to mention how she's been ignoring her meds and her general emotional well-being. That's bound to be way more interesting than the latest Seahawks news, yeah?"

"Aggghh!" She tossed up both her hands. "Fine, okay? You win."

Not that she was going to make it easy for him. She glared

when he pulled her hand to his lips and pressed a rough kiss to her knuckles. Nervy shithead. The Mr. Darcy act didn't eclipse his George Wickham maneuver. "Just get it over with," she muttered.

Zeke didn't reply to that, and she was grateful. With commanding efficiency, he moved his hands to her hips in order to pull her to a prone position. Rayna squeezed her eyes shut. Just being in this physical position was enough to pull the trigger on the panic bullets again. She pulled in deep breaths, visualizing Wonder Woman bracelets on her wrists to deflect them. That wasn't as effective as remembering Zeke's words. She was safe. She wasn't in Thailand anymore. These were her sheets at her back, not a concrete floor. Nobody was going to trap her or do anything she didn't want, or make her feel—

Unnerved. And more than a little terrified.

Her mouth went dry as he tugged at the waistband of her sweats. They came down easily for him, making her wonder just how many times he'd performed the move. He made her panties follow with even more practiced speed, coming off in his grip with a trio of soft *thwicks.*

Rayna pressed her lips together as the cool air brushed her naked skin. For every slick move he pulled, her body broke out in mortified goose bumps—though she'd spill her savings account before revealing this was the first time she'd ever been bare like this for a man's gaze. She wasn't a prude. She and virginity had parted ways the summer after she'd graduated from high school, but it had happened in a pitch-dark room. That was just fine for a girl who'd grown up fighting off her brothers so much, she often had better muscles than her lovers. She'd fast made friends with the shadows when it came to sex.

There were no shadows now.

But this also had nothing to do with sex. Not a damn thing. *Not a thing. Not a thing. Not a thing.*

She timed the mantra with every frantic breath that left her as Zeke set her clothes aside and then turned back and settled his weight between her legs again. She braced herself for what he'd do next. For the push against her legs, the vulnerability of her body, the humiliation of his gaze on her disgrace. The way he'd prod at the piercing, reminding her that a part of her ordeal would never leave her. That the nightmare would never really go away.

He lowered his fingers to her skin. Against her hips.

Bewilderment dragged her eyes open. Again, the man's size made him take up most of her view, but Rayna's focus was seized by more than that. In the last minute, his face had changed again. The hungry puma was gone. The protective grizzly wasn't back yet, either. But what she stared at wasn't another beast. He was all man. A man who took her in with a gaze like heat beneath coals, instead of his typical sparks and intensity. A man with a full-lipped mouth that seemed finally at rest, instead of quirks that obeyed the slightest changes of his temperament. A man who slid the pads of his fingers along her skin, slowly and reverently, almost like a kid learning a new texture.

"You're beautiful, you know." He traced her hipbones with his thumbs.

Rayna sneaked her tongue out to rewet her lips. Beautiful? He was tossing that out to describe *her* when *he* looked at her like this, touched her like this? "Th-Thank you."

She gulped deeply. To her shock, Z matched the action. He paused his hands and then rotated his head, face intense, as he glanced to her sweats and panties. He blinked as if realizing what he'd just done...and was silently admitting that this might not be a good idea after all.

She needed to listen to that instinct, too. This was her opportunity. She could roll away right now. He'd probably let her. They'd laugh awkwardly, and this moment would officially be in their past. They could go back to standing on opposite sides of the bridge that connected them, enjoying the view while safe on their respective shores and traveling across from time to time for visits...but never touching in the middle. Never throwing off the balance. Him, Dominant. Her, never going there. Yes, balance was good. Balance was necessary.

Zeke moved his hands again. Into the crevices where her thighs joined her torso.

Buh-bye, opportunity.

She twisted her hands into the sheets as her heartbeat set up camp in her throat. Zeke moved his hands down and pushed at the insides of her legs. She clenched in resistance.

"I'm only going to look, Rayna." His voice was so intimate she doubted someone standing at the door would be able to hear it. "I promise...if it hurts, I'll stop."

She swept her stare up to his face. He waited with those banked embers in his eyes, with that perfect slant of his lips, with his wide shoulders set, waiting on her patiently. Everything about him said the only thing on his mind was her health and safety.

If he'd tethered his Dom for the night, she could damn well do the same with her whiny infant.

She relaxed her legs.

Zeke opened them.

Rayna gulped hard and looked up at the ceiling. She mentally filed it as a necessary chore, like a root canal or a pap smear. The gynecologist at the base had a round sticker on the ceiling over her stirrup table, a conversation bubble that said *I Hate This*. That sign had always pissed her off, but now she'd give anything for even that distraction from the strong, sure fingers that parted her pubic curls, softly wending his way toward the circle of steel embedded in the hood of her most intimate flesh.

She bit the inside of her lip when he found it. Nobody had touched her there since that awful night in Thailand. The only reason *she* went near it was to wash the area. She certainly hadn't inspected the little ring like Zeke did now, softly twisting it, lifting it a couple of different ways to observe the insertion point in her skin...

And unleashing a wholly unexpected force in her body.

Force, as in an eight-plus on the Richter scale. Cracked cliffs of composure. Tsunami time.

Holy hell.

Thank God she already had a death grip on the sheets. Her increased torque wouldn't appear odd. Z didn't have to know that the reason she tortured her Mulberry four hundred threads was because of the jolt he'd just given her entire sex with his tender exam. The little flicks were like the switch on a stunning light display, flooding her pussy with new awareness, immersive heat...

Crap. How was this possible? She wavered between a wild need to know the answer and a screaming who-gives-a-shit. Her entire core was suddenly electric and alive, and she struggled not to cry out in pure wonder. She had no idea how she limited herself to the sharp breath she pulled in through her nose, which made Zeke stop his exam.

"You okay, honey?"

"Fine." She sounded like a chipmunk and hated herself for it. What the hell was wrong with her? And how on earth could she gain a second of pleasure from that *thing* they'd forced into her flesh? She cleared her throat and said more forcefully, "Yeah, fine."

Zeke still didn't move a muscle or, for that matter, a finger. "You don't look fine."

"Can you just focus and finish?" she snapped.

He tilted his head as if preparing to fire a comeback but gave her thick silence through the rest of his inspection, instead. Damn it. This had been *his* stubborn-ass idea, and now *her* psyche was the pinball machine of arousal, guilt, irritation, and confusion. As the man himself enjoyed saying all the time, this was some messed-up shit.

Fortunately, he only subjected her to another thirty seconds of the wordless tension—and the strokes to her libido that recruited even her toes into sheet-twisting duty. When he finally lifted his head, he wore a look she couldn't define. His mouth was still an unreadable line, though his gaze had changed hues again. His eyes, bright as emeralds, emphasized his ungodly long lashes and the tan he'd brought home from the mission. Great. Like she needed the reminders that the man's face was as captivating as his fingers.

"Well, I'm shocked," he said. "They got it right and did it clean." His lips lifted a little. The smile extended up, crinkling the corners of his eyes. "You're going to be fine, bird," he assured her. "It looks good."

Rayna admitted her own surprise. "Really?"

"Yep." He nodded. "Genital piercings heal fast, if they heal right."

The statement, along with the breath he let out after it,

enabled Rayna to finally ID his previous expression. Relief. From what she could tell, a bunch of the stuff. Despite this wholly uncomfortable situation, she smiled, too. It seemed he'd been really worried about her, so it wasn't just a chest-beating thing to get his testosterone card punched.

She was relieved too, though her mindset stemmed from a different purpose than Zeke's. *Much* different. She debated revealing it but realized this might be her only chance of attaining it. She'd never be in this position with Zeke again. And she'd never have the guts to ask it of anyone else.

"So if it's healed, you can take it out, right?"

She expected his smile to fall. It did. She expected his moment of contemplation after it, as well. But his shadowed scowl? That wasn't on the checklist. Nor was the retort he gave back in a guttural murmur.

"Why do you want it out?"

She actually laughed. "You're kidding, right?" She met his stare now, inch for unblinking inch. "You *have* to be kidding. You think I need a memento of that hell? A *reminder* of what happened?"

Zeke shifted his hands to the tops of her thighs. His grip was steady, matching his entire mien. "What they did to your body healed, but what they did to your soul hasn't. And you're not treating *that* wound, Rayna. Now it's becoming infected, dysfunctional." He jerked his head toward her bottles of meds on the desk. "And it's why you still need all that shit."

Hell. She should have kept her intention to herself. Just gone to a piercing parlor and let some stranger get the ring out of her. Now she had to deal with what Z's words did to her heart, the rip they widened inside. "What's your point?"

Zeke caught the hand she lifted to cover her eyes. "The

remembering is what heals you, Ray-bird. It's what makes you stronger. Better."

She sniffed, unsuccessfully battling tears. The torment got worse when Z intensified her horror by guiding her hand down, until she touched the steel circle that felt like an alien implant to her body.

"Feel it," he directed. "Do it. Feel your body. Love it again. You're so fucking stunning, Rayna. You're warm, you're vibrant, and you're *alive*. You did it. You survived." He took her index finger and swirled its tip around the little jewel embedded into the clit ring. "This piercing isn't your shame. It's your medal of honor. Touch it."

The tears came faster. He was a mush of colors across her vision, but in the mirrors of her soul, she'd never seen things more clearly. She could practically hear the storm canopies being thrown off her psyche, exposing the skies of her spirit, the heights of her strength. And ohhh yes...the pulsing needs of her body too. She set them free a little bit more, using her fingers to spread the wings of her sex, gasping as pulses of lust tore through her intimate tissues, now welcoming them. Rejoicing in them.

It was all because of him. Her wisdom. Her hero. Her friend.

But damn it, right now, she didn't need a friend. She needed more. If only for tonight, for this hour of liberation and light, she needed *him* as more.

"Zeke." It left her on a desperate breath. His fingers still twined with hers, though she now realized he was following her lead, not the other way around. "Please..." The supplication made their breaths mingle, too. She smiled as she pulled on his middle finger, leading that beautifully long digit toward the opening into her deepest core. The motion brushed his thumb against her ring, moving the metal directly on her clit again. She throbbed with wet need. "Shit!"

He moved over her on an urgent surge. His breath, cool as rain yet warm as summer, blew across her neck and face.

"Ray-bird." His voice was husky, his stare dark with his complete focus on her.

Rayna gazed back, trying to smile through her lingering tears. That effort went to hell when he caught a drop with his lips, wicking it from her with a little kiss. He did it to another. Another.

Forget crying now. Or breathing. She surrendered them both to wonderment. From the moment she'd met him, this man was gunning for a header of his own in *Webster's* under the word *ferocious*. This tenderness illuminated a new facet of him. How many more of these surprises would he unveil tonight?

She yearned to get started on that answer, but the man himself didn't seem to agree. Though his other still hand circled the sensitive membranes at her intimate entrance, driving her into the stratosphere from aching heat, he didn't enter her.

"Zeke, please!"

A sigh fell off his lips. "Rayna." It sounded damn near like an entreaty, too. A deep furrow invaded his brow. "Fuck... Rayna."

She dug her fingers into the longer hairs along his nape. "*You* did this to me. Now you have to help me!"

A ragged sigh shook his whole frame. He dropped his forehead to hers. "Honey, I'd love nothing better than to bury my finger inside you right now. I've fantasized about it, okay?

Lots of times. I've dreamed about what you'd feel like, taste like, be like. But—" He stopped himself with a huff.

Rayna grabbed his jaw. "But what?"

His eyes glimmered like hazel kaleidoscopes. The rest of his face tightened. "If I get my finger inside you, I won't stop there."

Hell. If his touch didn't have her soaked already, the confession would've done the trick. Her tunnel sluiced with new arousal. Her nipples pushed at her sleep tee. Her inner thighs burned. She writhed, ready to detonate, hating the word *stop* in so many ways.

"I don't want you to." She ran her thumb along his jaw, savoring the bite of his scruff.

A dark laugh quirked his face. "You know I've spent the last eight weeks with a bunch of rancid guys, right? You know my only lover's been my fist and that the only reason I even suggested getting you like this was because I got so damn worried about your piercing, and—" He dropped his head with a harsh grunt. "Shit. If this was an op, my approach would've had us both toes up with bullets in our brains."

"No." She dug her fingers beneath his beard, digging into his skin. "No talk of killing. No talk of death." When his gaze lifted into hers, she didn't hold back on letting him see everything inside her. The pure gratitude. The raw attraction. The scorching need. "We've danced at that edge before. Not now. Tonight, the dance is about living. About celebrating." She let her hands travel back, scoring his scalp again. "I know this isn't forever. I know you can't give me that. It's not what I want."

When conflict still glittered in his gaze, she took a determined breath and shifted her other hand—from her crotch to his. She shoved back her insecurity. This point *had* to stick. When her fingers closed around his erection, she stroked it as if his clothes weren't there and she held his bare, hard length in her hand.

"I only want you, Zeke. I need you. Here. Tonight. Inside me. Please."

CHAPTER THREE

It wasn't the first time a woman grabbed him like this. It wouldn't be the last. But holy hell, Z didn't know if another's touch would ever affect him this way. His thighs trembled. His heartbeat skidded. Christ, his toes were tingling.

He had to get a grip. She wasn't some goddamn lust fairy. She was simply the first body he'd been near in two months that didn't smell like a goat and fart like a cretin. So what if she'd been his go-to fantasy during those months, his escape from considering that the squad's targets had enough plutonium to decimate half of South Asia? So what if her body was more sleek, sensual, lithe, and gorgeous than even his best dreams? So what if that diamond nestled in her lush curls turned the peach beneath it into his new fruit to crave?

Shit.

His intention had only been to make sure she was safe, comforted, and lulled back into a peaceful sleep. He was a man of control, including his own body. He'd been able to play Dom with totally naked women for hours and never experienced what he did from ten minutes of this woman with her tousled hair and faded Princess Leia T-shirt.

Wasn't *that* the blinding flash of the obvious here? This woman. Rayna. The one who didn't get a category because she *was* a category. Light as mist but fierce as hail. Tiny as a sprite but formidable as a queen. Special. Incredible. A miracle.

His. Just for a few perfect hours, he'd have her in so many

ways he'd dreamed. She wanted it—and goddamnit, did *he* want it.

He almost tossed his head to see if there was a demon on one shoulder and an angel on the other. "Hell," he growled. "Ray-bird, I don't think you understand what—"

"Stop it. I'm not thirteen. I damn well understand what I'm asking for!"

"No." In one instant, he went from his half-respectful pose to sliding hard between her legs. "No, I don't think you do."

Thud. Thud. He locked her wrists down to the mattress on either side of her head, not compromising his hold or his stare. "I don't do smooth jazz and long, slow walks on the beach, honey. I'll fuck you like a Stratocaster solo, hard and long and sweaty, until your ears ring and you don't know which way is up anymore." Her pupils dilated and her mouth parted, and shit if that didn't turn him on in five fresh ways. "I won't tie you up. I won't use any kinky toys. But I promise your skin will carry my marks. My taste will linger on your tongue. Your body will remember, for a very long time, exactly who's been inside it."

He dragged his grip from her wrists to her elbows, leaving trails with his thumbnails on the way. Rayna shuddered and arched against him, almost stopping his next words from getting past his dry throat. "Be careful about asking for the fire, little bird, if you're not ready for the burn."

Funny that he mentioned fire. The woman met his scrutiny with eyes that were filled with the stuff, turning into someone he barely recognized as she panted hard. The flames burned brighter as he circled his thumbs to the tender flesh of her inner elbows. She cried out and writhed as if he'd stroked her whole clit. Fascinating. Exhilarating. So accessible, so real.

He loved watching her, observing what he could do to her.

Finally, she collected herself enough to rasp a reply. "You got flint and sticks inside those pants, Boy Scout? Or are you just going to talk all night?"

His grin busted his face so wide, it hurt. But only for a second. After that, he was too busy capturing her mouth with his. Commanding her lips to form with his. Meshing her tongue and teeth with his. She opened eagerly for him, giving back every degree of his passion. He moaned with wonder. For years, he'd kissed nothing but carefully schooled submissives who assumed they should let him do all the work, let him be all the kindling. How long had it been since a woman returned every drop of lust he gave from their first kiss? She astounded him. Ignited him. Scared the shit out of him.

He wanted more.

A lot more.

As they kept going at each other like teenagers at Gas Works Park, adorably breathy sounds erupted in her throat, driving him to the edge of insanity. But the woman wasn't going to settle for the edge. Since he still had her arms pinned, Rayna raised her legs for her cause. She wrapped both around him, dragging up his T-shirt with her toes, climbing his spine with the balls of her feet. The action forced his mouth from hers to make room for his astonished huff.

"Fuck." He pulled away long enough to help her finish the task, balling his shirt up and tossing it to the shadows. Her little gasp of admiration, joined by her curious fingers at the round three-part tattoo over his heart, shot his body full of electricity. He dipped back in and suckled his way to her neck, her scent swirling into his senses. Cinnamon. Cardamom. A little exotic. A lot erotic. "You never told me you were part Gumby, honey."

She trailed her mouth to the base of his throat. "Yoga is very helpful for stress levels when you're on the run from slave traders."

"Is that so?" He teethed her earlobe.

"Uhhhh..." She gasped and wriggled. "Uh-huh."

"Jungle yoga." He grinned against her nape. "That sounds real nice. Were you...naked?"

She lightly kicked his ass through his pants. "No! You ever been bitten by a baseball-sized bug, Sergeant?"

"A number of times." With no more warning than that, he moved his grip into the bottom of her shirt, shoving it up and then off. "No bugs in here," he drawled, drinking in the sight of her erect breasts. She colored a little, but that didn't stop him from dipping his head to one of the perfect mounds, dragging her nipple between his teeth. Goddamn, she tasted amazing. He took in more of her warm, delicious flesh as Rayna arched into him, tangling her hands in his hair again.

"But plenty of—oh, mmmm—bites." She finished it with a longer mewl as he slid his mouth to her other breast, tugging at the nub with similar demand. He joined his hiss to hers as she dug her nails into his nape and along his shoulders. Her eagerness was a goddamn stream of liquid fire on his body. To know she desired him like this, to feel it in her frantic touch, to see it making erotic shadows in her eyes, made his dick pulse just as if she were licking every inch of it with the tongue she sneaked out to wet her lips.

"Damn bugs." He slid a smile as he made short work of his belt buckle and fly. "They make people swell up...everywhere."

As he finally gave his erection its freedom, the breath audibly caught in her throat. Liquid flame dump number two, only this time, the hard-on flyboys aimed straight for his cock.

He joined her in the not-breathing-and-liking-it department as she stared at his tattoo. Her gaze hypnotized him as it ran over the twin barbed wire swirls that flowed just beneath his belt line, accented with eight dark blue drops. There were four on each side of the middle break, which was now dominated by his swollen length. As he stroked it from base to head with a grateful grunt, she let out a gasp.

"Zeke." Her jaw fell, clamped shut, and dropped open again. "You...you're..."

A strange sensation invaded his face. Hot. Tingling.

Holy fuck. He was *not* blushing.

Christ, Hayes. Like you've never gotten this reaction before?

Yeah, yeah, the response wasn't new. He just had no idea what to do with this version of it, a woman who didn't cap her surprise with greedy eyes and a come-fuck-me smile. Rayna's astonishment was genuine. Blush-inducing.

"I'm a big guy, Ray-bird."

"You're beautiful." She traced a finger along one of the tattoos. "All of you."

Her praise and her touch were a potent elixir. He spasmed, and the sweet heat of his precome emerged. He watched, fascinated, as Rayna moved her finger to the weeping tip of his penis and caught those drops. After she raised them to her tongue, she smiled like a kid who'd just discovered a new candy.

"You taste beautiful, too."

He cleared his parched throat. For what he had to say next, he needed every vocal cord that would cooperate with him.

"Touch me again," he ordered. "Every inch of me this time,

honey." When her lips parted a little in hesitation, Z guided her hand to his pulsing shaft. He'd promised no spanking or illicit toys. He'd said nothing about a little directed seduction—which scored a direct hit for eliciting its intended response, judging from how her nipples puckered and her inner thighs quivered.

She lifted her gaze as she stroked him with curious care. As amazing as her caresses felt, her stare affected him more. She watched him. Really watched. She clearly cared about the pleasure she brought him and was moved by it. No doubt, she could see the amazement in his stare, too. Of all the moments he'd fantasized about sharing with her between the sheets, this had definitely not been one of them. It was beyond expectation. Better than imagination.

And her shocked cry, when she ran her grip back up his penis, was more pitch perfect than he'd dreamed.

"What the—" She broke their eye contact to gape at the inverted V formed by the underside of his head—and the barbell nestled horizontally in the flesh there. Zeke pressed his lips to hold in a chuckle. A wise move. That made it easier to clamp his teeth as she continued to explore his piercing. Damn, if she rubbed that little spot beneath his bulb just one more time—

"Shit!" He spilled more precome onto her fingers.

She froze. "Sorry! Am I hurting—?"

"No. Sweet fuck, honey, no."

"This is why you knew so much about genital piercings."

"A little real-life experience goes a long— *Damn*! Oh yeah, right there. That's—that's perf—" He closed his eyes to let them roll back in his head. "Is this how it felt when I was inspecting you?"

She ran her thumb along his bar again. Her answer carried

a gloating smile. "Karma's a bitch, Sergeant."

Part of him wanted to laugh. The other half longed to flip her over and spank that adorable sarcasm into mindless screams—and pleas for his cock. God, what he could do with this woman if she were his willing submissive. The ways he'd harness her...teach her...pleasure her...

Right before he released her.

And hurt her.

It was much, *much* better this way. One night only. A hot fuck between friends. A welcome back to the States for him, a welcome back to sex for her. A memory to make. A path they'd never travel together again.

He was going to make the most of it.

With a wicked grin, he pulled Rayna's hand away from his erection. A frisson of curiosity glinted in her eyes. He loved that look... The mesmerized girl twined into the passionate woman, waiting to be shown a new discovery. He had one ready, too. He guided her fingers to it, slipping them into the valley of her labia. Her mouth parted more, an invitation he couldn't refuse. As he fused his lips to hers, he led her fingers deeper into her sex. Her trembles became shudders. Her sighs turned into moans.

When he was finished, he didn't go far. With his mouth a breath above hers, he watched the arousal take over her face and crunch her forehead in a bittersweet scowl. He'd dreamed of her like this so many times on the mission. In the deepest parts of the nights, during those sleepless hours when he wondered if the next day would be his last, he'd imagine her in this bed, thighs open, fingering herself, gasping faster and faster until she came, calling out his name with her explosion. Now that he realized she hadn't come close to making that a reality in the last two months, he was determined to help her find that nirvana in herself once again.

"That's it," he coaxed. "Touch it, honey. Rub your beautiful pussy for me. Stroke your clit with that pretty diamond. God*damn*, you're beautiful."

He was glad he hadn't bothered to empty his pockets yet. In two fast motions, he had his wallet whipped out and his backup condom in hand. As he pushed his pants all the way off, he ripped the foil in a motion more natural than scratching his balls. Not that his balls screamed for anything but release right now. They throbbed harder as he sheathed up, rolling the latex over his length before positioning his head at the soft, shiny entrance of Rayna's deepest core.

"Oh!" Her eyes flew open, long lashes framing eyes that had become dark green oceans. Fuck. A guy's soul could drown in a stare like that. Thank God he'd never see it again after tonight.

"Oh, Zeke." She breathed it she looked down. "Oh, *Zeke*!" The scream erupted as he pushed his tip into her, stopping just before his piercing breached her pussy.

"I'll try to make this easy, honey." He barely heard the dry tree bark of his words past the blood pounding in his ears. "I can't...guarantee I'll...succeed."

Another nudge in. Rayna tensed as her tissues stretched to accommodate him. He hated admitting that turned him on, but shit, there was no ignoring it. He loved this. Rejoiced in pushing her. Reveled in taking her body to limits it hadn't known before. Celebrated that his cock would mark her in corners nobody else had. For these few precious minutes, she belonged completely to him. Her world would become only him.

"Damn!" She exclaimed it as he slid deeper. Her tunnel clenched his cockhead tighter as the barbell in his frenulum said hello to the sensitive skin above her ass. He pulled out slowly but plunged back in with more force. Over and over he stroked and filled and fucked her, sinking his shaft more deeply each time.

Beneath him, Rayna went from exquisite to exhilarating. Her head arched back. Her lips fell open. Her thighs bunched, so beautifully tense as she tried to meet him thrust for thrust. As he claimed her sweet cunt with his dick, he roamed the rest of her with his mouth. He licked the salty sheen of her forehead. Bit into the straining column of her neck. Sucked each breast so hard her areolas were imprinted with his teeth marks.

He didn't want to stop there. He couldn't. He needed to ensure he was stamped on her body and in her memory. Deeper. He needed to get deeper.

"Spread your legs wider," he ordered on a growl, "and tell your eye sockets to get ready, bird."

Rayna wet her lips. "M-My eye sockets? Wh-Why?"

He didn't answer her. He showed her. He opened the firewalls, letting the blaze in his blood take over his ass, his balls, his dick. No more gradual inches. No more tentative prods. He slammed every inch of his length into her wet tunnel, grunting in pleasure as his head rammed her cervix. Trojan stallion, meet the gates of paradise.

Rayna's eyes burst wide in shock. "Oh my God!"

Well, *that* certainly registered down the hall on the big-brother-protective-posse radar screen. At the moment, Zeke didn't give a shit about Trevor. Everything was Rayna. Only Rayna.

He shifted his hold to both sides of her waist, openly

adoring the hourglass curve. Hell, she was magnificent. He almost hated to summon the breath for his next words.

"The Stratocaster's fired up, honey."

Rayna gave him a shaky laugh. "No shit."

"Does it hurt?"

"Yes."

His chest knotted. He lowered his fingers into her hips. "I don't want to stop."

"If you do, I'll never speak to you again."

"If I don't, that's still a possibility."

"Shut up, Zeke."

At first, he retorted to that by dropping his face to hers, twisting her lips in a brutal kiss. He barely let her free before growling, "I'm going to rip you open, Rayna."

The woman's little grin wasn't the reaction he expected. It caused him to pull back another inch. Though he'd seen her smile so many times, this expression was something brand-new. A challenge yet a surrender. Utterly soft yet completely fearless. Sweet God. He felt like a miner who'd discovered a new gemstone. Did he bellow in victory about it or savor the secret in wicked silence?

She didn't give him time to decide. "Do it," she pleaded. "Fuck me. Please!"

He gladly granted her wish. He'd just referenced a stallion—now he acted like one. He drove into her with bestial ferocity, not giving an inch of clemency or a moment of rest. He directed her body too, gripping her hard, pumping her pussy onto him, making her ride him as hard as he enjoyed her. High, aching mewls vibrated from her throat. She locked her hands around his shoulders and scratched the fuck out of his back. It was worth every painful inch. His senses spun. The room went away. The *world* went away. There was nothing now but the utopia of Rayna's kisses. The silken skin of her body. The stinging bliss of her nails in his skin.

The heaven of knowing he was about to come inside her.

The euphoria of feeling the tremors in her skin and knowing she was just as close.

He lifted his head again. Waiting for him were the gorgeous green oceans of her gaze. Zeke let himself get lost in them this time. Just this once, he'd know what it was like to drown.

"Give it to me." He dug his grasp deeper, grinding her faster onto him as he speared her with deep, long, hard passion. "Give it all to me, honey. Every drop of it is mine tonight."

"Zeke!" Her hands stopped where they were, though her nails turned into ten human power drills. "Zeke. Ohhh!"

He caught the last of her long cry with his lips, using the motion to tamp his volume as much as hers. Waking up Trevor's bro-dar was one thing. Blasting the guy's brain to pieces from listening to his sister's orgasm? Though Z often had an asshole side, it didn't extend that far.

He roared into her mouth as his climax screamed through his cock. His sex was flooded in white heat. His senses swam, his logic fled. He was seared alive, consumed by the heaven of her sex around his, her breaths twined with his, their bodies fused into one blistering, flawless flame.

When he trusted himself not to bellow the walls down anymore, he dragged his mouth away. His breath still left him on heavy pants. Hers, too. His body shook every ten seconds, racked by crazy aftershocks from what he'd put it through. Hers, too.

He lifted a hand to Rayna's face, wondering about the

strange sensation that overtook him when she lifted a tiny smile at him. He was breathing but couldn't get enough air. Everything but her seemed muted, unfocused.

Wasn't this a lot like drowning?

Shit.

He forced himself to roll to his back. Pillows and sheets, joyously soft and smelling like sun, caressed his skin. After he trashed the condom, he pulled Rayna over, tangling his legs with hers, pressing her breasts to his chest. His battle-bruised body almost didn't know what to do for a second. But only a second. It picked up on its new orders pretty fast. His muscles uncoiled. His breathing relaxed. His fingers roamed the entrancing landscape of Rayna's back. She trailed light fingers through his chest hair.

It was one of the most perfect moments of his life.

She stirred a little before whispering, "Thank you."

"Mmmmm." His voice sounded distant. Satiated. "Thank *you*, little bird."

Her fingers trailed down. They traced the knife-wound scar below his right rib. His memento of the sting they'd pulled on King three months ago. "I mean thank you for all of it, Zeke."

He brought his hand up and stroked her fingers, somehow feeling he needed to comfort her. Why had that gratitude carried such melancholy? Hell, no. It wasn't time for shit like that yet. The night still owed them a few more minutes of perfection.

"That's what I meant, too." He brushed her hair off her temple and kissed it.

She burrowed a little closer. "Please stay."

He had no idea what to reply. It was raining harder outside. It was soft, warm, fragrant, and very naked in here. *A paradise you shouldn't be getting used to, asshole. This was one time. One very good fuck. Now get the hell out before you drown in her for good.*

He took a deep breath, scrounging his brain for the usual niceties. *Early day tomorrow.* Yeah, that was always a good one.

"Of course."

Fuck.

One night. Friends with bennies. Nothing more. You know the drill. The pants come on after the condom gets trashed. What the hell are you doing? What the hell are you thinking?

He gave his brain a mental flip-off. She wasn't asking him to stay and *think*, right? She wanted him to stay. No more, no less. She'd begged with that sweet, husky need that always ate up his blood and made him long to find fucking Atlantis for her if need be. But she never wanted anything more than him.

And in this perfect, warm moment of now, all he wanted was her.

His brain finally relented. As soon as Rayna's breathing evened, he felt his consciousness slipping, too. With the sound of the rain echoing in his head, he plunged into the deepest sleep he'd had in months.

★ ★ ★ ★ ★

It was still raining. But he wasn't warm anymore. He let a slow smile curl his lips. His little bird would help with that challenge. He reached through the sheets for her. She had to be around here somewhere...

He realized the bed was empty when he heard her talking in the other room.

Revision. Rayna wasn't talking. She was arguing. And

trying to be quiet about it, likely due to concern about waking him, which was hilarious. Since his normal alarm clock was usually Hawk or T-Bomb sticking their socks—or worse—in his face, this was a welcome change.

Maybe not *that* welcome.

Trevor was still here. He heard the guy biting out his name like a piece of lousy fish. Didn't the fucker have a deposition to be at or some sap to carve up in court? It was ten in the morning. Trevor always had people to see and places to—

Wait.

"Huh?" he gasped, gaping at the clock again. Sure enough, the digits blared a one, a pair of zeroes, and then a two. Holy hell. Half the day was gone.

He dug through the linens for his pants and underwear before ramming his legs back into both. As he got into his boots, he visually searched the room for his T-shirt.

The *whap* of a slammed cabinet whipped his stare back toward at the door.

"You know what, Trevor? Maybe I should go get myself kidnapped in Asia again. Those pirates gave me more leash than you do."

The shirt would wait. He was out the door and down the hall in the space of a half-dozen strides.

The scene in the kitchen was about what he expected. The bright lighting and rustic French décor, down to a plate of homemade croissants and hand-iced cupcakes, did little to eclipse the dismal atmosphere between Rayna and her oldest brother. The guy looked like hell. His hair was more a haystack rolled in rust, and his eyes were rimmed in exhaustion. Zeke actually felt a twinge of empathy for Trev.

It vanished as soon as the asshat opened his mouth.

"Well, if it isn't Sleeping fucking Beauty."

He decided to ignore the comment, crossing to Rayna instead. She looked like an elf immersed in Santa's smoking jacket, wearing gray leggings and wrapped in a long-collared crimson sweater that was six sizes too big for her. She'd likely pilfered the covering off one of her brothers. One of *his* pullovers would look a hell of a lot better.

He ripped that fantasy up before it could get started. Focusing instead on this real-life sprite, he affectionately bussed her forehead. "Good morning."

"Hi." She tilted her head back, clearly expecting a more intimate greeting. So much for keeping his thoughts or his bloodstream in the realm of chaste. Still, he held back. Kissing her like that couldn't happen anymore. It didn't matter how tight his gut twisted as he watched her disappointed wince—or that damn wobble in her chin. "I-I'm so sorry, Z. We woke you, didn't we?"

He was grateful for the chance to lighten the air with a chuckle. "I haven't slept past five for at least a year, honey. Believe me, it was time for Sleeping fucking Beauty to get up."

Maybe the self-deprecation would inject a little helium to Trev's happiness balloon now.

"'Honey,' huh? What, you're Mike stinkin' Brady for her now?"

Or maybe not.

Zeke forced down a deep breath as he fished a coffee mug out of the cupboard. He set it on the counter with a *thunk* that wasn't exactly the stuff of guy bonding commercials. As he filled it, he tossed a calculated glance over his shoulder, one brow raised.

"Sleeping Beauty. Mike Brady. You're giving me quite a

range there, pal."

Trevor huffed. "On the contrary, Hayes. I don't think I've given you enough credit. *Half-dressed sister fucker* hasn't made the list yet."

"Trevor!" Rayna yelled. "For God's sake!"

Z dragged a hand through his hair. Shockingly, the comment didn't nearly torque him to the depths that it did Rayna. He didn't always understand the depths of love between siblings, but that didn't stop him from wanting them. Envying them.

"Ray-bird," he said, "catch an iceberg for a second. Your brother only cares about you." He turned and cocked a more direct stare at Trev. "Though if he has half the brain I think he does, he'll watch the land mines he's jumping while he does so."

A nerve jumped in Trevor's jaw. "What the hell does that mean?"

"I came out here half-dressed because I heard Rayna talking about a year of captivity as a preferred choice to your asshole behavior."

"You came out here half-dressed because you had your dick in my sister last night."

Rayna stomped forward and bared her teeth at her brother. "You are *not* helping your case, counselor."

"You think I care about *winning* this one, Rayna?" Trevor spread his arms. "I care about *you*, damn it!"

"Me? You mean your sister, the child who can't tie her own shoes? Or your sister, the grown woman capable of making decisions about the men who share her bed?"

Z had to give the guy props for getting to his feet with steady calm. "I mean my sister, the woman who has a heart full of compassion and care...and love. I mean my sister who would willingly give her incredible heart away to a guy like that"—he jabbed a finger toward Z—"only to find he'd ground it up and spat it out."

Zeke sloshed some cream into his coffee and swished the shit around. The action was purely for show. If he took even a swig of the liquid, it'd come back up in a second.

The man was right. Down to the last syllable. He'd avoided the truth of it last night in the name of being there for her. In a thousand ways, even Rayna had avoided it, too. There was no escape hatch anymore. The truth, spoken by her brother with nothing but love in the words, forced both of them to listen.

If only Rayna had gotten that memo, too.

"Get out." Her dictate punched the air like acid. She yanked away Trevor's coffee cup, marched across the kitchen, and hurled it into the sink. The mug shattered, spattering her Provençal trim tiles with black coffee stains. "You heard me," she spat when Trevor froze in shocked silence. "Get the hell out, Trevor!"

The guy attempted a snort. It came out more a geeky sputter. "Are you kidding me?"

"Kidding left this conversation a long time ago. Get out of my house. Now."

"Rayna!"

"Now!"

"*No.*"

Z hadn't meant for the command to sound like a boot-camp order. Or maybe he had. Maybe he knew nothing else would get through the fury that dominated her face, her stance, her voice. Hell. The last time he'd seen her like this was the moment after she'd shot King in the head.

He stepped and caught both her hands in his. "Bird, listen

to yourself. You're practically declaring war on your own brother."

Rayna's lips screwed together. "Because he's being a dickwad!"

"I won't refute you there." He shrugged at Trev. "Sorry, man. That part's true. I think Big Boss Creator Man just had it in for you and slapped it on your DNA."

She wriggled her grip in his. Zeke clutched her tighter. She needed to know how serious he was about his next statement.

"What's your point, Zeke?"

He looked down at their clasped hands. Shit. Now that the moment was here, he really did feel like hurling.

"He's a dickwad, honey. But he's also right."

Every inch of her body stiffened. He hated being the one who'd caused that shock. His remorse was so great, he forgot about holding on to her. When she wrenched her hands this time, she stumbled free with awkward momentum and crashed into the refrigerator. Papers slid free from the magnet clip things, fluttering to the floor.

"Z-Zeke?" She said it like he'd disappeared and she was searching for him. "What do you mean?"

He forced himself to look at her. Compelled his mind to take the reins over his heart, to remember that all the pain he saw in her eyes would only be a hundred times worse if he didn't have this conversation with her here and now. If he didn't set her straight about the limits of knowing a guy like him. If he didn't remind *himself* about those limits, too.

He swung his gaze at Trevor and lifted his hand, fingers spread. Trevor nodded, respectful for once, understanding the request. The guy could afford the magnanimity. It was easy to give a man five minutes alone with your sister if sensing they'd be the last.

When the door leading to the garage clicked behind Trev, Z reached for her. She slapped him away.

"You know exactly what I mean, don't you?"

She pulled her sweater tight, coiling the cuffs into her fists. "Like that gets you off the hook." She lifted her face until he saw the tears tracking down her cheeks. "Say it," she spat. "You do not get out of doing this, Sergeant. Say it. Every damn word."

Zeke downed a deep breath. "It's been said already, Rayna. By you. Last night. Somewhere between calling my number on the Dom disguise and begging me to go vanilla for one night—"

"Vanilla?" Her face went mutinous. "Gee. Thanks for the free scoop, buddy."

Take foot. Dip in shit. Insert in mouth. "It's just a term we use in the D/s community," he explained, "to describe the act without—" He shook his head. "And it's all wrong for what happened last night between us." Holy hell, was it wrong. Just letting in a few images of his hands on her skin and his cock inside her body were enough to make him shift from foot to foot, trying to adjust his fresh erection. He cracked his neck to refocus. "But before we went there, you told me you could deal. You told me you knew me. That you accepted what I'm capable of giving and not giving. Look, Ray-bird—"

"*Don't* call me that." She turned her stare out the window. The dark weather looked like a basket of spring fabric softener compared to the storms in her eyes. "Please don't."

Again, he stepped toward her. This time, she didn't flinch. He lifted his hand and brushed his knuckles along her shoulder. He dared breathing her in one more time. Shit. All her cinnamon-and-spice warmth filled him again, mixed with something new—the heady scent of her orgasm from last night. Every muscle in his body yearned to pick her up, haul her back into the bedroom, and do it all over again. No. There'd be a new twist this time. He'd order her to get naked while he fished some rope from his truck. He'd spread her atop the bed and make her shiver with need as he tied her up. He'd use her bondage ropes to drag her sweet body onto his dick, nice and slow, taunting them both, and—

And there was the arrow that pointed him to fate's shitty *You Are Here* for the day. If this situation were a mission, he'd be telling the guys to start writing final letters home.

"Look," he finally grated, "Trevor's right, okay? I'm sick to my fucking stomach that he is, but...I'm not good for you, Rayna." He shook his head. "Goddamnit, I wish I was, but—"

She slammed a hand to the counter. "Here we go again. Are you really going to pull out the different sides of the tracks spiel, Sergeant? *I'm not good for you, Rayna; I wish I was.* Really? What made you good enough last night but not good enough today?" She turned in front of the sink, arms slammed across her chest. "We slept together, Zeke. It was nice. Very nice. But it doesn't have to dynamite our friendship. I can get over it if you can."

Get over it. She thought it was that simple? This very second, he locked his legs to keep from crossing to her. His arms ached from resisting the need to crush her to him again. His cock swelled from the memories she invoked, even with her casual allusion to last night.

Hell.

If he stayed, nothing would be casual between them again.

Which was why it was time to pull out the guns he didn't want to use.

But sometimes, the best way to save a friend was to shoot them.

"Okay, great," he said, spreading his arms. "Nothing changes, huh?"

A smile lit up her face. Just what that choir in his gut needed before their encore of *King of Assholes, Zeke Hayes are Thee*. Rayna made a perfect muse for their next round by rushing over, circling her arms to his waist, and laying her head to his chest.

"See? I knew everything would be okay."

"Right. Everything's fine." He pulled her arms away so he could see her face again. "So...what? Tomorrow's Saturday. You suppose I grab a pizza, get here around eight, and we rent a movie or something?"

His biting undertone was lost on her. She shrugged and flashed a goofy grin. "Sure. If that's what you—"

"No. *No*, Rayna." He shoved her hands down. "That's not what happens tomorrow night." There was no way he'd turn his back on her for this, though distance was going to help. Maybe a little. Three steps back got him away from her intoxicating scent. Another step made the confusion in her eyes look less like darts aimed at his sanity.

"You know what's going down tomorrow, honey? I have a special appointment at a little place called Bastille."

She frowned at him, searching his face in clear confusion. Shit, why didn't she put it together? Was she going to make him spit it *all* out?

"Bastille. You mean, like the French prison?"

"The one known for its vast dungeons. Yes."

"Oh." Comprehension pushed her eyebrows toward each other. "I see."

She saw. Finally. Thank fuck.

He gave her a few seconds to process that knowledge—and jump to all the assumptions he needed her to because of it. "So, you still with this *let's be besties* program, Chestain? Is everything still A-okay?"

Rayna's features bunched tighter. "Why don't you just cancel?"

"Because I can't. I won't."

He hated himself for the snarl. The anger wasn't meant for her. Wasn't really meant for him, either. His sexual triggers were just...like this. He'd accepted it a long time ago, though there were times when it was still damn hard to do that. Now was one of those occasions—maybe the shittiest one of them. Tomorrow's session wasn't for education, edification, or satisfaction. Nothing remotely close. It was payback, pure and simple. Luna, the submissive who had automatically gotten his first appointment when he returned, had supplied the intel that led him, Garrett, and Wyatt to King three months ago—and gotten Rayna, Sage, and Josie back alive. The woman's price? One D/s session with Zeke. No time frame. No toy restrictions. No hard limits.

Luna hated limits. It was why he'd always refused to engage in the dynamic with her.

Because, God help him, he hated limits, too.

"You really look like you want to cancel it."

That was the second he turned his back on her. "I'm not going to cancel it, Rayna!" When he got to the middle of the living room, he pivoted back. "Fuck! What do you need to hear to understand this? I'm a Dominant. I can't stop being a Dominant. I can't be reworked, rewritten, or retrained, even if you click your heels three times and wish on a crapload of shooting stars. I'm not the guy in the cape. I'm not the goddamn hero you keep seeing just because—"

"Just because you *were* mine?" She stomped out of the kitchen, making the fallen papers swish in her wake. "Twice?"

"I was doing my job," he retorted. "That's it." He jammed a hand through his hair. "Look. I didn't grow up saving kittens in trees and walking old ladies across the street. I was a thug, Rayna. A street rat, living and fighting for every meal I ate. I was out for *my* ass only until a social worker cared enough to knock some sense into me. I joined up with the big green machine only because I wanted to impress her. I had no idea it would change my whole goddamn life. Everything was transformed for me, thanks to the army. Everything—except the D/s."

He sucked in a breath and squared his stance toward her.

"It's a lifestyle I can't change. I *won't* change." He reset his jaw. "Tomorrow night, I'm going to meet a submissive in the dungeon, strip off all her clothes, tie her down, and whip her until she's spun so far out of control she won't remember her own name. But she'll remember mine. It'll be on her lips when she falls down on her knees at my feet and thanks me for the scene. And I'll love doing it for her, Rayna. I'll love every fucking minute."

There was no sense in going beyond that. Rayna's potent silence told him so. There was no need to blurt that Luna was likely going to beg him for a hard pounding after she twirled down from sub space, and he'd refuse before making sure she had the most perfect aftercare on earth. There was no sense in trying to explain that after opening a submissive with a shell as thick as Luna's, the last thing he wanted to do was drive his cock into that mess.

He saw the conclusions painting their way across Rayna's

face and knew they were both better off if she thought the worst of him for it. Sure, he wouldn't screw Luna tomorrow. That didn't mean he wouldn't fuck another subbie one day. *Long* after today. *Very* long after Rayna Chestain was nothing but a distant and beautiful memory for him.

Especially if this was the last sight he'd have of her.

She'd scooted out a little more, stopping next to the living room window, through which a shaft of sunlight had suddenly burst from the storm clouds. The rain turned the beam into a rainbow. The colors washed over her adorable little frame in its bulky sweater, tight leggings, and bunched-up socks. The cyan in the rainbow hit her face. It made her features even more unreadable. In contrast, her hair was a fiery mane tumbling over her shoulders. They were covered by the sweater now, but it took a simple mental click to remember how they'd felt under his fingers, bare and sleek, as she'd drifted to sleep in his arms.

"Have fun at your appointment, then, Zeke."

"Right."

The sky wept harder outside. The rainbow faded from the room.

"Ray-bi—" He clamped his teeth hard. "Shit. Sorry."

"It's all right." She folded the bottom edges of the sweater on each other. Curled one foot atop the other.

"Listen, if you ever need me for anything..."

"Sure." She pulled her sweater origami apart. Her chin wobbled.

Fuck.

This is what you want. This is what she needs. For one of the few times in your damn life, you're doing the right thing.

Somebody just needed to give that memo to the invisible

bastard jamming the hot poker into his gut.

He grabbed his jacket and keys before walking out into the rain bare chested. The downpour was like ice. He welcomed it. The poker got fizzled for at least one second.

Fate wasn't so kind with the next moment. Or the next.

There was a saying on the squad that they had for times like these. He spat it out from frozen lips.

"This hell doesn't want your sorry ass, fucker. Keep the boots moving."

CHAPTER FOUR

This was going to be one of the best nights of her life. She refused to accept anything less. After all, she'd waited six years, three months, two weeks, and four days for it.

With that thought, Luna Lawrence smiled as she checked herself out in the full-length mirror of Bastille's submissives' dressing room. She looked good. Damn good. Her one-shouldered dark green club dress played up her purple eyes better than the black she normally wore to the dungeon. The dress's slick fabric showed off all the right parts of her body, including the rings in her nipples and the tattoos down her arms. The gold high-heeled gladiator sandals made her long legs look alluring and elegant.

Wow. Who knew? She'd had her doubts when Zeke sent over his instructions for tonight's scene. The man had been in full-on Master Z mode when he wrote the laundry list, which read like travel orders to Siberia at first. No leather. No latex. No black. No panties. Okay, the last one had been easy to oblige. But no black? Was the guy serious?

Of course he was. Zeke wasn't one shred comfortable about doing this, and the preliminary instructions were meant to drive in one statement on his behalf.

Tonight would be played by *his* rules.

Luna had grumbled but met every demand on the man's list. No way was she messing this up. She'd waited too long. Had wanted it too bad. Wanted *him* too bad.

She tugged at the dress and frowned at the weird sensation in her stomach. It felt like a flurry of dry leaves. Ha. The last time she checked, Seattle was outside the door. The term *dry* didn't exist within fifty miles. But *nervous* did. And *unsure*. Which made the insides of her thighs tingle in anticipation. In greater need to feel that man's body between them.

She couldn't wait.

How long had it been since she'd prepared for the command of a Master who'd earned the name? A man who knew that even the clothes on her body had to feel all wrong in order for her head to start feeling right? Who knew that the key to her submissiveness was triple-welded to her brain and all she craved was a Dom with balls big enough to take a blowtorch to those bonds?

Plenty of men had applied for the job. But on one hand alone could she count the ones who'd turned her mind to fireworks and made her dreams come true. Zeke wasn't represented on that hand. *Not yet.* Tonight, all that would change. Tonight, if her fantasies *really* materialized, all those faces on those fingers would be wiped away by the man who'd finally, *finally* realize that when paint touched its perfect canvas, it was best to thank fate and let the art explode.

With Zeke, she was going to be a Rembrandt.

The leaves in her stomach swirled harder.

The door to the dressing room opened, bringing a blast of the music now permeating the main room. The mix of sensual synth and soaring opera was mixed for the club by one of the city's emerging DJs. Lively conversation joined the song, a marked difference from the quiet of the club when she'd arrived forty minutes ago. Luna savored the noise. It was Saturday night at Bastille. A very special Saturday night. *At last.*

The folds between her thighs tickled with fresh arousal. Fortunately, the new arrivals in the room were Penny and Noah. Her friends each took a side of the mirror to give reactions to her makeover.

Penny normally went for an aloof Goth air, but right now her eyes bugged as if Luna stood there in a Mary Poppins costume. "Fuck. Me."

Luna rolled her eyes. "No thank you."

Noah held up both hands, showing off perfectly groomed nails. "And don't look at me."

Luna glanced back at Penny. "Was that a good 'fuck me' or a bad 'fuck me'?"

Penny tipped her head. "Just a *wow* one."

"Thanks for nothing, then."

"C'mon," Penny chided. "Does my opinion even matter? This is what Z wanted, right?"

"With one exception." Noah rolled the words out in a singsong before gliding behind Luna in a cloud of scented baby oil and a creak of leather shorts.

"Damn it." Luna smoothed a protective hand over her head. "Guess I forgot."

Penny smirked. "Uh-huh."

"Shut *up*." She fidgeted again. Her hair, a swath of black, lavender, and silver down to her hips, was her glory. It was no secret to anyone in the club. Nobody messed with her hair. Until Zeke and his instructions.

"Right," Noah drawled. "Just like I *forgot* Laird is bringing in that new *boi toi* from his gym to play with tonight—and I decided to wear my hottest leather Daisy Dukes because I wanted to."

"You can shut up, too."

"And you can hold still." Seemingly from nowhere, her friend flourished a hairbrush. He instantly went at her with it, gathering every strand into a high crown ponytail. "Sweet azaleas, what I want to do with this mane..." He pouted at her in the mirror as he started to braid the length, almost pulling off innocent with his blond schoolboy haircut and big brown eyes. "Don't we have just a few extra minutes? There's this coiled bun I've always wanted to try on you—"

"*No* coils, Daisy." Penny grabbed the brush from him before spinning Luna toward the door. "It's finally time for the lucky Master Z dungeon spin." Her friend lightly kissed her cheek. "You look perfect. Have fun, beautiful biatch!"

Her friend's words resonated as she headed out the door. The lucky dungeon spin. If her friends only knew how true the statement was. Penny and Noah had only heard the same line as everyone else—that Zeke was back from deployment and requested her for his homecoming Dominance session. She didn't realize Luna had gotten her true pass at the jackpot three months ago when Zeke had shown up at her door needing key information for a mission that clearly meant more than the usual. She'd helped him but had asked a price.

Tonight was his time to pay up.

Hell. The terms made her sound no better than the criminals she'd pointed Zeke to that night. And yeah, she'd tolerated some guilty twinges about their deal. She'd actually gotten to the point of scrolling to his name in her phone, tempted to be the better person for letting his body out of a scene that his brain clearly didn't want.

But there was the sticky. She hadn't waited on this man for six years because of half-baked hope. From the moment she'd first seen him stride into this club, an instinct had flared inside her like no other. She felt like a griffin from the fantasy books she'd sneaked out of class to read as a kid, spreading its wings and finally finding its lifemate. Regrettably, Z's griffin had still been snoozing.

She'd decided to be patient. *Really* patient. At times, she'd even been generous—like that afternoon three months ago. She'd given him the information for his mission even when she'd learned he was out to save another woman with it. But that didn't concern her anymore. After tapping connections at the base, she'd learned all about Z's mystery woman. A former army nurse who still worked on base in a civilian capacity. Cute but basic. Jogged in the mornings. Downed smoothies for lunch. No smoking, partying, or even regular clubs. In a word, *vanilla.*

Not the match for Zeke's griffin.

Her heart pounded in time to the new boot steps in the entrance foyer. She'd recognize the powerful footfall even if somebody threw a blindfold on her. She almost begged someone to do just that. Though it would kill her not to watch him enter the room, at least some of the water balloons in her body might change back to the muscles they once were.

"Shit," she blurted. The cushion upon which he'd told her to wait for him was next to the fireplace, across the room. There was no way she'd make it in time. But the bar was right here. She grabbed a cold beer and popped off the top. Maybe if she greeted him with it, maybe even from her knees—

"Wow. Thanks, little flower, but Amstel isn't my brand."

Shit, the awkward sequel. "Sorry. I thought you were someone else." She glanced at the guy's feet. Yep, there were the same heavy boots, same big-ass feet. They were attached to equally impressive legs and surfer-god gorgeousness, which would've had her running for whatever *was* his favorite brand on any other night. "There aren't too many size seventeens that walk through that door."

Surfer god grinned. He had one slightly crooked canine, which gave him a devil's air as well. "Good call."

"I know shoes."

"Ah-ha. Then the guy you're likely mistaking me for is my buddy, Zeke Hayes. Only guy I know in Seattle who also wears a seventeen."

She smiled back. "Yeah. That'd be him."

"You're in luck, then. Saw him out in the lot. He's parking his truck. He should be in here in just—"

"Thank you." She felt awful for not letting him finish but hoped the fast peck on his cheek made up for it. After a hasty dodge through the crowd, she made it to the cushion in time. The velvet square caressed her ass and thighs as she arranged herself, making sure the dress and her hair were still exactly what Zeke had specified.

She got in half a calming breath before a second set of boots thumped into the club.

It was both heaven and hell to wait here. In this location, she could keep her head lowered but still steal peeks from the moment Max opened the red velvet curtains to let him through. When that happened...

Holy. Crap.

Screw the downcast eyes. She couldn't stop staring. The backdrop of those drapes was achingly perfect for him tonight. He was regal. Beautiful. A black leather vest embraced his broad torso, covering a pristine white button-down opened into a deep V where his burnished skin practically glowed in contrast. The shirt's collar caught the ends of his hair, which hadn't been recut to army regs yet. Black leather pants covered his legs, leaving no hard, huge inch of his thighs, glutes, and calves to anyone's imagination. That included the beautiful long muscle that dominated their apex.

Before she could stop herself, she openly licked her lips. By every saint Da Vinci ever put to canvas, God had hung that man with a beautiful cock.

Like Hampton Court gone kinky, the crowd parted for Z like he was a young King Henry returned from Cambrai. In truth, Z had probably been someplace worse, so the adulation fit. Few in the club knew exactly what Zeke did for the army, but it didn't take a genius to piece things together when he disappeared for months without warning and no estimated return time. He was one of the elite, going out to battle the worst of the bad guys, which meant everyone celebrated his returns. But the cornerstones of his job, stealth and concealment, also meant he forced every inch of the smile he gave in return to everyone now.

He didn't look any more comfortable as he approached her. Working to regulate her breathing—ha, fucking ha—Luna pulled up her spine, dipped her head, and folded her hands atop her thighs. She checked the angle of her legs again. One was tucked against her backside, the other curled gracefully next to it. She was as *in place* as she'd ever be.

Even without Zeke's air-altering presence, she would've detected him drawing near. Though all conversations didn't stop, it felt like they got tucked beneath a heavy blanket. She expected the sounds that stood out in the resulting hush. Stunned gasps. A few curious whispers. And of course, the snarky giggles. *Master Zeke was playing with* her *tonight?* Like the good courtiers they were, everyone buzzed with their bets about the outcome.

Go ahead, you petty shits. We'll see who's satisfying him long after you've gone home to your dream lovers and vibrators.

There was no more time to indulge the musings. The scuffed toes and heavy buckles of Zeke's boots appeared in her view. The scent of him, musk and rain and man, filled every corner of her senses. So much for feeling composed.

"You got the memo." He said it in a murmur only she could hear. The intimacy was a pin on all the water balloons.

"Yes, Sir." She kept her head bent as he paced an assessing circle around her. "Are you pleased?"

Shitty timing on the question. He was behind her now. The disciplinary yank on her braid proved that, along with the scratch of his beard against her ear. "Are you in charge?"

"No, Sir." The words left her on a breath. Yeah, she was officially a puddle now.

"Then no more questions, Luna. The only words that leave your mouth tonight are 'Yes, Sir' and 'No, Sir.' Are we on the same page?"

She nodded, for words weren't possible. *Oh, God.* This was what she needed. A merciless leash. A Master who held it without a tremor. He knew that already, didn't he? He just... knew. As she'd been so certain he would.

Zeke released her hair, though he remained behind her. His legs pressed her shoulders. The force of his stare scorched the back of her neck. "In answer to your query, since it was asked so sweetly, I *am* pleased." He stroked the top of her head. "Did you comply with everything?"

The pause in his words filled in the subject to which he referred. Like she'd forgotten it for a damn second since he'd come in. Like the panty-less, pulsing walls of her pussy would let her. "Yes, Sir," she responded.

He stepped back. "Then lean forward and show me. Full ass presentation, girl. Knees nice and wide."

Her heartbeat rammed her throat, shoved there by a mix of terror and excitement. Fuck. He danced at the edge of terminology for slave positions. Would he really go there with her? Had he somehow reached that far down into her psyche, explored the deepest shadows of her desires?

Zeke's impatient cough left those questions hanging. Shit, shit, shit. They'd barely begun and she was blowing it. She pitched forward into the position he directed, pressing her forehead to the carpet, her arms flat from elbows to palms. She raised her lower body high, spreading her legs as he'd specified, which caused the slinky dress to slide and puddle across the top of her back. Nearly all of her body was now on display for Zeke. And everyone else in the room.

And all of them could see how wet she already was for him.

"Holy shit."

Quiet praise permeated the words, which would have warmed every inch of her if Z had said them. The drawl came from his friend, Mister Size Seventeens with the cute crooked tooth.

"Hey." There was a gruff slap, like the two men clasped hands. She couldn't be certain, since her eyes were barely an inch off the floor.

"You're a lucky bastard, Hayes."

She really liked that guy.

"You also know what other kinds of a bastard I can be." Zeke's response was full of tight meaning.

"So you say."

"So you've *seen*, Tait."

The other man snorted. "Fine. I get that you're concerned. But you're not in mission gear, this isn't a scum pond in Bumfuck Asia, and *she* is nothing like the pricks we're normally up against." Another distinct pause. She felt him gazing at her, as well. He audibly shifted in his pants. Was the guy really that hot from the sight of her? And did that please or disturb Z? "With all that beauty to harness, I don't think 'Psycho Zsycho' will want to come out and play tonight."

Psycho Zsycho? She should have laughed. Instead, a shiver claimed her. Every inch of her sex got soaked with anticipation, making her pussy tingle when the moisture hit the air. Sure, Z was a well-built man and a masterful Dom, but it was the violence beneath his surface that lured her like yin to yang...the animal in him, more than able to handle the voracious beast in her.

And now, learning his squad mates had *named* his animal...

Shit. Just shit. She curled her fingertips into the carpet in order to keep the rest of her body poised for him.

"The vote of confidence is appreciated, man," Zeke answered, "but you don't understand. Right now, I guarantee you that little beauty is wondering how fast she can meet the Zsych Man. And how long he'll stick around."

She indulged a smile. Damn, did that man know her. But why did he keep fighting it? Why did he keep denying what they shared? Everything they could be together? She was determined those questions wouldn't go unanswered tonight. He'd finally see her truth. He'd finally see *her*.

"She can wish it all she wants." The statement came from Tait. "But the last time I checked, you weren't her genie in a bottle." There was a meaningful pause. "You're here to give her what she *needs*, Z."

Luna gripped the carpet again. The anticipation of Zeke's answer rushed her stomach with delicious terror and drenched her sex with illicit heat. Would he get it? Would he know?

"There's the quicksand, man. Zsycho out of the bottle *is* what she needs."

She barely held back a grateful sob. He understood. He really did.

Tait wasn't so ecstatic. "Fuck."

"Now you know why I need a babysitter."

A drink glass clunked against a table. "I'd better not finish this."

"Bring it along. You'll probably need it later."

"Affirmative on *that*."

Like a meadow beneath an approaching storm, every nerve in her body stood on end as Z moved again. She shook but held her position, even when he crouched next to her. But when he skated a hand down her back, scoring her skin in a slow drag, her moan was uncontrollable.

His touch roughened. So did his breath. Her body rose and fell in time to his exhalations, her blood forming its lusty backbeat.

He didn't stop at the bottom of her spine. He rode the undulations of her ass, circling his long fingers around one cheek and then the other. By the fucking stars in heaven, he was going to give her an orgasm before he gave her a single welt.

No. No! She fought the rush. Tried to clench her pussy against it. She didn't deserve it. Not this fast. She had to earn the pleasure. She couldn't have the ecstasy before she endured the agony. They'd made that abundantly clear at Saint Cecelia's, hadn't they? Over and over again. You could take the girl out of boarding school, but boarding school never really left the girl.

She shook her head, wrestling back the memories in addition to the arousal. Tonight wasn't for those girls. They'd never rule her again. Zeke would banish them tonight. Forever. His hands felt so good. So powerful. So right. He made it even better as he straddled her again, looming while he curled his grip into her pooled dress and then tore the thing in half with one violent tug.

As the fabric slipped from her body, her breath rasped from her throat. She whimpered, melting beneath his brutality, soaking up his strength. She didn't stop even when he wound her braid around his fist again, using it as a handle for hauling her to her feet. But she wasn't standing for long. Another sweep of his arm twisted her around to face him—for all of two seconds. One more yank and he had her flung over his shoulder like a limp rag doll. Her face bounced against his back. Her ass, firmly anchored by one of his hands, pointed toward heaven. Appropriate, since that was where her mind was headed, too.

People greeted Z during his descent to the club's private play dungeons. He didn't say anything in return. She was grateful. Totally exposed and completely helpless, she wasn't in the socializing mood, either.

The man's energy intensified with every step. If he was a meadow storm before, he was a mountain downpour now. His stomps echoed off the stone walls like thunder. She felt every one of his breaths in her knees.

A tiny shred of her mind wondered to which room they were headed. They called this the dungeon level, but some of the rooms were just role-play sets. She sure as hell hoped he hadn't stripped her bare only to shove her into a French maid or harem harlot getup.

As soon as Zeke turned into a room, she knew he hadn't let her down. The temperature dropped by a few degrees. The visceral smells of leather and iron filled her nose. His footsteps resounded with ominous, bass-filled notes. *Yes.* They had to be in the Stockade, the Crypt, or the Keep. She didn't care which. All three rooms were designed for what she needed tonight. No ceremony. No luxury. Only his primal force unleashed on her willing body.

He wasted no time in getting started. As fast as he'd thrown her up on his shoulder, he let her down. Though he took a second to make sure she had her balance, there was no gentleness to his motions or his face. Part of her panged because of that before she shirked the feeling. She'd all but blackmailed him into this, so did she expect a sweet kiss on the nose and a light swat on the ass? *Blech.* She wasn't Lucy Ricardo, and Z sure as hell wasn't a bongo-beating nightclub crooner. *Thank God.*

The door thumped shut behind them, followed by another set of footsteps. She heard Tait settle himself on a couch in the little observation area in the corner. Again, the force of the second man's stare made her sex clench and her nipples pucker in hyperawareness. Shit. Zeke was serious. He really did want a monitor on their scene. She hated and loved how that made her shiver.

"Display."

He gave the direction with such calm power, she froze. Had she heard right? The command didn't hint at a slave position. It *was* one. Could she hope he really knew about her fascination with those shadows of the lifestyle? Could she dare think he would take her into them tonight? Use her in that raw, basic way?

During her deliberation, Z stepped to a side table. She hadn't noticed it until now, but a quick glance revealed what had to be every extreme toy in the man's kink arsenal. He tucked away a few things she'd been too slow to see, but the large coil of rope wasn't going into any of his pockets. She wet her lips in anticipation of how he *did* intend to use it.

He arched a thick brow. "I assume you understood the command, girl?"

"Yes! Of—Of course, Sir."

Crazy. She was truly nervous now. Her fingers trembled as she laced them behind her head, extending her elbows to the sides, securing her feet a little farther apart...opening herself to what he could do to her. She tried to concentrate on holding the pose, but as he circled behind her, she shook again. The storm was temporarily banked, but the man in which it roiled made her feel like a sapling in comparison. She needed him to tie her in with that rope. She needed to know she could fall apart and the power of his bondage would catch her, contain her, cradle her fall into joyful nothingness.

Z moved closer. Luna's eyes slid shut. Her skin prickled with expectation, awakening to his size, his hardness, his power. God, she hoped he wasn't gentle. She wanted to burn from those coarse hemp fibers...

He didn't wield the rope. Instead, he clamped a hand to her braid again. "Be still." His voice went low while his grip tugged high. Her scalp throbbed in delicious pain as he secured her hair to an overhead rig point that she couldn't see. Before the strands slipped too far, he twisted thick long leather cords around them, securing the connection with rigid tugs. Luna breathed deep. *Damn.* That smell. Leather was her chocolate, her oysters Rockefeller. It woke her up and turned her to goo in one glorious whiff. Just like that, she was even more aware of every movement Z made, of even the slightest brush of his huge, strong body.

He finally stepped behind her again. She heard him uncoil the rope and then measure its length with definite calculation. With every long, steady stroke, her bloodstream danced closer to the edge of her skin, filled with the imagery of letting him drive his huge cock into her at just that pace...

Hell.

Or was this the beginning of heaven?

Why couldn't she wish for both?

The question formed a beautiful dilemma as he laid the rope across the back of her neck. The hemp was everything she hoped for. Harsh. Hard. Heavy. As he reached over to crisscross the lines between her breasts, he settled his mouth next to her ear. She let out a shivering, needing gasp. *Tell me what you're going to do to me. Tell it to me in a filthy growl. Tell me in illicit, immoral detail. Please...*

"Time to go over the rules, Luna."

No wonder the bastard had tied up her hair. If her head was free, she would've snapped it with a glower to singe his skin off. She had to settle for hissing at him in disgust. "Yes, Sir."

Zeke chuckled. "I'd swat you for that tone, girl, but you'd love it too much." He looped the rope atop her navel and then yanked the lengths around her waist. "You know full well how I roll."

"Yes, Sir." She gave him the frosty cone version of it this time. If Mr. Safe, Sane, and Consensual wasn't going to touch her until the D/s legalese was complete, then Lady Attitude-With-Wheels was coming out for a spin, too.

"You have a problem with that?"

"No, Sir." She supersized the frosty cone.

"Then you'll have no trouble giving me your safe word."

Forget the frost. She unleashed the ice storm. "Are you fucking serious?" Rules, she would do. Guidelines, she would follow. But safe wording was the boundary she didn't want or need, and Z knew that. Hard limits? *Ha.* Safe words *were* her hard limits. He knew that. But clearly didn't care.

"That's too many syllables for a safe word," he drawled while continuing to cinch her in, twisting the rope around, laddering it up her spine with a series of masterful knots. Damn him, He knew how good that felt, how much she loved this. "But I'm confused," he went on. "That couldn't have been backtalk coming from you, right?" He secured his next knot extra hard, locking in her whole torso, squeezing her breasts between the ropes in front. "I'm not used to backtalk. That's also part of the rules. I like being obeyed." He extended the ropes along her shoulders, pulling her right arm straight and starting an intricate gauntlet down its length. "I expect to be obeyed."

Now she silently wished him to the bottom of the Sound. The way he bit out *expect* but finished it in such a sensual husk... the way he pulled the rope hard and then fastened the line to a hook protruding from the wall...the way he shifted his massive body around her with the grace and speed of a damn ninja... He was so magical, he broke down her defiance with disgusting speed. Worse, she didn't even mind. She couldn't summon the nerve to even clench her teeth as she finally whispered, "Yes. Yes, Sir."

"Perfect." He halted in front of her. Planted his feet. Lifted her chin with one of his fingers. He was so beautiful... Already, more of his beast prowled in the bronze shadows of his stare, played at his full, battle-roughened lips, unfurled through the majesty of his huge, gleaming muscles. Luna yearned to reach for him with the arm he hadn't bound yet. She could tell him, even with just the tips of her fingers, that he could dump a dozen safe words on her tonight and she wouldn't use a single one. She wouldn't banish his beautiful animal, even if it came close to killing her.

"Safe word?" he prompted again.

Ugh. *Fine.* She sighed and blurted, "Cinderella."

"That wasn't so bad, was it?" Though he pulled her other arm out and started whipping the ropes into its own gauntlet, he kept an appraising eye on her. "Slipped out easily enough, too. Have you been masturbating about glass slippers and dancing with princes, Luna?"

She let a bristled glare serve as her silent *fuck you.* Like that stopped the man from his scrutiny, burning it up her arm from the wrist he secured with a flawless cat's paw twist before knotting off the line using the eyebolt on the opposite wall. She didn't shy back from his stare. Let him look. He wasn't going to see anything he didn't know about her so far. Nothing that he didn't recognize in himself first.

He proved that as truth with the next words he gave, knowing and carnal and dark, as he moved back in front of her.

"Oh, yeah. Dancing's just fine with you, yeah? Just as long as the slippers are in shards and the prince has a blade at your throat." He lifted a hand exactly there, bracing her neck from ear to ear with his hand. Slowly, masterfully, he began to clamp down. Not so languidly, her pulse began to hammer her veins.

"Mmmm," she mewled. Technically, it wasn't a word. The sound was definitely more cat than human now, the feral creature into which he was turning her as he squeezed a little tighter...

"Yeah...you'll fill the night with dancing, won't you, Luna? Just as long as you keep wondering if your next breath will be your last...then soaring on the high when you realize it wasn't. You'll keep dancing, even when it hurts, because the pain is the reminder that you're alive." He softened the hold. He cupped her nape with his other hand, making her whimper again with need. "But it's your way out, too. It confirms you. Then it erases you."

For the first time, she hated him for binding her like this, for opening her so wide to him. It assured that he saw every inch of her reaction. The gratitude. The adoration. The arousal. The truth in every last word he'd spoken. The craving for all of it. She swallowed hard, swearing he wouldn't get her tears, too. *Nobody* got those.

Past taut lips, she answered, "Thank you, Sir. Yes."

He studied her for another long moment. The alloy in his eyes turned from bronze to gold. She had no idea what he was probing for in her face, but his lips parted to reveal teeth clenched in victory, as if he'd found it.

Then he left her.

She was stunned for a moment. And cold. The man was a walking radiator. The temperature drop made her nipples pucker tighter, her skin turn to pebbled pathways. Her mind reeled with trepidation, anticipation.

She listened to Z's decisive steps, now behind her once more. But there was more movement than him. Somebody shifted, as if readjusting themselves on leather furniture. Hell. She'd forgotten about his buddy. The appointed kink police. What was his name again? It didn't matter. The timbre in his voice spoke for him, penetrating the depths of her soul.

"Christ. I didn't think she could get any more beautiful."

Zeke answered with a deep chuff. "The fun's just begun."

The guy gave an angry groan. Luna sympathized. Every moment from here on was under Z's complete control. Though she'd begged fate for this, the reality of it brought exasperation along with the excitement. All her fantasies of this had played out with her timing, her wants, the actions she created for him to carry out. The hugest aspect of this, his domination, was simply impossible to create. Like it or not, it filled the room now, claiming every throb of her heart, every awakening every inch of her body.

Her breaths quickened as Z paced back over. She prepared herself for the whoosh of a crop, perhaps the swish of a flogger. There'd been a few beautiful whips on his toy table, too. Dear God, would he dare *start* the scene with one of them? Her stomach wrenched in fear.

Thwack.

The crack of the broad paddle ricocheted off the walls, ringing in her ears. Hell, that thing sounded big. And painful. *Really* painful. She got a little concerned, wondering if he'd tested it on his hand, hoping he hadn't cracked a finger or two by doing so—

"Shhhiiit!"

The scream spilled out of her the same second the realization hit. He hadn't indulged her with the mind fuck of the "test smack." Her ass *was* the test. In fiery, consuming intensity.

He had the nerve to press the damn thing to her skin again, tracing the edges of the burn with the tip of the thick wood. Luna squirmed beneath his taunting touch. She imagined him standing back there like a hammer that had grown muscles, now flashing a cocky grin at the nail he'd just tamed. But when he spoke, nothing but calm command defined the words.

"What do you say, girl?"

His composure was unnerving. Enraging. "Ummm, how about a warm-up next time, *Sir*?"

Thwack.

"Owwwww! Damn it, Zeke!"

"Still not the right answer."

Thwack.

She twisted her hips, hating him for this...revering him for it. Zeke stepped forward again, making her gasp in exquisite fear, though he refrained from swatting her again. He was utterly silent—but she sure as hell felt his stare. His assessment. His patience. Damn him. Bless him.

Finally, she let out a long breath. Her words were tight but sincere. "Thank you, Sir."

He came closer. Swept a hand across her burning ass cheeks. "You're welcome."

Ohhh, yes. That felt wonderful. She got ready to give him a blissed-out sigh, but sharp pricks suddenly rolled down her spine, jamming the sound in her throat. The telltale squeak of metal accompanied the pricks. She stretched the sigh into a grateful moan. A Wartenberg wheel. One of her favorites. And God, did he know how to use the thing. Z was relentless with the pressure, making sure the steel pins dug in nearly hard enough to break her skin. As she cried out from the delicious torment, a deep part of her begged him to do just that. What would he do if she really bled for him?

She sensed the answer to that just by listening to his breath. He was fighting hard to keep the steely Dom veneer. His exhalations clawed at the edge of growls, especially as he turned the wheel and ran it back up her torso. As he dug new tracks into her skin, her delts and lats twitched with fevered awareness. With every inch he scored, he pressed to the edge of cutting her but never did. It was making her insane—and she was pretty sure he shared the sentiment.

She whimpered in need.

Aggghh! Why didn't he listen?

She writhed and pushed herself back at him. She parted her legs, struggling to show him what he was doing to her, how hot and wet she was because of him.

He didn't care.

"Damn it, Zeke!" It burst out beyond her control. "Do it, damn you! Cut me open! Please!"

Her heart sank when she saw the wheel fly by as he threw it to the floor.

Her senses flew when he replaced the instrument with his fingernails.

He used just one hand. It was enough. He spared no mercy with those five prongs of determined flesh, firing them into miniature blow torches, especially when he crisscrossed the tracks he'd already made with the wheel. Another cry clamored at Luna's lips but he was already a step in front of her. Suddenly, he wrapped his other hand to her throat again, compressing with more exquisite purpose than before. He loomed close, a presence at her peripheral that was larger than life, a haunting saber tooth with his rough breaths and silken motions.

"We'll get there, subbie. But in my time, not yours."

Luna's arms tensed against the ropes. She knew what words he wanted, but giving them up felt impossible. She was already so vulnerable to him physically. Giving him more surrender, even verbally, was too much. "Fine," she sneered. "All right, all right."

He stilled the hand on her back and constricted the fingers on her neck. "You know, I'd almost applaud you for that audacity. *Almost.*"

He scooped around enough to meet her eye to eye again. His grip moved to the hook and bindings in her hair, freeing her from the bondage in a pair of deft tugs. That didn't mean he was done. After winding the braid around his fingers again, he yanked. Her head snapped back, releasing a new shower of shivers down her nape, throat, and shoulders. So much for feeling one speck sure of herself. Now capturing her from the front *and* back, Z directed exactly where she looked and what filled her vision—which, for now, was nothing but him.

For which she should be rejoicing...right?

A funny thing happened on the way to the rope bondage. All her dreams of this night had never made room for one key element: the magnitude of this man's energy. The potency of his presence. The dark splendor of his beast, taking over more of him. He was so perfect it hurt to look—but shutting her eyes was as futile as breathing. The second her lids descended, he growled and wrenched her hair tighter.

"Eyes right here, girl. Right. Here."

Her obedience wasn't without reward. His lips twisted in a smirk that made her breath turn from a wad in her throat to a boulder in her chest.

"Very nice. You'll stay like this until I tell you. I want to watch you through this next part. Best to remember the rules again on this one. Especially the clause where I expect to obeyed."

"Yes...Sir."

Miracle of miracles, she prevented the punctuation on it from being a shaky question mark. His instructions took on another tone she'd never heard from him before, frost and fire mixed so seamlessly she couldn't determine what to prepare for. His lips curled higher, telling her it was where he wanted her, too. Wavering on *his* strings. Teetering on *his* ledge. Slowly, achingly, fulfilling her dream—on *his* terms.

As she worked to accept that thought, he unwound her hair and brought her braid forward, draping it between her breasts. His knuckles brushed her skin, making her quiver. She released a rasp of shock. Simple caresses weren't supposed to do this to her. She wasn't a silk and ribbons girl. She was barbed wire and steel chains, a creature built for Doms who bit as hard as they barked. Z knew that, too. Knew it and craved it as much as she did. So why was he pulling the lame seduction moves? Why did he follow that stroke on her breast with a duplicate caress? Why did he slip his other hand down in order to fondle the other peak in the same manner? Why did he keep up the mushy-gush treatment, even when she let out a protesting snarl?

Probably had something to do with how he planned to rip that sound in two. Or a thousand. That was what her voice felt like once a pair of nipple clamps seemed to appear in his hands from nowhere and were guided to the tips he'd coaxed to full attention.

Without a second of warning, her crests went from aching need to receiving mind-halting pressure. She screamed, wondering if she resembled one of the immortals from *Highlander*, with lightning bolts ripping her apart. The pain went from mere torture to what-the-fuck-is-*that* within a second.

"Holy shhiitt!"

Z was still as a damn monk. She got her head under control long enough for a chance to look down and gauge if his cock was behaving like Friar Tuck, too. If she was going through this and not getting a damn inch out of him, her snarl was coming back if she had to hog-tie it in her chest.

Her gaze never got as far as his crotch. As soon as she saw his fingers on the strings of the clover clamps attached to her breasts, tightening their sadistic clutches on her nipples, her snarl came with no problem.

"I'd think twice about continuing that if I were you, girl."

She bared her teeth as she lifted her glare. He released the strings but continued batting at them, taunting her, his eyes aglow. He knew exactly what his arrogance did to her, didn't he? He was confident of every drop he elicited in her pussy now, with his massive body in front of her and the clamps pumping an agonizing elixir through her whole torso.

Through those clenched teeth, she issued, "Wasn't thinking of continuing anything, Sir."

His lips quirked. "No?"

Unbelievably, she summoned a smile. The endorphins from that, blended with the adrenaline from the pain, curled a tendril of delirium through her brain. "Words aren't the only way to talk, Master."

Z chuckled. "Very nice point. They certainly aren't." Through foggy vision, she watched his hand dip into his pocket again. "Which is why you won't mind this at all, hmmm?"

Before she could follow his movement, he showed her the "this" to which he referred. Luna grunted in surprise as he fitted a hard silicone bit gag between her lips with expert speed. He had the nerve to laugh softly again, the mirth lingering on his lips as he cinched the buckles to hold the bit in place. When he finished, he slid his fingers back to the sides of her face, tilting her up for his scrutiny.

He began stroking her bottom lip with his thumbs. The motion clicked as *her* cue to do something, right? But what was it? It was time for her to glower at him again, right? Or stamp her cute sandaled feet at him? To pick something out from the "bratty" column to drive a new thorn into his fur, so a bigger chunk of his civility finally fell off and he—

Stared at her exactly as he did now.

Ohhh, hell.

As he swiped her lip the second time, Z traced the seam between her teeth and the bit. That made his snicker stop. When that happened, Luna pulled in a shaky breath. Zeke's smile faded. She was glad she'd filled her lungs, because when his lids lowered and his irises went molten, air was officially added to her body's No Admittance list.

Stare at me like that forever.

"Very nice, Luna."

Forever and a day.

His husky words wove pure magic into her body. She needed to acknowledge him, but no sound stirred except a soft moan from deep in her throat. For some reason, that made his lips rise again. But this time, his smile didn't tease. It was more like...

What? What *was* he thinking? Hell, she barely connected to what *she* was thinking. All right, *that* was funny. What thoughts would those be, exactly? The ones consisting of *nunh, he's so beautiful,* or *gah touch me again, Master*?

He'd told her they'd do this in his time. By his rules. It had been so easy to *Yes, Sir* him, without absorbing the truth into her soul. She believed him now. She adored him for it now. She needed more of his domination now. And could do nothing to demand it.

Even when he dropped his hands from her and disappeared.

She whimpered in frustration. The ropes around her arms, once friends, were the sentinels that prevented her from knowing where he'd gone or what he was doing. She dropped her head, glaring at the dark, throbbing red nubs of her nipples, still bound in his clamps. Her mind swam, still hostage to the spell of his control. Though she could hear his steps and feel his presence, she craved his touch again. Longed for his words. Needed the next sweep of power and blessing of pain he had to wield.

She hated every second of it.

She loved every second of it.

As her mind plunged deeper into her surrender, a deeper moan erupted from her throat. She drooled a little past the gag. She tugged at the ropes, savoring every burn they gave her skin.

Until Zeke slammed against her spine again.

Her breath rushed out as he splayed a hand to her stomach. His other hand trailed lower. Two of his long fingers dipped into the valley of her buttocks. They stopped at the rim of her tight back hole. Luna pulled in air through her nose as he slowly pressed at the sensitive nerves.

At the same time, he trailed his other hand into the layers of wet arousal between her legs. A thousand sparks shot through her pussy, her thighs, to the ends of her toes. "Ahhh!" The cry came from her but sounded like the scream of another, a being spun of pure sensation, created solely to be his special welcome-home toy. Oh damn, *yes*. More of the world spun away. She forgot the dungeon, left the world behind, even the awful memories of Saint Cecelia's that had threatened before. Right now belonged to Zeke—his touch, his hands, his control...especially as he captured her most sensitive button beneath his fingers.

She released a high, long keen.

"Good girl." His voice was dark as coal as he squeezed something cold into the opening of her ass. *Hell.* The only smell she loved more than leather was leather mixed with lube. As he worked the tapered tip of an anal plug against her entrance, he ordered, "Be still now, subbie."

Despite the morass in which everything from her clit to her cranium now swam, she tried to swing a glare backward. Be still. Really? Sure, boss. She'd get on that as soon as she got over the fact that first, his fingers were turning her pussy into a not-so-small electrical storm, and second, he was preparing to invade the tiniest cavity in her body with something—

That stretched it far beyond comfort.

"Unnnnck!"

The syllable was a miserable fail at the F-word. It did the trick all the same, easing off the tempo on her body's wild megamix of pain, frustration, and nympho-level arousal. Her womb, teased by two forces outside her control, throbbed like a savannah without a tiger to rip through it. Yet Z twisted the plug in deeper, stuffing her more full than she'd ever been back there, hurting her so exquisitely, so erotically.

"Uhhhhnnnn!"

She bucked against his grip, feeling that he hadn't gotten it in all the way, unsure if she could take the rest.

"Girl, what part of 'be still' did you not understand?"

Hell.

With heaving lungs and trembling legs, she gave in to his command. And learned that her ass could indeed take the rest.

"Aggghhh!"

Stars shimmered behind her squeezed eyelids as he seated the plug completely. He pressed the base to her ass cheeks with an approving grunt, letting his fingers linger along her skin. "Perfect."

His voice was lower. Grittier. Mesmerizing as the lightning he continued to spread through her sex, helping to gather the downpour over her savannah. Terrible torment. Throbbing rapture. She wanted to burst so bad...

"Mmmmph." The pressure from the plug turned into a steady, beautiful burn. Everything was a mad mix of pain and pleasure. In the black behind her closed eyes, she spiraled higher into the storm. She was pulled by relentless winds, flying across the veldt. She was lashed and helpless, at the mercy of the beast now driving her on with a bamboo cane at her ass. His feral breaths ripped through her blood. His guttural commands filled her head.

"Feel it all, Luna."

Another stinging blow. Another scream from the depths of her soul. *Yes. Oh, yes!*

"Take it all, Luna."

Another. Harder. Sharper. Her penitence. Her deliverance. *Yes, Master. Anything you want to give me.*

"Shatter for me, Luna."

The bamboo came down. His fingers pushed inside. The storm crashed. The climax claimed. She was devoured.

Yet before the pulses in her sex died away, his mouth was back at her ear. His breathing was heavy, harsh, pure animal. It matched the next *whack* he rained on her, going for the virgin flesh of her upper thighs this time. Relentless. Driving her to another limit. Ramming her past it.

"*Now* you've had your warm-up."

CHAPTER FIVE

Rayna didn't want to be here.

Sally couldn't have been thrilled about it, either. But the therapist looked as serene as the Dalai Lama in one of her office's big leather chairs, blond curly hair pulled up loose, and a Foo Fighters sweatshirt pulled over faded jeans. From behind her trendy oversized glasses, her eyes were warm and kind.

That didn't stop Rayna from continuing to feel like a giant shit.

"It's ten o'clock," she muttered.

"We've established that," Sally answered gently.

"On a Saturday night."

"That, too."

She grimaced. "I can't believe you insisted on meeting like this."

"I can't believe you thought a phone call would handle it."

She tugged at a thread in the tan T-shirt in her lap. Zeke's T-shirt. He'd left it in her room this morning. Not surprising, considering his commitment to his bat-out-of-hell flight from the house. She hadn't found it until she'd finished scrubbing the kitchen, scouring the bathroom, and cleaning out the den closet, only to find she still wasn't tired enough for the TV lullaby that had saved her from returning to the bedroom last night.

As if fate still had it in for her, she'd walked into the

bedroom and found the damn shirt like it was a homing beacon. To compound the mistake of picking it up, she'd smelled it. In an instant, he'd filled her senses again. She was meeting his brilliant hazel gaze. Exploring his burnished skin. Letting him fill her body. Letting him see more of her soul.

Burning their friendship because of her damn hormones.

Twenty minutes after that, she'd dialed Sally. Gotten desperate enough to call her therapist's cell at eight p.m. on a Saturday.

"I would've been fine," she murmured, "after a little bit. I just needed to talk and—"

"Rayna."

"What? I wasn't in total crisis, okay?"

"*Rayna.*"

"I was in a little rough spot."

"You were in tears."

"It was a bump."

"*A lot* of tears."

"Okay, okay." She started making accordion folds in one of the T-shirt's sleeves. Sally didn't say anything for a very long pause. Crap. The woman was watching her. Being watched was intimidating. It meant she was a target. That any minute, three of King's men would swoop in, hold her down, spread her legs, and—

This jewel isn't your shame. This diamond is a symbol of your miracle. It's your true medal of honor...

She forced down a shaking gulp. Clung to the words, begging them to echo some more in her head, hating them when they did. Her fingers hurt from gripping the beige cotton. *Shit.* She was stronger than this. He'd been the one to show her that. And he'd be the first to tell her she had to do it without him, too...

"Ugh. I'm a mess." She fidgeted, considering a get-me-out-of-here moment of her own. "Look, I'm sorry I bothered you, Sal. I'll call one of my brothers. This isn't fair to you. You're gorgeous. You must have a date lined up or something."

"Yep. A really good one." Sally chuckled. "He's very adept at putting a movie on pause, keeping dinner warm, and understanding that when his woman is a shrink for MRW services, her hours aren't nine to five."

"Sounds like a keeper."

The woman's face softened. Her lips crinkled in that "I've got a delicious secret" way that only other women understood. "We'll see."

Rayna nodded at Sally's shirt. "Does he like the Foo Fighters, too?"

The woman squared her shoulders. "Are you going to play deflection until I call you on your shit?"

She shrugged. "You have to admit, I'm good at it."

Sally didn't return the mirth. She let a sizable pause go by. "Who belongs to the shirt, Ray?"

She let her gaze fall again to the beige lump in her lap. Tried to tuck in the spots where she'd dampened it with her tears. This heartache was so ugly. And stupid. And useless. "You mean who *belonged* to it." She ran a finger along the worn collar. "Me," she finally said. "It belongs to me. He left it behind. Which means it's officially mine now, right?"

"Is that a good thing or a bad thing?"

"It's a *no* thing."

As Sally's brows ticked up, she backpedaled over her thou-protesteth-too-much answer. "It's nothing, okay? It has to be. It's what I agreed to, all right? And the last time I checked, I was a grown-up who knew the difference between strings-free sex and stalker expectations."

One side of Sally's mouth kicked up. "So you slept with someone."

"What's so funny about that?"

"Nothing. I think it's wonderful. You're moving forward with life, getting on with what a normal twenty-seven-year-old woman should be—"

"It was Zeke."

After ten seconds, she got ready to repeat it. Maybe the bomb was really that huge. Though Sally looked more Zen-perfect than ever, she didn't even lift her pen to jot this in her ever-present session journal.

Finally, Sally stated, "So he got back early from the deployment."

Had the woman spoken like they were just trading costume ideas for the Halloween bash next week? "Uh...yeah."

"Bet you were glad to see him."

"Uh-huh. I was. And then I *slept* with him, Sal. Did you get *that* part?"

"Yep. Sure did."

"And you're not shocked?"

"I'm stunned that you thought I'd be."

She went silent while scrunching one of the T-shirt's sleeves into an accordion fold. Yay. The self-appointed stupidity medal just got bumped from silver to gold.

"Let me guess," Sally went on. "You two agreed it would be a friendly little tension reliever, right? Just a way to burn off some stress? But hindsight isn't bearing that out?"

She let the fold fall apart along with the edges of her composure. "Hindsight." It fell out on a whisper. An image engraved itself on her mind with not-so-nice severity. Z's broad, bare shoulders as he'd made a beeline for her front door. "Sure. That's a good way of saying fucked-up-to-shit, isn't it?"

"That's pretty harsh language."

She looked up. Hell, here came the tears anyway. "It's a harsh world."

Getting her bitter side on didn't help things one bit. The ache in her throat got heavier. The loss in her heart flooded deeper. Neither got better when she remembered the look Z stamped into her before turning from her. His stare, full of so much regret and discomfort, that she'd been certain of one thing. He'd likely been prepping it long before their night of reckless sex.

Great. Out of all the Special Forces studs in the world, she'd slept with the only one who dealt the goodbye fuck *after* the deployment.

She erased the wetness from her face in two furious sweeps. "Look," she muttered, "I understand what happened. I even understand why." After her easy catch of Sally's tissue box lob, she went on, "I just don't understand...all this." She waved one of the white swipes. "I have a lot of friends on the base. And some of them come with equipment that's handy at times..."

Sally smirked. "Helps to know a soldier with a good-sized...gun."

She returned a watery laugh. "Yeah. It does." As if she were getting naked physically as well as emotionally, she curled her knees to her chest. "But I've never had any problems putting them all back into their compartments. What's my problem now?"

Sally released a meaningful breath. "Zeke's a little too big for a compartment."

Rayna snorted. "No shit."

"I didn't mean that literally."

"Neither did I."

After another silence passed, filled mostly with her efforts to force the memories of Thursday night away, she hurled the tissues to the floor but kept the T-shirt.

"I hate this," she spat. "I hate feeling like this. All right, I admit it. I was just part of his job for a while. Maybe a part that lingered longer than most, but—" She rested her cheek on her knee. "I told myself it wouldn't be forever. I knew it wouldn't be, since the second we got out of that damn jungle. And nothing got any easier when I found out he's a Dom—"

She coughed to cover how she chopped back the rest of the word.

"He's a what?" Sally asked.

"A—a dog lover." She averted her eyes. "And you know how my back porch is a magnet for every stray cat in the neighborhood."

"Rayna." Sally's tone got layered with concrete all of a sudden. The woman leaned forward. "You're racing all over the place with this."

She raised her head and winced. "I've noticed, thank you."

Sally uncurled her legs. As she came forward some more, she L-shaped her elbows atop her knees. "What do you want here, sweetie?"

The ten-million-dollar question. If only searching her heart for the answer made her feel that way. If only she didn't have to search her damn *heart* for the answer. When had Zeke come to park his beautiful ass in so much of it? When should she have pushed herself back from his massive shoulders and told herself that they wouldn't be there forever? That one day, she'd be looking at the horizon without him in it?

She should have known. She should have seen.

She ducked her forehead back against her knees. "I just want to go back three months."

"You think that would give you the answers?"

"No. It would prevent the questions in the first place."

"Because you'd make sure to keep Zeke in his compartment this time. Is that it?"

The concrete was gone from Sally's voice. She didn't need it. The question did a fine job of crushing Rayna's logic on its own. "Shit," she whispered. "Maybe I'm just screwed."

Maybe she'd been that way from the beginning. Perhaps from the second the man had scooped her from the dirt in that jungle, some chromosome had gone rogue and let in stupid expectations through a back window of her psyche. That meant Zeke was more than right yesterday, accusing her of turning him into Superman—or worse—when all he'd been doing was his job.

Yeah. Screwed. That was her.

She lifted her head enough to shoot another despairing stare at Sally. "Why did I pick now to be an idiot about this crap?"

The therapist barely moved. "Why do you think *now* has anything to do with it?"

She should have looked away once more. She knew what Sally was getting at—and dreaded it. About three weeks ago, during a session where Rayna had been more confused than usual about the inability to disconnect from Z, an inquisitive look had crossed Sal's face. Two seconds later, she'd made a suggestion that first had Rayna giggling.

Hypnosis.

She hadn't laughed for long. Sally had stated her case with serious intent. The therapy was doing wonders for the guys who'd seen intense battle, and maybe a focus like that would help Rayna feel more independent of her attachment to Zeke. Still, Rayna had rolled her eyes and accused Sally of simply wanting to see her dance like a duck or break into a Beyoncé tune.

The subject hadn't gotten dropped for long. Sally had been persistent in her suggestions about the therapy. Like now.

But there was a difference tonight. Rayna was officially desperate enough to listen.

She straightened a little. Released a weighted sigh. "You really think it'll help, don't you?"

Sally smiled softly. "I think there might be something in your past that you don't see now that might explain why you're in bondage to these feelings for Zeke."

Bondage. Zeke. If the woman only knew how perfectly she'd tapped that vein. "You mean, like something I've repressed? But why?"

"Perhaps it's too traumatic to carry in your active consciousness," Sally offered. "Or it happened so fast, you've mentally filed it away as nonimportant." She tilted her head in contemplation. "Our minds are like a big sweater, woven with fibers of our experiences, present and past. Sometimes the tiniest of threads can unravel a whole sleeve before we see it."

Rayna scooted her legs into a crisscross. "You think I'm unraveling?"

Sally took a deep breath. "Not yet."

"Great," she snorted. "So I've still got half a sleeve left. Thanks for the assurance."

The therapist got up, crossed to her, and crouched. "I think you have a need to understand things, Rayna. To understand yourself. And after you've done that, you need to fix it. Goes hand-in-hand with your need to care for people. None of it is bad, sweetie. It's probably why you went into the medical field." When Rayna huffed, Sal grabbed her hand. "Answer me something. If you guys get a patient who isn't responding well to a medication, do you give them a sweet little 'too bad, so sad, maybe we can help you next time'?"

"No!" She glared. "We try something else."

"Even if the patient thinks you're going to turn them into a Beyoncé-belting duck?"

"This isn't the same and you know it."

Sally folded her arms. "It isn't?"

"Sal, an amputee with a shitty penicillin reaction isn't the same as—"

"That guy's nurse with a devastating one-night-stand reaction?"

She turned, refusing to let Sally see her grimace. Like that would prevent the woman from noticing anyway. Sally had made the remark to get her specifically to this reaction—this crossroads of confusion and defeat that gave her no other choice of what to feel next.

Total desperation.

"Okay, okay!" She tossed up her hands and sighed. "You win. I'll try this nonsense." She almost laughed at Sal's fist pump. "I said I'll *try*."

Sally grinned. "That's all I ask, sweetie."

"I suppose you want to get this done now?"

Sally nodded eagerly but stopped herself. "Wait. You haven't been drinking, have you?"

She chuckled. "Do the five huge iced teas from this afternoon's cleaning binge count?"

Sally scrambled to her feet. "Only if you need to hit the little girls' room before we start."

A little over thirty minutes later, Rayna found herself parked in one of the big chairs again, now seated just a few feet away from Sally and feeling a dozen kinds of dork at once. The lights in the room were dimmed. Sally had turned off the soft jazz station she usually played, making the building eerily quiet. She'd already guided Rayna through the hypnotherapy version of foreplay—breathe deep, stare at the candle, feel your eyes getting heavy, breathe deep *again*, stare at the candle *again*, feel your eyes slowly closing...

Ugh. Enough was enough. It was clear this game wasn't working. And didn't Sal say she had a hunk waiting for her back at home with a paused movie and a warm dinner? And likely a foot rub, too. Yeah, game over. She'd tried this new planet, but sometimes you had to kill off the crewman in the red shirt and beam back to reality. Now they could both go home and—

She couldn't move.

She thought about it. Hard. Told her body to get up and move for...wherever it was that wasn't here. Her limbs were rooted to the chair. No, that wasn't it. She was able to move. She could lift her hands and wiggle her toes, just didn't want to. She was really relaxed. Peacefully focused. When Sally asked her if she was comfortable, her head bobbed in an easy nod. Heck yes, she was comfortable. Too much so.

She really needed to get out of here. And Sally, too. She had to go—

Where?

Where was it Sally had to go? She'd known a minute

ago, hadn't she? It didn't seem important anymore. She was walking through a park on a beautiful spring day, just like Sally suggested to her. It had recently rained. She could smell the damp pines, the moist honeysuckle. A mild wind picked up her hair and rustled the pashmina around her neck. What an awesome day...

"Are you in the park now, Rayna?"

She smiled. "Yes."

"Do you feel safe there?"

"Totally."

"Perfect. Just keep walking and enjoy the day. What else do you see?"

"Mmmm." She looked around. "Playground. It's themed like a pirate ship. There are some kids on it." She lifted her hand to wave at the children before quickly scooting to the left. "Yuck. Somebody didn't clean up after their dog."

Sally's answering laugh came from far away, as if she'd stopped at the other side of the playground. But when she spoke, she was back within arm's reach. "Is there anyone with you? Anyone who makes you feel more secure and relaxed?"

She smiled. "Yes. Ava."

"She's your friend?"

"My cousin. But yeah, she's my bestie, too." Just like that, Ava materialized next to her. Chocolate curls swinging. Indigo eyes dancing. A fashion plate even at twelve, with her self-painted T-shirt and red high-top sneakers. Rayna laughed and sobbed in the same breath. She hadn't seen Ava in years, since her cousin moved to LA to work as a stylist on a TV show. To have her like this, flung back to one of the summers when they'd both been so free and happy, made her heart soar like one of the blue jays overhead.

"What are you two doing?"

She flipped her head, feeling thoroughly twelve and arrogant. "Just hangin'. The usual." She giggled. "Talking about boys."

"Of course you are." There was a smile in Sal's voice, adding to the sunny freedom of the day. As Rayna offered a stick of Juicy Fruit to her cousin, Sally directed, "Okay, you're going to move on. You're moving to a place where you're not so comfortable. Maybe the two of you leave the park. Maybe Ava isn't even with you anymore."

The day got darker. Clouds skidded over the sun. She clutched Ava's hand. "No. She's still with me." Wrong. The sun hadn't been blocked by clouds. "Tunnel," she muttered. "We're still in the park and there's a tunnel. We normally love it in here. It's like our secret cave, but today"—her throat clenched—"it's not."

Their footsteps didn't reverberate the way they normally did. "Who's here?" she murmured. The air reeked of cigarette smoke and sweat. She wrinkled her nose.

"But what, Rayna?" There was a slight pause. "Come on, sweetie. Talk to me. Is someone in the cave with you and Ava?"

★ ★ ★ ★ ★

She thrashed her head back and forth. No! *She didn't want to see this, let alone experience it again. Summoning strength she didn't feel, she jutted her chin.* "Stay close, cuz. They're just stupid boys. They're not going to—"

"Rayna, watch out!"

The tang of terror filled her mouth. The horrible taste was worsened by the tobacco and grime on the fingers of the gang's leader, who sneaked behind her as fast as the tall rat he resembled.

"Dibs on this slut, guys. I like redheads. The trendy tart looks like she'll be double the fun for both of you."

"Get your hands off me!"

"Rayna? Rayna!"

She couldn't figure out who that was anymore. It sounded like Ava but resonated like Sally, too. What was real? What was going on?

The other two boys were closing in on Ava. The one who held her already gave a low chortle. She snarled and tried to get her teeth into the guy's finger. Fail. He rearranged his grip, squeezing until her molars tore into her cheeks.

"Quiet, bitch. Don't make me do this the hard way."

"Mmmppff!"

The guy was stronger than his wiry frame let on. When she stomped her right foot atop his, he just laughed and kicked her in the heel with his steel-toed boot. The pain shot her up with more adrenaline. She poured it into the elbow she drove to his gut. Direct hit this time. He groaned and doubled over. She was free.

For fifteen seconds.

She went straight for the two shitbags who descended on Ava. She whirled one of them around and drove her nails into his cheek, praying she peeled his skin off his skull as she tore down. He howled, making his buddy look up and let Ava go.

"Run, Ava!" she screamed. "And don't stop!"

Thank God her cousin obeyed. Now she just had to deal with her own consequences, which came with furious speed.

"You stupid little snatch." It was gritted by the guy with the red gashes down his face, leering as she got dropped to her back *with leader boy's steel-toed stompers. She grunted as she hit the dirt, the air punched from her lungs and balance ripped from her senses. The roof of the tunnel was a twisted canvas of dark oil and fresh moss, pigments that could've been pulled right out of the fear and agony in her spirit.*

"No," she whimpered. "Please don't!"

Her hands were slammed back, locked beside her head by leader boy, who stood on her wrists. She choked, overwhelmed by the stench of mud and dog crap from the soles of those hideous boots. His chuckle dripped with derision as he unzipped his pants.

"You take her first, Taylor. Her blood for yours, yeah? In the meantime, she can look up at the next meat for her oven."

Taylor laughed. A switchblade fwipped out of its holster. In two seconds, he slid the blade through her shirt and tore it off her torso.

"I can't believe this is happening." Her rasp echoed in her head. Her sob sounded even worse. "Help me. Somebody please—"

There was a shriek, but it wasn't hers. The switchblade clunked to the ground between her legs. Taylor was suddenly gone. No, not gone. Torn away. What the hell? Since her wrists were still pinned, she could only see what her upstretched neck would allow—which was Taylor getting flung against the wall.

Was she imagining this?

Taylor hit the rocks like a hurricane had blown him there. Impossible. Superman only existed in comic books, right? Not that leader boy gave her any time to rationalize that. He scooped up the switchblade and hauled her across the floor by her hair, but stopped after four steps.

"Stop where you are, asshole, or I'll give this stupid squaw

a scalping."

Fear was an ice floe in her veins. The only operating parts of her body were her chattering teeth and her heaving lungs.

"Rayna! Sweetie, you have to tell me what's happening!"

Sally was back. Oh, thank God! Maybe she could help. No, she couldn't. Where was she? Far away. She was still so far away.

"Help me. Somebody has to help me. He's going to—"

There was a massive lunge, like a bear rushing the tunnel.

"No! Don't move! Can't you see? He'll—"

The shriek belonged to her this time. The pain was awful but didn't touch the horror of feeling a chunk of her hair stripped from her head at the edge of a switchblade.

"Rayna!" Sal's voice shook. "I'm going to bring you out of this now!"

"No!" She held out a hand, fingers spread. "Don't!"

Why had she done that? She wanted to stay here? *Trapped in the hands of a scumsucker who'd been ready to rape her a minute ago and was seconds from slicing into her scalp?*

Her memory provided that answer the next second.

The hurricane that had flattened Taylor wasn't done yet. And holy crap of all craps, that force of nature had taken human form. At least that's what it looked like, as the guy went at her attacker with a snarl that was only half biological. She was certain the other half was meteorological. Raging. Roaring. Such a wild difference from the faded jeans, plain tennis shoes, and worn black hoodie he had on. Rayna shook her head in deeper disbelief when he made the gang leader drop the knife by twisting the bastard's wrist until the bones cracked. The hoodlum doubled over, clutching his hand. The human hurricane planted his foot between the guy's butt cheeks and shoved him until he joined his gang mate on the ground.

Wisely, the third thug had made himself very scarce.

"You know, Kier, you should be happy I'm in a nice mood today. The way you two dickwads are moaning on each other, I could take a movie and sell it for big bucks to Sissy Boy Video."

Rayna was rooted to her spot. The voice in that body sounded like a teenager, but the muscles in that body—oh, God. Her twelve-year-old hormones got a jump to light speed as her gaze traveled up his formidable legs, traced over his proud back, took in the angles of his fisted arms, and finally followed the plateaus of his shoulders to his hooded head.

"I need to know who he is."

Her murmur was a deceit. There was a scream beneath every syllable, which still didn't explain the panic that hit when he turned. She ducked her head behind her knees. Her frantic breaths bounced off her thighs as she listened to the three strides he took back to her side. He crouched and skimmed long fingers over her shoulder, setting off tremors of hot and cold through her whole body. He was so big. So confident. So male.

And she was being a total nimrod. Jeez, she'd grown up surrounded by boys. Male was nothing new to her!

Wrong. So wrong. This male was different.

She let the emotions go ahead and invade. In a weird way, she savored them. The smallness. The gawkiness. The inability to move or speak. Things she'd never felt around a guy before.

"Rayna." It was Sally again, calm but firm. "It's time to come back. This is enough for your first—"

"Wait. Please wait."

"Are you okay?"

His voice wasn't a storm blast anymore. It was a dark but calm caress, like the wind after an October rain. Power leashed again.

There was a ripping sound. Those magical fingers moved over her head, dabbing at the gouge at the back of her head. That spot had always been sensitive. It burned now, matching the stinging heat behind her eyes.

"Hey, you're safe now."

She needed to tell him she believed him. The encroaching tears stopped her. She needed to thank him. She needed to—

"Are you hurt? Can you stand? I can carry you, if you need. I just want to help, okay? My name is Zeke. What's yours?"

"Oh my God."

The next second, sirens blared through the tunnel. Red and blue lights flashed into the gloom. Flashlight beams joined them, swords of illumination around Ava's silhouette. Her cousin led the way for a handful of cops, now bellowing orders to each other.

"Ray! Are you all right?"

"I'm fine, I'm fine. Thanks to him. Oh God, Ava! He was amazing! He..." Her voice trailed when her cousin frowned. She spun, throat clutching when all she saw were the dents in the dirt from where he'd hunkered next to her.

"Rayna, you need to come back now."

★ ★ ★ ★ ★

She opened her eyes at Sally's firm command. Her vision was still hazy with tears.

"What is it?" Sally reached for her hand. "Can you tell me what you saw?"

For a long moment, she could only shake her head. Emotions rained on her brain, her heart. Shock. Joy. Confusion. Delirium. Absurdity. Clarity.

"No wonder," she whispered.

"What?" Sally pressed.

"No wonder it's different with Z. No wonder I've felt this way."

Sally stroked the back of her hand. "Do you need to talk about it?"

She nodded. The action came slowly at first. But by the time she shoved out of the chair, determination powered the move. "Yeah. I *do* need to talk about it." She grabbed her purse. "And I know with whom."

Sally rose, as well. "Rayna, listen. I know you're excited about this, but sometimes letting these revelations rest a while—"

"I think fifteen years is a pretty good while, Sal." She beamed a full smile at the woman before pulling her into a tight hug. "Thank you," she whispered, "for not giving up on the hypnosis. Now go home to your man."

Sally's answering look was pinched. "Though 'home' isn't on your mind, is it?"

Her smile grew. "Not by a long shot."

★ ★ ★ ★ ★

A little under an hour later, after some tenacious web searching, she stood in front of a building in the warehouse labyrinth beyond South Spokane Street. The structure's few windows were shrouded by black drapes. The door was painted the same color. A faint but steady bass line drifted into the night. The melody behind it was beautiful but did nothing to stop the nerves chasing each other down her spine.

No doubt about it. The determination that had gotten

her here was disappearing as fast as the stars behind the night mist. If "here" was even the right *here*. She checked the address on her phone again, not that the warehouse had any corresponding number on it. Yet the GPS pin rested directly on top of the spot in which she stood.

In short, she was either walking into Bastille, one of Seattle's naughtiest BDSM dungeons, or a kickin' rave party with God-knew-what spiked in the punch bowls. In either case, she'd look like an alien and feel even weirder. Goodie.

She took a deep breath. An expression popped off her lips that she and Sage usually saved for patients with rolling blood veins.

"Suck it up, bang on the sucker, then plunge in, Sergeant."

She knocked on the big steel door.

Her greeting was answered faster than she thought. Her breath hitched and her nerves tensed with the expectation of being greeted by an Igor or worse, raking her over with bulbous eyes and a lascivious grin.

No sign of Igor.

Not by a really, really long shot.

Her greeter was like a huge slab of granite, only carved more beautifully. The skull-close cut of his black hair magnetized her study right to his eyes, their color giving new meaning to the phrase *piercing blue*. And the grin? *That* was where the guy's inner Igor showed itself. Lascivious only skimmed the look he slid over her.

"Well, hello there."

"Hi." Rayna cleared her throat and tried to smile. "I'm sorry to bother you—"

"Let's make something clear, Little Red Riding Hood. *You* are no bother at all."

The man knew how to pick imagery. He opened the door wider with a confidence that was one hundred percent Big Bad Wolf. Rayna stood where she was. Didn't take a rocket scientist to remember the ending of that fairy tale. "I'm, ummm, looking for a place called Bastille."

Wolf Man inclined his head. "You're not looking for it anymore." He crisscrossed the air with his finger. "X marks the spot. Why don't you come inside, beautiful? It's getting cold."

She shrugged off the hand he cupped on her shoulder. "Who are you?"

The guy laughed. Damn, could his dimples get any deeper? "Shit," he mumbled, "where are my manners?" He dipped his lips over one of her hands. "Max Brickham. Bastille is my castle, and I am your servant. Perhaps you'll return the pleasure of knowing your name now, Miss—"

"In the wrong place." She swallowed and tried to slide free from his grip. Her resolve deepened when a long male moan punched the air from somewhere in the club. She couldn't tell if the instigation was pleasure or pain. Did it matter? "Uh, yeah," she stammered. "That's me. Wrong place. *Really* wrong time. I'm so sorry."

What had she been thinking? Hadn't Zeke reminded her yesterday, in damn clear terms, what he did with his Saturday nights? Had she really gotten all the way inside the door of this place before that memory slapped her like one of the paddles mounted on the lobby's wall? Each of the boards had a number on it, along with club members' signatures that relayed its correspondence to another year Bastille had been open. There were seven paddles in all. It was weirdly sweet. She wondered if Max put up a Christmas tree each year too, decorated with kinked-out customizations of Hallmark collectibles.

The man chuckled as if the nonsensical image hit him as well. "It's not that bad, Red. You haven't dropped your basket... yet."

Great. Wolfie was on an innuendo roll. Rayna tried pulling from him again. No dice. Though the man's hands were as big as paws, his hold was that of a practiced paladin. He clamped her fingers tight but stroked her palm with a thumb that was all feathery seduction.

"Th-thank you for your time, Mr. Brickham. It's been nice to meet you, but I think I'll just—"

"Tell me your name?" He tugged in his bottom lip with the grin this time. He knew the boyish charm angle, too? She wondered why there wasn't a woman or ten draped on his arm.

Despite her nerves, Rayna laughed. "Good heavens."

"We can certainly make time for that. But I need to know your name first."

"Rayna!"

Max dropped her hand like he'd gotten caught in the cookie jar. The voice clearly wasn't new for him—nor was it for Rayna either. For a year of her life, when the world was nothing but African jungles and the tribes who would enslave her there, her only friend was the diminutive blonde who stopped about six feet away, rocking a pair of black stilt heels, pink fishnet stockings, and a rose-hued minidress with black corset ties up the back. Her face, framed by her glamorously curled hair, was frozen in a gape.

"Well, well, well." Max folded his arms as those ocean blues danced with amusement. "You're a friend of Sage, huh?"

"She's my *best* friend, Brick." Sage rushed forward. "I'm just wondering what the hell she's doing here."

Rayna seized the opportunity to scoot back. "Zeke," she

blurted. "I was looking—well, I was hoping—"

"Zeke?" Max's brows jumped with new interest. "You know *him*, too?"

Rayna disregarded that. She looked to Sage. Just saying Z's name again, along with her friend's arrival, reignited the determination that had gotten her here to begin with. "I need to talk to him, Sage. He's here, right?"

Sage took her hand. "He is," she gently confirmed. "But this may not be the right time—"

"Then I'll wait until it *is* right." When her friend winced, she persisted, "Do you know what it took for me to find this place, let alone the personal psych-out just to knock on the door? So do you think I'm here just to ask him about catching the *Star Wars* marathon downtown next week?"

Max's jaw dropped. "There's a *Star Wars* marathon? And *you're* going?"

Sage rolled her eyes. "Don't get her started, Brickham. Do you know how many times I've had to listen to the 'Han gets frozen in carbonite' scene, word for word?"

Max dropped to a knee and took her hand again. "Marry me."

Sage rolled her eyes. After yanking Rayna from him, Sage gathered both her hands up. "Listen...Ray..." Her eyes, normally bright as spring, were a somber celadon. "Z could be a while."

"Because he's with a submissive?" She smiled a little when Sage gaped. "I know all about it. And I'm still choosing to wait."

Max growled while getting back to his feet. "Damn that fucker! Back in the country less than three days and he has a waiting line."

"No, he doesn't." Sage pulled her deeper into the club, past a red velvet curtain and into a shallow alcove. "I love you," she said, "so I say this *with* love. You don't want to see Z tonight, Ray. It's complicated for him right now, and—"

"Sage!"

The bellow came from fifteen feet down the same hallway. Rayna turned with her friend as a familiar face emerged from the shadows: the golden, chiseled features of Garrett Hawkins. "Shit!" Sage exclaimed before rushing to her towering, black-clad fiancé. With equal alacrity, she bowed her head into his chest.

"Sorry, my Sir. I was on my way to get Z's beer, and—"

"Screw the beer," Garrett interjected. "That's why I came to find you. I've never seen him like this. He's gonna need something stronger."

Rayna swallowed, unable to move again. Garrett's syllables were rolled in gravel and finished with doom. She'd never heard him sound that way before. Or any of the guys on the squad. They didn't talk to each other or about each other like that.

An anvil dropped in her stomach. Garrett was *worried?* About Zeke?

She mentally peeled the glue off her feet and stepped out. "What is it?" she demanded from Garrett. "What's wrong with Z?"

The guy's tawny brows descended over his eyes. "Fuck." He glowered at Sage. "What the hell?"

"Don't look at me! I only went for beer."

Garrett hissed and raked a hand through his hair. "Rayna, this isn't a great time for—"

"She wants to wait," Sage cut in.

"You can't wait." Garrett's lips flattened. "You don't want to wait. Rayna—*Rayna!*"

His yell consumed the hall, even making her ears ring, but she almost told the guy to save his breath. Vocalizing her resolve and then hearing it reiterated from Sage fused new girders into her resolve to see Zeke, no matter how long it took. What she'd learned in the session with Sally...it was remarkable. Uncontainable. In a way, it was perfect that she was here to tell him about it. This dungeon was no less foreign and daunting than the cave where he'd been her hero for the first time. The thought poured cement into her drive.

Funny thing about cement, though. The stuff took time to harden. And in that period, images were pressed into it that would last a lifetime.

Like the moment she saw Zeke again.

She turned the corner and came across an area with couches that were centered on a sprawling fireplace. There were a lot of plush blankets and big velvet pillows. If a few bowls of popcorn got thrown into the scene, it would've been an idyllic slumber party setting.

With the exception of the naked woman who got carried into the area by Tait Bommer.

They were followed by a person who vaguely reminded her of Zeke—if she could use the term "person" for him right now. The shirtless, sweat-covered creature in front of her was someone who looked like him but barely seemed *him*. His steps were bestial tromps. His breaths were harsh heaves. He didn't just occupy the air. He wrestled it from the universe and claimed it—and wasn't nice about it, either.

Rayna couldn't take her eyes off him.

"Shit," she whispered. Hell was certainly preparing a place for her right now, because her eyes weren't the only body part obsessed with him. Every one of the nerve endings between her thighs came alive in need, making her clench back a gasp. She watched him cross in front of the fire and fantasized about tackling him right there, in front of everyone.

The tension got worse the next second.

Tait laid the woman on her side along one of the couches. He settled at her feet. There was room for Zeke on the cushions near her head, but Z didn't sit. He kept lapping the circle of ottomans in front of the fire, eating up the space like a dynamite fuse that wouldn't blow.

Tait threw a questioning look at Garrett.

"Let him burn through it," Garrett murmured to the guy. To Sage and Rayna, he added, "Holy fuck, I hope he burns through it." A scowl creased his brow. "On the other hand, that means he's gonna drop hard."

Rayna looked to Sage. "He's going to what?"

Sage tugged her closer so she could speak softly. "After an intense Dominance and submission scene, when the adrenaline and endorphins fall, the participants often take a physical or emotional tumble. Sometimes it's both." She nodded toward the couch. "Tait's made sure that Luna's got a shitload of aftercare: Gatorade, ointment, blankets. It's Z we're all worried about."

Sage's confession made Rayna gape back at Z. She couldn't fathom him dropping from anything, especially knowing what he'd been like as far as fifteen years back. But before fifteen *minutes* ago, she couldn't imagine confronting the man in this state. His frenetic energy stirred the flames beyond the grate every time he passed.

One thing finally halted him. Luna herself. Her eyes, half-closed and unfocused until now, opened a little wider. She sobbed and reached for Zeke. He crouched to her side in a second, running a long, gentle thumb along her forehead. Even from where she stood, Rayna saw the dark concern in his eyes, the silent questions across his face.

When the woman shifted a little, Rayna understood why.

She stifled another gasp. Luna's back, butt, and upper thighs were twelve shades of red. Dark slashes formed a sadistic crossword puzzle in her alabaster skin, with bruises and whip marks taking the place of consonants and vowels. It was all so ugly, it was beautiful.

But Luna's face riveted the eye more. By anyone's ranking, the woman was already stunning, with a full mouth, thick eyelashes, and high cheekbones. She became awe-striking when she opened her huge lavender eyes, tears glittering, and stared at Zeke with open adoration. His reaction wasn't so gooey. His jaw and shoulders tightened. Still, he spoke to Luna with measured care.

"You did real good, little girl. You were great."

"Zeke." Luna's sigh was soft as a prayer. Her smile made her look like she'd dragged on the best doobie ever rolled. "Thank you. Oh, God—"

"Ssshh. Rest."

"But I need to tell you—"

"*Rest.* I won't ask again."

Zeke exchanged a glance with Tait, who nodded reassurance that he'd stay with Luna. That seemed a really good thing, because Z gained his feet again like an untamed animal. He skipped the circuit around the ottomans to stalk down another dark hallway. Rayna rushed to watch his silhouette in that corridor. His arms were coiled, his hands turning to fists. He slammed the wall twice before careening to the opposite side of the hall, yanking open a door, and staggering into the room beyond.

Garrett lunged to follow him. Rayna did the same. At the guy's threatening glare, she squared her shoulders and pointed at Sage. "Save it for her, Hawkins. Do *not* try to stop me."

With a dark glower, Garrett stepped back. Rayna sprinted down the hall. By the time she got into the room, Z had sagged against a large steel cage there, gripping its bars like he was already locked inside. The chamber was outfitted like the Taj Mahal in satin drapes and a giant round bed, but it could've been the damn Four Seasons and she wouldn't care. Her only focus was the man she rushed to, pressing herself against his massive, heaving back. When Zeke flinched, she pulled out the perfect words to whisper. Things a teenage hero had used to soothe her fifteen years ago.

"It's okay. I just want to help. I'm here, and it's going to be okay."

A weighted moment passed. Another.

Of all the reactions she finally expected from him, his outraged snarl definitely wasn't on the list.

CHAPTER SIX

Anger. Confusion. Torment. Guilt. *Shit, the guilt.* This was what it must feel like to be the Incredible Hulk, only there was nothing incredible about it. Not a single fucking thing.

Things went even worse when a bird got into the dungeon. Not just any bird. *His* bird. Z thought he'd imagined it at first, somehow summoned Rayna's scent and presence through the force of his imagination, considering how many thoughts had been filled with her since the beast had completely taken over.

He tore through his brain, trying to reassemble what had happened. It'd been sometime after he spiraled Luna through her third climax. Her sobs had filled the room as he traced her whip marks with one hand and cupped her mound with the other. He'd crooned his approval and actually meant every note of it, for both her and him. He'd given her what she needed yet kept his head screwed on straight. The debt had been paid, and Psycho Zsycho was nowhere in sight. *Thank fucking God.*

Yeah...*there.* It was that moment, letting those words intrude, that started his supersized mistake. He'd dropped the mental defenses without considering how high his senses were really revved, how it could all sneak up on him in one dumbshit second and fill his imagination with the sole face he was struggling to block from this night he'd been duty-bound to live.

Inside a second, Rayna was everywhere. Blown up in his mind to the size of a goddamn megaplex screen. Not just any picture, either. He saw her gasping into her pillow as he possessed her body with his. He heard her screaming with ecstasy in the orgasm he gave her. And when Luna had moaned, wordlessly begging for more, he'd only heard Rayna's husky alto beneath the sound.

The same voice that vibrated in the air now, so real and terrifying. With every word, she reminded him of the leash he'd let the monster have—of exactly what he'd done to take Luna to her fourth climax. The strikes. The welts. The lashes. Her sobbing need for all of it. *His* hunger to give it to her. And the dark, savoring pleasure he'd gotten from every twisted second of it.

Psycho Zsycho hadn't just come out to play. He'd nuked the whole goddamn playground.

He roared at the fucker now. The effort spiked him with enough adrenaline to push from Rayna. He staggered a few steps and fell onto a little bench that Max surely must've gotten from Liberace's estate sale. He would've laughed at the gold velvet cushion if he wasn't so afraid of what might spew from him along with it. Tears or puke; they were equally humiliating.

To be sure he did neither, Z forced words out. "What...the fuck...are you doing here?"

For a long second, she was silent and fidgety. She was so gorgeously out of place in her pink hoodie, white sweats, and cushy winter boots. He didn't have the strength to go subtle with the stare he swooped over her. Fuck, what he'd give to get her inside those bars, cuffed and stripped, awaiting his pleasure.

Luckily, she grabbed that gist loud and clear, too. Her fingers were tense as they worked her sleeve ends against her palms. "I—I had to talk to you."

"Now?"

Emerald fire flared in her eyes. "Yes, damn it."

She darted a glance around the room. Summoning a moment of lucidity, he wondered what her impressions were, of what she must think of the ornate spanking benches with their red wrist cuffs, the round bed with the spreader bars and chains, the small stage that was preset with a submissive's V chair and a St. Andrews cross. All of it was so much his normality, of the planet he lived on. It was so different from hers. Did it horrify her, as it had the few vanilla women he'd dared bring here? He couldn't remember their names now, let alone the disappointment he'd felt in their disdain, if any. But having to think about Rayna fleeing in shock and disgust...

A barb lodged in the lining of his gut.

Fuck. This was so much easier when he'd been dictating the terms, when he called the shots. When *he* left *her*, not when she stood appraising a room in the club that was like his second home, and thinking—

What?

Well, she wasn't hyperventilating. But a longer scrutiny told him she wasn't truly seeing everything, either. That was the furthest he dared go in the effort. Staring at her more meant she'd captivate him more. Which would lead to him getting her onto the bed with him. Or better yet, into that cage.

Christ. The things he could do with her in that cage...

He barely held back a groan. Just when he thought his erection had found its manners, the fucker pounded at his pants, cheered by the chemicals left over from the insanity that'd gone down with Luna. Mentally, he was a mess. Physically, he was a machine primed for anything. A goddamn lethal combination.

He breathed hard, trying to summon words again. "Rayna, I'm working at the nice-guy thing here, okay? It's *not* a good time."

She twisted the zipper of her jacket. When she took a breath, her breasts strained at the T-shirt beneath, as perfect and round as he remembered. *Shit.* He closed his eyes. Like that was going to help—especially as she shifted even closer, filling his senses with her warm cinnamon scent.

"Are—are you okay?"

He lurched off the bench. "No, damn it." Fuck, she smelled *so good.* "You really need to—" He flung an arm up, muscles coiling, fingers trembling. "Stay there. I mean it!"

Another wrong move. If he was rational right now, he would've realized that. The woman gravitated to suffering and a need to eliminate it, like Mother Teresa poured into Aphrodite's body. Instead of backing off, she picked up speed.

"Zeke—"

"It's not a goddamn request!"

Desperation was an ugly CO. The bastard guided his arm to the whip rack before he could summon a shred of restraint. An Axel El Diablo ended up in his grip. Under normal circumstances, the whip would've felt incredible, a piece of high craftsmanship in his hand. He didn't waste time on that now. He flicked the thing with vicious speed, making the triple tails singe the air like a blow torch through rice paper.

Finally, *finally,* she skittered the right direction. Back. At last, her face contorted with the emotions that needed to be there. Shock, confusion, fear. Oh yeah, couldn't forget the fear, no matter how much it made him feel like spewing his dinner. Maybe it *was* a good thing that she'd come. That she'd finally seen, touched, and smelled all of this. That she now got how his planet could never share the same galaxy with hers, let alone the same solar system.

Nausea hit him again. A bowling ball of a headache joined it. More dizziness followed. The confusion of seeing her here, followed by the realization she wasn't an apparition, capped by his free fall from the helicopter of Top space, had him reeling like the end of a three-day op without sleep. No, this was worse. There was no bad guy to show for the ordeal. Only a head full of pain, a cock full of lust, and a gut full of frustration. And yeah, he heard his heart's screams about its omission from that list. He snarled inwardly at that. *Nothing's changed since yesterday, you bonehead. Where Rayna's concerned, you* don't *get a vote.*

He needed some air. He needed some solitude. Goddamnit, he needed a wormhole and clearance for the other side of the universe.

At least he could easily get the first two. After jamming the whip back into the rack, he wheeled and stalked out the door out to the room's adjoining patio. Not every room in Bastille had one; he'd just gotten lucky to stagger into this one, where Max had erected a walled pavilion that continued the harem theme outside, much to the delight of club members who enjoyed under-the-stars fornication. Nobody "daring to bare" outside tonight. Those fuck-friendly stars were in hiding too, leaving just a black midnight and a chilled October wind.

Z gratefully sucked in the cold, dumping himself into a chair fitted in protective plastic for the winter. The covering was damp. It had rained earlier, and he smelled more on the air. Thank fuck for that. The scent was a blessed one-eighty from the spiced temptation of Rayna's essence. He bent his head back, letting the drizzle drench his face, allowing his equilibrium to swim.

"What the hell are you doing? It's freezing out here."

Her voice didn't stun him now. He would've been surprised, if not relieved, if she'd left now. That didn't make the ache in her tone any easier to handle.

"Go home, Rayna," he growled. "I know you need to talk. I'll call tomorrow, okay?"

There was a rustle as she sighed. She'd probably folded her arms, getting all gorgeous and huffy on him. *Fuck.*

"I got the message the first time with the mighty whip stunt, okay? But somebody's got to keep you from dying. Might as well be me."

Incredulity prompted one of his eyes open. Oh, yeah. Huffy. Gorgeous. Damn her. "What the—"

"You've been sweating. In leather pants and nothing else. Now you're sitting in midnight rain, shirtless and hatless, all but inviting hypothermia into your bloodstream for a nightcap."

"Thanks, WebMD."

"You're being stupid."

"I'm a soldier, damn it. I'm used to a little rain."

"Let me help—"

He stopped her by slamming a fist to the stone table. The glass stones in its fire pit jumped against the cover tarp from the impact. Both his eyes were open now. And shit, so were hers. Those deep green fantasies were even more exotic in her fury, especially when she parted her lips at him, too. He wanted to tame that mouth in at least fifty ways. He was hungry to bite it, growl orders against it, open it wide for the invasion of his. And that would be just the start.

"If you 'help' by even one more step, what I'll do to you would be—"

"What?" She bore down by another step. "What *would* it be, Zeke?"

He dropped his head. Stared at his curled fists. How easy it would be to just open them up and reach for her. To tangle his fingers into her beautiful strawberry strands and drag her back inside by them. To lay her out on the bed and kiss her senseless while he cuffed her down, yanked those sweats off, freed his cock, and—

With a guttural moan, he hit the table again.

"It would be what neither of us needs."

Despite the dictate in his tone, Rayna didn't budge. Hell. She wasn't going to let up on this sheet check, was she?

Fine. He knew how to do this. He did it for a living, goddamnit. Inwardly, he streaked his face the color of the jungle and imagined his loaded gat in his arms with a shitload of hostiles on his ass. With that new fortitude, he lifted his face and drilled her with a steeled stare.

"Go home, Rayna. I mean it."

For a long second, she still didn't move. For another, she shifted only those incredible lips of hers. Their hopeful defiance vanished, replaced by a bitter twist. They tightened as the depths of her eyes started to glisten silver, though the tears never liquefied. Without another word, she turned on him and disappeared inside the dungeon.

Zeke waited for the relief to come. It didn't. He dropped his head back and peered into the thickening mist. "Thank you for coming, ladies and gentlemen," he snarled. "That officially concludes the Zeke Hayes fuck-up-alooza for the night. Be sure to buy your T-shirt on the way out."

A new flood of light from the building jerked him upright. Rayna appeared again, head aglow with a burnished halo, shoulders set, head high. She let the door close without giving him a passing glance. Instead, she fished her car keys from her purse.

He rose, but she still didn't look at him. Her only movement was a nod at the pavilion's little side gate. "I assume this alley will get me back out to the street?"

"Affirmative," he muttered.

"Good." She paused long enough so he caught a glimpse of her profile—and the tiny wobble of her chin. "I don't want to see...everyone again." Even without her pause, he would've deciphered her subtext. *Everyone* meant *Luna*. "Tell Sage I'll be in touch."

He let out a frayed sigh. Pathetic. But it was either that or the command, right on the tip of his tongue, for her to stay. "Yeah," he mumbled. "Will do."

The clang of the gate behind her was filled with brutal finality. Thanks to the soaked pavement, he heard every wet *thwop* of her retreating steps. The high alley walls took care of the rest, pinging back every word she softly railed at herself during that walk.

"Great. Way to go, Rayna. That went about as wrong as it could have, huh? Maybe, girlfriend, you do need to go back to the jungle. Maybe you really are just a stupid little squaw."

He forgot to breathe again.

Funny how that happened when words acted like arrows in a guy's chest.

He spun around. His brain whirled too, feeling like an onion peeled by a coked-up chef.

Stupid little squaw.

Rayna was a crazy-smart woman, but even she didn't have an expression like that lying around for fun. She'd used it on purpose. Because it meant something to her. Because she'd heard it before.

And damn it, so had he.

"Shit." It was a hoarse punch of sound into the fog. He wagged his head, maddened by his inability to match the trigger to a memory. He only knew his heart suddenly pounded and his body dropped its lethargy like a snake shedding skin. As he turned and stared through the fog, his stomach filled with its special bile for those occasions when something or someone needed protecting. The last time he'd felt all this at once, he'd been carrying Rayna through the jungle, speeding her as fast as he could to the transport back to Bangkok—only minutes after he'd met her for the first time.

Right? Or not?

Christ. Did she know the answer to that? Was that what had brought her here? What *wasn't* he remembering? What hadn't she told him? *No, you bastard. You mean, what didn't you let her tell you?*

"Rayna." Her name barely made it out past his constricting throat. On the second try, he forced out a full bellow. "Rayna?"

The summons rang along the alley walls, but she didn't answer. He couldn't hear her boot steps anymore. Thanks to the thickening mist, he couldn't see her, either.

Another moment went by. No discernible *whump* of her car door or quiet start-up hum of her hybrid.

Shit. The Triple Crown of dread pounded harder in his gut. Burned deeper in his veins.

He raced for the gate and hurdled it. When her shriek sliced up the alley, he broke into a full run.

CHAPTER SEVEN

Rayna shouldn't have assumed the night wouldn't get crappier. As she emerged from the alley and crossed the sidewalk to her Jetta, a man emerged from the shadows behind her, proving that assumption wrong.

Really wrong.

Horror spurred her stunned cry. A second later, she choked it short. This couldn't be real. Her mind had been wrung like putty tonight. This had to be a sick aftereffect of that. Or maybe, please God maybe, she was just dreaming. Maybe all of this—the bizarre session with Sally, the massive mess of a confrontation with Z, and now this—was just a hideous dream. All she had to do was wake up.

Do it. Wake up. This isn't real. He *isn't real.*

But the monster with the tailored suit, proud stance, and slicked black hair curled a very real and disgustingly familiar smirk at her. It spread across a face of smooth sienna skin and part-Asian features that could be considered exotically handsome, if they didn't mask a soul that was blacker than an adder's.

How is this possible? She'd wiped that sneer from the bastard's face three and a half months ago—when she'd fired a bullet into the face that framed it. She'd watched them zip a black body bag over its lifeless pallor before they dragged him away, filling her with a relief that was so complete she'd been sapped of the energy to even wipe her tears. A couple of FBI guys had stayed with her, murmuring praise for her courage in putting the monster down. She didn't have the mettle to tell them the truth, about how courage had nothing to do with it. She couldn't verbalize how she'd become someone else when watching King drive a dagger into Zeke's gut, her body and thoughts filled so savagely with rage that she'd turned into an unthinking animal.

The agents had assured her King's torment was part of her past. He'd be great worm food in a week, and they were already transferring his twin, Mua, to the darkest cell they could find inside the max-security block of the Clallam Bay Corrections Center. It would be Armageddon before the cockroach saw freedom again.

Apparently, Armageddon had begun.

"Ms. Chestain." The criminal drawled it in a silky tone as two men materialized and flanked him like security at the elbows of a Fortune 500 CEO. They fixed her with stares that matched their muscles for steely hardness. "You are even more lovely in person than in your pictures, my dear. I've gazed at so many, you know. Surely you remember my brother's enthusiasm for photographing his treasures before he parted with them?"

Revulsion knifed her. King's photo sessions would haunt her forever. The monster would croon at Sage and her like they were in a Parisian fashion studio instead of his jungle warehouse, making them pose in their chains, recording their humiliation beneath flashbulb strobes and oily compliments.

You're not there anymore. And this isn't happening. This can't be happening.

She shook her head. That forced the memories away, but the three men in front of her, stepping slowly closer, remained horribly real.

"I'll scream," she threatened.

Mua smiled. "Oh, please do." He stopped but motioned his henchmen to continue. "My fantasies of this moment have been filled with many of your cries, dearest, though I wonder if they'll touch the real pleasure of hearing your terror on the air. I highly doubt it. Being locked in a stone box does become limiting, even with the dream of avenging one's brother's death." As the hulks approached and backed her against her car, the bastard emitted a silken hum. "So please, my little Rayna, indulge us with a vocalization or two."

Out of sheer defiance, she only glared—officially completing the circuit on her stupidity tonight. Terror blazed through her as the hulks moved with speed that defied their size, snaring her arms in meat-hook grips. Fighting them was a lesson in pain. She had no doubt they'd snap her bones if forced. She pulled in a lungful of air, reconsidering the scream, but the taller goon clamped a hand over her mouth. He didn't let up there. His fingers squeezed into the back of her jaw.

"Shut up, slut."

Thanks to her freshly ignited memories of King, it only took those three words to ignite her from dread to rage. The fire exploded into the bite she twisted into the inside of the henchman's middle finger. The lunk howled and released her, allowing her a full-scale fight against the other guard. She went for the obvious, raising a knee toward his groin, but Mua's men were better trained than his brother's. The asshole was ready. He quickly caught her knee and hooked an elbow beneath it. In a dizzying sweep, her whole word was upended. Her breath was pounded out of her from behind, and her view consisted of nothing but mist-shrouded streetlights.

She blinked, realizing the assailant at her back was actually the hood of her car. The smaller guard now shoved her knee close to his chest, keeping her pinned to the hood with his other hand with his palm shoved between her breasts and his round face consumed by a leer.

"Didn't King's notes say she was the docile one?" he drawled. "Well, if this is docile, I'm a fuckin' monkey. No wonder he had such a high ticket on the pair of 'em." He let his fingers trail over the swell of her breast. "Such a hot package. I bet she's a fine little ride."

Her head continued to spin. Her blood was a tribal cry of fear and fury. *The docile one?* That had probably been true—at one time. When she and Sage were first captured, she'd been the one to calm Sage, to exhort to her friend that compliance would keep them alive. But what kind of living had it been? Shackles and fear, humiliation and dread, the constant unknowingness of what the next minute, let alone the next hour or day, would bring.

She wasn't going back to that. She wouldn't. She'd make them kill her first.

With that resolve locked into her mind, she glared up at Round Face. "You got the *little* part right, asshole."

The guard's nostrils flared. "Don't tempt me to show you otherwise, baby."

"I'd love that. But I don't think there's a microscope handy."

She had at least three more zingers lined up, but Round Face erased them with a backhand that thrashed her head to the side. Rayna grunted with pain. Stars cavorted in her vision.

"Idiot!" Mua's shout was a razor of fury. "I said no marks on the merchandise!"

"What're you so pissy about? Nobody's gonna look at the bitch from the waist up."

The bastard was making this too easy. Rayna rolled her face center again, cocking a weak smile, "Well, nobody's looking at you *below* the belt, buddy."

Being prepared for his next blow didn't lessen the impact of it. As the agony radiated, the stars in her vision mutated into cartoon-style birds. She was stopped from laughing by the creature's bloodred eyes. They told her conscious mind what her gut already knew. If she kept goading the goon on, her death wasn't going to be pretty or painless.

Maybe if she scraped up the strength for one scream, it would reach down the alley and—

What? Zeke was ready to go back into the club as she left the patio. He was on his way back to Luna now, if not tucked at her side already. He wouldn't be listening for her any more than he'd heed a flushing toilet.

Mua's roar thickened her hopelessness. "Barbarian!" he shouted at the henchman. "Were you raised in a puddle of shit? When you are on my time, you are not an animal!"

"Well said, cocksucker." The words cut into the air like a sword of black steel. Very sharp, very pissed-off black steel. "Good thing I'm not on your payroll, then."

Rayna craned her neck and tried to focus her vision. "Z-Zeke?"

Her sob was diluted by a bestial snarl that seemed to come from everywhere at once. The next second, Round Face's weight was yanked from atop her. Before the bastard got out half an oath, he was cut short by a punch she'd only heard in movies as a sound effect. The real thing made the air shudder and vibrated down to the pit of her stomach, too. When Round

Face blew out a rickety moan, she decided the nausea was worth it.

Until the next moment.

She raised her head enough to recognize that the incredible had come true. Zeke really stood there, his wrath so palpable that the mist itself followed suit, turning into violent rain. Round Face still lay on the asphalt, clutching his gut and his groin at the same time, but the larger henchman clearly hadn't gotten the *back off* memo. The guy came at Zeke with single-minded purpose, eyes slitted black, teeth bared white. He was surrounded by the night's heavy tears, which made a perfect camouflage for the thick silver chain he swung in one hand.

"Zeke!" she screamed. "Watch—"

Her breath clutched as the bastard whipped the weapon with a vicious underhand. Zeke caught the chain with stunning reflexes but not before a half-foot of it whipped around his forearm with a sickening *chink.*

"Oh my God!" The words tumbled out as she scrambled off the car and started toward him. Two steps later, she froze in her tracks from the force of his fiery glower.

"Run!" he ordered. "*Now*, Rayna. You know what to do!"

Her sobs stuttered and then stopped in her throat. The boom of his voice was a reset button on her instincts. He was right. She did know what to do, and standing here like a melodrama damsel wasn't it. She needed to get him some help. Lots of it.

Despite the anguish of having to leave him, she spun and ran back toward Bastille's entrance door. She half expected to fight Mua himself on the way, but the cockroach seemed to have disappeared, a fact that disturbed more than comforted.

The cold made her hands sting as she beat frantically on the club's steel door, but she didn't let up until it was opened. Her breath of relief was cut short. Max's hulking form didn't fill the doorway. A curvy woman, looking like Rihanna's doppelgänger complete with gold boots and a matching fetish mini, flashed a friendly smile.

"Hi. Can I help— Oh hell, sweetie, what happened to your face?"

"Where's Max?"

Rihanna frowned. "He's at the back bar. Who are—"

"I need Max. And Garrett Hawkins. And the police." She was shocked at the control in her voice. Her heart hammered and her nerves were strung tight. As she stalked past the counter, she scooped up the phone on the counter and thrust it at the woman. "Call them. We need them out front, five minutes ago. Do it!"

By the grace of the universe, Sage appeared again. "Ray, how did you get back—*ohmigod*, your face! What's going on? I thought you and Zeke were in the—"

"We were. Now we're not. Sage, I need Garrett. Z's in trouble."

"Z's what?" Her friend blinked. "I don't understand. How can—"

"Get. Garrett. *Now*." Dread trumped calm again. Round Face was probably getting his second wind by now. The image of him and Chain Man going at Zeke together charged her like a Pamplona bull. "They're going to kill him!"

"What?" The exclamation came with the Midwest inflection for which she'd been praying. Garrett. Fate had smiled and hauled Max with him. "Who's getting killed? Holy fuck, what happened to your face? What's going on?"

"Thank God," Rayna blurted. "Zeke. He—"

It was all she had to say. The two men raced out the door in a cloud of gritted oaths. Rayna was right behind them, with that bull pummeling every one of her heartbeats. Had she moved fast enough? Were Garrett and Max in time to help Z from getting pulverized, or would they find him sprawled in the street, bloodied and beaten? Her mouth was dry. Her head careened. Her imagination screamed.

None of it was ample preparation for the real scene they encountered.

There was blood, all right. Lots of it. Impossible to miss across his bare torso, even in the rain. Rayna's stomach turned as she forced herself to look. But after a frantic scan of him from head to toe, she couldn't figure out where the goons had gotten him, aside from one nasty nick between his shoulders. His legs were stiff, wet logs against the pavement. He braced his arms out at forty-five-degree angles, his shoulders so rigid the rain formed puddles atop his muscles. Breaths ripped in and out of him, making the chain in his fists clank a little. The goon who'd just been wielding it was curled in the gutter nearby, groaning softly.

Confusion struck again. Rayna didn't know whether to hang on to her terror or surrender to a wash of lust. He looked movie-god good. Maybe that meant the rest had also been pretend. Maybe the stress of this whole night had finally sent her over the edge and she'd wake up inside the club somewhere, realizing she'd dreamed everything and—

Round Face took care of that delusion the next second. He reappeared from the same shadows that had first spawned him, stalking at Zeke with the same determined pace, though the reason for the guy's disappearance was clear. He'd gotten a wardrobe change. His tight black Henley was now covered by the gear of a Seattle cop, complete with badge, shoulder radio, and fully stocked weapons belt.

Like Z even saw all that. Or cared.

He crouched low and spread the chain wider, half a smile sliding across his full lips. "Aww, baby, you came back for more. I'm so happy."

Round Face grinned past his shiner with entirely too much ease. "Enjoy the humor while it lasts, motherfucker."

Forget the lust. Rayna grabbed Sage, clutching her friend to avoid letting her knees buckle. "What the hell is he doing?"

"My question exactly." The utterance came from Garrett. "If that asswipe is a badge, I'm the goddamn mayor."

"You're not and he's not."

Max's interjection was far from reassuring. Rayna flashed him only a second's glance before looking back to Z, but she made the glare count. "I can back that up, but what are *you* talking about?"

Max strung out a dark growl. "He's one of Mua's guys."

Sage gasped. Garrett's whoosh of shock followed. "Mua?" he fired. "How the hell does he have *guys*? And how do you know him?"

"How do *you*?"

Their astonishment got put on hold as the darkness across the street gained human form again. Rayna's heart froze, but the figure wasn't Mua. It was a new stranger, again garbed in black, only this guy wore a rain jacket emblazoned with the KOMO 4 NEWS logo. A plastic-covered TV location camera was planted on his shoulder. As Round Face rushed Zeke and got himself a gut full of chain for it, the camera's recording light flashed on.

"Shit." Rayna sputtered it at the same time as Sage.

Garrett spoke again, his voice lined with gravel. "I helped take down his snake of a twin brother, three months ago."

Max flashed him an awed glance. "That was you?" He shook his head. "Motherfucker of awesome. The hero who took down King is one of my club Doms."

Garrett snorted. "I said I helped. You've got Rayna to thank for the 'awesome' trigger-pulling part of it."

"Holy hell. Serious?"

"Head up her fan club later, Max. I need to know why you turned three shades of white when you said Mua's name, and how—"

"Hell." Max's interruption coincided with the first wail of a police siren. "I'm gonna be three shades whiter than that if all those police get here and find Z doing this. Goddamnit, Hawk, go give him a verbal Quaalude. He's gonna kill that jerk. Not that I wouldn't mind, under any other circumstances."

"How do they even know?" Sage asked. "If that asshole is a fake officer, then who called them?"

Rayna winced. It wasn't just from her bleeding cheek or her friend's question. Max's tension went beyond the aspect of a guy concerned about half the Seattle PD swarming the street in front of his kink club, not to mention its discretion-centric members. She sensed that he knew why a one-man news crew had showed up *before* the cops, as well. The only way she'd find out for certain was to come clean.

"It was me." She grimaced as they all peered at her in confusion. Damn, her face hurt. "You can resign from the fan club now, Max. I told your receptionist to call them, just now when I went to find you guys."

"No." It was more a command from Max than a negation.

"Yes," she insisted. "Great legs, pretty eyes? Getting ready to belt out 'We Found Love in a Kinky Place'? I practically taped the phone to her face."

"And I guarantee you she peeled it right off. Mira knows better. My whole staff knows better. We don't call the cops for help, Rayna."

A violent oath burst from him as Zeke took another rush from Round Face, who got a hand around to his back and twisted a screwdriver into the existing wound there. Rayna screamed as fresh blood rushed down his spine, but the asshole might as well have thrown gasoline on the weapon and tossed it into Zeke's brain for all the stopping power it yielded. Like a gargoyle broken out of its stone shell, Z let out a gothic bellow before twisting the chain around the guy. He used that leverage to flip Round Face into the gutter next to his friend.

"Hell," Max spat. "This isn't good. Not at all."

"Wait," Garrett interceded. "What the hell? Why not the cops? You running something illegal out the back door, Brick?"

"No, goddamnit," Max growled. "When we call the police, there's a price, okay?" He grunted. "And it's not always money."

Sage stepped forward. "What do you mean?"

Max prefaced his reply by peering around, looking like the raindrops themselves might have tapping devices on his utterance. "I mean that King had at least half the police on his leash, whether it was bribes, extortion, or both. And now that he's gone—"

"Mua's moved into that throne." The certainty of it permeated Rayna's words, just like the new layer of bile coating her stomach.

"Fuck. Me."

The moment Garrett finished gritting the words, red and

blue lights flashed between the buildings, turning the street into a soaked, surreal disco. The police sirens howled closer, threatening to drown even the din of the rain.

Max ran to where Zeke was booting the two goons' guts a few more times for good measure. "Z, you need to get out of here. Now!"

Zeke glared back at Max but didn't see him, lost behind eyes that were so afire with violence Rayna could see their glow from where she stood.

"Damn it." Max pointed down at Round Face. The badge on the guy's chest was shiny and obvious. "Those bastards will be here any minute. Even if they don't belong to Mua, you know the shit that's going to fly, right?"

Garrett raced to his friend. "Zeke. *Ezekiel*. Listen to me. Listen to Brick. He's right, man. You've been set up. They'll arrest you and use that footage to convict you."

Zeke didn't move. The sirens got louder. The nausea in Rayna's core turned to aching dread. She forced herself forward by a few steps, close enough to hear how he answered Garrett.

"Is Rayna safe?"

She closed the distance to him. "I'm right here, Z. I'm fine."

He whipped his head and lashed his stare to her. Her breath caught for the fiftieth time in the last ten minutes. Water sparkled on his eyelashes, nose, and lips, a weird and beautiful contrast to the violence that etched every plane of his face. Only one instinct outweighed her longing to run her fingers over every noble feature. She grabbed his massive bicep and jerked him around. Though she had to stand on tiptoe to do it, she started assessing his gash as clinically as she could.

"You need stitches."

"Not gonna happen," Garrett asserted. "We're on borrowed time, Ray."

"Garrett, this wound is deep!"

He grabbed Zeke by the other arm. "You have to get out of here, Z."

Max rushed forward. "Final jeopardy, boys. Alex Trebek has to get the fuck out of the building."

Rayna fumed. "He needs this injury looked at!"

Garrett's glare was a blue glow against the night. "If he doesn't cut a chogey now, the prison doc will be the one 'looking at' him." He jerked on Zeke to force their gazes to lock. "You wanna keep her safe, Z? You can't do that from jail. You think Mua hasn't twisted all this around to his advantage now? He followed her here tonight. He'll follow her again, and he'll probably get her the next time. And you'll be nowhere nearby, will you? That prison cell is going to give you blank walls for you to play fun mental movies for yourself. You can imagine Ray drugged out, trussed up, and tossed into the hold of a plane bound for Bangkok again."

That got Rayna to drop her hands from Z. A sob spilled before she could hold back. Zeke wrestled from his friend's grip. He threw the chain down with a vicious jerk. "You're a harsh asshole sometimes," he snarled at his friend.

"I love you too, honey. Now you gotta pop smoke."

Z didn't waste time on a comeback. He swung his stare back at Rayna. She returned a tremulous smile. The intensity on his face dissolved, giving way to a look of raw anguish. She started backing away until he pulled her back and raised his hand, gently outlining the bruise on her cheek with his thumb. A crazy, deep part of her was moved by his pang for her. A bigger part overrode it with the reminder that she had no right to tie down his emotions, his fingers, or any more of his time. This insane incident didn't change a word of what he'd said in his harem den.

She only wished her heart was listening to her brain. Instead, the thing was on a clear channel with her body, which shirked its shivers the second Z tucked her good cheek against his chest. Her senses gave in to a peaceful softness. Her blood was suffused with the warmth that belonged solely to him. The chaos and rain of the night vanished. If only for one moment, they were reconnected.

One perfect, precious moment...

The first police sedan screeched around the corner. Max pulled at Zeke. "Can we spare the sappy movie ending? Z, if you don't get your ass out of this street in thirty seconds, you're going to be the lead story for tomorrow morning's CNN feed. I'll bet my left nut you're already being loaded up and edited at KOMO. Anyone want a wild guess at who's feeding them the news angle?"

"Shit," Garrett muttered. "Mua's probably in the control booth writing the script for the anchors."

Max turned Zeke's hand over and slammed a set of keys into it. "Get out of here. You're taking my car."

Zeke gaped. "Oh, hell no."

"Don't argue. They'll be looking for yours *and* Hawk's." The club owner cocked both brows. "More importantly, nothing's gonna get you out of town faster than they can get checkpoints up."

"Good point," Z muttered. He clapped Max on the shoulder. The guy nodded in silent acknowledgment of the gratitude.

Nearly at the same time, Zeke slipped his hand into hers. He gripped her tight, pulling her across the street and back into the alley behind Bastille at a run that spattered puddles in their wake. Max, Garrett, and Sage followed. By the time they got to the little parking lot behind the harem room and its patio, her heart was pumping with two elements: adrenaline and apprehension.

She swallowed hard as Zeke tugged her near a gleaming silver car that really did look fast enough to beat the police. The round Jaguar logo and the initials *R-S* gleamed on plates embedded into the front grill. Witnessing the way Max gazed at the car like a man about to put his thoroughbred down, she sensed the two men had a relationship way beyond kink club owner and star staff Dom.

Max proved her even more right by literally giving Z the shirt off his own back, too. He shirked his tight gray T-shirt, revealing a physique as beautifully sculpted as his friend, though his shoulders and chest were also defined by a maze of Maori tattoos. Other than that and the slight difference in their hair colors, the men could be brothers.

There was no time to delve into it now. She meshed her fingers tighter into Z's, clinging to every last second before he had to get into the pseudo-spaceship.

"Thanks, man," Z said to his friend. "I mean it, Brick."

"Yeah, yeah. Send me pictures," the guy returned. "But whatever you do, don't stop at home. Don't stop *anywhere*. Delphine's got a full tank, so that should get you pretty far."

"Delphine?" Rayna muttered it as Zeke turned to her.

"Don't ask." The flash of mirth in his eyes turned to copper intensity as he looked down to her again. His lips went tight as he stroked her bruised skin again.

"Stop it." She grabbed his fingers.

His face tightened. "Does it hurt that bad? Damn it, if that cock knocker gave you deep-tissue damage—"

"No. I meant stop fretting over me when you took a damn screwdriver in the back from the asshole and won't even let me—"

"It's easily handled on the road, bird."

She longed to slap him. He was tossing his health aside like a snack he was packing for a road trip. But she sighed and reminded herself he was Special Forces. God only knew what medical attention he'd been required to give himself at Mach Five.

Instead of whacking him, she lifted a gentle hand to his jaw. "Where will you go?"

To her surprise, a quizzical grin teased his lips. "Don't you mean, where will *we* go?"

She stilled her fingers. Forget that. Her whole body froze. "What?"

He braced his hands to her waist. Rayna stared at him without blinking, half expecting to find little gold flecks that meant he was teasing. But there were none. He was calm and serious as he softly thanked Rihanna—er, Mira—for bringing out a bottle of ibuprofen, a tube of antibacterial cream, and a huge gauze bandage.

"You think I'm going anywhere without you, knowing Mua's out and roaming free, with the police's blessing?" He finished that by slamming down a few of the pain pills while Mira slathered the cream on his back, pressed the bandage on his gash, and handed off the leftover supplies to Rayna.

It wasn't reassuring to watch her fingers shake as she accepted the pile. Her breath was a fearful bite in her chest, too. Despite that, she argued, "You can't move as fast or as invisibly with me."

He opened his hand, where he'd held back four ibuprofen. "Take these. Sorry there's no water." His sardonic glance at the sky wasn't lost on her. The clouds roiled overhead, seeming to fight with each other about what mode to be in: pouring or torrential.

"Zeke, you need to think—"

"No." As she watched, his humor gave way to granite cliffs again. "No, *you* need to think." He grabbed her again, this time in determined grips to her shoulders. "I'm not letting that prick or any of his minions get within ten miles of you."

She struggled for a reaction to that, any reaction, but the force wasn't just evident in his words. His conviction poured from him like a radiation cloud, stopping her breath. She told herself to resist its searing impact, to remind herself it was only his soldier's ferocity and his dedication to honor that made him say all that. Even if some deep part of his soul remembered that scene in the tunnel so long ago, he wasn't consciously accessing it now. He wasn't committing to anything with her, other than his duty by her.

Rayna finally gulped again.

Maybe...for now...duty had to be enough.

It sure as hell won over the consideration of watching him drive away and then stepping foot in a city where Mua was slithering free—and hell-bent on getting his pound of flesh for King's death by selling hers.

"Okay." She finally gave him a shaky nod. "But only until they get Mua and your name is cleared."

Zeke's lips quirked up for a flash of a second. He yanked her closer and pressed his lips to her forehead. "Good girl. Now take your meds."

As he pulled away, a surge of alarm hit her. "Wait. What about my own car?"

"It'll be part of Seattle PD's crime scene in ten minutes," Garrett explained. "We'll do what we can to get it back. In the meantime, leave your keys and phone with Sage. We'll dump them in a locker at the airport. That'll keep a few of them busy for a while, thinking you've tried to catch a flight somewhere."

"A few hundred flight manifests and a few miles of security cam tape?" Zeke nodded in satisfaction as he pulled on Max's shirt. "It'll put some hair on their chest. Or not."

Rayna did as they told her, despite feeling naked from the second Sage took her items. Being absent from her phone wasn't a huge tragedy, except for the seven-part panic switch known as her brothers. She was about to remind Zeke of that *minor* snag, when he handed his own cell to Garrett and said, "I'll call when we get there. You still have the sat phone number if you need it, right?"

Garrett nodded. "Check." He locked hands with Zeke before pulling him close, bumping shoulders in their soldiers' version of a hug. "Be safe—"

"Or die trying," Z finished.

"Not an option," Sage scolded. "For either of you." She yanked Rayna into a fast but tearful embrace. "It'll be okay," her friend whispered into her ear. "We'll get this straightened out, and I'll see you in a few days."

Rayna attempted a smile. She wasn't sure if she was successful. She wasn't sure of anything anymore. A year and a half ago, she'd been kidnapped by foreign rebels and nearly sold into slavery. Three months ago, a soldier had rescued her from that fate. Forty-eight hours ago, she'd gone to heaven and back in one night with him. Yesterday, she'd never expected to see him again.

None of it felt more insane than this moment. She looked at her legs, still in the sweats she'd pulled on this morning, sliding against the leather of a car worth more than she made in a year. She watched Zeke gun the engine with practiced ease, the driver's area full of his big body and his graceful strength. She marveled at how he effortlessly maneuvered the Jag through the slumbering city streets and then into the sleepier suburbs, toward a destination only he knew of—and in which she trusted him completely.

Insanity...right? But had she been given a choice? Sure, if going back home tonight in a state of complete dread qualified as a choice. If choosing to watch Zeke—the Zeke who'd saved her from a gang rape in the park those many years ago, the Zeke who'd carried her out of King's jungle—ride away as a fugitive at Mua's manipulations was a choice.

No. There was only one choice now. Only one path.

She was going to help him figure out how far Mua's corruption extended—and after that, they'd take him down again. If that meant she had to face Mua personally, so be it. But God help the bastard if that ever happened, because she wouldn't hesitate to rid this world of him exactly as she'd ended his brother. Nobody messed with the people she cared about and got away with it.

CHAPTER EIGHT

Luna roused from her fog of semiconsciousness, fighting reality as if she were being pulled from a perfect dream. But the stinging stripes that crossed her spine and ass, as well as the blue bruises around her nipples, were the beautiful reminders that it had all been real. That *he'd* been real.

That he'd been a more perfect Dom than she ever imagined.

"Zeke." She whispered it against a pillow on one of the couches in Bastille's sitting room. She'd been here plenty of times to recognize it, even without opening her eyes. Her voice shook like a damn fifteen-year-old after her teen idol had left town, but she didn't care. This hurt. Sub drop was one thing, but crash and burn was another.

Damn straight it hurts, girl. When you fly to the moon, you have to re-enter the atmosphere somehow. And you're not wearing much of a space suit, are you?

She shivered and pulled the flannel blanket tighter around her nakedness. She wasn't expecting the large, warm hand that appeared to help her. It was attached to a formidable forearm, a toned bicep. She looked up into the face of Zeke's friend, Mr. Huge Feet, and his Byzantine brown eyes. The guy Zeke had recruited as their play room babysitter for the night. He stared at her like the rest of the room didn't exist, though it was starting to get crowded as other couples drifted in after finishing their kinky fun for the night.

His seriousness was a far cry from the eye roll she'd heard earlier in his voice, back in the living room after Zeke voiced his concern about the scene limits. She'd wanted to do the same thing, except the carpet would've been her sole witness. It all worked out. She'd been able to flash the look fifteen minutes later when Z had the nerve to mandate a safe word.

Z had clearly known more than both of them.

Another tremor hit from her fingernails to her toenails. She closed her eyes as flashes filtered back to her from the scene. Every moment leading to the first orgasm returned with brilliant clarity. That was the easy part. She'd been lucid then. That was before Z told her it was only the prelude to his game... and the world had begun to spin. He'd dragged her along peaks and valleys of sensation like a lion toying with its food before splitting it all the way open. He launched her to the heights where only the pain and her screams existed, only to pull her back with his growls and his touch...and her next climax. Then he'd start all over again, stringing her senses higher, clamping and spanking and whipping until her blood sang in her ears and flames licked at her skin. She'd gasped and even tried to scream, but by then her mouth functioned less than her brain.

That was when the lion had let her tumble into the jungle.

She felt a little smile lift her lips from what she could scrape together from memory and store in her soul for the rest of her life.

She'd already climaxed for him three times. Of that much, she was sure. A submissive rarely forgot orgasms that made their knees so weak they were grateful for the bondage that held them up. Her recall was especially vivid because something had changed about Z after that third explosion as well. Something came unhinged, as if he freed a new part of himself along with her. Her body had instantly recognized it. She'd become an aching, writhing mess of sensation, especially as he finished layering sharp little crop bites along the insides of her thighs.

When he'd unlocked the bit gag and replaced it with his three middle fingers, she'd hungrily accepted his invasion. She remembered the musk, sweat, and leather on his skin and how the sinful taste lingered across her tongue. His other hand had still wielded the crop. With dark growls, he had curled the slapper up through her legs, raining ruthless blows directly on her sensitive pussy.

It was all the invitation her mind had needed. The sub space had swallowed her like the damn Amazon. She'd swirled in colors and sounds, plunging deeper into a vast wilderness of sensation and emotion. And yes, Zeke had even gone there with her. His breath was hot on her neck, his snarls echoing in her ears, and his hands...oh God, his hands had kept weaving their untamed magic over her, taking her deeper and deeper into paradise...

Until that wretched safe word had burned her out of the forest. *Cinderella.*

She blinked as confusion eclipsed the memories. Who'd evoked the damn princess? Not Z. And it sure as hell wasn't her.

She opened her eyes and glared at Babysitter Man.

"It was you," she charged.

He frowned. It defined the dip in his top lip even more. "Me what?"

"You called the safe word." She didn't hold back the accusation this time.

He reset his face in resolve. "Damn straight I did."

"Why?" She punched a glower across hers. "Are you new at this, Ron Weasley? Why did Z tap you for this? Do you not recognize sub space when it's consuming a woman in front of you?"

He shoved his bottom lip out. Damn it, did he pay for his mouth to have dance lessons or something? And why did she even keep noticing?

"Tait," he finally said. Just that.

"What?"

"As much as I dig Ron—because he gets the hot chick at the end after all—my name is Tait. And I knew exactly where you were at when I dropped the safe word." He averted his gaze but only for a second. "I didn't take my eyes off of you during that scene."

A weighted moment passed. Though his lips stopped dancing, his eyes flashed with strange, deep squalls of conflict. He added lowly, "I couldn't."

Luna squirmed. She didn't want to feel good about that, even a little. Clinging to her ire was a much better fit with the emptiness at the edges of her heart. "So?"

Tait didn't back down. But neither did the golden storms in his eyes. "It wasn't you I was worried about."

"Z's been with Max for years. He's one of the most responsible Doms in the scene."

"Which was why he asked me to spot tonight. He knew it might go—" He stopped as if fishing for the right word. "Well, where it went."

"Which was nowhere I didn't want it to," Luna retorted.

"Which would have caused you some serious physical damage, Luna." There were no mysterious lights in his eyes anymore. Only angry darkness. "Perhaps permanently."

"That was *my* risk to take, Quidditch boy."

"No." He dropped a hard hand atop her knee. "It wasn't yours anymore, from the second you shot into sub space. There's a reason why the word 'safe' tops the mantra for this lifestyle, sweetness. Zeke made sure I was there, because he knew I wouldn't forget it." He released a slow breath. "Because he knew there was a good chance that he would."

"You're wrong." She seethed. "Zeke would never—"

"What?" he cut in. "Permanently hurt you? Maim you?" Faster than she thought a man could move, Tait had leaned in and over her. He braced a knee on the cushion in front of her stomach and a hand at the side of her head. "Do you know what we do for a living, Luna?" He dug his fingers into her scalp and his thumb into her jaw. "Do you know where we go, what we're asked to do sometimes? And do you know who's leading the pack most of the time? That's right. Hooah, Psycho Zsycho. I'd follow the man into hell because I know he's going to have my six anywhere, any time. And you know why I know that? Because I've seen him go to hell inside himself to do it. When he does"—if it was possible, his stare got flooded with more shadows—"well, it's not a cute little demon, that's for sure," he stressed. "It's a creature he's had inside him for a very long time. A time filled with a shitload of ugly business."

For reasons she doubted Tait would ever understand, Luna smiled. "You think I don't know that? You think because I'm a painter with lavender hair and a great leather wardrobe that I don't 'get' the shit beneath that man's military posture and dog tags?" She shook her head. "You don't know anything, Weasley. You don't know *me*."

Jabbing in the Hogwarts angle yielded the effect she wanted. Tait slid away, though she noticed how he took care not to jostle her back and thighs as he did. Damn it, why did he have to be so considerate?

"Maybe I don't," he said. "But that doesn't matter. I would've fucked Z up good if he didn't comply with the stop."

Her stomach fluttered in a really uncomfortable way. It got worse when she slipped her hand into his, squeezing out a feeble attempt at thanks. He didn't lift his head, though the look he gave her through his long copper lashes burned deeper than the welts across her back. He didn't break concentration even when a tray full of drink glasses shattered to the floor, caught by the wrong edge of a new flogger being tried out by a Dom across the room.

Luna gave up a little smile. It felt comfortable to be here like this, with Tait's sun-warm touch and crooked smile. It almost felt right.

Almost.

There was a significant piece of the scene that blared *wrong*.

She released a long breath before voicing it.

"He isn't even in the building anymore, is he?"

Tait's eyes flickered with conflict again. He finally responded, "No."

She tried to pull her hand away. He held fast. "Please let go."

"It's been a strange night, Luna."

She fired a dark laugh. "You can say that again."

"Some bad shit went down outside. Z was in the thick of it."

"Of course."

"Hey, it's the truth. He called me from the road. He was really concerned about you. He wanted you to know—"

"Stop." She finally got her hand free. A little fury went a long way in the battle of the handclasp department. "Save it." She closed her eyes again. "I knew what I signed on for tonight, okay? I knew what the deal was. I'm happy. Besides, I'm not a cuddler."

Like her wise-assery even mattered. Tait wasn't a stupid guy. He'd fill in the blanks between what she said. Every word she spoke was true, too. She had no right to be irked, miffed, or insulted by Zeke right now. He'd fulfilled his part of their deal to the letter. He'd given her the play session she'd dreamed of for six years and had made it all well worth the wait. It wasn't his fault that he didn't reciprocate what she felt beyond the dungeon, too.

It wasn't his fault that she'd hoped tonight would change that.

Tait's comments, *all* of them, suddenly repeated in her head. She shot a probing stare back at him. "Did you say 'on the road?'" At the guy's nod, she pressed, "Why? Where's he going?"

Tait's mouth did that twisty dance thing again. "Like I said, it's been an odd night."

She scowled. There was something he wasn't telling her. "Who's he with?"

Tait meshed his fingers with hers again. "Rayna Chestain."

The air *whooshed* from her lungs. She managed a jerking little nod, too, but it was a shitty attempt at hiding how she'd yearned for any other name as his answer.

And how she'd known with sickening dread that it wouldn't be.

How medic girl had gotten here, let alone seasoned her vanilla to suit Zeke's palate, wasn't worth two thoughts to rub together. Yet here those thoughts were, stealing the perfect end to Luna's perfect night. She was tired. Defeated. And clinging to the hand of a total stranger while the Dom of her dreams drove into the night with his redheaded damsel in distress.

Again.

"Right," she finally mumbled. "Rayna. Of course."

"Truth sucks ass sometimes." Tait ran his thumb over her chafed wrist. "But you don't deserve less, little flower."

Irritation flared. Like she needed more of *that* shit. "*Don't* call me that."

"Why?"

"Because I'm not a goddamn flower, that's why."

This was the point where he'd finally let her go. Some lovely slam involving the words *cold* and *bitch* would spill off his poster-perfect lips before he decided to enjoy his evening with one of the little hotties in mall-bought kink wear who'd been eyeing him from the corner. Something she'd never be. Something she never was. A mold fitter. A submissive who couldn't please anyone.

She gritted her teeth against the aching heat that pressed in her chest. Shit. *Go away; go away.* But like a case of violent food poisoning that was coming up the way it went down, she felt the dams of indifference crumbling inside.

"L-Listen," she stammered, "I appreciate you hanging out with me, Weasley, but I need to—" She swung her feet out, planted them, and then stood. The blanket chafed her back, making her head swim with dizzy pain. She weaved and prepared herself to hit the floor. She was going to lose it. Damn, she was going to—

She didn't fall. Tait and his really significant chest made sure she didn't. He wasn't as broad as Z, but what he lacked in width, he made up in boulder-like density.

"Luna! What the hell?"

Before she could think of a smartass answer to deter him, the persistent dork gathered her, blanket and all, into his arms. She wanted to struggle, but the pressure was building faster now, and his body offered all the strength she no longer had. With pathetic desperation, she wrapped a hand around his neck and squashed her face into his shoulder.

"Get me out of here," she whispered. "Please."

"Hang on, flower." His voice filled her ear with a matching murmur. His long, forceful strides assured that the buzz of the common room fast faded, followed by the creak of a door, two more of his steps, and the blessed click that sealed them into the privacy of one of the vacated play rooms. A place where she could finally let the dam break and the tears come.

Through every one of them, Tait gave her exactly what she needed in return. Silence.

CHAPTER NINE

Silence. It wasn't such a golden thing, especially with Rayna and especially now. The air in the car was thick with all the shit they needed to clear, but Zeke let the muck get worse as he pretended the increasing twists in the road required his complete attention.

The excuse was weak as piss considering the work of art in his control. The five hundred and fifty ponies under the hood worked with powerful precision, making the Jag stick to the turns like silk on damp skin. Thank God for Max and his generosity. The sooner he got Rayna to the cabin, the better. Mua had come too damn close to taking her tonight, a horror that hadn't happened because of pure dumb luck. He wasn't going to let the fuckwad have that chance again. Ever.

Mua. There was a name he'd thought permanently deleted off his "Assholes I Need to Worry About" list. Now every other thought was scourged again by the slimebag, his smirk a brazen taunt, his voice a cock punch, his eyes a glaring reminder of the number-one item on *his* to-do list. To recapture Rayna.

That formed the shit-perfect segue into the crap filling the rest of his thoughts. Irony's nice little dig. The words Rayna had mumbled before she left the patio, that got him chasing her so he eventually saved her, were still a relentless refrain in his mind. But his efforts at successfully figuring them out were useless, love taps at a door that needed a goddamn boot slam.

Because your boots aren't the ones for the job, asshat.

He grunted. It was fucking frustrating to have an instinct that was always right.

He slowed the Jag to make the sharp left that would continue them on the Cascades Highway. To their right, the river was immersed in the night's blackness. To the left, the rain didn't make the view much better. The few lights that were on at the Buffalo Run Inn and the Marblemount Diner soon faded in the rearview mirror.

He took a heavy breath. Maybe it was time to end the silence.

Rayna beat him to the job by ten seconds. "Damn it."

He glanced at her. Though she'd only muttered the words, the glow from the tablet in her lap highlighted every facet of her pained grimace. Max kept the devices around like most people kept sunglasses or breath mints, so it didn't surprise him when Rayna had pulled that one out from under the passenger seat. She'd turned it on a few minutes ago and had been tapping at the screen ever since.

"You okay, bird? Are the meds wearing off?"

Fortunately, it looked like Mua's goon had meant to induce fear more than lasting damage when he hit her. That didn't stop the son of a bitch from booking his ticket to the end of Z's fist if they were ever in the same room again. Tempting as the fantasy was, he looked forward to calling Garrett in an hour and hearing that the FBI had not only thanked his friend for the tip but had a plan in place to bring down Mua and his network for good. Not being in the thick of that action, even now, made him feel like a fish out of water, but he'd gladly flop around for a few days for the reward of looking into the forests of Rayna's eyes again and telling her the monster was gone for good.

For now, just one more glance gave him the answer to his question. She wasn't okay, but it didn't seem related to her bruises. She attacked the tablet with another angry swipe. "If I ever see that dickwad again, I'll drill him with more lead than I did his brother."

He felt his eyebrows jump. Yes, she'd shot King. But since then, he'd seen the woman's commitment to compassion on shitloads of occasions. Once, he'd tried to whack a field mouse in her garage, only to be pummeled and ordered to set it free in the backyard.

"Okay." He cautiously strung out the syllables. "Should I ask for elaboration?"

She stabbed the screen again. "The bastard only started at KOMO. Every news outlet in the city has the story now."

Zeke shrugged. "We expected that."

"But they're all wrong!"

"We expected that, too."

"No!" she protested. "Not like this."

He shot a concerned stare at her. There was a sob in her voice, and it continued across her face.

Without hesitation, he pulled the Jag over.

Once he'd stopped, Rayna curled her knees to her chest. "I want to kill him, Zeke," she whispered. "I swear to God, he's not going to do this to you. Not because of me."

A strange calm took over him. He recognized the feeling well. He'd gone there a handful of times already in his life, on missions when his death was pretty much a given outcome.

The soul-deep acceptance had been what stabilized him enough to survive all those times.

From the depth of that calm, he said, "Let me see it, Rayna."

She didn't move. He reached and pulled at the pad. At first she fought him but finally gave way, seeming to comprehend she would never win a tug of war like this.

The screen lit up with the home page for the *Tribune*. He winced with embarrassment at the first photo they showed, his military ID photo from about four years ago. He looked like he had a pole up his ass. He'd felt that way, too. Farther down in the article, there was another picture that didn't make him feel much better. It was a grainy screenshot from the video footage taken by that pop-up camera man, undoubtedly one of Mua's wolves in a media fleece. It showed him standing over both of the bastard's henchmen, the chain still in his hands, violence branded across his face.

The words between the two photos were an even bigger bog of bullshit.

Soldier Goes Insane, Instigates Brutal Downtown Beatings

Two men are in intensive care tonight at Harborview Medical Center after an altercation with a US Army officer just returned from a stressful overseas mission.

Sergeant Ezekiel Gabriel Hayes, stationed at Joint Base Lewis-McChord, engaged two men taking a cigarette break outside a downtown nightclub earlier this evening. The men gained consciousness long enough to state that Hayes appeared agitated and angry. They speculated he might have been under the influence of cocaine or methamphetamines. The men's names are being withheld from the media until their families can be notified.

He snorted. "Don't hold your breath, guys. I hear it takes a while to find 'family' in hell."

"Not funny," Rayna snapped.

He continued reading.

A friendly conversation apparently became heated when a woman, Sergeant Rayna Chestain, a member of a medical corps unit at JBLM, emerged from the club as well. When Hayes began lascivious advances on Chestain, the two men tried to assist and were assaulted by Hayes. He retrieved a heavy chain from his car, as well as brass knuckles and a tire iron, to continue his attack.

After incapacitating the men, Hayes forced the woman into another car, tagged by eyewitnesses as a dark blue Sierra truck with upgraded hubcaps and license plate TRO1ACY. Though the police have set up checkpoints on all major highways, Hayes's location is unknown.

A manhunt has begun, jointly operated by the Seattle Police Department and the army. Hayes is to be considered armed, well-trained, and extremely dangerous. If identified, do not approach this dangerous suspect. Dial 9-1-1 or—

He flipped the tablet's cover shut.

Okay, he'd had more comfortable moments in his life. But his anxiety wasn't due to this cartload of lies. His job, often his very life, depended on using deception and custom-created personas. He just wasn't used to being public about it. *Really* public. And dragging someone he cared about into this goddamn spotlight with him.

"Well, fuck," he finally muttered. With a sigh, he turned to stash the tablet behind her seat. He was pulled up short on the way back, her stare burning into him.

"Well, fuck? That's it?"

He frowned. "For now."

Rayna dug her fingers into his forearm. "How can you be so calm about this?" With her other hand, she tilted his head in order to peer back at his bandage. "This has got to be bleeding again and taking all the fluid from your brain, too."

As wonderful as her touch felt, he pried her hands away. "I'm fine. You can check it out in full soon, Flo Nightingale. Just not now." Though reason dictated that the night was their friend more than foe, he couldn't get over the feeling that they were exposed as a water truck in the Sahara right now.

She twisted her fingers into his. "Damn it! This is unfair!"

Zeke looked down at their joined hands. Her tapered nails were painted pink. It was a few shades lighter than her jacket and reminded him of little girl birthday party streamers. "You're right," he replied.

"Damn straight I'm—"

"It's totally unfair to you."

"No. Wait. I meant—"

"I know what you meant." He lifted his head, bringing his gaze inches from hers. She smelled like pink, too. Her cardamom spice had a spun-sugar softness wound with it, a sweet contrast to the treated leather of the car. "And I know what *I* meant." He untwined one hand to tenderly frame one side of her face. "You should've gone to a hospital and been checked out for all this. By now, you should be home in bed, helped to sleep by painkillers, warm in your sheets, and dreaming of what Halloween parties you're gonna go to next week."

She huffed. "I don't know whether to belt you or kiss you, Hayes." Despite her threatening words, her throat gave up only a rough whisper. "Over half of Seattle is going to think you've downed the jungle juice for good, and you're worried about *me*?"

He didn't say anything. Rain began to cascade over the

car...and heat sluiced through his blood. It poured from the spigot of her touch and her words. Damn it, when she talked to him like that, husky and low, like sharing a secret just for the two of them...he yearned to make it just that. A moment only for the two of them.

Not the right way to think right now, man. Not the right thing for you; especially not the right thing for her. You're stronger than this. You have to be.

"I think there's been enough of that belting shit tonight, honey."

So much for the dutiful self-talk. And so much for the parting of her lips, only by a half inch at best, as if wondering that she interpreted him right.

Her half inch was his damn mile.

In two seconds, he had her mouth buried under his.

Fuck...*yes*. She even tasted like pink. A buffet of cherry cream and cotton candy, of spun sugar and whipped meringue, of summer and sweetness in the dark, shitty winter of this night. Of his whole goddamn life. She was more perfect and delicious than he remembered. More pliant, more responsive, more incredibly open with the passion she gave him in return, spearing its way through his body and straight into his cock.

His mind flooded with a fantasy. He'd shove the sweats to her knees. Pop back her seat. Order her to turn around, and grip it while he slid into her from behind. With his fingers on her clit and his hard slaps on her ass, she'd pulse all over his cock while filling the car with her orgasmic screams...

That was all fine and good until they broke apart for air. Her face, lighted by the dim glow from the dashboard, was filled with longing, desire, need—

For all the things he still couldn't give her.

You are a selfish, depraved bastard.

"I'm sorry," he gritted. "Hell, Rayna. That shouldn't have—"

She grabbed his hand before he could yank it away. "It's okay. It's more than okay. Zeke, listen. I have something I need to—"

"It shouldn't have happened." He gave the words as if they were a command, issuing it as much to himself as her. While he restarted the engine and gunned the Jag back onto the highway, he set his jaw and concluded, "And I promise that it won't again."

CHAPTER TEN

The weather got worse as they drove another hour north. It was a perfect companion for Rayna's mood. Her chest was a thunderhead of frustration, her mind on fire with a thousand stabs of angry lightning.

With a strange jolt, she remembered pizza dough. An uncooked slab of it sat at home in her refrigerator. She was going to make a giant, gooey, pineapple and pepperoni pie as a self-pity snack as soon as she got off the phone with Sally. That had only been six hours ago. She'd almost disconnected the call before Sal picked up, because she began to think the pizza would be enough to help her deal with the weirdness of her feelings surrounding Zeke.

Shit. *Weird* didn't begin to describe how she felt now. Conflicted? Probably. Torn between appreciation and exasperation? That one was good. Completely baffled about what she was going to do in the middle of the Cascades Forest with him? *Ding, ding, ding.* Someone give Sergeant Chestain a prize.

Just when it didn't seem the highway could get darker, Z swung the Jag onto a murkier side road. The pavement gave way to gravel and dirt, which had now turned to rain-soaked muck. Mud spattered the car's windows and front windshield.

"Is Max going to speak to you again after this?" she cracked with grim humor.

"He knew where I was going," Z muttered.

"The middle of the Haunted Forest?"

When they rounded the next corner, she winced through an attack of spoke-too-soon.

Zeke directed the car up onto a paved surface again—a driveway formed of interconnected flagstones. It swept around in a wide horseshoe shape that had a spacious three-floor cabin at the apex. There was nothing remotely "haunted" about it. The deep A-framed building had a glass wall that took up its first two floors with an intricate stained-glass pane fitted into the triangle shape of the top floor. The front porch was bracketed by natural stone pillars and contained a spacious swing that was currently protected by a rain cover. Hanging baskets across that area were still surprisingly abloom, brimming over with verbena that seemed impervious to the downpour.

She felt an instant, welcoming presence from the place. A firm strength, as well.

Zeke threw the car into park but didn't cut the engine. He gazed over as if trying to assess her reaction to what she saw. She didn't try to hide her smile. His uncertainty was a bit different. And a lot endearing.

"Wow. I get to enter the inner sanctum of the Zeke Hayes private lair."

His eyes narrowed by a fraction. "How do you know it's mine?"

"Oh, it's yours."

He shot her a nonplussed glance. "Stay here while I get some lights turned on. The entry will be slick in this piss party, and I don't want you falling into the stream."

"Falling into the—huh?"

He'd already left the car and was sprinting through the

rain.

After a few seconds, lights from the cabin spilled into the torrent. Rayna watched Z moving through the rooms on the ground and second floors, scooting around the furniture with wide and easy steps. He clearly had a comfort level here. She wondered how often he came up to enjoy the hideaway.

She also wondered who came with him.

The twinge in her stomach didn't get time to fester. He was at the car door less than a minute later, bearing a jacket he'd gotten from inside, holding it over her as she got out and bolted for the house. The flagstones gave way to a wood-plank bridge. Sure enough, the din of the rain got joined by the clamor of a rushing stream that she judged to be about fifteen feet below. Also as he'd predicted, the boards were slick. Even in her tennis shoes, Rayna slid and nearly went down. Only Zeke's hold, solid as a steel pole around her elbow, kept her balanced enough to make it inside on her feet.

She wasn't sure what to expect once she'd entered the cabin—but this wasn't it.

If there was such a thing as décor porn, she was sure Zeke was capable of corrupting millions with his forest-cabin version of it. Recessed lighting led the eye toward a sunken living room with a huge leather couch that was flanked by overstuffed love seats, all done in inviting shades of brown, russet, and dark blue. Large seating pillows on the floor were covered in complementary fabrics. They were arranged around the fireplace, which soared through to the second floor, its mismatched stones forming an eclectic piece of artwork in their own right. Reflected in the floor-to-ceiling windows across the room, she caught a glimpse of the dining room and kitchen, both possessing the same inviting colors and comfortable woods. On the walls were unique pieces fashioned out of a combination of copper and driftwood. The one over the couch depicted a sunset with a family of deer. On the wall next to her, waterfowl took flight off a lake.

One word tumbled off her lips. "Wow."

Zeke scooted past her to the thermostat. "I hope that's a good wow," he said while flipping on the heat.

"Here's the part where I really get to hit you, right?" After he joined her in a soft laugh, she blurted, "Zeke, this is— I mean, I never expected—"

"I know what you expected." He lifted a knowing smirk. "I like hanging out at Bastille, honey. But I wouldn't want to live there."

"I wasn't talking about the club." She gave him an inquiring stare. "Come on. Even your apartment near the base isn't—"

"I don't live there, either." He walked to the bar area, set into the alcove beneath the stairs, and swung down a bottle of Scotch along with two glasses. "That's just a parking space for my body when I'm not here or out on a mission. Here, drink it. In case you don't know, that's good shit, so do it slowly."

She made a face into the glass. "I'm strictly a wine girl, thanks."

"You're so blue, I'm going to call you Smurfette in a second. *Drink.*" He took a small sip from his own glass. "It'll warm you up—and give you some liquid courage."

"Courage?" The distraction of her curiosity lent the ability to tip the Scotch to her lips. Holy shit, he was right. It was like drinking fire and tasted just as horrid. Between a couple of chokes, she asked, "For what?"

"For calling your brothers."

Damn. She'd forgotten about that detail. "You promised I

could look at your bandage."

"After you call your brothers."

"Now who's doing the stalling thing?" She smirked at his peeved scowl. "I only need to call one of them, you know."

"Close enough for rock and roll, honey," he called while pacing into the kitchen. While he was gone, Rayna took another hit of her Scotch. Dear God, people drank this stuff on purpose? The only benefit she could fathom to the act was how every inch of her body acknowledged each warm sip. By the time he circled back into the living room with a sizable satellite phone in hand, her third sip was proving his theory true about the liquid fortitude, as well.

"You ready?" He extended the phone.

She took a deep breath. "Not really."

Z's eyes laughed at that, though the rest of his face was sober. "I'll be right here."

As you always have been. She yearned to say it aloud but knew where her weighted words would lead. He'd roll his eyes. Tell her she was full of shit. She'd finally get so fed up, she'd blurt out everything from the hypnosis session, and God only knew where that would lead right now. Z fiercely guarded the things that different people knew about him. Cross the lines into a life compartment in which you weren't supposed to be, like her visit to Bastille, and you suffered the not-so-pretty repercussions.

Right now, she was preparing for a metric shit ton of backlash from another neurotic man in her life. She just had to figure out which one.

She had seven choices on the big-brother hotline. Actually, six. After the scene that went down in her kitchen on Friday morning, Trevor was off the options list. She crossed off Dallas, as well. He was eleven months behind Trev, a chronological proximity than made him just as much a butthead, especially since ATF had crowned him Special Agent in Charge on the squad. Finn and Shane were rarely reachable, a fact that had nothing to do with their Alaska addresses. Finn was simply surgically attached to his helicopter, and Shane took the "ranger" part of his national parks badge to a different level of serious.

That left Rhys, Jenner, and Arah. Her heart leaned toward Rhys, but he wasn't a morning person, and a glance at the clock confirmed it was four in the morning. That took Jenner out of the mix, too. He loved the dawn as much as his twin hated it, to the degree that he'd chosen a life as a fishing-fleet captain. He was probably prepping his first nets out on the Sound right now.

Arah won by process of elimination, as he usually did. Rayna almost smiled as she punched in the number for the brother who was separated from her by eighteen months. She wondered what part of the world in which she'd find her guitar god of a brother today.

He clicked the line open after one ring. "Rayna!"

That answered her question about whether her siblings had been contacted about all this yet. Stress drenched the voice of her normally laid-back sibling, who spent most of his time writing songs about peace, love, and chakras.

"Okay...wow." She tried a teasing tone. "Were you sitting on top of the phone or something?"

"Where are you? What's he done to you? Did you escape?"

She laughed. She couldn't help it. "Escape? Arah, listen; I'm fine. The shit they're reporting—"

"I'm on my way to Seattle now. I'm in San Francisco on a

fucking layover, but that gives Ava the chance to catch up with me and—"

"Ava?" Her astonishment punched both syllables. "Damn it, not cool. Why did you guys bother her? She can't miss a day on the set. Bella Lanza is the most demanding diva on TV right now—"

"Who's recovering from a nose job in Malibu, so chill. Ava's her stylist, not her assistant, so Bella's ordered her away until the swelling goes down. As far as the 'not cool' and the 'bothering her' part, pull your claws back. The news affiliates in LA have already picked up the story. Thanks to your sergeant being a total chunk of man candy, there's a good chance the trashy entertainment peeps will carry it soon, too."

At first, she only groaned from the taffy-tough twist in her stomach. She hated taffy. "He's not a 'piece' of anything," she muttered, though every taste bud in her mouth watered as she caught Zeke's curious frown. *And he sure as hell isn't mine.* "And he knows what he's doing, okay? You guys *have* to stay out of this. I mean it." When her brother's anxious silence stretched more than five seconds, she persisted, "Arah..."

He pushed out a hard grunt. "Fine. Trev and Dallas are already working with the police, all right?"

"No!" She yelled it before she could think about it. Since Zeke actually grinned at her with pride, she tore back in with a growl. "*Not* all right! Arah, you can't trust them. None of you can. A lot of them are in the back pocket of a shithead criminal named Mua. He's trying to capture and sell me again, Arah. Please, you need to listen to me!"

There was a pause that gave her hope, though she could practically taste her brother's incredulity through the phone. Hell. If she was Arah, she wouldn't believe what she was hearing, either. Police officials in collusion with criminal masterminds? People out to kidnap her, to sell her into slavery? It sounded like a TV show instead of her life. She prayed Arah would heed the desperation in her voice.

Finally, her brother asked slowly, "What are you saying, Ray?"

Thank God. "It's all lies," she told him. "The scene they're showing in that feed...it's not the truth. Zeke was saving me from those two men, not the other way around. They work for the twin of the bastard who imprisoned Sage and me in Thailand. He should be in prison, and according to all the records, he is, but he's not. I saw him with my own eyes just four hours ago."

"So why don't you go on TV yourself and say that?"

"Remember the part where I said he was still after me?"

"But why?"

"I can't tell you that."

And that *wasn't* a lie. So many details from their Thailand rescue had been tagged as classified by the CIA that it was easier to tell her brothers only the surface details of it all. And the follow-up nightmare in that Medina mansion, which had ended up with her shooting King, hadn't even happened according to the army, the police, and most of the feds.

"Arah," she pleaded after her brother's vexed snort, "you have to trust me on this. And you have to tell everyone else that, too. I'm completely safe. Zeke is hiding me, not abducting me."

Her brother let a tense pause go by. She could hear the airport behind him with its paging system, rolling suitcases, and beeping courtesy carts. It was all so normal, yet it sounded surreal and distant from the high-wire act that her life had become—again.

"If you want me to trust you, Ray, then tell me where you are."

She grimaced. Z noticed and took her free hand. His firm, unflinching strength suffused her. "I can't do that either."

"Why the fuck not?"

"Jeez, Hamilton." Yeah, it was time to go for the undercut of the middle name. "Is douchebag fusion the new musical trend right now?"

"You didn't answer my question."

She swallowed and squeezed Z's fingers harder. "Because there's a better than half chance he's listening to us even now, Arah."

"Rayna, for the love of—"

"I've already been on too long." Z's darkening frown told her that much. "I can't run the risk of him tracking this signal, okay?"

"Rayna!"

"I love you."

She ended the call, shutting the real world off once again.

For a long moment, neither she nor Zeke said a thing. The room began to warm. She wasn't sure if it was the heating ducts, the Scotch, or the proximity of the man who once again had transported her to a place of refuge and safety. She needed to thank him. She yearned to hold him. Instead, she jabbed a toe at the carpet and muttered, "So what now?"

Z let his hand slip from hers. She told herself that she was imagining his reluctance about the move. "I'll get the first-aid shit out. You can go to town on my neck, candy striper. Sound good?"

Despite her exhaustion, his indulgent tone made her feel safe enough to giggle. Maybe they actually could work their way back to being friends again...

"Yeah," she murmured. "That sounds real good. Thank you."

His mien stiffened a little. "But right after that, you get into the shower—or a bath if you prefer. While you're cleaning up, I need to call Hawk and Captain Franzen. I'll get the run on how they're tracking Mua and make sure both of us are pulled off AWOL status for as long as possible."

"Damn. I'd forgotten about that not-so-little slice of red tape."

One side of his mouth quirked. "It helps to have kidnappers in high places, honey."

She shot him another laugh. Zeke, clearly pleased with himself for inciting it, sauntered toward the stairs. She gave herself the privilege of watching him for a second. Sweet shitloads of sexy, the man was captivating. His leather club pants moved with his Sequoia tree legs like a second skin. His biceps and pecs fought the constraints of Max's T-shirt. Nothing in any of his movements betrayed that he had a three-inch gash in his back, let alone hadn't slept in over twenty hours.

And all she wanted to do, even in her own sleep-deprived state, was get her hands all over him again.

Not a good plan, Ray. Not at all. She fished through the fuzziness in her head to get back the words he'd issued in the car, after that toe-curling kiss they'd shared. *Shouldn't have happened. And it won't happen again.* So the man was beautiful *and* smart, especially about this. No matter how perfectly their bodies fit, they simply weren't going to snap right when it came to the same sexual "Like" button.

She prodded her brain to agree. Shoved at the damn thing.

Submissiveness? On a regular basis? *Her?* Right. And tofu was a great side dish for steak.

Tonight, she'd seen in glorious, living color exactly what that term meant. She closed her eyes and willed herself to pull up the images. She recalled what Luna looked like when Tait brought her in after the session with Z. The marks on the woman's back...the limp languor of her body...the sparse rasps off her lips...

She blinked, and all those memories vanished like magic act doves—all but the most disconcerting one. The expression that had blanketed Luna's face. The peace in it. The adoration in it. The connection in it, reflected in Z's own face as he'd knelt to her...

"Rayna?"

She blinked and looked up. He'd stopped on the landing halfway up to the second floor. His features didn't hold a shred of that intense stare he'd exchanged with Luna. He'd even dropped the smirk of five minutes ago. Now he regarded her only with friendly, even pragmatic, expectation.

Ugh.

"Huh?"

"First-aid kit's up here."

"Uh...okay."

She followed him up the stairs. At the top, there was a large area that was just as comfortable as the ground floor. One side was lined by the balcony-style overlook into the living room. Tucked into the far corner was a window seat with plush pillows and a chenille lap blanket. But occupying most of the eye's attention was the entrance that beckoned into the bedroom. Correction—the straight-out-of-her-wildest-dreams bedroom.

There was no way any person, let alone a linens lover like her, could avoid gaping at the bed. Its Mission-style headboard was balanced by a dozen huge pillows in butter and honey tones. They were stacked horizontally down the center of a puff comforter that looked soft as fawn skin and colored the same rich hue. The room's drapes matched it, as did the cushions on a semicircle-shaped couch that was positioned in front of the stacked-stone fireplace. A flat-screen TV took up the space over the mantel.

"Holy...wow."

Zeke walked ahead of her into the room. "At the risk of redundancy, good wow or bad wow?"

She glared in irritation that wasn't entirely a joke. When he tossed a snicker back at her, she stomped over and punched the meat of his shoulder.

"Hey!" His expression became a glower. "What the hell?"

"You had that coming," she accused. "And stop looking at me like that. I didn't even knick you."

His response seemed a humorous move at first, too. As he backed her up against the wall, Rayna let out more giggles—until he actually had her pinned there. One direct hit from his focused copper gaze, and her laughter petered out.

"You only think that because I hide the knicks well." Though they were likely the only human life for miles, he said it at a volume solely for her ears. "But I have them, Ray-bird."

"I know." Her trembling whisper blended with the damp musk of the rain in his hair, on his skin, dripping down his leathers. "Believe me, I *know*." With her stare still locked in his, she scooped one hand around the side of his neck. "Zeke, there's really something that I have to—"

"Shower," he cut in.

She blinked. "Huh?"

His intimate murmur was gone. So was the crack, however infinitesimal, that he'd opened into the core of himself...only for her. Not the easygoing soldier-on-leave self she normally saw, or even the dungeon-leather-and-chains-Dom self of earlier tonight. For a few seconds, she'd beheld the guts and heart of the man who lived far beneath all that. The man who'd once been a teen, gazing at her with those intense eyes on a stormy afternoon in a park tunnel.

Did he remember, too? And if so, why did he keep shutting her off like this?

"Huh?" she repeated in an even dumber blurt.

"My neck can wait," he declared, "but you're shivering like a can of pop that's been used for soccer practice." He looked down at her soaked, dirty clothes. "And all this is getting washed. Twice." His brow knitted tight. "Shit. Now there's a cluster of what-to-do, huh?"

"A...cluster? Of...what?" She sounded idiotic. Confusion and exhaustion were making her brain a puddle. She swayed on her feet during the minute he took to fish through the drawers of the dresser next to the bed. Nothing was any clearer when he turned back with a long-sleeved flannel shirt that had red-and-yellow parrots printed all over it. They were depicted in flight across fields of bright-turquoise flowers. She almost let out a manic snicker. It was hideous.

"This'll keep you warm. It's one of my favorites. The socks are great, too. They're designed for high-mountain hiking, but I've broken them in. Really soft."

She held the shirt up. It was going to fit her like a tent on a sapling. "This is yours."

He flashed her a visual *duh*. "Were you expecting

something different?"

"Maybe," she answered, then amended, "Probably." When his *duh* twisted into a *what-the-hell*, she explained, "C'mon, Z. You don't have a stitch of anything that other...ermm... houseguests might've left behind?"

As understanding entered his features, so did a soft smile. Hell, she loved getting that look from him. It lit up everything, including his eyes, and made her feel like she was the only one who put it there.

"If you're referring to Garrett, then I'm afraid none of his threads will fit you much better." He fingered some stray tendrils off her forehead. "He's the only 'houseguest' I've had besides you."

She blamed her fatigue for how her whole body reacted to that little brush of his fingertips. Still, she managed to quip, "Your mask is slipping, Darth Vader. Better come clean now."

"And your ass is begging for a good blush for that, little bird."

The rain suddenly stopped. Maybe it was just as stunned as she was—though Rayna wondered if the astonishment on her face came close to the wonderment on Zeke's. No, she was pretty certain her bewilderment outweighed his, for in that moment, three insane realizations hit her.

She'd loved what he growled at her.

She'd loved how it stopped her breath.

She was terrified at the image it burst in her mind. Because she loved that the most of all.

Her ass beneath his hand. Her naked flesh, blooming for his touch. Her screams feeding his soul.

"Yeah. Maybe I'd better get in the shower."

He reacted to her rasp with a clipped nod. His gaze had

gone dark as burnt copper. His bottom lip was shoved against its mate, and his jaw was a hard square. "Damn good idea."

He left the bedroom before she could say anything else, disappearing down the stairs. He pounded the steps so hard, the decorative reeds in the urn at the top rattled each other. Rayna glared at them.

"Hey, kids," she grumbled. "Looks like the word of the day is going to be *awkward.*"

★ ★ ★ ★ ★

Things went from bad to worse after she got out of the shower. She headed downstairs to find Zeke throwing a couple of blankets and a pillow across the sleeper bed into which the living room couch converted. When she'd thanked him and gratefully sank onto the mattress, sleep encroaching fast now that she was warm, he'd given her a string of snarled "Nos" before snatching her up, blanket and all, and carrying her back upstairs. She'd gotten out no more than three words of protest before he'd cut her off with a sharp, "Good *night*, Rayna."

As he'd shut the door on her, she'd fumed, punched a pillow, and muttered, "Next time, just cut to the chase and tell me to fuck off, Hayes."

Before sleep torpedoed the rest of her consciousness, she promised herself a good long meditation session tomorrow—or, more correctly, later on today. She needed to lob a shitload of mental detangler on this mess called Zeke Hayes. The fact that he was now her roommate for a few days only hastened the urgency, especially the not-so-little part about thinking of his hand on her backside—or any other part of her body. He'd made all of that clear, hadn't he? His kinky world wasn't hers to tread on. She needed to stay in her own box with him. It was probably better that way for them both.

On that thought, she passed out.

That was when, even from hundreds of miles away, Mua got to her again.

In the dream, she was walking through thick midnight mist again. But this time, she wasn't in the city. Her surroundings looked like a canyon, stark and steep, the high walls making each of her steps resonate in frightening emptiness. Mua materialized from the gloom just as he had before, with Round Face and Chain Man by his sides. Rayna backed away but was stopped from behind by arms that curled around her neck and waist with greasy surety. A camera floated in the air in front of them. A tongue slid along the curve of her ear before a seedy voice commanded, "Smile, little bitch."

King.

Her legs buckled. Her lungs seized. Her heart stopped. Her mind turned to paralyzed ice.

No. No. No!

One simple syllable. *Say it. Scream it.* But she couldn't. She...couldn't. Her throat was glued shut, strangled by terror. Her mouth struggled to move, to simply process air. *What air?* She couldn't breathe. She couldn't move. He was going to get her. He was going to sell her. He was going to make her disappear forever.

"Noooo!"

Her scream burned in her throat and rang in her ears as she shot straight up in bed.

She reached for the glass of water on her nightstand. It wasn't there. That wasn't even her nightstand. She whacked her hand back to her heaving chest and peered around. Where the hell was she? Everything was still dark and murky. Clouds roiled past a glass window, dumping rain in deafening sheets.

She cried out in confusion and kicked at the covers. There were so many of them, so heavy and thick. Lightning flash bombed the room. Thunder bellowed. She shrieked in full again, her senses caught in the ether between nightmare and sentience.

A set of arms formed from the shadows. Terrifyingly strong, just like King's. They grabbed her shoulders. She screamed and twisted free. "No!" The force of her voice gave her strength, yanking her back toward reality. "No, damn you!"

"Rayna."

The voice was gentle and firm—and achingly familiar. She stilled for a second. Major mistake. In that second, her wrists were captured in dual iron grips and then pinned to either side of her head. She flailed and kicked, but her quads were subjugated by a log-sized thigh.

"I'm not the docile one anymore, damn it. No! *No!*"

"Rayna, honey...listen to me. Look at me."

She kept fighting. Bucking her whole body. Squirming and writhing. Sucking down air in giant, desperate gulps. Those inhalations made her smell the monster, which was confusing as hell. He didn't smell like sweat, mud, and halitosis. He smelled like cedar, smoke, and mountain wind.

She swallowed and opened her eyes.

Then let her mind wake up. And her heart fall apart. "Zeke."

His face warmed with a gentle smile. "Hey." He slackened his hold on her wrists.

"Your cabin." Relief flooded from her with the words. She grabbed the front of his T-shirt, pulled him close, and nestled her head into his chest. "We're at your cabin."

"And you're safe, bird."

Right after he rumbled it, he shifted to roll off her. Panic speared her like a rogue icicle. The worsening storm, which had turned the afternoon into an eerie night outside, didn't help. She dug her fingers deeper into his shirt.

"Don't go. I can't—"

"All right." He smiled softly, his teeth contrasting with the stubble that was quickly becoming a full beard. "I'll be right here, okay?"

He patted a couple of pillows. They were as close to the edge of the mattress as possible. She whipped her head back and forth. "No. Too far. I'm still scared." Her voice was small and pathetic, but she didn't care. "And cold." She ran her fingers along the little gap between his T-shirt neck and his skin. "And you're so warm."

He expelled a long breath. "Rayna, you know what I'll do if—"

She wrested his argument by showing him what *she* yearned to do. With one hand yanking on his shirt, she drove the other into his hair. She wrenched his face down to hers, fully ready with an open offering of her lips and tongue. Their mouths fused. Their breaths mated. As the storm raged outside, they stirred a wanton, hot hurricane inside. Rayna let the tempest take her, rejoicing as it ripped through her blood, fired through her sex, and decimated her resolve.

"Zeke," she finally pleaded. "Help me forget it. I need to make it all go away. Please!"

She watched his jaw tighten and his eyes flare. A squall of dark humor passed across his face. "Fuck," he whispered. "You're not talking about a chick movie and a foot rub, are you, honey?"

"No." She moved her hand to his face, digging her fingers into his beard. "I want you to make me forget...just like you made Luna forget."

CHAPTER ELEVEN

Zeke stared at her hard for a long minute. Now *he* had to be the one dreaming. For the last forty-eight hours, she'd been the merciless erotic torment in his mind, but now she was his wildest desire come to life, right here in his arms. With her lips parted, her eyes imploring, and her body this close and warm... *Fuck. Dream come true* was the tip of the goddamn iceberg.

But weren't dreams the soul's way of reminding you what you couldn't have? Who *was* the depressing dickhead who'd said that? Oh, yeah. That was him.

With a resolution he couldn't be further from feeling, he uncurled her fingers from his shirt and then cupped the ones at his face long enough to press a kiss on her knuckles. "Honey, as much as every bone in my body would thank me to do that...I can't."

As he forced himself to sit up, her bewildered stare followed every move he made. "Why?"

How could she speak one word but scratch at fifty corners of his composure? Even if her trembling tone didn't tip him off, he saw the self-doubt on her face, the way she glanced down at her body, encased so adorably in his shirt and nothing else, and compared herself to Luna's "charms." And clearly noticed every difference that he did. Then instantly came to the ridiculously wrong conclusion.

"Damn it, Rayna." He cracked his neck. Wasn't working. His thoughts still bounced in his head like ping-pong balls in a carnival guppy booth. "It's not you, honey, okay?"

"So it's you?" she retorted. "Is that it? And I'm supposed to believe that how, Mr. Prom King of the Seattle kink crowd?" She shot a derisive laugh at his stunned gape. "There isn't a lot Sage and I don't share with each other, Z. I've known since before you went on the last mission. But even if I hadn't, the rocket-science degree wasn't necessary to witness it at Bastille last night." Her glare dissolved, and again she tore at his edges with her questioning eyes and wobbling lips. "But there's no subbie waiting line right now, is there? You can't have your pick of the bench. But you can have me, and—"

He surged to his feet. "My pick of the bench?" Straining the outrage from it was impossible. "Is that what you think? That I just stroll into the club and decide what workout I want for the night? Like choosing to go run on the treadmill or play some basketball?"

She twisted the drooping sleeve of his shirt. Goddamnit, why did she have to look so sweet and small and sexy in it? "I don't *think* anything, Zeke. I just want— I just—"

"You just *want*? Okay, you just want what? Are you able to verbalize *that* much?"

"Stop talking to me like I'm seven. These aren't words I'm spewing on a whim. I didn't decide to pop them out because I liked the sound, okay?"

"Right. Because you were thinking so lucidly after having a nightmare that had you nearly tearing up this bedroom."

He was being a semi-asshole. Maybe more than *semi*. Still, she responded with tight calm, "From time to time, Sage shares a few things with me about what she and Garrett have as Dominant and submissive. I already know there's a lot more to it than what people assume. Now I've had a chance to witness it firsthand, too."

He moved to the end of the bed and locked his hands behind his back. "That's nice. But you didn't answer my question." After stepping one leg out and bracing himself in a full drill-instructor pose, he leveled his stare back into hers with unflinching intent. "What. Do. You. Want. Rayna?"

She earned a new chunk of his respect for not surrendering an inch of her own gaze. Despite the Gung Ho Mo Fo act he flung at her, she gave back as good as she got, drawing up her shoulders with admirable precision. But when she spoke... her words were complete woman. One hundred percent a pleading, sexier-than-hell husk.

"I want you to look at me the way you looked at Luna last night."

Gut, meet a boot named Rayna Chestain.

His breath left him on a heavy rush. So did his anger. But the void left behind didn't remain empty. He recognized the feeling like rounding a corner and seeing an old schoolmate— the one who liked to get in a couple of punches before letting him move on.

"That's not a request I can grant, Ray-bird."

She rose up on her knees. "Why the hell not?"

"Christ." It roared out of him. He threw up his hands. Another emotion two-by-foured his core without the bully's help this time. Despair didn't need a sidekick. "Did your 'firsthand' experience include what I did to Luna last night, Rayna? Did you see the marks on her body? *All* of them? Did you think about how she got them, about what I did before—" The look that crossed her face, as if preparing herself to be slapped, clutched the words short in his throat.

"Say it," she rasped. "Before you fucked her. There. I did

it for both of us."

"I didn't fuck her." She blinked, seeming to believe him, though his ominous growl didn't give her much choice. "I wasn't her Dominant, Rayna. I was her Top. There's a massive goddamn difference."

She let out a breath in frustrated puffs. Her lips twisted. "But when you stood in my living room and told me you were going to Bastille and what you were going to do, I thought—"

"I know what you thought. It was exactly what I wanted you to think."

He pivoted and crossed the room. Though it was the middle of the afternoon, the world was a swath of pewter mist and black clouds. A perfect backdrop for this conversation.

Conversation? No. It wasn't going to be that. She was silent and still now, and he needed to just leave it at that. He had to close her down from ever thinking they could explore a D/s dynamic together. He knew damn well what would happen if he ever crossed that line with her, ever accepted her at his feet and demanded a *Yes, Sir* spring from her lips. As beautiful as the beginning would be, none of the end results were remotely good.

Yeah, he should have left it at the silence.

But her mute hurt tore at his edges. Pulled and jabbed and peeled at his scabs.

Shit.

"Letting you think I was going to screw Luna was an easier way to break things with you, okay? I needed you to see what I am, Rayna. How I'm wired." He swung his gaze toward her again. "And how that equates to a disaster for *your* wiring."

As he expected, she was waiting for him with eyes that looked like crushed emeralds—tossed on top of a bonfire. "So you just decided to sever my wiring," she charged. "Is that it?"

Hell. That mind of hers. Nothing was a bigger turn-on, and nothing made him want to throttle her ass more. Hard. With a slotted paddle.

"I'm not going to jump on this carousel with you. It's going to leave us both dizzy and pissed. You don't understand half of what you're asking me for, and—"

"God!" She climbed off the bed so fast, she thought nothing of the peeks she gave him at her bare sex as she did. He stood locked in a mix of stunned and stimulated as she advanced and smacked the center of his chest. "They give you three golden rules in BDSM, right? Safe, sane, consensual? Congratulations, Jesse James. You've already stolen the third from me, and you're well on your way to making off with the second."

He openly fumed at her—and seethed with disgust at himself for doing so. God*damn*it, the brat had hit him twice, and he just fumbled like the fucking new guy with bad intel, disbelieving what was happening but unable to pick up a damn radio and order a proper extraction. Gawking. Helpless.

No. Way.

He hadn't been helpless for a very long while. He sure as shit didn't plan on starting a trend of it now.

Rayna had made the mistake of leaving her hand suspended midair in front of his chest. Now she drew it back a little, as if contemplating whether to pummel him again. The follow-through was a no-brainer. He whipped his own hand up, swallowing her fist inside his own.

"You want to discuss your sanity, bird?" He shook his head with steady surety. "Trouble is, you haven't gone insane. You've gone bratty."

Her eyes widened. She flinched and attempted to pull back. He grinned and clutched her tighter. Yeah, that aroused him. A lot. But this had nothing to do with his pulsing cock and everything to do with teaching this little girl a lesson. Sometimes—many times—that involved mission recon above the waist.

Not that she made the effort one click easier. Instead of fighting him more, she tossed her fiery hair and gritted her teeth in sexy challenge. "Bratty, huh?" One side of her sleek mouth quirked up. "Aren't you big bad Doms supposed to put brats in their place? Teach them a lesson?"

Damn it. She was really, *really* asking for it.

Openly sparring with you doesn't mean she wants you to subdue her, Hayes.

Even if she did, it'd be too damn dangerous. Tait wasn't here. *Nobody* was here. That was the fucking point. Zsycho couldn't come out to play if there wasn't a babysitter, especially with Rayna. Especially with how incredible she'd feel under him, snarling at him...then finally, breathlessly begging him...

With a tight growl, he slid his hold from her fist to her wrist. Using the extra stability for strength, he yanked her closer to him, nearly punching her nose with his as he forced her to stare at him. "Is *that* what you want, Rayna? A lesson? From me?"

She drew in a rickety breath. But her eyes glittered with pure sass. "Hmm. What do you think, Master Z? Do I need one?"

He shook his head again. The move wasn't so patient this time. "Ohhh, honey..."

"Well?"

"It doesn't fucking work that way, Rayna. Five minutes

ago, you were about to kick in my family jewels because of fighting off the cockroach twins in your sleep. Now you want me to turn off the lights and take you to subbie dreamland. But if we hit a land mine on the way, your psyche is the casualty. Do you get that? Has Sage explained *that* part to you?"

In spite of the challenge, he made no move to let her go. She didn't shift, either. Her chin jutted higher, almost daring him to go on.

"You're pulling bratastic on me right now. Doing a damn fine job, too." He tapped her head with his free hand. "But there are a lot of emotional insurgents in here waiting for you to pop your parachute, Rayna. If you're ever on your knees for me, that brat walks out the door. *All* the way out. You won't get to hide. You won't get to pick the reaction you think I want or some cute answer from a story Sage has fed to you about what she and Garrett did one night in the dungeon. I don't teach lessons like that." He watched her pupils dilate in response, so gorgeous and intoxicating, making it impossible to conclude in anything less than a low but determined thunder. "So be damn careful of the one you're asking for now."

The message finally seemed to get through. Thank God. Apprehension and expectation played over her face. He was about to let out a breath and slacken his grip—when the defiance surged back into every inch of her stance.

"So...what? Is that supposed to scare me?"

Hell.

He let her go and moved back. One wide step. Another.

Now you need to turn around and leave completely. Now. Get your ass downstairs before you start really contemplating how good it would be to chop that saucy attitude to pieces in screaming, writhing, climaxing, sinfully submissive chunks.

"Yeah, bird. It sure as fuck is."

She didn't move except to slide both hands to her hips. Christ. She was breathtaking. Her stance defined her luscious curves in every damn way. Was she actually tapping one set of turquoise-polished toes?

"Well, it doesn't."

Goddamnit. Yeah, she was tapping. And glowing. And tempting him with every rise of her beautiful breasts, every tug of teeth at her cinnamon-dark lips, every drop of need in her open, honest eyes.

She wanted this. And damn it, he did, too.

He pivoted and took another step toward the threshold. Rayna coiled her fists tighter at her hips. That pushed the shirt harder at her breasts, stretching the parrots that matched her stubborn toes. Fuck. His shirt got to feel up more of her than him, and *he* was the one getting glared at like Caligula? This was wrong. On a number of shit-laden levels.

"Well, it should." He sneered it viciously enough for the Caligula rep.

"Got that part, Sergeant. Are we moving on now?"

For a moment, he was plunged back into disbelief. For another he just blinked, unable to splice together the sweet friend who'd gone fishing with him in August was this mouthy rebel who tempted him with every lift of her chin and toss of her thick red mane.

In the third, his fury slammed him back into action. As he regained the distance back to her, he tore off the T-shirt in which he'd been sleeping. "You want to throw down on this, Rayna?" he charged. "Then let's do it." Ignoring her open gawk at the sudden exposure of his chest, he seized her hand and forced it against the tattoo between his pecs. The small black circle, divided into three equal slices that bore a dot each, rose and fell with his incensed breaths. "Touch it," he ordered, "since you seem to know so much about it. The triskelion means something to me, Rayna—something so deep that it's stamped into the skin over my heart. *All three* sections of it. Safe, sane, consensual. They're embedded into me. They're part of me."

She nodded. "I—I know, Zeke."

He tugged her chin up with a finger. The brat was gone. Fresh tears glistened in the jade pools of her eyes—and that was actually a good sign. Maybe she was really comprehending the depth of this subject, especially for him. "You do?" he challenged. "So *that's* why you're standing here in a cabin in the Cascades with me, miles from any human let alone your phone or clothes, freely offering yourself to me?" He tilted his head. "Did I get all that right?"

Shockingly, her face broke into a soft smile. "Zeke—"

"Because you see, honey, that 'consensual' part implies a little something called trust."

She pulled his hand away from her chin and curled one of her own around it. Her other hand still rested atop his tattoo.

Atop his heart.

When she spoke again, her tears flowed as steadily as her words. "Let me be clear. I know what I'm asking. I know where I am. Right here, alone in a cabin with *you*, Zeke Hayes. Without my phone. Without my clothes. There's really only me. And with all of me, I trust you. Not stupidly, not blindly. I am giving you the trust you've earned from me, over and over and over again."

He expelled a weighted huff. "And here we are again. Back to the hero thing." He pushed back, disentangling his hand.

"You need to listen—"

"No, *you* need to listen. Stop making this into something from a movie or a sappy novel. What went down with King was doing my job."

"And what went down with Mua was, too. Right?"

He knew she'd go there. And was ready. "Tied into the same stinking mess," he admonished. "You and I both know that."

Rayna blinked at him through fresh tears. "So how do you explain what went down with Kier?"

Forget the boot in his gut. Her words were the talons of a crane now, ripping into him, picking him up and flinging him fifteen years into the past.

Kier. Holy fuck, he hadn't heard from or seen that asswipe since they'd both squeaked by with their high school diplomas, though the guy had been a filthy spot on his radar for years before that. Between shuttling drugs, fencing fake watches, and beating up half the school, the guy always found time to hang out in the park and spin up creative ways to make life hell for anyone who dared to cross his unofficial turf. Like girls who just wanted to enjoy a walk on a sunny day...

Stop where you are, asshole, or I'll give this stupid squaw a nice little scalping.

Way to go, Rayna. That went about as wrong as it could have, huh? Maybe, girlfriend, you do need to go back to the jungle. Maybe you really are just a stupid little squaw.

He lifted his head and looked at Rayna with a stare that forced the years to fall from her face. He willed himself to see her as a girl blooming into her teen years, with that red hair hanging a little longer and bangs caressing her eyebrows. She was wearing capri pants and a fuchsia top. Dirty tears tracked her cheeks. And Kier was hanging his bare, dirty dick over her face.

"That was you."

His voice was a hoarse effort. Rayna's reply was no stronger.

"That was me."

"How—"

"Sally. I went to see her. I finally let her hypnotize me."

That made him laugh. At himself. "The hypnosis *I* kept telling you get?"

"Yep."

The time-travel crane went to work again. It tore him open just as deeply as it dumped him back here with Rayna, gaping at her through a haze of shock, incredulity, amazement. No wonder she'd come to see him at the club. No wonder she'd kept looking at him like her goddamn wishing star had just crash-landed.

Maybe it had.

For both of them.

And maybe it was time to do something about that.

Without wasting another word, another breath, he closed the distance to her again. Before he was done planting his feet, he curled his hand into her hair and yanked hard. A little cry burst from her, swirling to him like an enchantress's smoke. Like the cobra called by that smoke, he plunged his mouth to hers. He bit, sucked, and licked, countering his violent hold with smooth caresses to her face. She bent for him without constraint, showing him with her body what her lips had already given.

Her trust.

The most precious gift she'd ever handed to him.

As the rain began again, the room darkened. Zeke pulled away to watch the gray and silver shadows play across all the lively, gorgeous curves of her face. He sucked away a few of the tears that clung to her cheeks and then delved his gaze into her eyes, giving her something in return.

An order.

"Take this thing off. Then kneel for me, honey."

CHAPTER TWELVE

"Yes, Sir."

Saying those words for a man had never been a spark in Rayna's mind, even after what she'd learned from Sage about the world of D/s, but right now, they felt completely natural. Magical. And so, so perfect.

Because she'd uttered them for Zeke.

Because she knew what they'd do for him.

Because she needed to know what they'd do for her, too.

She thought the admission would grant her a clinical distance about this, make this threshold feel safer to jump over somehow. Yeah, and wearing a parachute made it less terrifying to hurtle out of a plane. Detachment wasn't happening. Tremulousness, nervousness, and awareness *were* happening, along with the sense that shedding the dopey shirt off was stripping more than the shield to her nudity. Something significant in her mind dropped, too. Too late, she realized what it was. Her inner uptown girl. That horny, cavalier, this-is-just-sex girl from Thursday night wasn't here anymore. This wasn't just sex anymore, either.

This was surrender. A gift that showed him how deeply he'd woven himself into her heart, how dark the ink of his heroism was tattooed upon her life. She made the offering with the fullness of her soul because she knew what it would mean to him...but also what it meant to her.

Yes. God help her, she wanted this with every cell in her

body. Not forever. Probably not even tomorrow. But right now, nothing felt more right than dropping to her knees before him, fixing her gaze on his rough bare feet, and waiting, breath held, for what he'd do with her next.

What *would* he do with her next?

By the sound of his puma's growl, she sensed his dark answer for that. But he was stealthy and still otherwise, continuing to stand over her, which made her shiver in anticipation...and drip in arousal. It took a shaking breath and pressed lips to hold back her whimper as desire clenched every inch of her wet pussy.

"So stunning," he finally told her in a husky grate. "Thank you, bird."

As he lowered a hand to the top of her head, kneading his fingers into her scalp, Rayna managed, "My—my pleasure, Sir."

His massages stopped. He slid that hand to the side of her face, bracketing her jaw with his thumb and forefinger before lifting her face up. "Not yet, sweetheart." His answering gaze was burnished with possessive smoke. "But soon. Very soon."

He pulled away from her and settled back into his A-frame stance a few feet away. Defying her control, her gaze lifted from his feet. Up his carved and mighty calves. Over the defined tendons and muscles of his thighs. Lingering for a long moment on the hard force that punched at his nylon shorts before raising to the arrow of hair that bisected the defined ladders of his abs. When she looked even higher, it was to view his coiled arms atop the dark breadth of his chest. Across every inch of him, there were scars, nicks, and bruises, some silvered from long-ago battles and some painfully new. He was a walking scrapbook of violent battle and contained power.

He could really hurt her, and nobody would know.

Why did that make her nipples go painfully hard and her channel push out even more wet arousal?

Finally, she couldn't bear the unknowing silence anymore. "Wh-What happens now?" She glanced up at him though she'd heard that was a major subbie no-no.

Zeke emitted a deep hum that didn't make things easier for her nerves or her nipples. "It's already happening, bird."

"Huh?"

"Ssshh. Just breathe," he instructed. "And just be. Right now, it's your job to simply let me look. And believe me, honey, I'm looking."

The sultry cadence that entered his voice made the cold rain suddenly seem a summer cloudburst. She was washed in liquid warmth, feeding off his sensual strength. It was a little confusing. Wasn't *she* the one required to give over the power here? Then why did she feel powerful enough to fight an invading army by herself? The thought made her squirm a little, only increasing the flow of tantalizing tingles through her bloodstream.

"Nervous?" Zeke asked softly.

"A little," she admitted.

"Then other things are making you wiggle, too."

Her head fell. She couldn't even look at his feet when she admitted, "Yes, Sir."

"Let me see."

"I— What?" she stuttered.

"You heard me, bird. Let me see your aroused pussy. Spread your knees wider and lay your back against the floor so your cunt is pushed up for my inspection."

She'd expected orders from him, but not like this. And his tone? No more seductive silk. He really was Vader now, without the creepy hyperventilation. His deep, guttural tone said he expected to be obeyed without question.

She didn't ask any questions.

With quivering limbs and a shaking heartbeat, she moved her knees apart before lowering her back to the floor.

"Raise your hands above your head," he said, reading the confusion in her awkward hand flails. "Join them together, flat on the floor."

Once she'd complied, she held her breath and waited for the next instruction. None came. Zeke barely moved, aside from stepping closer to line up his toes with her kneecaps. Two minutes ago, she'd been unable to rip her gaze from him. This changeup took care of that obsession. She riveted her attention on the ceiling, just trying to maintain the position, though she was hyperaware of every breath on her lips, every pulse in her blood, every molecule of air that hit the moist tissues she'd opened for his examination. With her arms positioned overhead, she was completely exposed to him from the waist up, as well. He took full advantage of the moment. The weight of his stare was as hot as a bath in candle wax, encasing her in its heat one inch at a time. She'd never been commanded to assume such a vulnerable physical position before.

It didn't come close to what he was doing to her on the inside.

She was scared. Excited. Trembling. Rejoicing. Unsure. Unfettered. Small, so small, yet poised on the threshold of something significant...magnificent. Beyond that doorway, something glowed just out of her reach, a captivating but terrifying light.

"Oh, honey." Zeke's rough rasp tugged her an inch closer to that magical portal. "You *are* glistening, aren't you? And I haven't even told you what I have planned for your sweet little body yet."

She attempted a nonchalant shrug. "M-Maybe it's okay to just surprise me."

"Maybe it's *not*." There was half a laugh in the words, but it definitely danced on a stage of black humor. "You're going to hear what I've got in mind, bird, because I want to see how your body reacts to it. Then I need to hear your lips consent to all of it."

She fired off a dismissive huff. "We've been through this. Zeke, I—"

"You trust me," he retorted. "I know that. And thank you. But this isn't negotiable, bird. Not by a long shot."

She took her turn to laugh. "'Negotiable?' Really? You want to draw up a little contract while we're at it, Sergeant?"

He scooted his toes to the insides of her knees and widened his stance, making her spread farther for him. "That's 'Sir' to you from this point forward, honey. And yes, we'll stop and draft a contract if we have to. This isn't the part you rush through. This honesty is the keystone of the bridge. Got it?"

She pushed out a frustrated snort. "Of course I got it, okay? Zeke"—she rushed to correct herself—"*Sir*, when are you going to get it through your head that I've thought about this? That, maybe just once, I really want this?"

She expected him to pull the toe-scooting thing again. Maybe add a grunt this time. Maybe, just maybe he'd smile in pleasure and get on with—whatever the hell he was going to get on with.

She should've remembered that this man and the word *expected* weren't on speaking terms with each other.

The thought ricocheted through her brain as Zeke acted

with wildcat speed. In one sweep, he'd moved to stand above her head. In another, he crouched and grabbed her wrists. In a third, he whipped her around to face the leather couch. The velocity of it all caused her to lose balance and pitch forward. She was able to stop her fall by gripping the top of the couch. He flowed his body in perfect synch with her, pressing his breaths to her nape, his chest against her spine, his thighs along hers. He shoved the hair off her neck before biting his way to the curve of her ear.

"When are you going to get it through *your* head that I've wanted this, fantasized about this, since the night I met you?" He plunged both hands down to grab her inner thighs. With feral force, he pulled them open, settling her naked backside against the hard, huge length that defined his crotch. "That even in that hospital bed after the stabbing, my cock turned my gown into a goddamn central supply tent because of what I thought of doing with you...and to you."

He didn't give the words half a second to sink in before he demonstrated for himself, scraping his fingers along the sensitive flesh on both sides of her labia. Those intimate lips quivered in response. Joined with the way his legs kept brushing the backs of her knees, his assault became a torment of blissful agony. Dear God. Zeke's College of Power Exchange was in session, and Breathing was on the optional courses list. Speaking? Not part of the curriculum.

"Even in Korea," he went on in a grate that turned the rest of her bloodstream to mush, "hell, *especially* in Korea, I dreamed of all the ways I wanted to take your body and turn it inside out. How I wanted to tear inside your mind, pull out all your pain, then—"

She felt him suppress the rest on an agonized grunt.

Rayna protested by surging herself back and rolling her head against his shoulder. *Then what? Holy hell, Zeke. Tell me before I have to throw myself over the balcony in order to ease this fire you've set in my body.*

The new frisson of tension through his frame told her he might just be on that mind track. Thank God she was right.

"I'm going to start out by keeping you right here, bird. I'm going to bend you over so your ass is nice and high for me. Then I'm going to make it beautiful and pink by spanking it with my bare hand. After I warm us both up, I'll be doing it fast and I'll be doing it hard."

She moaned for him. Or thought she did. She couldn't hear anything for a moment beyond his smoldering breaths in her ear and the rush of arousal to her bloodstream.

"When your pussy is dripping from that, I'm going to make you get on the bed. You'll be facing up so I can watch every sigh on your lips as I secure you to the four corners of it. Then I'll watch every scream as I subject your skin to a bunch of very interesting sensations."

Rayna already gave him the sigh he predicted. "Do—Do I get to know what they are?" she managed to squeak.

Zeke gave her a deep chuckle. "What happened to the girl who wanted to be surprised?"

She got her head to cooperate with a short nod. "She's still here...somewhere."

A rumble of pleasure vibrated his chest before he slid his fingers back up her body, scoring her skin with his nails on his way over her hips, stomach, and rib cage. When he got to the tender nubs of her nipples, he finally stopped. The masculine thunder rolled through him once more as Rayna gasped from the heaven of his touch.

"As I line my cock up to your tight, wet tunnel, I'm going to pinch these, Rayna. I'm going to watch your nipples pucker and redden for me while your cunt gushes, begging for my dick. It'll tell your lips to plead with me, too—but you won't. From now on, your words are mine, too. If any of this gets overwhelming or painful, you'll call out one word to me. That word is *Kier*."

"What!" She nearly unleashed the scream he wanted from her, as well.

His reply came with an arrogant lilt. "You're not going to forget it, right? And if you use it, I'll *know* you need to stop."

"Damn straight," she grumbled, though she wasn't allowed to wallow in her irritation. The next moment, her ass was set on fire by a swift, determined *smack*. "Oh!"

"Your words are mine, remember?" If he was arrogant before, he was in complete Marc Antony mode now, spinning her so he could peer down at her like his prized Cleopatra. And damn it if her whole body didn't crave him just like dear Cleo, too. "You can say 'yes, Sir' if you understand, subbie."

Subbie. His affectionate drawl turned her inner Cleopatra into a fig in the Saharan sun. "Yes," she whispered, sprawling her fingers along his biceps. "Oh yes, Sir."

"So you accept the intentions I have for you this afternoon, freely and openly?" After she nodded, he went on. "That means you are willingly submitting your body and your mind to me, Rayna. You're placing yourself completely into my care. You know that choices will not be yours. You will be mine to claim, to mark, and to fuck as I wish."

She was glad she had a good grip on his arms. They kept her from swaying at the impact of his words, which already swirled such a thick erotic haze into her mind that her vision went cloudy. Gazing up at him didn't make things easier. His dark hair tumbled against his jaw. His gaze penetrated her like a pair of solid bronze javelins. His wide, dark torso made her feel small and helpless in all the oh-so-right ways, especially as he dug his fingers into her hips with increasing purpose.

"Y-Yes," she finally got out. Shit, even the chest hair that tapered between his pecs was perfect, stabbing between her fingers with coarse tension.

"Yes...what?"

"Yes, Sir."

She dipped her head again. It felt natural, almost right. Best of all, it brought out the rugged vibrations from deep within him again, making its way through to her body, causing the tips of her breasts to shiver like flowers answering to the wind.

"God *damn*, that sounds beautiful on your lips." He roamed his grip up her body and back down. His battle-roughened fingers abraded her hips, her waist, her shoulders, and the sides of her tingling, taut breasts. "And I'm going to fucking love hearing you say it, over and over again. Right now, you'll position yourself on the couch again for me, exactly as I had you before. Rest your forehead on your arms, and push your gorgeous ass into the air for me."

He backed the directive up by turning her to face the couch again. "I'm going downstairs to get some things. You'll wait for me like that, and you'll think about how I'm going to touch you exactly how I please. You'll think about how incredible this spanking is going to feel on your beautiful skin."

Incredible? She was glad Z couldn't see the pucker on her face as she arranged herself back into the position he'd specified. It was one thing to fall into this stance by accident due to his passion but another to willingly brace herself again, her legs open and her body exposed...to an empty room. It felt awkward. And more than a little ridiculous. Surely he could have just told her to sit on the bed and wait for him, right? What good was this going to—?

She stopped the inner rambling when she heard him rustle around downstairs. The clangs and bangs suggested he was in the kitchen, though she couldn't be sure. He pulled out drawers and opened cabinets, interjecting his journey with wicked chuckles—which drove her curious tension even higher.

To her wonder, the mental friction carried repercussions in her body, too. Since she was alone in the room with nothing but her breath for company, her mind fast became an empty mental playground for Z's words to play in. They took full advantage of the chance, too.

Think about how I'm going to touch you...

That one jumped on the teeter-totter that alternated between her breasts. The syllables traded the blistering taps between each nipple, sucking away her breath each time they did.

Exactly as I please...

Down the slide and straight into her sex was that one's pleasure, fingering her clit with its hot assumption as if the words were Z's own fingers. As every pore in her body opened and shivered, she gasped.

You'll think about how incredible this spanking is going to feel...

That one gave her no choice about doing anything else, turning the slide into a waterpark as the deepest channel in her body rushed with a new river of arousal. She grimaced with the effort of holding back a needy mewl, forgetting about her effort of deciphering what Z was up to, only wishing he'd finish fast and get the hell back up here. When another full minute went by and he still seemed content to whomp around downstairs, she started twisting her hips a little, answering her pussy's need for more stimulation.

"Ohhh, bird." Though his baritone hit the air with no more volume than a mutter, it seized every muscle in her body. "That's *not* exactly how I left you."

"But it's what you turned me into." The desperate need between her thighs punched the override button on his rule about her words. "You ordered me to stand here thinking about your touch and your hands, and—"

"And this is how you get when you think about those things?" Though his voice was mild, his fingers weren't. He pushed two of them inside her channel from behind. No warning preceded the move. No hesitation hindered it.

"Ahhh!" she cried. He shocked her. Invaded her. Consumed her. Though he touched her nowhere else, her entire body reacted to his harsh penetration, his total power. Her legs trembled. Her stomach coiled. Her senses reeled.

"That's not an answer." Mild jumped off the deck of his tone now. His puma was back and consuming that space, snarling every word with predatory focus. "Answer me, Rayna. Is this what your body does when you think about my hands on it?"

"Ohhh." The exclamation slipped from her as he twisted his fingers, possessing her tunnel with ferocious strokes. She willed herself to nod, and then rasp, "Yes...yes, Sir. This is what my body does when I think of you touching me."

"Your skin always pebbles so beautifully like this? Your tits tighten and get this hard?"

"Y-Yes, Sir."

"And your gorgeous thighs...they always flex like this, so they make your ass clench, too?"

"Yes, Sir."

"And your cunt drips like this, turning into the sweet cream that's calling to my cock even now, honey?"

"Yes!" It erupted on a sob, high and needy as her body gripped his rough fingers, drawing him deeper inside. Higher. Harder. *Yes...*

"Hmmm." He damn near drawled it, making her want to shriek. How could he stand there sounding like the walking poster for *Keep Calm and Dom On*, when she'd never been so turned on from a man's fingers? Only two of them, at that? "You know what that means, then?" he asked, joining his other hand to the cause by pressing it into the small of her back.

She wanted to fling back a quip so sexy and smart it made him laugh a little, easing the air between them to something less terrifying than an electric transformer about to overload. But where would that leave them? She'd be hiding behind sarcasm instead of showing Zeke her truth. Using humor instead of letting him see this naked, unsure sparrow that didn't have a damn clue about what to do for him now, about what to say. But if she saved her pride, she'd dismantle their honesty. She'd be yanking out the keystone of their bridge.

She drew in a wobbly breath. As she let it out, she answered him with all the trust her heart could muster. "N-No, Sir. I have no idea what that means."

His reply came after a weighted pause. Zeke slipped his fingers from her pussy before he issued it in a growl that clenched at every cell of her sex and curled into every fiber of her spirit. "It means you're a very naughty girl."

Whack.

Thank God she'd just taken the effort to breathe, because she couldn't now. Her throat clutched from the emphasis he gave in the form of his hand on her left ass cheek—or what remained of it. This blow made his previous slap feel like a summer breeze.

Within seconds, he delivered an equally blistering blow to her right side. Again to her left. Down once more on her right.

At last, her stunned lungs found air again. "Oww!" It wasn't fast enough to prevent his third round of scorching smacks. "Zeke! S-Sir! Shit!"

As she squirmed, he increased the pressure on her lower back. The reasoning behind his hold made sense now, in a not-so-assuring but oh-so-arousing kind of way. But how was that possible? How could she let a man hold her down again, *ever*? And even worse, how could she feel so damn good about it?

Because they were Zeke's hands. Because her mind knew, her *soul* knew, he was here to take care of her. And in the dominion of his hands and the command in his next words, she felt how she took care of him, too.

"Naughty girls get spanked, subbie. Especially when their ass looks this good and their pussy drips this wet—and they make their Dom go half insane just from walking into the room and looking at them."

So much for flippancy. So much for forming any significant words beyond the tiny "Oh!" she squeaked before he gave both of her buttocks another taste of the Zeke Hayes spanking special, this time with a dose of the extra-fiery sauce. Ohhh crap, did the man know how to turn that meat in his biceps into whips that scalded every inch of her backside. It wasn't long before the flames caught on the kindling of her nerves and licked up her body, making her quake and shudder with each stinging kiss from his palm. It was so corrupt. It was so carnal.

It felt so damn good.

"Holy fuck." His growl was a hot and brutal crack in the air, stroking her senses like a blissful blow in its own right. "You look more beautiful than I could have imagined, bird." He raked his hand up her spine, his touch becoming a gauging caress. "You feel okay, too?"

That hand met her scalp as she gave him a half-delirious nod. He plunged his fingers to the back of her head, digging them in to push it down between her shoulders. "Outstanding," he murmured. "Yes. Lower this completely. Fucking beautiful. I love seeing you bent for me...surrendering for me." With his other hand, he smoothed the skin that burned the most from his treatment, pressing the heat deeper into her bottom, her thighs, and the most tender parts of the valley between her legs.

"You're perfect, Rayna. So goddamn perfect." His touch turned into a rough buff. Soon he curled his fingers, digging his fingernails into her sensitive skin. She hissed from the hot, sweet torment. "Such a beautiful shade of pink," he growled. "But now I want to make it red."

"Mmmm!" She hoped her long, desperate moan conveyed how damn much she agreed with that.

"You're amazing, honey. So strong. Such a miracle. You can take more, and I'm going to give it to you."

He gave her two seconds to process that before starting the blazing blows again. He meted them harder than before, making the air pop like a battlefield with each loud crack. Her body, mind, and spirit exploded in a matching maelstrom. Lucid thought was a lost cause. The blackness behind her eyelids exploded in orange, red, and white. The colors sharpened as heavy tears seeped from their corners.

He kept up the fiery pace. The tears seeped onto her lashes. He rubbed in the heat with flowing, forceful fingers before starting again, ramping his impact higher. The tears spilled over and rolled down her cheeks. It was brutal, wonderful insanity.

Holy shit. What's happening to me?

Trying to understand was as useless as controlling it. She wanted to blame the wild surge on the physical agony he was dealing, but every drop confirmed the truth: the inferno he opened on her skin was just the beginning of everything else he flared in her. The bewilderment. The amazement. All the feelings that rose from her soul in visceral, incredible ways, the memories she'd been stuffing into dreams and dimming behind medications, now rushed her soul like the wind that whipped outside...and burst as unhindered emotion.

For the first time, the doors of her senses were blasted open so wide, the past disappeared. The future was nothing but mist. Nothing existed but this moment and all it demanded from her. The pain. The clarity. The excruciating agony, the blinding clarity.

Like a baby taking its first breath, she gasped.

She was new. Restored. Reborn.

The revelation burst through her chest and heaved through her lungs. It exploded from her on a sound between a choke and a shriek. Lovely. She sounded like a dying seagull but was helpless to care. The tears came in shuddering waves, drenching her, cleansing her. She rode every redemptive wave, loving every lash that set her faster on the journey...

But needing more.

Craving something beyond his hands. Longing for—

Exactly what he gave her.

The bite of his fingers at her scalp. The knife of his teeth into her neck. The twist of her head in his hold. Then the slice of his mouth on hers, bruising and consuming, ramming her lips apart so he could stab his tongue into every recess she could take him. The salt of her tears soaked the seam between their lips, enhancing every delicious drop of his rugged male taste, causing her to open wider for him, to moan deeper for him.

When he dragged away, his lips only backed off by an inch. He jerked at the back of her head, raising her higher. His gaze was dark and intense as summer sun while taking in every inch of her face, including the wet trails down her cheeks. He bracketed her with his other hand, pressing his fingers into her jaw and temple, giving her no choice about letting him see exactly how he'd excavated her mind, her soul, her heart.

"Little bird." The words were an intoxicating mix of reverence and violence. "Fuck. You're already halfway over, aren't you?"

She was conscious of blinking at him. Sort of. She didn't know what mesmerized her more—the power in his touch or the rough magic in his voice. "Over...where?" she whispered.

He poured the bronze heat of his stare over her again. The force of his scrutiny zapped lightning down the middle of her body, bursting into a million shards of heat in the middle of her clit. She shook from the impact, erupting with a whimper of restless need.

Zeke answered with a hard, heavy breath. "Change in the mission plan, honey. I'm not going to make it to the bed, and something tells me you won't, either." As he took her mouth again, he spun her around and wrenched her close, forcing the juncture of her hips against the pulsing ridge between his own.

"Fuck." He rasped it into the inches between their lips as they pulled apart. "You even taste different now." He suckled again at her bottom lip. "Your surrender has turned your mouth to pure honey. So sweet..." He licked it from corner to corner. "So goddamn delicious."

As he swooped his tongue inside once more, he dropped to his knees in front of the couch, making her sit on it in front of him. His words made her aware of how *he* tasted, a combination of wind, spice, and lust that captured her senses so completely, she didn't realize he'd slipped a length of soft rope behind her back. Cognizance came when he looped the ends around her wrists, deftly cinching them back to lock against her hip bones. Her new position thrust her torso directly at him—which, judging from the carnal caramel streaks appearing in his eyes, wasn't a damn bit by accident.

He added confirmation to that by dipping his mouth to one of her hard, jutting peaks. She watched him from beneath heavy lids as he used the flat of his tongue in a sensual figure eight around the tingling nipple. When it was hard as a piece of strawberry candy, he bit into the engorged tip.

"Ohhh!" Her head fell back, rolling her eyeballs the same direction. The stab radiated through her breast and tripled her heartbeat.

"You feel different, too, subbie." He murmured it while skimming his mouth to her other breast. "You're hard for me in all the right places. Like here"—he tugged on her nipple with relentless pressure—"and here..."

While she struggled to process the sensations from his mouth and refocus her vision, he slipped a hand down once more. With the ease of a sniper's heat laser, he found the most sensitive places in the valley of her sex, rolling his thumb against them with tantalizing assurance.

"Shit!" She lurched forward, needing to clutch him, claw him, make him feel every tremble he induced and shudder he inspired. When her arms caught against her bonds, she groaned in frustration.

Zeke went on like she'd barely sneezed. "You smell so fucking amazing, too. Submission's turned your pussy into a little garden of lust, hasn't it?" He trailed his fingers deeper, tracing them along her trembling labia. "Open your legs, bird. Open them wide for me, and let me smell how much you want me."

She moaned again. "Untie me first," she blurted. "Please... Sir. I need to hold you. To show you—"

"I know what you need to show me." He lifted his gaze, full of such burnished, beautiful depths, and locked it into hers. "But we're playing by my terms right now, not yours." He trailed tender kisses atop her thighs, along the fringes of her pubic hair. "Open up, honey. Spread wide for me."

She used his face as her anchor. Borrowing the strength that defined every inch of his bold features, she compelled her knees to move outward. The motion caused her bruised ass to brush the couch's smooth leather, radiating heat through every layer of her sex until it ignited even the deepest caverns of her womb. She took a huge breath as Zeke did. As he exhaled, his eyes slowly closed. His thumb pressed harder against her clit.

"That's the best perfume you could ever wear for me." He snaked his finger up to her lips and stroked his thumb along the ridge of her upper lip. "Smell that, subbie. Breathe in how beautiful your cunt is to me." He followed the tangy line he'd painted with the tip of his tongue. "You're so hot. So wet. Like a peach cream tart, thick with need for me."

"Yes." The end of the word was lost to a sigh as she stretched out her tongue to meet his. Her taste buds were filled with his rich, virile taste, mingled with the fruit of her most intimate essence. The flavors instantly made her ache to taste him in other ways, and she squirmed against her bonds again in an effort to break free so she could touch him, hold him, suck him.

That wasn't going to happen anytime soon.

With an impatient snarl, Z grabbed her thighs, which had gone to aroused paralysis beneath his assault. With one vicious shove, he splayed her all the way open for him. In another sweep, he roped both hands around her buttocks and pulled. Her breasts slammed against the wall of his chest. Her crotch hit the enormous bulge in his. A gasp fell from her. A groan fell from Z. He cut both of them short by spearing his tongue inside her mouth, claiming her with primeval fury.

By the time he tore free from her mouth, he'd already grabbed a handful of her hair and yanked hard. Rayna's shriek erupted into the thick air of the room.

"Again." He growled it before taking the column of her neck in a feral bite, making her cry out again. "Scream for me again, little bird. Higher. Louder." He wrenched his mouth to the other side of her neck and dug his teeth in harder.

"Shhiiit!" Rayna yelled. "Oh, Zeke! Please!"

"What?" he snapped.

"Sir!" she revised. "Please. This is— I need to—"

"What?" His mouth was back at her throat, demanding it against her sweat-slick skin. "Tell me what you need, subbie."

"I—I— Set me free. *Please.* I need to touch you. To feel you."

His hair scraped her neck as he shook his head. "Uh-uh. Not your job. Not right now."

"But—"

"*Let it go*, Rayna." His guttural command came with another harsh yank in her hair. Her face was now a vertical plane over which he loomed, cutting at her brows, her nose, and her cheeks with jabs of his teeth until he came to her lips again. "*You* are *mine* to touch right now," he said against her mouth. "Your beauty is mine to worship. Your mind is mine to inhabit. Your body is mine to use." He took her in a biting kiss before commanding, "Now tell me you understand."

She drew in a stuttering breath. It was a perfect emulation of the tatters of her control. "I—I understand."

Shadows moved across his face as the storm turned into a squall. Wind whipped at the windows. His gaze, darkening to russet, swept over her entire form. His lips parted to reveal his clenched teeth.

"Now beg me to take you."

As thunder shook the world, desire burned up her veins. "Yes," she whispered. "Take me, Sir."

He slipped his hands from her head to the band of his shorts. "Beg me to fuck you."

She swallowed. "Fuck me. Please."

With a feral grunt, he pulled his cock free. It burned at her pussy in seconds, the hot, moist tip sliding into her tissues, seeking her welcoming entrance.

"Damn," he gritted. He leaned back for a second to scoop a foil packet off the floor. Inside five seconds, he'd torn it open with his teeth. In another five, he slammed the condom over his full, thick shaft. Rayna couldn't help staring at his hard glory. She dug an anticipating bite into her lip.

Zeke grunted. "You keep looking at me like that, bird, and I'm going to explode right here."

She took a chance on a sultry grin. "I'm a naughty girl, remember? Isn't this part of the job description?"

His dark brows ticked. "Making your Sir come in his condom instead of your sweet body?" He clawed all ten fingernails into the welts he'd left on her ass. "Oh, you *do* want a punishment, don't you?"

She gasped as he used his grip to grind her clit up and down his hot, huge erection. She lost the ability to think, much less maintain the smirk. Her body clenched, teetering on a wire between sanity and sensation. His words now made sense. *You're already halfway over.* She understood now, because she'd tumbled more than halfway. The beautiful, black abyss in her senses was now a pull she couldn't fight. And didn't want to.

"I only want what you do."

His nostrils flared. His stare turned to impenetrable shadow. He pulled back his hips. When he rolled them back on a single lunge, he filled her depths with his cock.

"This," he rasped. "I want this. It's all I've been thinking about for two days. All I've been craving since the moment my dick left you before."

A fresh burst of tears pooled in her eyes. "Me, too," she said. "Oh, yes...me, too."

A look mixed of pain and joy creased his features. "You're so beautiful," he uttered. "So goddamn perfect...bound for me like this, open for me like this, taking every inch of my dick like this."

"Yes," Rayna whispered. "All of it, Sir. Please."

He rammed his lips over hers again before ordering, "Beg

me for it again. Plead with me to shatter you."

"Yes," Rayna responded. "Yes. Make me come with your cock!"

His jaw hardened to dark stone. He curled his fingers into her hips, gripping her with inescapable force. He handled her like a toy for his pure carnal pleasure, and she gave herself over to the joy of being just that, her breath escaping her on harsh gasps in time to every brutal crash of their bodies. With every thrust, his cock seemed to grow. His flesh shoved at hers, forcing her to accommodate him, giving her no quarter for comfort or ease. He took. She gave. Then he gave so much back to her. Fire. Friction. Tightness. Tension. Heat that built and grew, pulsed and pounded...

And released.

"Oh!" She cried it in pure shock. The orgasm overtook her from the inside out, radiating in a shockwave that really rendered her limbs to the consistency of a yarn doll. "Oh my God. What the *hell*?"

Zeke bent his head to kiss her hard. "Let it come, little bird." His voice was husky and thick. "Fuck. That feels so good. Let it come, because when you do, I'm going to burst deep and hard inside you."

"Zeke!" His nasty words worked their magic. A second climax claimed her, more intense than the first. It ripped her mind free from what remained of its moorings, sending her over into the abyss of surrender. She was lost in an ocean of raw sensation, overcome by pure white heat as Z poured his come into her a moment later on his own long, roaring groan.

She was washed in new beauty again—but this time there was no analyzing the flood, let alone controlling it. The tears poured, untamed and unabated, as a blend of sorrow and elation tore back so many shackles in her heart.

She wanted him inside her forever.

But all too soon, he slipped away.

She mewled in protest as he pulled out. With an efficient swipe, Z pulled off the condom. She didn't know where he put it, only grateful that he barely budged from her side as he did. With equal efficacy, he released her arms from the rope and then stroked them, his gaze scanning every inch of skin where he'd cinched it around her. Apparently satisfied she was all right, at least in a general physical sense, he gathered her in his arms and carried her to the bed. Once she was there, he laid her carefully on her side before climbing in behind her.

The feel of his huge body did nothing to stop the flood now bursting from her senses. She dragged in air, hoping to calm the storm down, but her ragged breaths were just a blatant reminder of how thoroughly he'd turned her inside out.

What the hell had just happened?

Would she ever be the same again?

Would *they*?

"Ssshh." Z issued it into the hair he'd started to finger comb off her face. His tone was deep and resonant, as if he'd just read her damn mind. "Let it all come, bird. Let it all out. I'm not going anywhere."

She twisted to face him. With a watery smirk, she asked, "Is that an order, Sir?"

His answering chuckle made his whole face go warm and sexy. "Sure as fuck is."

She laughed, too, which provided the tears with another escape hatch. Zeke rolled her over, gathered her close, and stroked her hair as she choked her way through another sob fest.

"I'm sorry," she finally blubbered.

"I'm not," Z murmured back.

"I don't understand all this."

He lifted her chin with a finger. When she looked into his eyes, the passion that had darkened them swirled with rich caramel hues. "I do." He gave her a fast kiss. "And it's probably the best gift you've ever given me."

She narrowed her eyes. "Better than the Yoda T-shirt I found for your birthday?"

He broke into a grin. "Yeah. Even better than that."

"Explain?" She tilted her head.

"Later." Anchoring the back of her head with his hand, he tucked her against his chest again. "Rest. I'm going to get up in a few and find some cream for your ass. Then you'll sleep. *A lot.* Then we can talk."

Though his voice was still full of command, there was no mistaking the encroachment of real life on them once more. She sighed deeply. It wasn't like she hadn't expected this part. She'd knelt for him with the full knowledge that no woman would ever hold that the space at Z's feet forever.

Knowing it and accepting it were two different things.

She turned her cheek against his chest and gazed at the couch across the room. And conceded that she'd never look at that thing the same way as long as she was here.

And wondered if she'd look at *anything* the same way again.

And realized, even with the entire Seattle PD and a vengeful madman looking for them, that no moment in the last twenty-four hours terrified her more.

CHAPTER THIRTEEN

He woke up alone. And was puzzled why that bothered him so much.

A glance at the clock told him it was two a.m., though that wasn't the reason for the disconcertment. In Special Forces, one lived by the timetable of the mission. This was often the team's lunch hour. The immediate circumstances weren't a valid excuse, either. After funneling so much of himself into the needs of a subbie, it was often a relief when they sneaked off to freshen up, letting him relock himself the way the he liked best: in silence and seclusion. The good ones figured that part out pretty quick.

But she isn't just a "good one," is she?

She is the perfect one.

"Fuck." He threw his forearm over his eyes, as if that would blot out the memories of her kneeling for him, opening for him, climaxing for him...giving herself to him. "You need to stop this right now, moron," he told himself. "Perfect or not, it's past tense now. It *was* good. It *was* a damn great adventure. End of story. She scratched her D/s itch, and you were the lucky bastard who got to help. She's done. You're done. It was great. Move the hell on."

Even considering anything else with her would be a catastrophic mistake. His past was knife fights and naps in garbage dumpsters. Hers had been homecoming games and cupcakes. His present was missions, bullets, and terrorists.

Hers was bandages, healing...and cupcakes. The last time he checked, bullets didn't go well with frosting.

That didn't stop him from wanting one last embrace.

Where the hell was she?

He sat up in bed, realizing that he didn't hear her in the bathroom. A quick look across the room didn't reveal a light under the door, either.

He swept back the covers and left the bed in one flow of movement.

Since he'd put his shorts back on when he'd gotten the cream for her ass, he only had to throw his T-shirt on now. He did that while crossing to the doorway to the landing. Once there, he stopped and listened to every corner of the cabin.

Aside from the post-storm drips off the roof and trees outside, he heard nothing.

There were no lights on downstairs, either.

Where the *hell* was she?

Following protocol from years of training, he clamped down the urge to yell for her. Instead, he padded to the upstairs lockbox, quickly keyed in the code, and yanked out the Springfield .45 caliber stored within. With a fast flick, he opened the chamber and loaded a couple of bullets. He slid his thumb to the safety, preparing to flip it off if need be, and then took the stairs down two at a time, absorbing his weight with his knees and regulating his breathing so he made no more noise than a feather.

Which was what he felt like when he got to the ground floor and saw her again.

Moonlight shone through the back deck window, though the silver streams danced with the storm clouds, making the living room look like a mystical rainforest. Rayna, covered again to her knees in his Henley, stood in the middle of it—if that was the proper term for her pose. With one leg raised with its foot braced against her other knee and her hands pressed over her heart in a diamond shape, she reminded him more than ever of a fairy-tale bird.

She was gorgeous. Amazing. If he hadn't been all over her and inside her six hours ago, he would have even doubted she was real.

He couldn't decide whether to keep staring at her or order her to the couch so he could redden her ass again for scaring the shit out of him.

Not scratching that itch again, jackass. Remember?

The next moment, she took care of his dilemma anyway.

"Put down the gun and come join me, Sergeant Hayes."

Her voice was as ethereal as the light that surrounded her and soft as the smile she tilted at him. The fact that he stood there with the weapon didn't seem to stun her in the least— which dazed *him* so much, he complied without a word. She rewarded him by extending a hand, pulling him next to her.

"You should be sleeping, bird."

She arched both brows as she angled him to stand as she did, facing toward the panorama of cliffs and mountains that seemed to undulate beneath the clouds and the full moon's glow. "Are you really going to try that one on me, SF boy?"

"And are you really going to call me 'boy'?"

She turned her face up to him. Her eyes were full of dark-emerald solemnity. "Then what do I call you?"

Hell. That was the sixty-million-dollar question, wasn't it? He looked away instead of answering her, all too aware of the words that pushed way too close to the edge of his discipline. *You can just continue with "Sir." How does that sound? Or maybe I'll just tell you how it sounds. Maybe I'll tell you about all the submissives who have offered it to me in so many scenes but how none of them filled my spirit with the satisfaction you did. How my body has never been pumped with such need. How the word never gave me what your lips did...*

"What are you doing?" he asked instead.

"Just getting the chakras in line."

She centered her stance again. This time she kept both feet on the floor. Without letting his hand go, she lifted her arms like a swan about to take flight. If his evasiveness ticked her off, she chose to play it close to her vest. Well, her chest. Like he could avoid noticing the sight, between her pose and the deep V of flesh exposed by the neckline of his shirt. *Damn it.* From his vantage point, he could see all the way in to the dark gold circle of her left areola, including the deep pink streaks left behind by his teeth. He smiled in grim triumph. He couldn't touch her anymore, but she'd sure as hell remember he had, at least for a few days.

It would be so easy to use their handclasp to drag her close again. To ram her against him, devour her in a kiss, shove that shirt up past her waist, and—

"Come on, Z." Her voice fell back into its gentle mist again. "Join me."

The steamy fantasy bugged out like a greenie grunt under heavy fire. "Nah. Thanks. I'm good."

"Yes, you are." She curled a silky smile. "But how're your chakras?"

He seriously needed to just let go of her. But goddamnit, he couldn't. As his arm went along for the ride through a sweeping circle of hers, he muttered, "Bird, I don't do chakras."

"Really? Because you sure as hell tangled with a few of

mine."

Shit. How did he address *that* without coming off like an elephant on rice paper?

With a nervous snort, he rotated and adopted the same pose as her. "Is that good or bad?"

He watched her face carefully as she considered an answer. Her forehead crinkled just a little before she replied, "A little of each. So breathe in the next time we go up, okay? Hold it, then let it out slowly."

He rolled his eyes. "I...don't—"

"In," she decreed. Up their arms went. He snorted his way through obeying her. "Now let it out. Slowly."

"Christ," he grumbled—though damn if the action didn't spread a nice layer of warmth through him. As she lifted his arm again, he ditched the snort in favor of really filling his lungs all the way.

And sneaking in a stare at her.

And marveling at what he saw.

With her hair a bright mahogany mess, contrasting with the porcelain serenity of her profile, she was as fascinating to him as the first day they'd sat and talked in the garden at the embassy in Bangkok. He took in the little curves at the corners of her lips, the gentle rise of her neck, the straight strength of her shoulders. There always seemed something new to notice about her, something else about her beauty that took his breath away.

And here she was...all his. Dressed in his damn shirt. Still covered in his bites.

Filling his cock with craving her beneath him again.

"Z."

"Huh?" he stammered. "What?"

"You're not breathing."

A shrill ring saved him from having to answer or apologize. The satellite phone.

He rushed into the kitchen to pick it up. The ID showed Garrett's landline, but he still didn't say anything when he picked up. It was anyone's guess as to how far Mua's influence stretched now.

"Zsycho? *Annyeong*?"

He expelled a relieved breath. There was only one person who spoke Korean in a tone as pretty as his face. "Runway." He used Ethan Archer's radio call sign in return. "Hey, man. What the hell are you doing at Hawk's place?"

"Helping you out, assface. Most of the team's here. It's our new command center, I guess."

His mind jumped three steps ahead to the next conclusion. "Which means you're not using the team facilities at base."

Ethan's own rough breath clouded the connection. "No." Defeat weighted the word. "That's part of the reason for the zero-dark-fuck-me call."

"Don't worry about it." He grunted against the thick, dreading ball curling in his gut. "What's the word on this rodeo?"

"Not *bueno*," Ethan supplied. "Your horse is limping, Z." He paused for a second. It sounded like a bunch of people had just come into Garrett's condo. "Hawk, Slash, T-Bomb, and Moonstormer just got back from running Franz back to the base. He had to file you as AWOL, Zeke. I mean, officially."

The ball turned into a lead brick. He knew Runway couldn't see his nod, but he went through the motion anyway. "Yeah. Got it."

"He didn't want to, man."

"I know," he returned. "But I expect things weren't pretty when he took all our findings to the Chief of Police."

"And the mayor," Ethan added.

"Shit." He couldn't hide the surprise from that one. "Does Franz think Mua's got a squeeze around nut sacs that high?"

"He wasn't ruling out the possibility, especially when the mayor backed up every page of the book that the chief wants thrown at you."

Goodbye anxiety, hello rage. Two things happened in that second to cause the twist. First, remembering the incident that had led to this mess to begin with, how those bastards were preparing to leash Rayna up and drag her back to Thailand like an escaped zoo animal. Second, watching her round the corner in front of him now, her face darkened by apprehension—and the purple bruise at the side of her face that still bore evidence to their cruelty.

"If the asshat wants to throw books, let him come," he snarled. "Hawk is always telling me to read more anyhow. We'll all learn something too, such as how half their police force is on the take from a criminal who's supposed to be locked up in their highest security box."

"We're all on that tack with you, Zsych." There was more scuffling, as if the other guys heard Ethan say his name and were literally gathering around in a circle of support. "He's not getting away with this bullshit anymore. Franz has given us the keys to the jeep and told us to throw down the throttle on exposing him, along with every ankle-grabbing fuck stick in the PD or otherwise who's jumped in his mud puddle."

"Outstanding." The support of his team, who were the closest thing he'd ever get to brothers, filled his chest with a furnace of gratitude. He relaxed enough to let Rayna push him down onto a barstool so she could do a recheck and bandage change on his own souvenir from the Mua-nettes. "So what am I doing next?"

"Uhhhh..." Ethan grunted. "What do you mean what are you doing next?"

There was a brief scuffle on the line. The next voice he heard was Garrett's. "You maintain that twenty, Zsycho," he barked. "Your invisibility is our best ally. With them all on the prowl for you, we have much less clog on the line for these firewall jumps into their system."

Z scissored his jaw and nodded again. "Agreed," he said. "As much as I hate admitting it...agreed."

The chatter behind Garrett faded. Even so, his friend lowered his voice. "Level with me, Z. You gonna be okay for a few days while we get this twister roped in?"

He snorted. "If I say no, you going to check Rayna and me into the goddamn Four Seasons?" He followed it with a chuckle that felt a little manic. "I'm sure I've been in rougher scrapes than this. Just remind me what they were when this is all over."

Garrett was quiet for a long moment, which tossed the brick of dread back into Z's stomach. They both knew what he was trying to reference by *rough scrapes*. They also both knew he'd trade those hundred times he'd almost lost his life for this single moment of looking at the end of his military career. And his personal freedom.

Angrily, he fired, "Look, everything's hunky-dory here, okay? I've got cash stashed in the safe. I'll run down to the general store for food and supplies. They're floating my military ID pic on the news blasts, right?"

"Yeah." Garrett let out a laugh now, too. "The one you

look nothing like most of the time."

"Especially now. With a hat and glasses, I'll blend even more with the locals." He glanced back over to Rayna, who was done with her futzing at his wound and now scooted up onto one of the kitchen stools. She gave him a sweetly supportive smile while wrapping his shirt around her knees for warmth. The action let him see a tiny piece of her ass, so cute and tawny and pinchable. That did *not* make his next words easier to say. "Hawk, did you ever make good on that plan to sneak Sage up here?"

There was another lengthy pause. "Aw, hell," his friend finally spat.

Z frowned. "Hell what?"

"I'm not getting that paddle back now, am I?"

"*What* paddle?"

"The one you found." Garrett snorted. "Right? The one I got at the vendor night at Bastille, the leather-wrapped number with the end shaped like a heart that I left up there? Bastard. You know Sage loves that thing. You found it, and now you're holding it hostage. All right, what do you want for it?"

Even under these circumstances, he'd usually laugh at that. But now, knowing he had at least a couple more days in this place with Rayna, that paddle, and a whole kitchen full of kinky utensils that he hadn't even used on her yet...

That he couldn't use on her, *ever.*

Hopping the border and disappearing into the Canadian tundra was looking less torturous by the second.

"I don't want the damn paddle, Haystack Jack," he retorted. "I was just hoping Sage left some clothes behind."

"Oh." Garrett emitted a sarcastic snort. "Well, in that case, can't help you, man." When Zeke sliced a growl through the line, he cracked, "What the hell? You think I let her pack *clothes* for a weekend in the woods alone?"

Z rolled his eyes. "One day, I'm going to regret exposing you to all this, aren't I?"

Garrett laughed. "I think I would have managed the way myself eventually."

"Yeah, just remember the buddy who put the first flogger in your hand, you stubborn smegma."

"No way I'm forgetting you right now, darling. You're hotter than the Kardashians and all twelve *Bachelor* finalists right now."

"Gee thanks, my little love muffin."

"Bite me, Hayes."

"I'd really rather not." Especially because he could only think of one body he longed to be biting right now. "But speaking of kinky aftermath—"

"You wanna talk to T-Bomb?"

Sometimes it was damn good to have a wingman who read your mind like a Jedi. "Check," he responded to this friend. "Thanks, Hawk."

After half a minute, Tait's voice came on the line. "Hey, Z." His tone was strained.

"Tait." He turned away from Rayna and pulled in a deep breath. *Awkward* just got installed over the conversation in neon letters. "Listen...I need to thank you for having my six last night with Luna. Well...night before last, technically."

Tait shot back an angry growl. "Are you really doing this shit? After you saved my bacon twice in Kaesŏng *last* Saturday?"

"Not the same game and you know it, man. There are times and places for Psycho Zsycho, and—"

"And from what I witnessed, Luna had no complaints about him showing up in that play room."

Something sneaked into the guy's voice that Zeke didn't recognize. If they were women, he might even think a certain green monster had perched on T-Bomb's shoulder. "Are you square with what happened, man?"

"Yeah." Again, Tait's answer came too fast and easy. "Of course. It was a fucking awesome scene, Z. You were good with her, really amazing. I learned a few new things, too."

"Okay." He said it slowly. "So how's Luna? Was *she* square with everything?"

"As square as she could be." Tait took another breath as if to add to that but huffed into silence.

"What?"

"What do you mean, 'what?' Dude, she was using Harry Potter references on me. *That* woman, with her goddess hair and her endless eyes and her sexy wit, was reduced to Hogwarts analogies after being under your hand for an hour."

He felt his eyebrows jump. Half of him wanted to take Bommer's clear-cut infatuation, mush it up into a pile of shit, and rub the guy's surfer god face in it. Fortunately, the other part of him won out.

"Yeah, okay," he muttered. "I need to talk to her."

"Ya think?"

"On the top of the to-do list, okay? Just as soon as I don't have every cop, civvy, *and* military craving to put a bullet in my ass."

With that as a perky little conversation ender, he hit the over-and-outs with Tait, coordinated another call time with Garrett in twelve hours, and cradled the phone with a weighty exhalation.

Rayna scooted around to stand next to him at the counter. She lifted the tips of her fingers to his forearm and scraped them lightly through his hair. Damn it if even that simple gesture from her didn't ignite his blood in forty different ways again.

"So we're on the lam for a little while longer, Clyde?" She embellished it with a tiny giggle. Zeke struggled to match her mirth but couldn't summon the feelings. They were jammed by an embargo on his senses, enacted by a joint effort between his cock and his mind, uniting as one front, behind one petrifying thought.

How the hell was he expected to stay here with her for one more hour, let alone a day or two or three, and keep his hands away from her?

You already know the answer to that, asshole.

Because if you don't, you'll destroy her. Forget about everything you'll do to her body. Consider the damage you'll wreak upon her mind, her heart...

Consider the devastation she'll wreak on yours.

CHAPTER FOURTEEN

"Ooohhh! I like this one."

Rayna giggled as she held up the T-shirt to her chest, grabbed from a bin of ridiculous tourist garb in the little gift store where she and Zeke were the only customers. It sure as hell beat the baggy sweatshirt he'd given her as a replacement for the Henley, along with her semiclean sweats and muddy Skechers runners.

Z glanced at the shirt, jabbed a tuft of her hair back under the Mariners baseball cap, and issued an answer without skipping a beat. "No."

She gave him a mocking gape. "No? What the hell, Hayes? It's the best line from all the Indiana Jones movies. You know, this shirt is probably a classic."

"Classic piece of crap."

Her jaw dropped again. "You just said that about Professor Henry Jones Junior, buddy."

"Pffft. Whatever."

"Ohhh, I get it. You're one of those Jedi boys who thinks Han Solo kicks Indy's ass, right?"

He grunted. "Han Solo isn't afraid of some stupid-ass snakes." He pondered a sweatshirt embellished with sparkled butterflies and flowers along with the words *Cascades National Forest: A Blooming Good Time*. "Han Solo isn't afraid of anything. Just sayin'."

"Except Leia."

The second it came out, she realized she wasn't entirely kidding. Fortunately, Z didn't get her subtext due to his own search through the bin. "Why would he be afraid of Leia?" he muttered. "She's the love of his life."

"And she knows that...how?"

"What do you mean?"

She glowered at him, strangely irritated. "*The Empire Strikes Back.* Cloud City, remember? He's about to be encased in carbonite. They have no idea how long he'll be frozen or if he'll even survive the imprisonment. It's dangerous shit. *She* comes clean, confesses she loves him. And he—"

"Okay, look." He abandoned the bin in favor of thumbing through a rack of hoodies on hangers. The action made it necessary for him to lean closer to her. "Leia is the leader of her people and usually has a blaster strapped to her thigh. It's not like she needs hearts for dots in her words or astral sonnets. Han knows that."

The smile with which he finished only worsened her weird case of rankled. Nevertheless, she tossed back a little smirk of her own. "Which is exactly why she scares him."

Before he could get out a comeback, she started back down the aisle. Just before she rounded the corner near the hunting rifles, she called, "Get me the sparkly sweatshirt and you're a dead man, Hayes."

★ ★ ★ ★ ★

An hour later, with several bags of nonperishable groceries and new clothes in the Jag's back seat, her mouth was filled with an incredible burst of flavor. She lifted a gaze of pure rapture at Z.

"Holy shit," she gasped. "You were right."

Z leaned back against the driver's side door and cocked a grin. "Bet your ass I was."

"This is the best damn pizza on the planet."

"Worth the extra half hour down the hill?"

"Mmmmm." She took another bite and rolled her eyes in pleasure. "Yes, Sir!"

Unbelievably, Zeke set his pizza down into the box that rested on his lap. She looked up in surprise—until her gaze got to his face. His parted lips and darkened gaze brought a meltdown of comprehension. And remembrance. And deep, needing lust.

And unease.

"It—just popped out," she murmured.

"It sure did." His voice was equally low. And coarse. And damnably, deliciously sexy. He didn't falter his stare, making her feel like the cheese on the pizza. The box rested against his broad, firm abs. She fought off a sudden urge to toss the thing into the back seat, climb over, and plunge her hands under his jacket just to feel his hot, hard skin again. She dared glancing up at him, biting her lower lip to keep her chin from wobbling and betraying her thoughts.

Like *that* helped.

"Rayna." It spilled from him on a rasp. "God*damn*it. How do you do that to me?"

She frowned, trying to discern whether he'd just bashed her or complimented her. "Do what?"

He shook his head. The action stirred thicker tension into the air. "*That.*" He rubbed his chest hard. "With just your eyes... *Hell.*"

She looked back down. It didn't thin her cloud of need at all. Nor, she realized, did she want it to. This needy burn in her body for him... She *liked* it. Though she knew it was insane, even knew her body might end up bearing the same welts she'd seen on Luna, she needed *him*.

"Z?"

"What?"

She peered up at him again. "Before that day, with Kier... I'd never been to that park."

"I know."

"I never went back after."

"I know." He gazed out the windshield as he repeated it. The scudding skies etched his bold features in dark gray light, making him look more a troubled warrior than ever. Her fingers itched with the need to touch him, to soothe those dark edges away from him. "I went back a few times," he confessed. "Looking for you."

"You did?"

He rolled his head, cracking his neck. It didn't ease the taut lines at the edge of his face. "I never knew what had happened. Whether you were okay."

It was easy to control the little tingles that danced through her chest. Fighting the thrill that rooted in her stomach was another thing. "You worried about me?"

He didn't answer her right away. His brows bunched as he picked apart one of the napkins, piece by thumbnail-sized piece. "You can blame the ballet for that."

If he'd just told her he was secretly a European prince, she wouldn't have been more stunned. "Excuse me?" She couldn't help the laugh with which she finished.

"Kier and I were street mongrels, Ray. You know that part already." After she nodded, he went on. "We were actually friends for a long time as younger kids. We were unified by our belief that there had to be a way out. Trouble was, once we hit middle school, Kier's escape hatch was lined with drug dealing, gun running, booze, and dropping out. I chose a different path. It involved the ballet."

She tossed him a teasing sneer. "You joined up with the Pac Northwest Ballet?"

"Not exactly." His lips quirked. "My social worker was a fan." He dragged a hand through his hair as an excuse to hide his embarrassed grin. "The rec center always got donated tickets, and she told me I was a great date. The night after Kier and I bumped heads in the park over you, I went to see *The Firebird* with Meryl. The ballerina who played her had hair as beautiful as yours. The entire time I watched the show, I thought about my own firebird from the park. I thought about... you." He lifted a wistful grin. "I was so pissed at the end when the bird didn't magically morph into a princess or something. She was shorted by a feather and a prince. What the hell was up with that?"

She couldn't help giggling. "Maybe the prince saw a blaster on her thigh and figured she was good to go."

Zeke scowled and shoved half a piece of pizza into his mouth. After gulping it down, he looked over and queried, "So you were okay, then? The police got you home?"

"Yeah." She issued the answer fast, flustered by what his fervent tone did to her. Actually, more than flustered. She wanted to launch herself into him, flattened pizza be damned. She wanted to grab his hair, kiss him, and beg him to put his hands on naughty places on her body. She wanted to show him that last night had only made her want more of him. And yes, more of his domination. Maybe much more.

But she couldn't give him more.

Because every time he claimed her body, a little more of her heart went with it.

And whose fault is that, Rayna? He's been damn clear about what he can do for you—and what he can't. If you get caught in the tractor beam of Zeke Hayes, don't cry when you're caught and then executed by your own foolish feelings.

She needed air.

Now.

In a rush, she jerked the handle, shoved the door open, and got out of the car. As she expected—and dreaded—Z scrambled out, too.

"Ray-bird?"

"I'm okay." She forced a light tone. "Sorry. It was getting warm in there."

"Yeah." The wet ground squished beneath his boots as he approached. "You sure you're all right?"

When she didn't answer after a long moment, he shifted closer. Her breath hitched from his heat, so familiar and strong...such a perfect fit with the very fibers of her body. It was likely why she let him pull her around to face him. He circled his other hand to the small of her back. With semiautomatic instinct, she lifted her hand to his shoulder.

One side of his mouth tilted, along with the corresponding eyebrow—just before he swept her into a perfect waltz.

"What the—"

"Did I mention Meryl also used me as her ballroom dance lessons partner?"

Rayna laughed and then squealed as he spun her even faster. After they circled once through the clearing, scattering wet leaves as they went, Z slowed their pace, guiding her into something like a back-and-forth prom night sway.

But as his dancing calmed, his stare didn't. Once more he scrutinized her deeply, his dark lashes dropping as his irises filled with bronze intent.

"What?" Rayna finally stammered.

"What *what*?" He curled her hand in against his chest. Even through his thick jacket, he warmed her skin. His fingers enveloped hers in unflinching strength.

"Why are you looking at me that way?"

"In what way? Enlighten me."

His voice dipped lower. Rayna turned her gaze down. If she looked at him now, she'd blurt something ridiculous. Something that stemmed from what she *hoped* his intent was, and nothing of the truth.

"What is it, Rayna? You can tell me. But I'll be clear about something. I'm not buying the 'it's too hot in the car' excuse anymore."

She forgot to breathe as his voice seeped into her. The authority of it, mixed with such deep protectiveness, sounded just like the order he'd given her last night. *Kneel for me, honey.*

Just like then, her heart kept racing. Just like then, she was a little afraid and a lot aroused. She closed her eyes, savoring the strands of heat and ice in her blood.

She took his hand and pressed it to the side of her face. When she opened her eyes, letting her gaze lock deeply into his once more, she almost formed her mouth around the truth he demanded.

Please. I know it can't be forever, but I need...all of it. Your bondage. Your body. Your control. Your strength.

I need you.

Instead, she clenched her teeth around a smile before gently kissing his knuckles. "I'm fine. Thanks for your concern.

Let's just get going, okay?"

CHAPTER FIFTEEN

An icy wind cut across the high cliff. It was bitterly cold; the clouds would likely open up again soon.

Luna put an odds-on bet that she'd get sick first.

She pushed the binoculars away with a wince. "Enough," she rasped. "I've seen enough."

It had qualified as "enough" once she watched Rayna and Z got out of the car. Could they have simply taken a walk or gotten a friendly breath of fresh air? No way. He'd gotten her to dance with him. Rayna had looked stunned, as if she couldn't believe Z could move, let alone dance. What, like it wasn't common knowledge? Had the woman not done her damn homework on the man?

But the dancing was easier to take than the touching. Having to watch him stop and stroke her face so gently...then give her that hot, heavy stare as she'd kissed the backs of all his fingers...

Shit, shit, shit.

How was this possible? How had this cup of vanilla frosting slathered herself in front of the Dom who was supposed to be hers? Where had things gone so horridly wrong, especially after their time in the dungeon had been so right?

It was supposed to be different now. He was supposed to have seen, to have understood. Once he'd had her in his hands, felt the potency of her submission and the strength of her devotion, he was destined to forget all the rest and surrender to their connection…just as she had.

Rayna Chestain had changed all that.

A tortured cry sprang from her throat.

Mua's snicker felt like alcohol on her open wound. He dumped salt on top of it with his musically inflected, "Are you all right, darling?"

She inched away from the edge of the cliff. Though she mentally knew how essential she was to the man and his "plan," instinct screamed she shouldn't trust him for a second.

"I think I'm going to throw up," she whispered.

"That's unfortunate." He stepped away. "Please do it over there. I despise the stench."

She stumbled back, but her empty stomach only cooperated with a painful retch. It was for the better. There wasn't time to waste. The next minute, she watched the distant silver speck of Max's Jag leave the parking lot of Annie's Pizza and turn east on Cascades Highway. Mua appeared next to her again, holding a tablet that showed a GPS-style map with a red dot traveling the same route.

The man emitted a low laugh and called to the three men next to the SUV behind them, "Excellent work, Vadim." The middle thug, who had a face as round as a pie tin, accepted the praise with a short nod. "It seems our target has acclimated well to the beacon."

Luna scraped back her wind-whipped hair to get a better look at the screen in Mua's grip. A shiver gripped her that had nothing to do with the day's dropping temperature. "Th-That dot is really being transmitted from inside Zeke?"

"Indeed."

She shook her head, wondering if her mind was going to implode. "I'm still having trouble comprehending how this happened. And why."

One side of Mua's mouth tilted as he brushed a stray pine needle off his wool-blend overcoat. The move was as refined as the Italian name which undoubtedly lined the garment—and gave her a supersized version of the creeps. The man spoke and dressed better than his brother, but the wolf beneath the fleece was spawned from the same disgusting gene pool. She almost hated herself for opening the door to him this morning.

Almost.

Sometimes getting someone to see the light meant you had to go to dark places for them. Really dark places.

Zeke was worth the dark places.

He was worth anything.

"It was quite a simple choice," Mua finally answered. "As you know, darling, time is a precious commodity to me right now. Leaving the country is a paramount priority for me—though doing so with Sergeant Chestain is equally significant. I'm sure that scenario fits into your plans as well, hmmm?"

She wrapped her arms around herself. "She's not going to get killed or anything, right? I'm not a murderer. I'm not going to be your little helping bitch for that."

The man chuckled. It actually made him look like a handsome magazine ad. She wanted to retch again for even considering the idea.

"I assure you, lovely Luna, her well-being is of prime importance to me." He handed the tablet to one of his men and then turned fully back to her. "As a matter of fact, our original plan was to simply slip her away in the middle of the night. We were but hours away from mobilizing on that when Sergeant Hayes arrived at her home. After he departed the next morning—"

"Wait." She gulped against the lump that dumped in the pit of her stomach. "He left...the next morning?"

Mua looked away, blatantly false in his "sympathy" for her. "I could show you our surveillance shots of his departure, though they are a little odd. He forgot his shirt. Seemed to barely have his boots on—"

"I don't want to see the damn pictures." She ignored Mua's knowing leer. "Why didn't you just take her then?"

"Her brother was still in the house." He sighed. "Seems she has one for every day of the week."

She wheeled on him as irritation joined her pain. "Right, right," she snapped. "Got that picture, okay? Snow White and her seven adoring mutants." She glared in response to his amused smirk. "So you followed her on Saturday night. She ended up at Bastille"—*and I don't want to know the reason why*—"and that's when you moved in?"

Mua's only confirmation of that was a little arch of his brows. "It became apparent, rather quickly, that Rayna wasn't willing to depart peacefully with us. When Hayes appeared and interceded, Vadim displayed brilliant thinking to move us forward with this test of the tracking chips upon which we'd been working."

She looked from him to pie tin guy. "And you just had one conveniently lying around?"

His expression didn't change. "I brought one, yes. The intention was to use it on Rayna." He flicked a glance at the tablet, seemingly satisfied with wherever Z was headed. "She would have been our inaugural recipient. When Vadim inserted it into Hayes instead, he saved us from risking a valuable commodity in the name of research."

Luna shifted her gaze to the ground. Rayna Chestain

was really only a name to her, but it was a better designation than *commodity*. But caring for the woman, even by this sliver, wasn't part of the plan. Chestain was ruining everything again. The only person who mattered here was Zeke. She had to make him see the depth of *her* devotion. When he realized she'd forged a deal with a demon for him, had agreed to get this dirty for him... *This* would be the magic formula at last. It had to be. He had to see everything she'd done for him. After this, he just had to know how much she loved him, right?

She looked back up but directed her gaze at the tablet. "I still don't understand where I come in," she said. "You said you needed me to help activate the chip." She waved at the screen. "But it's clearly working. What is there left for me to do? Aren't you just going to follow them, go get Rayna, and—"

When Mua clasped her arm to break her off, she wondered if his perfect handsomeness was due to him being a robot. His grip was crushing.

"Darling, if all I want now is to 'get her,' why would I have authorized Vadim to put the chip into Hayes?" His eyes narrowed by dangerous fractions. "Procuring Rayna again is only going to be half my pleasure. Watching her bow to my will and obey every word I say, down to the moment I watch her crawl on her knees in the chains of another, shall be the other. She'll do all of it without ever spitting at me again, too." He gazed out over the Cascades peaks, many shrouded now in thick mist. "Hayes is the key to her perfect compliance. Her weakness is now our strength." A slow smile spread across his smooth lips. "In the end, Rayna will be mine and Zeke shall be yours."

Hearing him say it aloud made her heart squeeze with elation. She turned, unable to hold back her eager smile. "So how do I help?"

Mua chuckled and returned her look, flashing movie-star-perfect teeth. "Patience, lovely girl. For seventy-two hours, we run on silent stealth. After that, Hayes's system will have assimilated the chip in its first phase of effectiveness."

"You mean it does more than that?" She nodded at the tablet.

Mua cocked his head with unwavering confidence. "We've only just begun, darling."

Vadim pushed off the car and set his stare on her, too. He waggled his brows. "A kiss for luck and we're on our way?"

Inwardly, she apologized to Karen Carpenter. On the outside, she gave the asswad a look that told him his balls were on the line if he took a step closer.

"Oooo," Mua interceded. "Touchy, touchy, lovely Luna. Vadim only wants to help."

The henchman lowered his eyelids and leered. "I'm good at helping."

"Tell him to help from over there," she retorted.

"That won't make it terribly easy for you to practice for your part," Mua answered. "Since it's going to involve embracing Zeke, I assume you wish to get everything just right."

Her guts did knot-tying practice again. Her chest heaved with disgust. But she forced her feet to step closer to Vadim. "If your hands go below my waist, your balls will be singing *Bohemian Rhapsody*."

"Mama mia," the guy drawled.

"Shut up."

I'm only doing this for you, Zeke. You understand, don't you? Of course you do. Sometimes we do shitty things for the ones we love. Because in the end, it's worth it. In just a few days, we'll have our happy end—and all this will be worth it.

CHAPTER SIXTEEN

Zeke was used to writing off a lot of stupid hunches to the paranoia that was sewn into his DNA the second he signed on for Special Forces. Not this time. No stupidity here. No paranoia, either.

The air in the cabin had gone from weird to outright uncomfortable. He was pretty certain it had started before they even got back here—during their little dance in the pizza parlor lot to be exact. The way Rayna had stared up at him, as if seeking something but sensing she wouldn't find it, had ripped through his gut like a shithook's rotor. Every muscle had jerked with the longing to flatten her to the car's hood and demand she give up every thought that darkened her eyes so much. Then he would have kissed her in gratitude for the disclosure, promising her more rewards once they got back here. Though there would be that matter of her flippant language in the gift shop to address, preferably in the form of a few good swats to her inner thighs...

One night of indulging the dynamic doesn't make her yours to do that with. To think of doing that with.

So here they were at the crossroads of Uneasy Avenue and Tension Boulevard. Rayna's car was clearly stalled at the light, stuffed with so many thoughts that the windows were clogged with the mounting pile. In his car? An arsenal of rifles, primed and waiting to blast those damn panes out.

Dinner was simple, boxed macaroni and cheese that

she managed to inspire with spices and some packaged sundried tomatoes, though they ate it in stilted silence. Z got himself a reprieve from her taciturnity by asking about the kids with whom she volunteered once a week at the base's Child Development Center. With Halloween days away, the excitement was high. They'd already made candy collection bags, as well as little ghosts for the classroom. Audrey was going to be Strawberry Shortcake. Rajan was pumped to dress up like Spiderman. Then there were her "creative" kids: Logan wanted to be a walking cocoa machine complete with working spigot, and Veronica had her heart set on being some creature called Derpy Hooves.

He thought he had her loosened a little again, enough to try to get inside her head once more, when the conversation fell upon the subject of the kids' annual trip to the pumpkin patch—which was happening tomorrow.

With a tight wince, Rayna had excused herself.

With a tighter wince, Z relocated himself to the couch.

Passing the next four hours with a marathon of *Ice Road Truckers* didn't ease the weight on his mind by one ounce. Or the pressure in his body. Though the mental shit was a confusion he didn't want to untangle right now, he sure as hell knew what was going on in his nerves and muscles—especially the one between his legs.

He was getting hooked on a drug called Rayna Chestain. And damn it, he had no idea how to rehab himself out of it.

He finally dragged his ass into the downstairs bathroom for a shower. Making the temperature ice cold helped him as much as a cheap condom during wild animal sex.

"Nice, asshole," he muttered while tucking the towel around his waist, as well as the boner that shoved against it.

"Could you do any worse for mental metaphors?"

He opened the cabinet to grab a fresh towel to hang on the rack. And groaned.

Lying on top of that towel was the heart-shaped paddle Garrett had left up here. There was a smaller wood spanker, a strict leather flogger, adjustable nipple clamps on a gold chain, and a pair of soft leather handcuffs.

"Garrett Hawkins, you're a dead man."

He grumbled it as he held the clamps up. The chain that connected them glimmered in the light. His mind instantly filled with the fantasy of putting them on Rayna. *Oh, yeah.* The matching gilt tints in her skin would glow as she endured the pain for him, as her nipples went from copper to crimson for him...

He let the clamps drop into the sink as he dipped his hand to his cock. If he didn't get release from this pressure now—

He'd gotten only halfway through his first stroke when a crash from the kitchen filled the cabin.

"Fuck."

A thousand images filled his mind, none of them good. There was no damn way Mua could know they were here unless the cockroach had gotten to Garrett or Franz or had his minions hack into the team's personal records. Neither scenario had a bright side of any kind. And if the din wasn't Mua breaking in, it had to be something like a pissed-off raccoon, mountain lion, or bear.

"Fuck." He repeated it as he skidded around the corner to the kitchen.

There were no marauding forest creatures. No armed and clumsy Mua henchmen, either. The wound in his upper back, now throbbing due to Rayna's debridement and butterfly-bandage treatment of this morning, thanked him for that.

But suddenly, ripping open those dressings seemed a really good plan. He wondered if he could go back and pick that box as the alternative to what he did encounter.

Rayna stood next to the sink where the running water was fast filling one side with wash bubbles. She'd changed back into his Henley, though he'd gotten her a set of pajamas in town. Next to her bare feet were both their dinner plates, in pieces now, surrounded by squished macaroni and spattered cheese. Her head was dipped but not so low that he didn't see the harsh wobble of her chin and the heaving breaths in her chest.

"They just slipped," she stammered. "I'm so sorry."

"They're just dishes." The angry blades in his retort weren't intentional. He didn't care about the goddamn dishes. It incensed him that she thought, even for a second, that he would. "Are *you* okay? Did you get hurt?"

She shook her head.

"Then what's wrong?" He went to her, skirting the shattered china. As soon as he touched her shoulder, dread sliced his gut again. "Christ. You're *not* okay. You're shaking like a—" He stopped himself. Awareness blared through his brain, hot and intense. "Shit. You don't have your medication, do you? You went to the club straight from Sally's. You thought you'd be going home."

"I don't need my medication." She squeaked the words before lifting her head a few inches. "Where are your clothes?"

He reached around her and slammed the faucet off. Since the suds were nearing the lip of the sink, a line of them stuck to the underside of his arm. "I just got out of the shower."

"And look." A manic giggle spurted off her lips. "Now you're all soapy again." Inside another second, the laughter turned to a sad moan. She sucked in a choppy breath as she stared at the bubbles dripping off his triceps. "Holy crap, Zeke. Your arms are really nice."

"Thanks. Are you sure—"

"I should get something to clean that stuff up." She turned away, sliding along the counter until she was clear from him.

"Uh-uh." By instinct or by necessity, his Dom baritone broke free. He took one step to recover the three she'd taken away from him. "You're going to scoot your ass to the other room and realign your chakras again, or whatever the hell you need to do, while I figure out a way to contact Sally and have her call in a prescription for you."

She shoved against his chest, making his eyebrows jump. "I don't need the damn medicine."

He followed her stomping journey into the living room. "Really? Because you're weaving like a goose on acid, honey."

"I *don't* need the medicine."

He unfurled a threatening snarl. "Rayna—"

"*I don't need the medicine.*"

She whirled back toward him, now raising her face fully. He stumbled back a step from the force of the sight. Huge tears welled in her gaze. Her eyebrows bunched in torment. Her lips battled each other as if disagreeing on how to hold back emotions that seemed a living beast inside her. She tore him apart with that stare. Reduced him to the same raw need with which she stared at him.

"I—don't need—the medicine." The whispers came out between her quaking steps back toward him. When she came close enough to touch him again, she bowed her head. "I need..."

She slid to her knees.

And dropped her forehead against his feet.

"I need this," she rasped. "Please, Zeke. I know you're not signing on for forever...but as long as I can have this from you, I need this."

He was pretty damn sure he stopped breathing. But as long as his eyes kept working, he'd be good to go. He couldn't get enough of this sight. He'd certainly commanded a few submissives to honor him in this way before, but none had ever offered their surrender so willingly, so openly, so perfectly.

The significance of her action pierced him like a dagger in a bull's-eye.

Rayna Chestain *was* a submissive. And she was discovering it right in front of him. Discovering it, welcoming it, and honoring it with every exquisite inch of her body and every generous shred of her soul.

And then giving it. *To him.* A former street rat who used this dynamic as therapy for his fucked-up past and a constructive purge for his current demons. A guy with an office that was lined in jungle wallpaper and sported mud carpeting. A trained killer who could wield an M4 as well as a flogger. A Dom who didn't deserve her—

But sure as hell wasn't going to turn his back on her now. Just as he'd freed her from Kier all those years ago, he'd release her from the assholes who violated her mind now. And dear fuck, he'd love every minute of it.

He found his breath. Pulled it in with steady intent. Only after that did he direct, "Rayna, lift your head." He tugged a finger under her chin. "All the way. Look at me."

Tears tracked down her cheeks. He traced one with the pad of a thumb and spoke directly from his heart. "You move me, little bird...in so many ways. Do you know that?" When her face crumpled as if she'd cry again, he pressed on. "Are you sure this is what you want? Rayna, I'm not going to drench this in any sugar. Now that I've had your submission once, I'll want more." To emphasize that, he tunneled his fingers into her hair and pulled hard. Her head fell back, letting him see all the depths in the magical lakes that lived in her eyes. "I'll push limits. Are you ready to let me do that?"

She swallowed. Then smiled. "If you don't, I already have a few bratty one-liners ready to zing free."

He didn't try to control his responding grin. "Well, all right, honey. Let's get started, then."

"Thank you, Sir. *Oh!*"

Her exclamation coincided with the brutal tug he gave on her head to pull her back to her feet. Once she was balanced again, he let her go—and dropped his towel.

"Oh." Her repetition carried half the volume but twice the astonishment of the first. "Oh, my," she murmured, her lips parting as she took in his erection.

"Eyes up here, bird." Z directed it while pushing up the bottom of her chin. He gave the command out of necessity as much as respect to the dynamic. Her spill had only diminished his hardness by half, and she seemed damn determined to make up the gap with her worshipful stare. At this rate, he'd barely have her tied down before needing to give her a thorough dose of his hard, thrusting religion.

"That's probably a good idea, Sir. I don't do well with being deprived of sweets I long to lick."

"Fuck," he muttered.

"Told you," she quipped.

"For the record, that wasn't bratty. That was teasing."

She gave an impish shrug. "What's the difference?"

"I punish teases worse than I punish brats."

Her lips pursed. "But why is it teasing if follow-through is intended?"

His cock ached deeper and visibly jerked. Rayna curled a victorious smirk.

"*Now* you're being a brat."

He didn't wait for her to form a comeback. It was time to claim control, and he did just that. With one yank, he hauled her up against him. In the same motion, he crashed his lips over hers. He wasn't gentle about a second of it, making her accept the full assault of his tongue, his teeth, his breath, his passion as he rammed his shaft against her warm, soft stomach. She moaned from the contact, slipping her hands up to his neck. Z didn't let them stay there for long. He seized both her wrists and rammed them behind her back, making her realize what kind of submission he expected from her...craved from her.

Many minutes later, he pulled up from her lips. She looked at him through half-lidded eyes, though her arousal blazed from every emerald speck of them. Her mouth was as red and luscious as a pomegranate from his treatment, driving caveman-style triumph into every inch of his dick.

"You intoxicate me, brat," he growled. "And I'm getting more drunk by the second."

Rayna bit her bottom lip. "Then maybe you'd better let me drive."

He let her have a wry tug of his brows for that—for a second. It covered the time it took for him to secure both hands into the neckline of his Henley. The baggy fit ensured that his fingers scraped her breasts as he did. The sneak preview didn't matter. As soon as he tore the shirt down the middle, her full, naked peaks were all his to gaze at anyway. And goddamn, what a view.

"Don't think so, subbie." He hurled the torn shirt across the room. "That took care of the shirt. As for those panties"— he flicked a finger toward the bathroom—"adorable but not needed. You can get rid of them in there while you grab the toys. After you've got them, deliver them to me without a word. From now on, the only thing out of your lips is 'Yes, Sir,' 'No, Sir,' your safe word, or direct responses to *my* questions. No reprieves tonight."

She looked him like he'd just spoken Swahili. "Toys?" she blurted. "What do you mean by toys? And how did—ahhh!"

He made her chop off the question with her own scream, reacting to the bare-handed smack he delivered to the center of her ass. "When I said 'from now on,' I meant it, honey."

"Yes, Sir." She rubbed her ass as she walked away, looking pretty damn cute about it. His soul soared from the giddy pleasure of inciting her ire—and her obedience.

As she disappeared into the bathroom, Z moved quickly to the handyman's bin outside the slider to the deck. The temps had dropped exponentially since sunset, but he welcomed the blast of chilled air on his naked skin, assisting to bring the heat in his blood under control. He wasn't going to rush this. He planned to watch her writhe and moan and climax for him for quite a while before he let his cock explode deep inside her.

The zip ties were exactly where he'd left them this morning. He'd taken them up to the bedroom last night, but she'd been so responsive and beautiful, his initial plan had gone to tatters. That wasn't going to happen now. He couldn't wait to see her bound for him.

After a full minute passed, he shot a puzzled look at the bathroom door. "Ray-bird?" he called. "Everything okay?"

The door opened slowly. She emerged at a similar speed.

The saucy demeanor was erased from her face. She kept looking to the pile in her hands—paddle, spanker, flogger, clamps—as if she carried an armed IED. A mix of worry and reverence defined her face, confirming to Zeke that he'd made the right call in sending her in after the implements. Five minutes ago, she'd been pretty lippy. Five minutes ago, he wasn't sure she comprehended everything he had planned for her. He was fairly certain that wasn't the case now.

"Thank you," he murmured when she handed over the pile.

"You're welcome," she whispered. "Sir."

He rubbed the side of her neck, coaxing her to look back up to him. "Are you a little more clear about how tonight's going to play out?"

She took a measured pause before responding. "Yes, Sir."

"I'm going to use these on you, Rayna. I'm going to make your skin turn pink and then red. I'm not going to stop until you scream and feel like you're going to lose your mind. And then you *will* lose your mind." He squeezed on her nape. "So are you still ready to submit to me?"

"Oh *yes*, Sir."

He couldn't help his open grin. His pleasure radiated back to her, provoking a breathtaking blush that started in her face and progressed down through her neck and chest...into the tips of her sweet, perfect tits.

The time for dawdling was *really* over.

He dropped his hold to her hand. Guided her over to the big pine dining table. They'd shared macaroni and cheese here a few hours ago. Now the feast was going to be her body, and he officially declared himself the world's luckiest glutton.

He kicked out the chair that bracketed the end of the table

and set the toys on it. With both hands freed, he grabbed her by the waist and lifted her onto the table. He half expected her to start firing the one-liners again, a nervous move common to many fresh subbies, but she watched him now in respectful silence, keeping her hands on the table at her sides...letting him gorge on the sight of her nude perfection.

He didn't use the term lightly. Good God, her body had everything he loved. That gorgeous slope of a neck he could suck and bite for days...firm, gently rounded shoulders...breasts that were the ideal stop between tiny and huge...a curving paradise of a waist atop hips and thighs that were muscular by necessity and more than able to handle him fucking her at his fullest passion.

He frantically grounded the fireworks of that thought's resulting fantasy. It was too late to do anything about the effects it had on his cock, which jutted more at his wide-eyed subbie. Damn, he loved how she looked at him, as if every time she beheld his body, it was the first time.

He smiled in cocky pride.

Rayna smiled shyly back.

"You ready?" he asked softly. After she nodded, he picked up the two leather cuffs and ordered her with quiet directive, "Wrists." Less than a minute later, with the bands of black now attached, she formed a sight that reminded him of why he loved domination. Pale skin and dark leather. Spirited eyes and silent patience. An imp's smile on a goddess's body. All his to command, conquer, and pleasure.

"Perfect," he told her, savoring the glittering joy he set free in her eyes. "Now lie back all the way for me, honey. Keep your ass close to the edge of the table, though. When you're comfortable, raise your arms over your head."

She complied, trembling a little, which amped his arousal by another sharp notch. He welcomed the torment of it, knowing the suffering would have its surcease when he buried himself inside her and gave over to her body's hot, tight magic.

Soon. Very soon.

As she complied with his order, he moved around to the other end of the table. Once there, he secured a set of cable ties around the top of each table leg and then looped more ties together to form chains that connected to the *O* rings on her cuffs. As he worked, the only sounds she emitted were soft but shaky breaths. *Fuck yes.* He savored many things about this process, but this moment was one of his favorites. The twilight between vanilla normality and dark fantasy...where hidden desires became fiery reality...where man and woman became Dominant and submissive.

He slipped assessing fingers under her cuffs. Her circulation looked good. He dropped his examination to her face. The color there was beautiful, too. Her eyes were bright and adoring. Her cheeks were stained with a perfect flush. He smiled down at her. "Nothing's too tight?"

"No, Sir," she murmured. "It feels good."

"Excellent." He leaned down and pressed a kiss to her forehead. He could see her disappointment about not getting the kiss on the lips again, but they needed a few clicks of emotional distance right now. If he fused his mouth with hers again, especially in her bound state, God only knew what would tumble out of his soul and go instantly AWOL on him.

He stepped to the opposite end of the table. As he'd asked, Rayna had kept her bottom close to the edge. Her legs hung over the side now. He spread them apart and shifted himself between them. Though he told himself not to do it, his gaze strayed to the perfect pink bloom at her center. He pressed a thumb to its shimmering beauty.

"Oh!" she cried out. "Ohhh, Sir..."

"A little aroused, honey?"

"Yes!" She gasped and writhed.

"You want more?"

"Oh God, yes!"

"Then you'll have to earn it." He withdrew his finger in order to push her legs farther apart. "Sounds fair, right?"

"Y-Yes." She licked her lips while tilting her head, clearly trying to figure out what he was doing. Zeke only answered with a serene smirk as he joined more zip ties together to circle her legs just below her knees. Before he did anything else, he stopped and met her gaze with his own.

"How bad do you want to earn it, bird?"

She huffed. "Are you serious? Can't you see the evidence right in front—ahhh!"

Her shriek was adorable. He treasured the sound, making a vow to swat her mound a few more times just so he could hear it. Right now, he had a point to make. "I can see every drop of hot, shiny arousal in your beautiful pussy, honey. But seeing it and hearing it are two different things, aren't they? I'm going to ask again and give you the benefit of responding properly, because I'm feeling nice tonight. Once more...how bad do you want to earn more strokes on your clit?"

She rolled her head straight again, her breasts tight and heaving with her fast gasps. "Really bad, Sir. Please tell me what I need to do."

He caressed her outer thighs to show her his pleasure in her confession. After a few moments of that, he charged, "Show me how far your legs will spread, yoga girl."

She complied at once—fulfilling his wildest expectations. As he'd hoped, she was flexible enough that her calves met the edges of the table just before each corner.

"That's a very good start." He injected a smile to his tone while fastening more zip-tie chains that connected her calves to the table's front legs. Her body became an open wonderland to map with his own special markings. Holy shit, just thinking about the tracks he was going to give her flesh...

His cock quaked. He gave his balls a harsh squeeze to keep himself contained—though picking up the nipple clamps pretty much canceled the benefits of the effort. He couldn't wait to see her breasts captured by them.

He walked around to stand close to her face again. Yeah, she'd begged him hard for this, but wanting it and getting it were two different things. The check-in was key, especially because of what he had planned for her next. And after that, too. And maybe after *that*...

He hovered directly above her so she could see the serious intent of his query. "How does it feel now, bird? You still okay?"

To his delight, her eyes were still twinkling. She actually curled a little grin at him. "I still feel very good, Sir."

Z smiled back before letting his hands fall to both of her breasts. Though her areolas were puckered already, they compressed tighter for his fingers as he rolled her rosy tips into erect red pebbles. "Yes," he said with a wicked smirk, "you do feel good. But 'good' can be defined a number of ways."

Her eyes went wide as he pulled the clamps into her view. She swallowed and wet her lips again. So much for trying to squeeze his balls now. She was beyond beautiful, and he was beyond hard.

"You ready to earn more strokes, Ray-bird?"

"I—I think so, Sir."

"It's okay to be a little scared."

"How about a lot scared?"

He first answered her with a groan. "The sadistic demon on my shoulder says that's just fine, honey."

"What does the angel on the other side say?"

He chuckled. "The angels gave up on me a long time ago. The only thing on my other shoulder are the devil's cheerleaders."

"Gee. Great to hear—oohhh *shit*!"

Her voice flipped from sarcasm to suffering in the second it took for him to close the first clamp around her nipple. The sight of her lying there, muscles twisting as she struggled to process the vise's bite into her sensitive flesh, caused a torment of a different kind inside his own body. He bunched his ass cheeks hard in a desperate battle to keep his dick in check.

"Breathe, subbie." He fed it to her on a taut wire of tone. "Close your eyes and tell your body to accept it."

She was stunning as her eyes slipped closed for him. Three inhalations later, her breathing evened. As she released the fourth, he fastened the clamp to her other breast.

"Ohhh!" She writhed again.

"Ssshhhh, honey." He flattened a hand on her stomach. "Breathe."

"With all due respect, Sir, that isn't working!"

He rubbed his hand a little lower, making soothing circles on her pelvis. "It wasn't a request, Rayna," he said. "You'll obey what your Sir has commanded without any more protest, right now."

She still flashed him gritted teeth but settled back against the table, letting her breaths come more evenly.

"Now take all that adrenaline rushing your veins and let it float into your mind," he instructed. "Let it take over all those synapses and neurons. You're going to be a little dizzy from it, but I've got you tethered right here. You're not going anywhere I don't want you to. You're safe, okay?"

"Okay." Her whisper was tense. But the cords of her neck loosened and the muscles beneath his hand relaxed. She sighed, her senses clearly starting to swim in the vertigo he'd told her to expect.

"That's good, subbie. Really good. It's important for you to learn processing. Just in case your Sir decides to hit you with something else unexpected."

He let his voice warm with humor on the last part of that—just before he gathered his four main fingers and thrust them high into her pussy.

"Dear God!" she screamed.

No shit.

He ripped a page out of his own book to breathe down the amazement from getting to finger her again. Like that did any good. It was impossible to be cavalier about the magic of touching her, of watching how she reacted to his skin against her, inside her. She held nothing back, as generous in her submission to him as she was in her friendship with him. He was rocketed to another galaxy. Humbled. Awed.

So fucking turned on.

When he pressed his thumb directly against her clit, her passion blasted him beyond the galaxy. He floated in a separate universe, lost to the force of her little mewls, her long sighs, her cream-perfect body.

"Tell me."

For a moment, he couldn't believe the words had tumbled

from him. He'd never used them on any subbie beneath his rule, because he didn't need to. In his job, retaining details meant the difference between surviving the mission or dying from a stupid mistake. It was effortless to carry the talent with him into the dungeon. One look always told him everything he needed to know about his sub's state of mind and body.

But with Rayna, looking wasn't enough. He needed to hear the words in her mesmerizing alto, longed for the connection back to her through those verbal threads.

"Tell me," he repeated. "Give it all to me, honey. Tell me how I make you feel."

She let out another sexy-as-fuck whine before answering. "Incredible. Unbelievable. It's pain but pleasure. Pissed off mixed with set free. I never knew it could be like this. I never knew it *was* like this."

For a second, he stilled his fingers. He guessed that was typical when the rest of one's body couldn't move, either. Which was probably the case when the universe found its way in past the emotional space suit and wrapped its brilliance around a guy's soul. And made him feel as powerful as a star gone nova.

He couldn't wait to take her higher.

"Perfect," he assured her. "Really perfect. Thank you, subbie."

With slow reluctance, he withdrew his fingers. Though she didn't say a word, her chest vibrated on a quivering breath, as if she already knew what was in store for her.

"Breathe again." He directed it with the conviction that filled him from being totally connected to her. The way she'd processed the pain from the clamps gave him another notch of justification for picking up the flogger and making sure the paddle was nearby, too. "Here we go, honey."

He watched her chest rise and fall, the chain between the clamps dancing in the light as she obeyed. Her body gleamed with a sheen of nervous perspiration. He trailed the flogger falls over every stunning, golden curve from her collarbone to her ankles, exulting in her tremors, soaking up every note of her anticipating, anxious whimpers.

In the thousands of miles and dozens of countries life had taken him to, he'd seen some breathtaking sights. He couldn't remember any of them as he gazed at the bound, beautiful submissive before him now.

"Breathe." He commanded it again as he circled the flogger over her thighs, warming up her skin with gentle *thwacks* of the leather.

"Y-Yes, Sir." Her eyes fell shut. Her muscles coiled and retracted, processing the new sensations he gave her.

And her pussy glimmered with new drops of arousal.

Z's senses soared. "Your skin blushes so perfectly for me, subbie." He didn't break the figure-eight motion of the flogger, allowing him to hit her thighs with equal impact. "Damn. So pretty."

Rayna didn't reply with anything but a tight sigh. That was okay. Her body spoke everything for her. Her quads and derriere clenched from each impact, making it impossible for her pussy not to be stimulated. With each constriction, the muscles in her sex got to be better friends, turning her into a fusion of stings, stimulation, agony, and ecstasy.

Z kept up the pace. And steadily increased the power behind each stroke.

After several minutes, Rayna's husky gasps turned into agonized cries. "Zeke!" she finally screamed. "Sir! I don't know how much more I can—"

"A lot," Zeke interjected. Though he tossed aside the flogger, he delivered a pair of sharp slaps to her inner thighs. While he pressed her flesh to distribute the heat, he intently studied her body and face. Rivulets of sweat trickled along her torso. Her carotid thundered. But most telling was the soaked flower at her core. "You can take a lot more, Ray-bird, and you will. For me. I'm not going to stop until your thighs are as crimson as your sweet, hot cunt. And you're going to love it. You're going to fly. And when you do, I'll keep you tethered and safe with my cock, buried deep and hot inside you."

She audibly gulped. "Okay. Yes, Sir."

He gave in to the craving to slap her pussy again. His action inflamed the juicy tissues, making them red as a pomegranate. "Not good enough," he growled.

"Wh-What do you mean?"

"Say it to me, Rayna. Give me the words. Tell me you can take more. Tell me you want more."

To encourage her, he slicked a thumb into the center of her sweet fruit, aiming for the nub that would give her the pleasure to counterbalance her pain.

"Ohhh shit!" She bucked against him like the kickback from an RPG. "Sir! That's— Oh God, that's so— Please don't stop!"

"The words," he prompted. "What do you want, honey? Tell me."

"Yes. Ohhh, yes. I want more. I can take more. Hurt me. Redden me. Give it all to me. Take me higher. Please!"

Higher. Dear fuck, yes.

His senses spun. Never in his life had a submissive's words shot him up with such power. Never in his life did he feel so euphoric, so wild, so free.

He needed to give it all back to her.

It was the only goal in his mind and body as he snatched up the paddle.

The dark rose flesh of both her thighs called to him.

"Get comfy, honey." It curled out of him as dark, savoring smoke. "And for God's sake, you'll need to breathe."

He was gentle about the first few swats.

Then she moaned.

He kept himself in check during the next three or four strokes.

Then she screamed.

What a perfect harmony it made to the brutal smacks he released on her beautiful red skin.

After no more than a minute, her shrieks turned into high gasps. Her eyes fluttered shut. Her head lolled to one side.

With a growl of dark triumph, he tossed aside the paddle.

"Yeah, subbie," he crooned. "Take a nice long flight in that cloud. You earned it."

He stepped back between her legs, lowering a hand to each thigh. With every inch of flesh he rubbed, a blast of possessive fire overcame him. The flames licked through his body, sizzling every nerve, burning up every muscle...and pooling in his dick. Even after he clenched his jaw and swallowed hard, the fire got worse. As a heavy drop of precome discharged from his bulb, he knew even going at his balls with vise grips wasn't going to help this time.

He slid his hands back. The globes of her ass fit perfectly in his grip. The lips of her sex teased mercilessly at his dick.

"Christ," he grated. "Ray-bird, I don't know how much longer—"

"Fuck me."

Her whispered plea whipped his stare to her face. She gazed at him with heavy-lidded eyes, her breaths coming fast through parted, glistening lips. "Please fuck me, Sir. Now."

Yeah. *Fuck yeah.* He was more than ready to fill her requisition.

She moaned. He shuddered. Her cunt was a furnace, cranking up the heat in his cock by fifty degrees from the first thrust. Still he dragged her body tighter and harder against him, ramming her onto his erection over and over. When the pressure in his sac tightened to an unbearable degree, he released her ass in order to lean over and drive horizontally into her.

His gaze fixed into hers again. She gave him a tentative, sweet smile. He returned one of gleeful, sadistic intent. With a deft twist, he pulled on the chain connecting her nipple clamps.

"Shit!" she screamed. "Zeke, what the—"

He silenced the rest of it with a harsh smash of his mouth. He kept his lips sealed to hers while releasing one clamp and then the other. As blood rushed back into her breasts, another yell exploded out of her and right into him.

It was the most arousing thing he'd ever felt.

"Fuck, yes." He snarled it against her skin before soothing the pain in one nipple with the flat of his tongue. As he tasted the other in the same way, the tip surged against his tongue. The taste of her consumed his mouth. The heat of her surrounded his sex. The pounding of her beautiful, submissive heart spoke to the deepest core of his spirit.

"Sir," she cried. "I can't hold it back. I...can't..."

"Don't you dare," he ordered. "Let it come, honey. Come for me, sweet subbie."

"N-No. You, too. C-Come with me. Please?"

Her tight, broken words and her shaking, drenched body spoke right to all the triggers in his. The burn in his buttocks and the clench of his balls gave him the DEFCON warning about the explosion about to decimate his cock.

"I can't, honey." He brushed the hair off her forehead. She was so goddamn beautiful. He longed to stay buried like this for hours more. "I'm in here bareback."

"It's okay."

"It's *not* okay. There's no way I'm pulling a pump and dump here, honey. If you think I'm the kind of guy who—"

"Zeke, I haven't had a period in five months."

"Huh?"

She actually rolled her eyes. "Can we not go into it right now? Captivity. Stress. My body. Not a great match, okay? They're trying to fix it, but I haven't taken those damn pills in a week now, so—" As she quivered again beneath him, her head jackknifed back. "Goddamnit, Zeke, I need to come! And I need your cock inside me when I do. Please...please!"

If the shock of her health confession didn't grab him, her deliberately dirty language sure as hell did. He lowered his mouth to her tits again, this time to bite into them as he let the blood surge his shaft, pushing at her wet, tight walls.

"You feel so fucking good." He suckled at her with hot greed. "Every inch of you is so perfect. So golden and perfect."

She sighed, trying to lift her head and kiss him back. "You, too." She squirmed with delectable frustration. "Zeke—Sir— let me touch you, too. I need to get my hands on you."

He gave her a wicked smile. "Request denied, subbie. You took all the pain in bondage. Now you'll take the pleasure, too— just like you're taking every inch of my dick in your sweet, hot cunt." He gave her a twisting kiss before settling himself fully against her spread, slick body. "Now tell me you understand."

Her eyes flashed with rebellious fire, but she replied, "I understand, Sir."

"Tell me you want my cock to fuck you deep."

An adorable smile tugged at her lips. "I do," she whispered. "I want your cock to fuck me deep."

"Tell me the pain was worth it."

"The pain was perfect. Yes. Very much worth it."

He started rolling his hips with each thrust. Primal triumph struck when he saw the effect it had on her. Somewhere far beyond the room, he heard the growl of thunder and the patter of rain. It was part of another world. His universe became the sighs from the back of her throat. His solar system was now composed of the pulses from deep in her body. His world was now the magic of pleasuring her.

"Now tell me you're coming for me, bird."

She shook her head. "Not unless you're with me."

"I'm right here. I'm with you. My come is yours, Rayna. And your climax is mine."

"Yes," she sighed. "Yes!"

"Now," he bellowed. "*Now!*"

Her tunnel shuddered and exploded. Zeke filled it with the blinding flood of his orgasm. His body was torn from its moorings. His mind was robbed of its sanity. For a brilliant second, the heaven to which he'd sent her was the same nirvana in which his senses danced. He was consumed. Amazed.

Terrified.

The trepidation curled itself into thick silence as he rocked inside her for long minutes. Rayna's wordlessness scared him even more, until he pulled up to look at her again.

He couldn't remember when he'd seen her features at such peace.

He realized, with blazing clarity, the answer to that was *never*.

He reached up, unbuckling her wrists from both the cuffs without taking his eyes off her as he did. Finally he murmured, "You okay?"

As she lifted her hands to his shoulders, she smiled like a kid who'd just gotten away with inhaling a chocolate bar. "Better than okay."

His first instinct was to kiss her senseless.

He coughed and looked away instead.

Three words. She'd unraveled him again with just three words.

They weren't even *those* three words, but something deep in his gut told him that the vocabulary was beyond the point. The warm serenity in her voice, the summer grass beauty in her eyes, the soft strokes she gave his shoulders along with it... They all conveyed her true meaning. That the other three words were bubbling, waiting for their turn.

And when they did brim to her lips...what then?

He didn't do this. He *couldn't* do this. Even thinking of it made the sweat on his back turn cold and the high from his orgasm fade into panic.

He mumbled an excuse about getting her legs free as an excuse to pull out and back from her. But he could've auditioned for a *Star Wars* walk-on as a maintenance droid for all the grace or thought he gave the motions. After he helped Rayna gain her feet, he sent her upstairs and told her to get warm in bed. He'd be up in a few minutes, he said. Maybe they'd pick out a movie from the online queue and—

"Liar."

He spat it beneath his breath as she reached the top of the stairs and he got to the kitchen. Anger swooped into his chest in backlash to the reprimand.

Yeah, yeah. Fine. You lied. So what? She was untied and standing; you weren't officially her Dom anymore, anyhow. Besides, it was only a little white one.

And a hell of a lot better than the nasty-ass big one.

Not that he was in danger of letting those three words slip out, even by accident. Not as a dumb mistake. Not as a casual second thought. Not as a drunken blunder. Not ever.

Because you know damn well what happens when you allow those words into your life, asshole. Life turns them into a fun little game of craps, doesn't it?

And when life's at the table, the house always wins.

He found dozens of ways to turn "a few minutes" into a solid hour. By the time he got upstairs, Rayna was tangled in the blankets, fast asleep—as he'd hoped.

As soon as he walked over and gazed down at her, his decision for the delay was revalidated. She was as delectable as a naked little fairy, her brilliant hair fanned across the pillow and one hand curled against her neck. One breast peeked from beneath the covers, beckoning to him like a ripe berry.

He yearned to climb in next to her. To wrap himself around her and feel that smooth porcelain skin against his again. To smell the spices in her hair mixed with the musk he'd left behind on her. To crush her close to him and not give a damn that he was stepping closer to the door of that alluring craps game. To hope that this time, maybe life was too busy screwing over some other poor sap and he'd actually win the gamble.

"No."

He backed away. The effort was painful at first, but looking to the tattoo on his pelvis made those steps easier to take. Barbed wire and tear drops. The pain and the loneliness of eight long years on the streets. Ninety-six months he'd survived because he'd learned to stay away from the craps table. There was no way in hell he was going back now. And if he cared at all for this woman, there was no way in *fuck* he'd drag her anywhere near it, either.

Oh, yeah. He was a losing bet in the hearts and flowers department. Rayna wasn't a dumb shit; she knew it as well.

But as he settled onto the couch with the blanket from the upstairs window seat, he accidentally sat on the remote control for the TV. The motion made the screen flare to life again—and showed him what movie she'd picked out for them to watch together.

The Empire Strikes Back.

CHAPTER SEVENTEEN

Rayna suppressed a little giggle.

Less than a week ago, she'd inwardly compared the man to a puma. At the time, he'd certainly represented for the wildcats in about ten different forms of sexy. She wasn't sure whether to classify this as the eleventh...or a new category altogether.

Z had obviously fallen asleep on the bedroom couch. She had no idea why he hadn't just come to bed, but maybe all that intensity did something different to a Dom's brain than it did a sub's. He'd seemed weirdly amped when they finished, whereas the last time she'd been so relaxed, she'd been nineteen and high on painkillers after having her wisdom teeth pulled. Needless to say, she'd been down for the count from the moment she'd gotten up here.

Now, nearly ten hours later, the mountains outside were bathed in sun and the man inside was lost to soft snores. She smiled as she drank in the glory of him. Z was sprawled beneath a lap blanket across the same spot where he'd pounded into her on Sunday night. That was *Sprawled*, capital *S*. One of his legs was hooked over the back of the couch. His other leg dangled over the end, his toes brushing the floor in time to the inhalations filling his massive chest. His arms, so ripped they looked flexed even in sleep, were folded across the bronze expanse as if he were preparing to issue orders to a lucky subbie in his dreams.

She wondered if she was that subbie.

She turned away and rolled her eyes.

How pathetic can you be? A couple of times at his feet, amazing as they were, didn't turn you into wonder subbie, okay? You're still you. Rayna Chestain. Accomplished medic. Survivor of kidnap, captivity, and seven overbearing brothers. Marching to another man's sexual drum, no matter how mind-blowingly great the experience, isn't part of your total life picture.

Now she just had to decipher why that dropped a ball of lead into her stomach, forming into claws that tightened around her throat.

She took a deep breath and prepared to turn for the bathroom. *And you're going to do it without looking at him again. Because looking will mean fantasizing. And fantasizing will only lead to—*

"Ray-bird."

It was a groggy mumble, barely audible, but it whipped her stare back in a fervent second. As soon as she gave her conscience the middle finger, she rotated her body, as well.

Z hadn't moved. His dark lashes were still solidly closed. The rest of his face, usually quartz-hard with focus, was even more beautiful in the grip of deep and peaceful sleep.

"Shit," she whispered, shaking her head. She'd imagined it, hadn't she? Pathetic. Why would a Dom like him, so powerful and assured and capable of drawing out a sub's most illicit desires, be thinking of a vanilla dork like her in his sleep?

"*Rayna.*"

Her breath snagged. The lead in her stomach turned into fire.

She had *not* imagined that full-volume moan—nor the way his upper leg slid down and helped its twin to writhe with need.

"Fuck...Rayna...yes."

Or the way he bucked his hips so violently, the blanket fell free from his body.

"Shit," she repeated. The majestic strength of his legs was amplified by the tension winding through them. The springy hairs along their lengths helped to define thighs, calves, even knees that were as sculpted as a gladiator's. And at their crux was the burnished length that now held her gaze as willing captive. His cock only twitched a little right now, but even in its half-flexed state, it was stunning to look at. It was so perfectly proportioned, pulsing with strength though it still lolled against his thigh. Her heart revved as she imagined rubbing it. Licking it. Tasting it...

She stifled a needy sigh. The memory of an after-work girls' night came back to haunt her. Sage and one of the base's lab techs, Jenna, had gotten all swoony about the beauty of cocks, even in their not-so-aroused states. She'd labeled her coworkers a pair of aggro-psycho-nymphos, which had earned her the tab for the next round and a pair of she'll-find-out-one-day nods.

That day had absolutely arrived.

Fascination pulled her closer to him. Zeke let out another slumber-heavy groan. His penis shifted past the twitching phase. She licked her lips as she watched the blood flow into his long muscle, lifting it off his thigh, practically beckoning her with its forceful jerks.

"Oh...hell," he grated. "Rayna, please."

The raw need in his voice dragged her legs down. Though he was still sleeping, it felt like the most natural thing in the world to kneel for him. "Sir." She placed her hands on his lower thighs, careful to be gentle about it. Though he obviously wasn't dreaming about a mission or battle, she was well aware of the dangers of rousing a Special Forces man from deep sleep. "I'm here. What do you need?"

His only verbal answer was another long moan. But visually he gave her much more to go on. His breaths changed from full and relaxed to choppy and harsh. His thighs clenched. His erection sprang higher, its swollen, silken head adorned by milky-white drops that broadcast exactly what movie played in his mind. She had a feeling it had nothing to do with laser blasters or carbonite freezes. Thank God.

"Rayna. Damn! Oh honey..."

She pressed her fingers into his legs, responding to the ache in his voice with the care of her touch. "Sshhh. I'm here and I'm going to make it better."

As she gave him the vow, she moved up and over him, dropping reverent kisses up the staff that now pulsed with dark bronze and red hues. His skin tightened beneath her lips. His thighs hardened. His body quivered, emanating potency and power that surrounded her, rolled through her, made her giddy from the high of getting to harness it with the ministrations of her mouth.

As she got to the shiny mushroom at his tip, she circled her tongue, savoring the tangy essence of his precome. Z let out a stunned snort.

"Mmmphh! Huh? What the—" He choked and lifted his head. His gaze shot down to meet hers in conscious astonishment. "Holy fuck," he uttered. "If I'm still dreaming, someone pass the Ambien."

She let her gaze warm as she pulled his wide, throbbing length into her mouth. He was delicious, a heady combination of salt, spice, and musk that bathed her tongue and filled her senses. She wanted to fill herself with him. Drown in his taste. Succumb to his heat. Give herself completely for his pleasure.

Beneath her tongue, his thick veins throbbed and his piercing danced. Zeke let out a harsh oath as she toyed with the balls at the ends of the curved steel, directly stimulating the chambers beneath that continued to swell from her exploration. She ran a hand over the contracted ridges of his abdomen. Felt him heave from harsh, hard breaths. Rejoiced in the cataclysm she stirred with every touch, lick, and stroke.

"You're playing with fire, Ray-bird. Do you know that?"

She hummed around his cock before letting the sound morph into a languorous, "Mmmhmmm."

She heard him swallow hard as she lowered over his thick stick of flesh. With a sudden yank he pulled her off, though he let her toy with his tip as he growled, "Let me be clear. I don't let myself 'get blow jobs,' honey. Keep this up, and I'm going to fuck that hot, wet heaven of your mouth. It'll be a full team assault. No mercy, no softness." As if to emphasize his point, he grabbed the sides of her jaw, one side in each hand, digging his fingers into her cheekbones. "You have ten seconds to decide."

He practically snarled the words in his heavy lust. An equally charged silence gripped the next ten seconds, where the only thing that changed was the slow, smiling kiss she lowered to his swollen, wet cock. She knew she shouldn't be enjoying what that did to his gaze. The way it narrowed with dangerous intent... The fire he'd warned her about now a live flare framed by his charcoal lashes.

His lips parted. For a moment, she thought he was about to smile at her in return.

Wrong assumption.

"Time's up."

Really wrong assumption.

Gone was his shuddering I-woke-up-to-a-blowjob tone. Master Zeke was back in the house—more accurately, in every inch of the body that rose into a full sitting position, legs braced in a massive V, dragging her to rest right at its crux. That was surely her cue to continue, so Rayna lowered her head to continue her ministrations to his cock, but she was stopped by his powerful fingers beneath her chin, forcing her to look at him again.

Her throat closed on a mesmerized choke. He was unrelenting darkness, hardness, intensity, brutality. He was breathtaking.

As she drank in his masculine beauty, her nipples and her clit hardened in tormenting tandem. In some crazy recess of her mind, she made a note to seriously suggest the gladiator gig as his first civilian job after the teams.

"Your safe word is 'red,'" he finally said. "'*Red,*' not '*Kier.*' I don't want you sparing a single fucking thought on that dickwad right now."

She felt her eyes go wide. Just as fast, she let them fall. Though her body was coursing with arousal and excitement like *Crazy Taxi* at level two hundred, her mind instantly downshifted and left the driver's seat altogether. Zeke was driving, and she was beyond joyful to let him. Her trust was his. Her surrender was his. Every inch of her body was his to command, to use, to dominate.

She nodded and rasped, "Yes, Sir. I understand. My safe word is 'red.'"

"Outstanding."

He gave her the word as fact, not endorsement. At the same time, he skated his hand from her chin to her nape. With his other hand, he anchored the top of her head by sinking his fingers into her hair from the forehead back. In both places, he dug into her scalp with circles of brutal possession, branding irons that scorched all the way inside her brain.

Rayna gasped and let her eyes slide shut. This didn't feel physically good. But she wanted it this way. No...she needed it this way. With every cinch of his bondage and grip of his captivity, Zeke replaced her nightmares with pleasure, her shame with survival. He showed her that the crucible could be good. Really, really good...

"Open your mouth." Again, his voice was low and nearly emotionless. He lowered her head until she felt his penis pushing at her lips again. "Relax your jaw. Breathe through your nose."

The next second, he was inside her. All the way inside. Though Rayna obeyed his directions to the letter, she could feel him pounding at her gag reflex with the fullness of his length. She concentrated on letting him get deeper into her throat. His vow had been spot-on accurate. He turned her head into a receptacle for his lust, shoving her down over and over onto his huge, hard pole. The pace was relentless. His cock was enormous. Her jaw hurt. Her eyes teared.

Her spirit soared.

"You like this, honey?" he said with rough tension. "Yeah, I think you do. Your mouth is so perfect for fucking, Ray-bird. So soft and wet and slick. Bet you love how hard and huge you've gotten me." He shoved her down and held her there, letting her feel his head pulsating at the back of her throat. "Bet it's made you hard, too. I want you to use your fingers and check. Stroke that erect clit for me. You're going to touch it until you climax for me—and as you do, you're going to swallow every drop of my come in that sweet, perfect mouth of yours."

She sighed in grateful acquiescence, though the man could've asked her to walk naked through the mall right now and she'd comply without question. The moment her hand cupped her mound, her fingers skimming over the silver bar that had such a different meaning even a week ago, a startled moan shot up her throat. She knew she was turned on, but from the second her fingers hit that moist, quivering ball of nerves, her sex clenched and her pussy turned to fire. She was ready to crash and burn right now.

"Don't." Zeke's charge pounded into her senses, another unnerving reminder of how he could read her more clearly than a CNN news crawl. "Hold it in, honey. Your orgasm belongs to me as completely as your mouth."

She whined as submissively as she could, trying to tell him she understood. The sound made him grunt in approval, though it earned her no mercy from the pace of his fucking. Harder, faster, deeper he pounded. His fingers were claws at her scalp. His cock was everywhere in her mouth. His hoarse, commanding breaths consumed the air.

"Now. Feel it all, honey. Take it all from me. *Now!*"

The climax hit her deep. Her sex convulsed and flared, dying and reborn in the same blissful, beautiful second. At the same time, Z pumped his seed into her with a roar of glory and a shuddering thrust. Everything went dark and then blinding white. Her equilibrium swam, yet she'd never felt more clear. She was a damn phoenix from ashes. She was destroyed yet overjoyed. She was—

The sobs hit her as fast as the comprehension did.

Zeke pulled out the second her shoulders started shaking. As soon as her mouth was empty, she erupted with high cries of astonishment and amazement. She drenched his chest as he hauled her up into his lap in a swift sweep, wrapping her in the lap blanket as she began to shiver. He didn't say a word. His hold was complete yet gentle, as possessive as it was ten minutes ago, absorbing every shaking sob and pitiful blubber.

When she finally collapsed her head against his shoulder, Zeke spoke. His voice was as soft as the caresses he gave her shoulder with the back of his hand. "You want to talk about it?"

She felt like punching him—before telling him to stop reading every need she had before she knew it existed. Instead, she curled her knees up and burrowed close as fresh tears plagued her eyes.

"I'm...a submissive."

The confession was as terrifying as she thought it would be. This wasn't like admitting she didn't like shellfish or only flossed every other day or liked masturbating in the shower. This was a huge damn door being opened in her soul, never to be closed again. She squeezed her eyes shut, hoping to find the *close* button again. Yet praying she never would.

Zeke turned his hand over and closed it around the top of her arm. "Yeah," he murmured, "you sure as fuck are."

She held her breath at that and wished she didn't know the reason why. More ominously, she wished that moment wasn't the one in which she'd predict exactly what *he'd* say.

"I can't be your Dom, Ray-bird."

His embrace suddenly felt like bricks. The same ones that crashed on top of her heart.

She rose, clutching the blanket with her. Confusion declared mutiny on her logic. Pain hit the override lever on her brain—and the thousands of things it told her about why Zeke was trying to speak his truth in as diplomatic a manner as he could.

Gazing at him now, gloriously naked and freshly satisfied *by her*, didn't put her in the mood for diplomacy.

"Is that so?" She flashed a grim smile while tilting her head. "All right, then. Can you explain what you've been doing for the last three days, if not being my Dom?"

His face, full of firm resolve, didn't change as he rose. "The last three days have been incredible, but they've been a dream. This isn't reality. You know it as well as I do, Ray-bird. We can't stay up on this mountain forever, and we sure as hell can't throw it on a trailer and drag it back to Tacoma."

The bricks in her heart started pounding together, pulverizing everything as they went. She spun from him. "Why not?" She hated the pitiful pitch in her voice. She hated him even more for causing it. *You rescued me from the dead. How hard can it be to move a damn mountain?*

His long sigh weighted the air. "Because you'll hate me even more than you do right now. Not tomorrow, probably not next week, but if we even attempt this thing long-term, I'll fuck it up. I'll fuck *you* up. It won't be pretty, and—"

"Pretty?" She whirled back around. "Seriously? You think I want *pretty*, Zeke?" She advanced and stabbed a finger into his chest. "You think I even remember what pretty is after what King did to me and what Mua is still trying to do to me?"

He wrapped her hand inside both his own. "I think you deserve a man, a Master, who's going to give you everything your heart desires and everything your soul needs." Before he spoke again, he dropped a soft kiss onto her knuckles. "I can't be that man, honey."

He pushed back from her with a violent growl. "I fucking hate saying this to you. I hate being the one standing here and telling you that I've tried already, okay? I tried the whole goddamn D/s dream on, and I burned it to shreds. Badly. I'm not going to do it again. I fucking refuse to send you up in flames." Her chest roiled as their stares locked. His eyes, usually adoring her or laughing with her or desiring her, were now filled with nothing but ashen sorrow. "Not you, Rayna. Not. You."

"Damn it," she rasped. "Do you think we're that flammable, Z? Do you think *I* am?"

That put his jaw on full lockdown. He swallowed hard. "Sit down."

"What?"

He pointed at the bed. "There. Now. Sit."

She really, *really* wanted to defy him. The twisted torment on his face canceled every viable reason to do so. Gathering the blanket tighter to her chest, she lowered to the edge of the bed.

Z braced his hands to his hips and sucked in a deep breath.

"Her name was Cherie," he finally said. "She was a hell of a lot like you, Ray-bird. Beautiful. Kind. She was a vet's assistant... She always had a dog or two around that she'd saved from euthanasia the night before. We met at a kink party down in Portland. After a year, I figured...maybe things could be good. I gave her a lifestyle name. Treasure. I had a collar made for her, inlaid with rubies. She moved up here for me." He took a determined step back in front of her. "You getting the picture now? We were unshakable, Rayna." A sad smile moved across his lips. "We were flameproof."

She threaded her fingers into his and gently pulled. Once he sat beside her, she took in every inch of his beautiful, formidable face before forcing out her question. "What happened?"

He pulled her grip out of his, digit by digit. With unwavering purpose, he flattened them all against his chest. "We didn't leave all the ugliness behind us in the city, bird. A shit ton of it came up with us. It's right here, beating in what's left of this heart. It's bloody and it's crappy and it doesn't get better, because that's what happens when your soul is sliced open at the age of eight, watching them bring home your dad in pieces from Somalia."

Her breath clutched. Somalia, roughly twenty years ago... *Shit, no.*

"Mogadishu?" she whispered.

His lips twisted. "Ding, ding, ding. Give the girl a golden trophy. The glaring military mistake that everyone up top wanted to sweep under the rug, including the families who had no husbands or fathers anymore. They tried some great parting gifts on us all, of course. I got to keep Dad's medals. Mom got a great gift out of the deal, too. A newfound craving for vodka."

She moved her fingers to his neck and squeezed, trying to show him how sharply his disclosure moved her. "Oh, Zeke. Oh, yuck."

"That's not where my vocabulary was going, but sure, *yuck* will do." He left her and paced to the window. His steps deepened his confession in their tight restraint. "After a year, she decided she was actually quite fond of that little perk. She wasn't home a lot, but it didn't matter. When she *was* home, she wasn't the person I knew as my mom.

"On my ninth birthday, I had a delicious dinner of Spam on saltine crackers followed by a friendly visit from Child Protective Services. Mom had decided to go to bingo night and took her own 'beverages' to the party. *They* decided that foster care was the better route for me—but the trouble was, I'd had a preview of what that foster shit did to a kid. His name was Kier Montague, and he'd beat the crap out of a couple of first graders the day before. And as we both know, he ended up on the streets anyway. I decided to cut to the chase. I'd already packed a bag for the contingency. Birth certificate, some cash, a couple of bags of Skittles, an easy shimmy out the bathroom window, and I was gone."

"Just like that?" She frowned. "Didn't you ever try to go back, to see if your mom—"

"I went back every night for a year." He slammed a fist to the window frame. His silhouette looked like a furious Michelangelo nude cut and pasted against an Ansel Adams slide. "I scrubbed the house from top to bottom, wanting it to be perfect for her when she decided she wanted to come home and be a family again."

Rayna dropped both hands to her stomach and clenched them. She hated what she said next, especially because she sensed it was the truth. "But she didn't."

Zeke shrugged. "I don't know. The city put the house up for sale, citing abandonment by the owner. After the sign went up, they locked it up like the goddamn White House." He turned and stared at her with finality. "I was on my own."

He turned back. Her stare fell to the ink across his lower abdomen with new understanding. "That's what your tattoos mean," she murmured. "Those are tear drops."

"One for every year between the day I left and the day I enlisted."

Rayna swallowed hard. Her chin started to tremble. The bricks had stopped trying to macerate her heart. They were a pile of useless chunks now, shoved into the corner next to her soul so she could finally see through the dust—at Z's pile, too.

"And you've been gone ever since." It was a revelation, not an accusation, though Z's glower told her otherwise. "You really haven't stopped running, Zeke, have you? Because the only time you tried, you couldn't deal with what it made you feel about that woman. You couldn't deal with feeling for a woman at all because of the last one you ever felt anything for."

He didn't reply until he'd crossed back over to the dresser, not sparing her a single glance in the movement. "I'm fine with feelings, bird. It's commitment I've got issues with, remember?"

A messy laugh sputtered off her lips. She raised a finger high. "Taxi? You got room for one party of seriously confused?"

He pulled out a pair of sweats with ARMY printed down the leg and jammed his legs into them. "I'm going to let that pass because you're angry."

"How about answering to it because I'm right?"

He wheeled back toward her. His stance was menacing, his hair wild as he dragged his hand through the unruly waves. "You calling me an unfeeling bastard, Rayna? I have news for you. I feel just fine, goddamnit. I have eleven guys who depend on me to have feelings and act on them when necessary. Their lives and mine depend on it."

She didn't blink as she returned his glare with a slow nod. "I know," she said. And she did. In the revelations he'd given her, she was able to connect more back to his finality about pushing her away now. More than she wanted to. More than her heart might be able to handle.

"Thank fuck for the day job, huh, Z?" she went on. "No wonder you're really good at it. Makes a nice little paint-by-numbers for the emotions. Take loyalty and brush it here.

Anger is best dabbed there, there, and there. Fear? It belongs right there. Joy waits to get put there. Perfect and neat. Nobody gets hurt. Nobody goes home in pieces in a casket. Nobody goes to bingo night and never comes home again."

He cinched the sweats in with harsh jerks. Every lurch of the movements told her she'd come close to, if not spot-on, the truth. She hated that surety because it put the emotional stick in her hand for poking the puma in the hardest way.

"That's why things were good with Cherie, too—for a long while. In many ways, BDSM is a neat box of its own, right? Even during the short time I was at Bastille, I saw that. There's a code. Manners. Ways of doing things, clear-cut sets of actions and emotions. A plan."

That yanked up his head. He returned his hands to his hips, too, doubling his daunting factor again despite the bedhead and the sweats. "You think *that's* why I'm in the lifestyle? Why I'm committed to making it better? Why I've mentored people in it?" His glower narrowed. "Because of boxes and plans?"

"I think it meets many needs in you," she replied, "the same way Cherie did. You wouldn't have called her Treasure if she didn't. But once the relationship expanded outside the dungeon and you couldn't predict every shot, things got scary. Maybe your heart started to open." When a pulse lurched in his jaw, she affirmed, "Oh, yeah. It opened a lot."

The other side of his jaw ticked. He cocked his head. "Should I cue the Coldplay ballad now? You going to wrap this up by saying how I took a chance with Cherie anyhow and opened myself up, but then she shattered me by running just like Mom? You going to sob about how I've roamed the world a broken man, vowing never to expose myself like that again?"

She shook her head with sad surety. "No, Z."

He dropped his hands though continued to flex them as if stretching out tension. "Good."

"Good? Well, that's a subjective term, isn't it?" When he answered her rhetoric with carefully cocked brows, she continued, "Broken isn't your style, Hayes. Broken means that at some point, you lost control." She didn't avert her gaze from him. "Which means that this one ended with you putting Cherie on a plane back to Portland, promising you'd call the next time you were in town—and how you've made it a point not to be back in Portland since."

His fingers froze at his sides...silent confirmation of everything she'd just spoken. Which made her next words complete agony to utter.

"Guess that leads to the logical conclusion here." She dropped her head, kicking at the carpet. "My own time on the magical Master Z timer is just about expired, isn't it?"

He punched out a heavy huff. "Don't you dare trivialize this. I won't let you, Rayna. Just because—"

"Just because what? I was a 'friend' before I was a subbie? Ooohhh, does that earn me an extra play allotment?" She palmed her forehead. "Shit. Maybe it works the *other* way. Hadn't thought of that. Do I get time lopped off because I know more than any good little Zeke subbie should? Because I've actually seen that some of him is—gasp—human?"

His hands curled into fists. "Goddamnit. That's enough."

She took a step back. Her damn chin quivered again. Fortunately, she felt too helpless to cry. "Yeah. I suppose it is."

Since she'd meant every word as an accusation this time, his seizing her wrist didn't come as a surprise. The way he wrenched her next to him, pinning her body against his by locking his other hand to her ass, was what sucked the air out of her lungs.

"Look. At. Me."

The syllables washed over her face with seething heat. She dragged her gaze up, trembling harder from the intensity stamped over every inch of his face. "I am what I am, Rayna." His lips barely moved. "You knew it when you stepped foot into this cabin with me. Maybe this conversation filled in a few blanks for you, but there wasn't anything you didn't know about what I could offer—and what I couldn't."

She gulped, trying to fight the fingers of disappointment around her throat. "So your point is what?"

He tightened his hold as well as his stare. "You wanted this, bird. You begged me for my domination, though you knew it wouldn't come with forever. You dropped willingly to my feet, *twice*, accepted safe words, and let yourself be bound and commanded and fucked." His eyelids got heavy as his gaze slid to her mouth. "You're also the one who woke me up this morning with your lips on my cock." He scooped a thumb under her chin and yanked. "Eyes still here. I'm not done."

She complied, but not without narrowing her eyes to slits. "Seriously? Because this felt like *done* about five minutes ago."

"Shut up." He shifted his hold, fastening his hands to both sides of her face. "And listen to me." Just like that, the puma sheathed his claws. His touch, now two thumbs that stroked her cheeks with gentle intensity, coaxed her obeisance inside three unnerving seconds. "I wouldn't trade a single fucking moment of it, Rayna. Damn it, I'd give my left nut to do it all over again. You were...so breathtaking. So courageous. So honest in everything you felt and experienced." He pressed closer, tilting her head back, filling her vision with his breadth and muscle and power. "It was a privilege, in so many ways, to be the first one to set your submissiveness free." His whole body tensed as he dipped her head back farther. "You're so goddamn special to me. You know that, right? You'll always be my beautiful firebird..."

"But now you have to put me on a plane to Portland."

The words left her on a whisper. She lifted the tips of her fingers to the edge of his jaw, breathing in his forest scent, soaking in the strength that had made her safe for so long and willing him to deny the searing finality of it.

His thick silence stretched longer.

The crack in her heart widened a little more.

He lowered his gaze to her mouth.

She swore if he tried to kiss her she'd bite off his tongue. Better that than the thousand pieces into which she'd shatter.

He still didn't say a word. Only tugged her chin forward a little more...closer to him.

A loud *whirp* exploded through the cabin.

The satellite phone.

Zeke let her go and stepped back. They blinked in time with each other, as if waking up from an insane dream.

Because maybe that was all this was.

The phone blared again.

"Garrett," he muttered before heading toward the stairs.

She winced and slammed her hands over her ears. That phone sounded too damn much like an alarm clock.

CHAPTER EIGHTEEN

"Psycho Zsycho, at your service."

He hoped the sarcasm would hide the fury in his gut.

Rayna's words had caught him well before the bag at first base. He'd been graceful about it—to a point. Yeah, he had abandonment issues. He'd more than earned *that* goddamn rank. But what about the rest of her rundown? "Boxes" for emotions? "Invisible lines" for his submissives? What the hell was up with all that?

Except maybe...that she was a little right?

Fine. But he was right, too. He couldn't be her training Dom. He couldn't be *any* kind of decent Dom to her. The last three days, having her totally to himself, had shredded any scrap of objectivity he had about the woman. Training her in this condition would be a farce.

What was that lame musical Franz had forced them all to watch one time when they were stuck in Malaysia? The one about the professor who tutored the street urchin how to talk right only to watch the mission go to shit at the racetrack anyway? It'd be like that, only his ponies would run right over Rayna's golden heart. They'd flatten her incredible spirit.

He wasn't going to let her flounder. He'd set the bird free, but he wouldn't let her fall. She'd have her pick from a handful of incredible Doms who'd practically fight each other to the death for the chance to train her. He just had to find a way to get that through to her while resisting the lust to tie her down for himself again.

Tagged out at second base. In a major, shitty way.

They both needed some time. As in freezing-shower, brisk-hike, and then hours-at-opposite-ends-of-the-cabin time.

After that, he'd have his brain twisted on straight again. He'd have a good plan formulated for her, some names of the better Bastille Doms to hand over, and his body wrangled in line with the new program. But right now, even after he'd spilled his guts and let her play jump rope with them, all he wanted to do was get her into his bed and treat her pussy to a nice, slow, tantalizing follow-up.

Not going to happen. Thanks to Garrett's impeccable timing, this phone call was out number three. Inning over. Time to move on and get into the rest of the game as best as he could. Whatever the hell that meant.

Listening to Hawkins chuckle and suck face with his fiancée at the other end of the line was *not* the best helper for his game face.

"Hey, assface. Can you tell your sub to disconnect her mouth from yours for a few minutes?"

There was a throaty female laugh. "I'm all too pleased to attach my mouth elsewhere on his body," came Sage's quip.

He clenched back a string of choice expletives. *Thanks for the memories, Sage.* His mind filled with an image of Rayna's lips sealing over his cock, of her tongue playing with his piercing, of her face lost to bliss as he lost himself down her throat.

"Ten minutes, sugar," Garrett murmured. "Then you're all mine again."

"Mmmm," Sage purred. "Does that mean I should go prep

the guest room?"

His friend let out a carnal growl. "I think that's a damn good idea, subbie."

"Fuck." This was getting worse by the second. Two weeks ago, he'd helped Hawk assemble a truss system in that "guest room" specifically designed for suspending a willing submissive and doing wicked things to her. Garrett hadn't spared any expense. The rigging was lightweight steel with a sturdy titanium shell. The guy could suspend a goddamn giraffe in his "guest room" if he wanted.

So maybe one day, one adorable bird wouldn't be a problem at all...

Knock. It. Off.

As his balls pounded in an attempt to take that order literally, he snapped, "You ready to give me a rundown or not, Hawk?"

Through another interminable moment, he listened to the distinct smack of a hand on an ass followed by Sage's delighted squeal. "Sorry, Z. We're taking advantage of some well-earned free time."

"Really? And I thought you were just getting in a few pages of your favorite Jane Austen tale."

"Actually, Sage has gotten me into Lexi Blake lately." His friend's voice carried a smirk. "You should try her out. You might learn a few new things. You haven't been spending *all* your time catching up on *SportsCenter*, have you?"

"Is my social calendar that riveting to you? Maybe you need to consider a pet, dude."

Garrett chuffed. "Have one, thanks. She's laying out rope in our play room right now."

"Fuck you, Hawkins."

"Ooooo, testy. Is someone discovering a new shade of blue between his thighs?"

He sighed. "Did you really call to discuss the status of my balls, asshole?"

"Hoo-wee there, Grumpy McGee. Man, it's so official. You need a night at Bastille. A *normal* one with a sweet, soft subbie. Especially before we bug out."

There it was. The statement that got his brain firing on some regular cylinders again. "Wait. What? Bug out?" He pushed off the counter and stepped out to the deck. The air socked him like a fist of ice, exactly what he needed to focus fully on the implications of Hawk's statement. "As in, hopping on a transport for a mission? That kind of bug out?"

"Roger," his friend replied. "We have forty-eight hours and some change. Got the text from Franz about thirty minutes ago."

He scratched the back of his head. "Okay, nifty piece of news. But why are you looping me in like I'll be anywhere near the base when the fun gets started? I'm still the official AWOL boy, remember?"

"Not anymore."

His breath left him on a whoosh. So this was what it felt like when they talked about world-sized weight leaving one's shoulders. He was a legitimate member of the First Special Forces Group again—a restoration he had no idea he'd missed. The whomp of emotion in his chest told him otherwise.

"You serious?" It was an effort not to choke out the words.

"A hundred and ten percent," Garrett confirmed.

As fast as it had vanished, the weight returned to his shoulders. He gladly bore the burden this time. Humility and gratitude sank over him like warm blankets after February jump practice over the Sound.

"I owe one of you fuckers about ten cases of beer." He declared it in as dry a tone as he could to hide the depth of sentiment. Like that was going to make a difference with Hawk.

"Shit." His friend strung out the word with derision. "I'm gonna chalk up your lack of manners to the fact that your last scene was with the pain queen of Seattle and now you've lost all sense of decorum. Do I need to give you a refresher course on how we do things? Have you forgotten so damn easily? Repeat after me, Sparky: *there's no limit to the good we can do—*"

"When we don't care who gets the credit," Z finished in a bear's snarl. "Colonel George Marshall. You want the time and date he said it, too?"

"Nah. Gold star in your box, Sergeant Hayes."

"Shut the hell up and tell me who it was, Hawk."

There was a long pause. He could feel Garrett's conflict through every satellite wave that connected them. "It was Rhett," he muttered. "But you didn't hear it from me, you stubborn pud. And I'm taking away your gold star."

An affectionate smile spread over his face. Rhett. Figured. The unit's tech guy wore his BDUs more like a tuxedo and asked for his beers as if ordering a martini on the rocks— but the arena where his style shined the most was any piece of an op involving a code to crack, a firewall to breach, or an intelligence labyrinth through which to sneak.

"Double-Oh-Seven worked his magic, eh?"

Garrett gave an appreciative groan. "Dude, it was beautiful. He found an exterior security camera feed from a building *three blocks* from Bastille. By the time he was done enhancing the footage, it looked like the camera was six feet away instead. There was no denying what happened. The attack on Rayna, the way you pounced to her rescue...it was movie magic, man."

"So the police had no choice about admitting the truth."

"Bastards' balls were nailed to the wall."

"What about implicating Mua in that shit? If he was in a single frame of that stuff—"

"Sure as hell was. More than one frame, too. It only shows the back of his head, but we couldn't—"

"Care about your goddamn lives?" Z cut in. A movement in his peripheral snagged him. Rayna had come downstairs, dressed now, and studied him with troubled curiosity from the other side of the slider. He turned and walked farther out on the deck. "Hawk, are you out of your collective minds?"

"Chill your grill, Zsych. We're not a bunch of hobos on this train." The guy snorted hard. "We didn't take the footage to the PD." His pause practically blared his shit-eating grin. "We went straight to the news outlets with it. Not local, either. I'm talking CNN's crew. And Fox. And MSNBC. Dude, they were more captivated than the day the royal baby was born. You're the newest vigilante hero of the nation."

He let himself sink into one of the covered deck chairs. It was soaked with morning mist. He barely noticed. "Huh?"

"You're practically Batman!"

"Not funny."

"Wasn't meant to be. As a matter of fact, we think it was enough to spook Mua, too. After the vid hit, the Seattle PD had no choice but to issue a public apology to you, hot on the heels of an APB for him. Clearly, one of his remaining inside minions got off a call to him, because one of the private air charter companies matched a photo of him to 'a handsome bloke' coming in right before the security nets got thrown down. They say he flashed a lot of cash for an expedited hop to Tokyo. Third battalion's already in Tokyo, so they're set to intercept once he's there. By this time tomorrow, that scumsucker's going to be carving his legacy into the walls of a max-security bunker."

He scrubbed a hand down his face. "Does this mean we can come home? That I can come back, report for duty, and do my job—and that I can know Rayna will be safe when I do, too?"

Garrett's empathetic hum, possible only from another soldier who loved what they did, was a welcome balm on his overwhelmed brain. "Yeah, Z. That's exactly what I'm telling you."

"Thank fuck." He stood again, welcoming the familiar surge of adrenaline that helped prep his body and mind for a mission. In this case, it also helped him start a timeline for getting some appointments set up for Rayna at Bastille, to meet with the right Doms and talk to the right submissives. Sage could help her with a proper wardrobe as well as the other basics. Gratitude flooded him again. He wouldn't be around to see any of it, which was a damn good thing. When he returned—*if* he returned—she'd be the happy property of a loving Dom who could give her everything she needed and deserved from the lifestyle. And eventually his gut would stop feeling like an overcinched loaf of bread because of it.

"Okay," he said into the phone, "we've got forty-eight before reporting in, right?"

"Uh, yeah." His friend's voice got edged with a weird lilt. "Technically correct—though there's a special project I've gotta ask your help with first, Z."

He cracked his neck. It didn't help clarify the mystery in

Garrett's voice. He let a long moment go by, allowing time for his friend to continue, but mild static was the only sound filling his ear.

"Okay, you going to elaborate any time in the next century? Because I've got every scenario going here from building a gazebo in your yard to disposing of a dead body."

Hawk snickered. "Points for creativity. But I'd rather tell you in person. How soon can you get to our place?"

"Does three hours give you enough time to dirty up your play room and then get presentable?"

"Hmm. It'll be tight, but I can make that work."

"Fucking sadist."

"Takes one to know one."

"Yeah, yeah," he muttered good-naturedly...but the thought hit, as he looked back inside and beheld the tousled, gorgeous redhead within, that right now he was the greatest masochist who ever lived.

CHAPTER NINETEEN

Lots of glass. Lots of light. Lots of white. Mua's mansion looked more like a place that should overlook the waters of Biscayne Bay instead of Puget Sound.

Luna squirmed atop a blinding love seat decorated with a pastel blue pillow. None of it felt right. Why did anyone in Seattle decorate their place like a hospital?

Only one answer made sense. Compensation issues. When a man's fortune was made on filth, it made sense that his household bleach receipts matched the booze orders.

She was getting a damn headache. Her heart began to pound.

Maybe it was her common sense coming back to life.

What the hell was she doing here? Why hadn't she seen the weakened defenses through which Mua had crawled in to get at her? Why hadn't she told him to go fuck himself and licked her wounds from Saturday in private?

Because she hadn't expected to be alone after Saturday. And Mua's smooth, slick smile was better than her empty, quiet loft.

Shit, how she yearned for that loft now.

She needed to get out of here. The whack job needed to find somebody else to play in this sandbox with him.

She'd furtively started looking for a quiet way to get out of here—when Mua's tech guy shut off the speakers that pulsed with the eighties technobabble and motioned his boss to the wall of gadgets, cameras, and speakers they all referred to as "the starship." Luna rose too, thinking whatever suddenly captivated the freak with the teased hair and the psycho killer eyes would do the same for Mua. If she got lucky, she could turn a trip to the loo into a walk out the front door.

Two things stopped her from the follow-through. First, a glance from Mua told her if she *thought* about running for it, she wouldn't be living in peace for an extremely long time to come.

Second, and *much* easier to swallow, tech boy cranked up the volume on the feed to which he'd been tuned. Because of that, Zeke's voice boomed through the room.

"...are you out of your collective minds?"

A rich baritone laugh answered Z, layered over mild static that denoted a tapped phone call. Luna forced her face to remain impassive. Garrett Hawkins. The guy sounded happy for once, something she felt like smiling *and* sobbing about. He'd been through hell to get to his joy with his destined love. She knew that struggle well.

The conversation between the two men continued. Luna steeled every muscle in her body every time Z spoke. It wasn't an easy task when the growls and demands he issued to his friend swooped her mind back to that magical hour they'd shared at Bastille. Her blood sang. Her pussy plumped. Every inch of her sex throbbed.

Mua slid her his I-know-what's-going-on-in-your-panties grin before patting psycho killer on the shoulder. "Excellent work, Stephan."

The guy chuckled as Garrett and Z wrapped their exchange with the confirmation that Zeke and Rayna would be coming back today. "The dumb shits fell for the decoy at the airport faster than orcs under a paralysis spell!"

Luna closed her eyes in order to mask her shudder. Thank fuck Mua hadn't told her to practice her special embrace with Stephan.

"They certainly did," the man murmured. "And now things are falling nicely into place, hmmm?"

Something in Mua's tone pulled her eyes back open. The man's expectant gaze awaited hers. He'd clearly directed the question at her as much as Stephan. She licked her lips fast. Her nerves still jangled, and her heart still stopped from hearing Z's voice again. Her body never reacted this way to anyone else. She was coded for him. He had to see that. He *had* to.

"You're really sure this is going to work?" She leveled it at him as a demand more than a question.

Mua's serenity remained unchanged. "One thing I love about my work is the certainty of human psychology and the beauty in making simple plans because of it."

She crossed her arms. "This plan is as 'simple' as a *Mission: Impossible* script, Mua."

He matched her pose. "The plan will work, darling."

She wondered why his assurance only made her stomach tighten. "And Zeke won't get permanently hurt? Even if worse comes to worse, the damage will be no worse than a Taser jolt, right?"

"We've been over this *several* times, Luna." He dipped his head, looking full of vice principal disapproval, giving her a delightful trip down the path of awful high school memories. "Have I not guaranteed that we'll both have what we want?"

Just like all those times in the VP's office, she craved a cigarette and compensated by squirming. Fine. For all the man's creepy vibes, he was right. Events were happening exactly as he said they would. His insight into *her* teetered on scary, which didn't make it easier to find a damn thing to like about him. But she didn't like wheatgrass shots or cleaning out the cat box, either.

Sometimes life required a girl to suck her shit up.

"All right," she finally conceded. "I'm in. I'm ready."

His reassuring smile returned. "Yes, darling. You certainly are." He moved his hand from Stephan's shoulder to her elbow. "Your bedroom is being prepared for you. Get a good night's sleep, lovely Luna."

She politely slipped from his hold. There was nothing flirty about his move—she mused the psycho killer with his skinny jeans and lush hair would be in more danger—but the man's touch still reminded her of being licked by a snake.

"You know, it's been nice of you to put me up, but I have a comfortable place of my own. I'd get much better sleep if I were in my own bed at my loft."

"That could be arranged."

She flashed a hopeful stare. "It could?"

"Certainly. I'm not a monster, Luna. And you're not a prisoner. In the interest of your safety, however, we'll send Vadim along for the night. I'm quite certain he'd like to see your little loft."

She moved back from him by a step, gulping against a wave of helpless anger. Damn it, she should be used to the stuff by now, but it coiled just as painfully in her stomach as the first time she'd let Mua lay out this crazy plan. But if everything worked...

When everything worked...

Zeke would be hers.

For that, she'd risk a damn ulcer.

For that, she'd let Mua plant a whole cactus garden in her stomach lining.

She raised her head and met the man's refined gaze. Then took a huge breath. Another.

"Which way did you say my room was?"

CHAPTER TWENTY

Rayna had never been so happy to see the gatehouse at Sage and Garrett's place.

The drive down from the cabin had been a giant training game in the art of awkward. And awful. After Zeke filled her in on the jaw-dropping news from the call with Garrett, he'd all but ordered her into a shower so they could get on the road as soon as possible. He assured her he'd clean up downstairs and leave her alone to bathe and change. She'd gone without questioning, though stopped at the top of the flight to sneak in a peek while he wasn't looking. She wished she hadn't. He scrubbed the dining room table where they'd shared so much passion as if it were now a murder scene.

She'd sobbed through every minute of the shower.

Things got even weirder during the trip itself. Z went straight for the Friend Zone as soon as they hit the main road, talking back to the radio DJs with dry one-liners and even asking if she was looking forward to seeing her own bed again. She'd managed an evasive hum as a reply—while her chest imploded and her muscles constricted with the effort not to bawl all over again.

Medically, she knew what was happening. She'd existed on a mental diet of adrenaline, endorphins, and exhilaration for five days, an emotional sugar high from which she now crashed. Hurray, she got an *A* on that test—which her heart immediately pleated into an airplane and hurled. He asked about her damn bed? How was she supposed to *look* at her bed again without remembering him in it with her, warming every corner with his big, magnificent body? How was she supposed to sleep at all without aching for his arms around her, his legs entwined with hers, his lips on her neck?

Was she supposed to think of taking another step as this new person she'd become without his touch to guide her?

The man apparently had an answer for that.

Z threw the subject into the conversation between a bouncy tune by the newest pop-folk darlings and one of her favorite wailing Halestorm songs. Talk about perfect. Or pathetic. Or both.

I like the kick in the face...

She got the rundown of the Doms at the club who'd be "ideal fits" for her.

Just know that I'll make you hurt...

Then the list of things she'd need to go over with Sage, along with "any other pertinent questions" she had.

When you tell me you'll make it worse...

She'd see, he told her. She'd be challenged. She'd grow. She'd be happy. And when he got back from this mission and showed up at the club again, she'd thank him for doing this for her. She'd tell him he was right about this.

She'd answered him by twisting the volume knob higher.

I don't miss you, I miss the misery!

Maybe if she let the radio scream it loud enough, she'd believe it.

As the song ended, Z threw the Jag into park in front of Garrett and Sage's condo.

"Yo, Fashion Sparkle Zekie! You made it!"

Garrett's warm Iowa accent broke into their thick tension.

Sage's squee of delight pierced the air, too. Rayna looked up and smiled. Her friend's energy was always contagious, though today Sage seemed ready to make the jump to light speed from it. Her dark blond hair was pulled into a cute, messy bun, and she wore a butter-colored sweater that enhanced the tawny glow in her skin.

"Hiiiiii!"

Sage pulled the Jag's door open and hauled Rayna into a hug. They pulled away and looked each other over out of habit, though now it was nice to see her friend covered in happiness and a few new curves instead of bug bites and plant scratches.

"Hi, yourself," Rayna returned. "Wow. Sweetie, you look great."

Sage grinned. "You took the words out of my mouth. Hmmm. Maybe Zekie should haul your ass up that mountain more often." Her smile turned into a wince as she glanced over to Z. "And while you're there, you can find a discreet way to burn some of those shirts."

Zeke tugged at the collar of his button-front shirt, swirled with a pattern of bright red and yellow squares separated by blue starfish. "I knew you'd like this one, Sage."

Sage rolled her eyes and tugged Rayna toward the door. "Sure. I'm completely into the 'Picasso meets *Sesame Street*' thing."

Rayna joined her friend in a devilish giggle. She looked back, wondering what her open taunt would incite in Z now, if anything. She hoped for anything other than the fake grin he'd been flashing since they passed Lake Stevens.

He wasn't grinning.

He stared at her with such deep intent she wondered how a hole hadn't burned open in the back of her head. His lips parted to reveal his locked teeth. In an instant, she was mentally back at his feet, kneeling between his legs, gazing at his face as he prepared to lower her mouth onto his body. Bound to him. Connected.

His.

She released a deep sigh. Attempted a smile.

He tightened his jaw and looked away.

She swallowed and told her heart it was time to stop beating again.

That was actually a good move, considering the scene she walked into next.

She assumed Sage and Garrett's living room was still in here somewhere. Yards and yards of dark gold tulle were strewn everywhere. Half a dozen gold urns, at least five feet high each, stood in a sentry line in front of the fireplace. More tulle spilled from them. Hanging on a portable clothing rack near them were at least ten formal dresses in different styles, all in royal purple. On the lawn outside, overlooking the complex's lake and swimming dock, there was a natural wood arch half-decorated in flowing bows of the same color.

"What the hell?" Zeke finally stammered. "You two having a party?"

Every female instinct in Rayna's body shouted the correct answer to that, but this wasn't her moment to spill. She grinned at Sage in expectant glee. The little blonde danced over to her fiancé and dipped her head against his chest, openly imploring him to drop the bomb on Z.

"Dumbass," Garrett muttered. "We're having a *wedding*."

Zeke's face lit up with a grin. "Serious? Now?"

"Tomorrow," Sage supplied. "Late morning, before the snow gets here. Surprise!" After Rayna crossed to her and they exchanged a squealing hug, she added, "Now you know why we needed you two to get back here!"

"Why?"

Rayna blurted it at the same time as Z. They shared a small chuckle because of it. And damn, it felt nice. Garrett and Sage swiftly followed with bigger laughs.

"You really are a dork sometimes." Garrett shook his head at his friend. He followed by clapping a hand to Z's shoulder. "Hayes, you're my best friend. You've saved my ass more times than I can count. So will you protect it one more time by being my best man and making sure I don't fuck this thing up?"

Z's face widened with a soft smile. "Fuck, yeah. I'd be honored." His voice was hoarse as he pulled Garrett into a fierce hug.

Sage approached Rayna with a trio of playful glides. "And Sergeant Chestain, you're *my* best friend. So—"

"I'd love to!" Her voice cracked with happy tears as she and Sage gripped each other tight.

Zeke erupted with a growl while fingering the fresh bandage she'd applied to his back this morning. "All right, all right, now that we've had the waterworks, let's get to the fun." He rubbed his hands together. "Grab some beers, dude, and let's go outside to plot the bachelor party."

"No," Sage interjected. She poked his chest with one hand and Garrett's with the other. "As soon as the other guys get here, you're going to go pick up Z's dress blues and take both sets to the dry cleaners. *Make sure* you expedite the cleaning. After that, you're picking out the cake and the guest book, going to the printer for the programs, helping Garrett with the playlist for the DJ, setting up the canopy over the patio—"

They all laughed when Garrett snatched Sage by the

wrist, grabbed the list she'd been reading, and gave her bottom a fast but hard smack.

"Hey! I wasn't done!"

"Yeah, you were." Garrett kissed her hard, his eyes turning to bright blue flames with possession.

"But—ow!" She squirmed as he dug a deep pinch into one of her ass cheeks. Beneath her breath, she seethed, "You *know* that hurts after this morning."

Garrett gloated. "Uh-huh."

Rayna, buoyed by the joyful atmosphere, couldn't help rocking on her heels and murmuring in a singsong, "Topping from the bottom. Never a good idea."

Sage's stunned stare got to her first. Garrett's was a half second behind. In tandem, they swung their looks to Zeke. Rayna twisted her lips to stifle a chuckle. She'd call him a deer in the headlights, but the analogy was all wrong for Z. By the time she decided on moose in the headlights, he was already directing a recovery grin at Sage.

"Okay, back to the important shit. You're not the least bit interested in planning the *bachelorette* party, Sergeant Weston?"

At that, Sage transformed. Her friend tossed Garrett a quiet, knowing look before responding. "Not going to be one, Z." She lifted a hand to her stomach. "Mommies have to be careful about how they define party, you know."

Rayna was certain her gape was similar to Zeke's. "Oh my God...Sage!" She hugged her friend again. "Really?"

Zeke repeated his own embrace with Garrett. "You humping bunny bastard."

Garrett chuckled. "Yeah, yeah, okay. But now you know why we're rushing this thing." He gathered Sage close and kissed her forehead tenderly. "My family needs to be protected...just in case the bad guys win on this mission."

"Shut your hole." Zeke whacked his shoulder. "The bad guys are going to eat our shit for breakfast. Lunch and dinner, too."

As if cued into action by those words, there was a testosterone-filled din at the condo's front door. Seconds later, even the tulle, the urns, and the rack of dresses couldn't drown the potent masculinity that dominated the air. Rayna felt her chest fill with quiet pride as Z greeted his men. As usual, Tait and Kell were practically attached at the hip; it made sense since they were the sniper team of the unit. Z gave an especially tight hug to Rhett Lange, which made sense considering the guy's technical prowess had saved Z's life—and probably her own. Next down the line was Rebel Stafford, who more than lived up to his name with his sinful black stare and double tattooed sleeves. Finally Zeke got to Ethan Archer, who'd been trying to blend into the wall. Not likely, considering the man often passed for a model with his chiseled features and stunning blue eyes.

She stepped close to Sage. "Are they *all* going to be in the wedding?"

Her friend giggled. "Only Zeke. They just wanted to be here when you and Z got back. And yeah, they'll likely coerce Garrett into some kind of a night out as his last hurrah of freedom."

Rayna smiled, though her eyes didn't leave Zeke. She didn't get to watch him very often without him knowing about it. The way he appreciated each of his men, focusing intently when they spoke to him... No wonder they'd follow him into the bowels of hell if he asked.

No wonder she'd fall to her knees again for him in an instant.

"I think it's just what he needed," she murmured to Sage before releasing a long sigh. "I'm just so glad my brothers aren't on their heels."

Her friend looked down fast and toed the carpet. "Uh, yeah. About that..."

Rayna wheeled on her. "Sage!"

The woman shot her bridal-manicured hands into the air. "They've been calling every half hour! What was I supposed to say?"

Before Rayna could pound her friend with another word of castigation, more wild male energy burst through the door. She inhaled hard and braced herself. The seven warriors watched their legion double as her brothers poured into the room.

Arah got to her first. "Thank fuck," he muttered, yanking her off her feet in a crushing hug. The others piled on top of him, gripping her from four different directions to make sure she was all right. They were all there—minus one.

"Hey," she muttered after shying away from Jenner and his fish stink. "Where's Trevor?"

Her brothers shared a significant smile. They peeled back so she got a clear look across the room.

Shit.

Trev was in the kitchen facing off against Zeke.

She smacked Jenner and Arah at the same time. "Are you freaking insane? I'm sure Sage told you they're planning a wedding here, assholes." She pushed them back so she could start stalking across the living room at her brother and her—

Damn. What did she call Zeke now?

It didn't matter. If Trevor laid one hand on Z and screwed up these memories for Sage and Garrett, she swore he was getting deleted off her phone, locked out of her house, and blacklisted from—

She stopped in her tracks. She was too stunned to move. She blinked hard. Then again.

Sure enough, Trevor hauled Zeke into a huge hug.

There was too much chaos in the room for her to catch everything Trev said, though she caught the more emphatic snippets, such as "saved her goddamn life" and "we all owe you, man," and something about keeping Z in a lifetime stock of his beer of choice.

Rayna shook her head, so tempted to indulge a full laugh. But if that happened, she knew the tears would come next. Fate had a crappy sense of humor sometimes. The very day Z earned Trevor's confidence was the day he didn't need it anymore.

She turned back toward her other brothers, who were still bunched together and smirking like a home transformation team getting ready to spring the Big Reveal on her. "What the hell are you mouth breathers up to now?"

Dallas flashed his sideways grin, putting her senses on higher alert. "If we said we have a bigger surprise, would you believe us?"

She folded her arms. "Define 'surprise.' You guys have used that term for everything from trying to pierce my ears yourselves to inviting yourself along on prom night."

Dallas scowled. "Prom night was fun."

"Both junior *and* senior year?"

It was the retort that pushed at Rayna's lips, only she got beaten out on uttering it by a saucy, slight-accented voice from somewhere behind Arah. A woman's voice.

She gasped. It wasn't just any woman.

"Oh, shit!"

She shoved her brothers from the front while they got jostled apart from the back. When a distinct pair of dark indigo eyes came into view, topping an infectious smile that was surrounded by a luxurious forest of dark brown hair, she let out a scream worthy of a fifteen-year-old. Ava did the exact same. They dived into each other's arms and shrieked some more.

That lasted for all of ten seconds.

Their cries were turned into stunned yelps as they were yanked apart with militaristic force. The qualifier was spot-on, since the force was Ethan Archer. He body-slammed Ava until she tumbled back onto the couch. Ethan followed her trajectory, though the mound of tulle into which they fell turned everything into the consistency of a water slide. The two of them disappeared onto the floor and under the fabric as all seven of her brothers *and* Zeke looked on with a smorgasbord of stunned laughter.

"Nice work, Archer!" Z called. "You got her!"

Rayna didn't bother shooting him a glare. "Ava?" she yelled. She paddled through the fabric, instantly worried when she didn't feel her cousin fishing from the other direction. "Ava, are you—" She froze after lifting a wad of the gold pile to discover where her cousin and the soldier had landed. "Oh my!"

Ava had landed on her back. Ethan wound up pretty much on top of her. Though he braced himself on both elbows, their noses and mouths practically touched. They both breathed hard, looking like they'd enjoy nothing better than getting sealed back inside their golden cocoon.

Envy stabbed in. Twenty-four hours ago, Rayna was sure she gazed at Z like that.

She covered the pain with sardonicism. "Sergeant Ethan Archer, may I introduce Ms. Ava Chestain?"

Ethan's black lashes lowered as he took in Ava's face. "Ava," he echoed. "That's really pret—" He huffed and then coughed. "Wait. *Chestain*?"

Trevor scooted closer. "She's our cousin, man."

Ethan snapped his gaze back. Ava beamed a gorgeous smile. "That's me. Cousin Ava. Nice to meet you."

Ethan glowered. "I thought you were a terrorist."

Ava bit her lip. Her hand fell to the bulge of Ethan's bicep. "Not a terrorist." She practically whispered it.

"No. Definitely not." Ethan's answer was just as intimate.

"You two going to get a room?" Trevor interjected.

"Just not the guest room." Zeke added it with a smirk in his tone and on his lips—while his eyes latched again to Rayna. He was back to staring with that golden fire that made her long for nobody and nothing but him. Half of her yearned to toss the tulle back on top of her cousin, grab his hand, and head straight for the spare room he'd mentioned. The other half was tempted to heave the entire ball at him before strangling him with it.

In the end, she decided on door number three. The frustration, fury, and helpless angst exit.

With a heave, she dumped the tulle mound back across the couch. With another thrust, she got back to her feet and dashed out the slider. Somehow, she got out a believable excuse about needing to get some fresh air. The pretext seemed to stick with everyone, even Trevor.

Everyone except Zeke. *Of course.*

He caught up to her as she hit the packed dirt path that ran around the lake. "Bird? You okay?"

She didn't break her pace. "Stop that."

"What?"

"You know what!" Everything darkened as they clanged through a gate in order to leave the condo complex and enter the woods. "You don't get to call me that anymore. You don't get to call me anything anymore, except my damn name."

"But I've been calling you that for months. Why—"

"Because nothing's the same." She flung the words like whip cracks as she halted and turned on him. "Nothing *will* be the same."

Damn it. Fresh air, her ass. The wind soughed through the trees and lifted his thick hair from his rugged face—and goaded the edges of her self-control. She had to purposefully drag in air in order to keep speaking. "I'm sorry," she whispered, "but you don't get the Friend Zone back, Z."

The words clearly tore into him—and her, too. Sudden and stinging as a fall into ice, the tears came and fell. Her words fell out on ragged chokes. "You don't get to call me 'bird' without me wanting to fall to your feet. You don't get to call me 'honey' without me craving to give you my wrists. You don't even get to laugh at the damn radio without me wishing your lips were against my ear as you do." She whirled, unable to keep looking at the tormented crevices that formed around his eyes, at the corners of his full lips. "And you don't get to keep sneaking those looks at me!"

She heard him take a step. "What're you—"

"Stop! You know exactly what I'm talking about! Those—those stares. The ones you level when you don't think I'm watching. The ones you steal at me when you don't think your soul's listening, either. But goddamnit, Zeke, it's listening, all right. I know it because I have to stare back, and I have to endure looking all the way down inside you again. And when I do, I hate you even more because it's so golden and...and... giving...and breathtaking...and the only one who doesn't see any of that is *you*!"

At some point, she wheeled back toward him. He didn't try to get any closer and actually reminded her of one of the trees that surrounded them, rooted in place but rocking in the wind. "I never wanted to hurt you, Rayna." His voice sounded like shredded bark. "God*damn*it. I'm trying like hell *not* to hurt you."

She swayed now, too. "I know."

"When I get back in a few months, this will all be better."

"Bullshit." She shot him a bitter laugh. "Sir."

"Z!" Garrett's bellow shot through the woods. "Dude, you out here? Let's get started on this list, man!"

After a long second, Z called, "Yeah. Give me five, would ya?"

Garrett didn't respond. The silence spoke his friend's impatience loud enough. Rayna kicked the ground, making messy divots of mud and leaves. She only stopped when Zeke threaded the ends of his fingers through the tips of hers and squeezed. She clenched every muscle in her body to avoid tugging herself into him, begging him to reconsider, telling him they could take this a day at a time, that this was worth trying for...worth fighting for.

"You going to be okay?" he finally whispered.

She forced in a lungful of the icy air. Gave him a shaky nod. "I'll make it work, Sergeant," she told him. "That's what you guys do against the bad guys, right?"

He chuckled quietly and pressed his lips to her knuckles. "Exactly."

"Okay, then."

She just had to pretend the bad guys were her own heart and spirit. For forty-eighty more hours, she was officially at war with herself.

CHAPTER TWENTY-ONE

Z needed a beer. Or twelve. Actually, he needed it an hour ago—at the moment he'd forced his legs to walk from those woods, away from Rayna. But hell, he really needed them now. After nine slices of wedding cake, he was fucking ready.

Only now, there was a hefty line at the dry-cleaning shop.

After he growled for the fifth time, Garrett backhanded him in the chest. "Chill, assface. *What* is your goddamn problem?"

"Oh, I dunno," he drawled. "Maybe I've got diabetes now. Seriously, Hawk. Eight different flavors? What the hell is lavender buttercream? Apple tiramisu? Cake is chocolate, man. Frosting is white. The roses are yellow, and—"

"Goldenrod."

"What?"

"The roses are goldenrod, you cretin. They have to match the napkins."

He would've laughed, but his shock eclipsed even that. "You are beyond pussy-whipped. I can't even figure it out. What's the term for what you are?"

"In love."

He fell into silence. He wasn't arguing with that one. Hell, he didn't want to. "Well played, fucker," he muttered, grinning at the look of total serenity on Garrett's face. "Well played."

As his friend took a second to preen, the line moved forward at last. Two girls moved in behind them, giggling openly. Zeke attempted to ignore their high-pitched titters, but they were gaping right at him. He got in a surreptitious peek at his reflection in the shop's glass front. Aside from the fact that his hair was way too long due to his cover on the Korean mission, nothing was out of place.

The girls laughed again. He rolled his eyes behind his sunglasses. Fuck. Nearly thirty years old, and he felt like a farty old man.

"Um...excuse me?" One of the girls, a little blonde in a tank top that exposed more than it covered, looked up at him with little bats of her lashes. "Can I ask you something?"

Zeke gave her a polite smile. Though he and Garrett were wearing civvies, they carried their dress blues on hangers over their shoulders, which meant they were representing the army as if they stood here in full work attire and boots. "Sure thing, miss." He glanced at his watch. "It's almost three thirty."

The second girl, probably a little older, wore too much eye makeup and an inch of lip gloss that reminded him of the damn lavender cake. "Ohmygawd, he thought we were asking him for the time," she said. "Ohmygawd, that's so humble." She twirled her hair around a purple fingernail. "And hot."

Z frowned. "Pardon me?"

The little blonde let out a sigh. "Um, I think what we're trying to say is...um, you *are* Zeke Hayes, right?"

"You totally are," the brunette insisted. "I mean, come *on*, Jade, look at him!" She gingerly poked his arm. "Ohmygawd, your muscles are way huger in person. And *so* hard."

He shot a gape at Garrett. His friend was already wiping tears of mirth from his eyes. He was getting *no* fucking help there.

"What you did to those two creepazoids on Saturday

night was amazing," Jade gushed. "When we saw you on the news, we were so proud to be Seattleites, just like you. I called my stepsister in Omaha and totally bragged that you're from Lewis-McChord. Your woman is so lucky. Do you think I could have her cell? I want to find a guy just like you, Zeke. Could she give me pointers on how to do it?"

"Uh, listen... She's not—"

My woman. The conclusion clung to the inside of his mind tighter than the inside of his mouth. The syllables wrapped themselves through the rest of him, too, ribbons that twirled through every nerve and muscle and breath...that were all imprinted with Rayna. Her bright beauty. Her cinnamon scent. Her husky laugh. Her pure, sweet passion. She was wound so deeply into him...

And now you're going to have to cut those ribbons out, man. Every single one of them. Soon, goddamnit.

"She's not what?" Jade queried with wide-eyed hope.

Just not now.

"She's...erm...not around. Yeah, uh...we're getting married. I mean, we have *friends* who're getting married. She's busy helping with all the plans. Not here. She's doing it...uh... somewhere else. I probably need to be getting back, too, and—"

"Could we have your autograph real quick?" Lavender Lipgloss asked it with a sweet grin. She was better at the eye-batting thing than her friend.

Zeke glowered. "What the hell do you want that for?"

Garrett stepped forward. "Sorry, girls. We haven't given him his medication yet today. Of course you can have his autograph. Got a pen?" He accepted a Sharpie from Jade and then handed it to Z. "Paper?"

"Don't need any." The brunette jerked down the neckline

of her shirt, exposing half of her full, pale breast. "Just sign right here, Sergeant Hottie."

To Garrett's credit, he didn't spit up any residual cake in laughter. But damn, did his eyes say he wanted to. They glittered with bright blue mirth as his lips twitched, also fighting not to explode with his obvious delight in this ridiculous scene. "Go ahead, Sergeant Hottie."

Zeke jabbed the pen back into his chest. "No."

"Huh?" The girl pouted her shiny lips. "Why not?"

"Hawk, I'm *not* signing that chick's left headlight."

"I think these are what you girls might need?"

Magically, a couple of issues of the *Stranger* materialized in front of the girls. While Z was grateful for something to write on other than their chests, he gawked at the paper's front page and realized way too late that Garrett was doing the same thing. The alt-culture periodical featured a shot of him from behind in the rain, the blood from the gash in his back running down his back. He looked like some idiot off a comic book, an impression that got driven home by the headline.

Batman Lives.

The mire in his gut stirred into a straight-up case of *holy shit* when he looked up to thank his savior.

"Luna."

She looked strange. She looked...normal. Aside from the lavender and silver streaks in her hair, which was pulled back with a nondescript headband, she could've been another pretty girl going about her day in this strip mall. She wore normal blue jeans that were topped with a pretty hand-painted T-shirt that he recognized as her own work thanks to the sleeping white cat depicted at the edge of one sleeve. Even her makeup was subdued. And kind of nice.

"Hi, stranger." She said it with a smile that bordered on nervous.

"Hey," he managed to stammer. "How did you— I mean what are you—"

"There's a great art supply place down the street. But I like the barbecue place in here, so I stopped to pick up dinner for later."

She gave the explanation as he whisked off a couple of signatures for the girls. As he let Jade snap a picture of him and Lipgloss, Garrett shocked the crap out of him by smiling at Luna. Since the second they'd met, the two had been repelling magnets. As soon as they got near each other, their disgust made the earth leave its axis.

"Thanks. Your timing was perfect, Morticia." Hawk added a wink to the nickname he usually flung at her in dismissive ire.

Maybe the earth's axis was doomed again, since Luna actually laughed. "Anytime, Cousin It."

Garrett scratched at his hair, which matched Z's in the thick-and-styleless department. "Ha-ha. Guess I'll own that one, at least for another hour. Then it's all back to a high-and-tight."

"Getting ready for the big day, huh?" She finished it with another laugh, in response to Garrett's stunned stare. "You and Sage were the subject of most conversations at the club last night. Congratulations, by the way."

Hawk's grin widened. "Thanks."

Zeke shifted forward. "As much as I hate to rip apart this alternate universe we've clearly entered, can I ask for a second with Morticia, Hawk Man?"

"No prob," his friend returned. "I'll handle the turn-in while you do that. So hand over the Batsuit, dude. I'll make sure they remember no starch."

"Thanks, Alfred." He gave the uniform to his friend with a satisfyingly harsh shove.

As Garrett chuckled and turned into the shop, Z dug his hands into his back pockets and nudged his head gently toward a little alcove near a door marked *Smoothie Bar Employees Only*. Luna followed his direction without a word, pressing herself against the wall.

Once he joined her, Zeke took a long second to look her over—carefully this time. She kept her head slightly bowed, her eyes fixed on his chest, and her hands gracefully to her sides. Oh, yeah. She had it all down perfect. Luna always did. She was flawless about the stance, the posture, the demeanor, the phrases. Regrettably, she thought that was all it took. Her impatience had torpedoed even second sessions with so many Doms. He'd told her that before, promising she'd always have his honesty.

That promise didn't stop now.

"So...hey," he finally repeated.

She watched his hands as he shifted them in his pockets. Her gaze darkened with disappointment. *Don't think about it, girl. They're staying right there.*

"Hey," she replied quietly.

"I'm glad we ran into each other."

She shot a glance up to his face. "Yeah. Welcome back." Almost like an afterthought, she added, "From wherever you were."

"Luna, about that—"

"Skip it." She held up a hand and curled it back against her neck. "I'm serious, Z. You don't have to do this. I understand, okay? Saturday night was great. Thank you...for everything.

But afterward, I wasn't a priority. I didn't expect to be. You had shit to take care of, and—"

He disobeyed his own damn rule to flash a hand up, slamming it over her mouth. "Damn it, you *were* a priority," he leveled. "Your submission was incredible. I'm humbled that you trusted me as you did. And I would have told all of that to you a hundred times if shit hadn't gone down like it did with that bastard Mua and his goons."

She nodded and lifted an unblinking gaze up through her lashes. The dark purple flecks in her eyes glittered as the late afternoon sun bathed her face. When he lowered his hand, she murmured, "You don't like him very much, do you?"

"To put it mildly."

"Why?"

He peered at her in curiosity. The question wasn't normal for Luna. She wasn't the nosy poodle type. She was the watchful cat in the corner, seeing everything and forgetting nothing. She only revealed her game if there was a worthy treat in the process. That meant he had to phrase his reply with care. The shit that had gone down with King was classified. For all intents, despite the viral video and the news coverage, what had gone down on Saturday outside Bastille was, too.

"Scars," he finally said. "Gashes that are long over but remembered forever."

The glints in her eyes were joined by a wet sheen. "Yeah. I know the feeling."

Zeke winced. The remorse wasn't required of him, but it showed up anyhow. He followed up on *every* play session with a subbie, no matter how big or small their exchange. For Luna, Saturday night had been big. Blowing-up-the-Death-Star big. And he'd flown right out of the galaxy.

"Luna, listen—"

"Didn't I say to skip it?" The cat came out of the corner, damn near hissing the words. "I said I understand, Z. You had bigger issues at hand than my sub drop. I got it, I got it."

He moved in and braced a hand to the wall next to her head. "You have every right to be tweaked. But I have every right to explain."

"There's nothing to explain."

"I had no idea Rayna was going to show up."

"But she *did*." Her lips twisted. "Didn't she? Oh, how lucky for all of us that Princess Rayna chose to grace Bastille with her resplendence!"

He cracked his neck. Why the fuck wasn't that working to knock thoughts properly anymore? "Be careful where you're going with this, Luna."

"Like you were careful on Saturday, Sir? Like you *thought* about *anything* when Her Highness got into trouble? Or did you just activate your royal guard card and fly to her side, hoping to hear her gasp in sweet thanks?"

He shoved away. For the first time ever, this woman really scared him. The vehemence in her voice, fired so completely at Rayna, awakened the grizzly in him. Like that bear, he exercised a choice. Walk away from the provoker or tear them open with a swipe of his paw. He decided on the former before the latter tempted him deeper.

"I'm going to pretend you didn't say that, girl. And maybe you should, too."

He pivoted, only to be yanked back.

"Zeke!" she sobbed. "Please, no!" He caught a glimpse of her crumpled face before she threw herself against him. "I'm sorry." She attempted to hug him, but the move backfired, with her arms wound awkwardly around him. "I'm really, really sorry."

Wetness soaked through the front of his shirt. Zeke sighed and held her in return. Fuck. He was *so* starting to lose his edge.

"I'm sorry, too," he mumbled.

She whispered her desperate thanks and held him tighter. Pain flared down his back.

"Ow." He got the word out on a laugh, half grateful for the excuse to set her back.

Luna bit her lip as she swiped at her running mascara. "Oh, God. I didn't hurt you, did I?"

"Don't worry about it. One of Mua's assholes nicked me with a knife on Saturday. You pushed on the most tender part of the wound."

"Oh hell, Z." She grabbed at his shoulders. "I didn't know—"

"Of course you didn't."

To his relief, Garrett appeared. "Z," he pressed, "we gotta fly. Sage just texted me with two new things for the damn list."

He grabbed one of Luna's hands and squeezed. "So are we cool?"

She smiled, but the look wavered as if her brain was directing her to do something else. Z told himself it wasn't his problem, that *she* wasn't his problem, but he worried. He made a mental note to chat later with Max about her. They'd see each other at Hawk's bachelor bash. The club owner would definitely be there, since he'd be getting his Jag back from Zeke at the same time.

"We're cool, Zeke," she confirmed. She wrapped both her hands around his. "We always will be, okay?"

"You bet. See you around, then?"

"Yeah. See you around."

He turned and made his way to where Hawk waited, the truck already started. He didn't look back. He already knew he'd find Luna still gazing at him. Watching him like the cat in the corner, waiting until her moment to strike was absolutely right.

CHAPTER TWENTY-TWO

"Just twenty more minutes."

The second Rayna said it, her eyes locked with Sage's in the mirror.

They squealed together.

That did nothing to help the warm sting behind her eyes. "Oh, Sage," she breathed, resting her chin on her friend's shoulder. "Oh, my."

She was a breathtaking bride. Her dark blond hair, now extra thick because of the pregnancy hormones, hung in long loose curls that fell from beneath a simple white headband adorned with purple and white wildflowers. She wore a white knit sweater that had gold threads woven into it, tied with a purple satin sash. Because of that, her gown's bodice was simple, flowing into a skirt of multiple lace layers that stopped midcalf in front, sloping to the ground in back. Her shoes, which were actually low-heeled white lace boots, completed the look.

"Sweetie, you're so beautiful."

Sage twisted her hands. "I'm so *nervous!*"

"Whaaat?"

The exclamation bounced through the room, as things usually did when they were issued by Sage's mom. Heidi Weston burst into the room like the doting, excited mother of the bride that she was, her gold dress swishing around her tall body and her joy-filled hazel eyes.

"Mom!" Sage surged to her feet and rushed into her mother's arms. Rayna watched them with a wistful pang. The last time she'd hugged her own mom had been at Sea-Tac, a month after her twelfth birthday. Mom had volunteered for an aid trip to Honduras, then devastated by Hurricane Mitch. Though she'd been immunized against malaria, there had been no time to start on pills, too. She'd died doing what she loved best: helping others who needed it the most.

"Rayna!" Heidi charged. "Get your backside over here, girl; don't think you're getting out of this."

She giggled but steeled herself. The guys at the base's sports bar hadn't nicknamed the woman "Mama Vise Grip" for nothing. Heidi hugged people with every muscle in her body. Today was no exception. Rayna gasped in tandem with her friend as they got squeezed together.

"Heidi!" A man's voice buzzsawed the air. "You want me walkin' her down the aisle or shuttlin' her to the med center for cracked ribs?"

An older, barrel-chested man entered, his uniform decorated with enough medals to trim a Christmas tree. Rayna joined Sage in throwing grateful glances to him.

"Baby!" Heidi ran over to him, foregoing the rib torture in favor of curling herself against his chest.

"Major Boone." Sage offered her hand and a smile. "Aren't you the dashing one today?"

The man's face crunched on a frown. "Sagie Pie, I've known you since you were twelve. Your mother's been wearin' my engagement ring for a year. Can we try for 'Dad' today?"

Sage's eyes glimmered. Rayna swallowed hard, witnessing her friend struggle with the request. She'd shared water rations, dirt cages, and complete life stories with this woman. To Sage, the only meaning that went with "Dad" was the alcoholic asshole who'd skipped on her and Heidi when Sage was ten. In a moment of ugliness that didn't belong with the day, Rayna entertained a secret fantasy that the man had hooked up with Zeke's mom and they'd died of alcohol poisoning together.

Her friend's watery sigh jerked her back to the moment. "How about 'Walker'?" she suggested to the major.

He beamed. "That'll be just fine."

Rayna fidgeted with the cowl neckline of her own dress. The dark purple wool hugged the rest of her torso, including the long bell sleeves. That theme was emulated in the flowing swirl of the tea-length skirt. "I still want to know the meaning of 'Sagie Pie,'" she quipped.

"Another day," Sage chuckled.

The major stepped back and admired her from head to toe. He jutted his chin as his eyes glittered over. "Dear God, Sage," he rasped. "That boy's gonna want to throw you over his shoulder and cart you off to the woods before any of us can utter a felicitation."

"Aww, Walker. Th—"

Sage interrupted herself on a gasp.

"The woods!"

Rayna cried it together with her.

"What about the woods?" questioned Heidi. "What's wrong?"

"My bouquet," Sage explained. "I wanted it to contain some wildflowers from the local forest." Her eyes misted again. "Ava and Ethan volunteered to go pick the flowers, but that was an hour ago." She swung a pleading look to them all. "The flowers are important. Thinking of this place...the lake, the egrets, the flowers...kept me sane so much of last year."

Her voice faltered through the last part of it. Rayna grabbed her hand and twisted hard. "Don't cry," she ordered. "You don't get to cry until Garrett does, missy."

Sage's gaze sparked with such bright green tints, she seemed a mischievous fairy. "You're sounding exactly like Zeke Hayes on some very scary levels, Ray." She broke out in a laugh as Rayna felt her whole face being dunked in the blush bucket. "Oh. My. God. *Rayna Chestain*! We are *so* talking about this during the reception!"

"Damn, dear." The mutter came from the major. "You're right. They really do have a language all their own."

Rayna knew a good chance for escape when she had one. "I'm going to go find Ava and Ethan," she announced, riveting her gaze to the floor as she scooted to the door. If Sage got another look at her now, her friend would detect the truth, *all* of it, in a second. Then she'd end up spilling what had gone down during Zeke's and her own trip to the woods yesterday. The last thing her friend needed today was a maid of honor sobbing for all the wrong reasons.

Fortunately, everything looked different on the path this morning. Nearly twenty hours ago, wind and autumn sun had been slashing through the trees, sharp knives of weather that were so perfect for the pain in her heart with every word, glance, and touch she'd exchanged with Zeke. Their lasts of everything...

This morning, the world seemed ready for a new beginning. A silvery mist floated over everything, turning the world into a hushed herald for whispered vows of love. Rayna smiled as she looked toward the water. As if they'd been summoned by special messenger just for Sage, three egrets flew in through the fog and took position on the dock.

She delved deeper into the forest.

"Ava?" she called. "Cuz, are you still out here?"

That was an instant lesson in unsuccessful. Her voice got absorbed by the mist, traveling two feet at best. Rayna smiled, enchanted by the atmosphere. If her best friend weren't getting married in fifteen minutes and her cousin didn't have the bridal bouquet, she would've gone exploring for a fairy prince and princess—preferably a couple who could order Sage and her impish imagination into line.

"Ava? Ethan?"

She shouted it a little louder.

"Hey, you two. Where— Oh!"

Her cousin and Ethan forced the cry from her as they seemed to materialize from behind a tree. She dismissed the hocus-pocus theory in an instant, since Ava was wearing half the tree in her thick hair and down her back. Her cousin's pale pink cashmere sweater showed off a nice collection of leaves, bark, and twigs, not that Ava noticed. She was too busy catching her breath and forcing her neckline to behave again. Ethan didn't look any less guilty. Rayna smirked as he mumbled something like an apology, pushing Sage's completed bouquet into her hands.

"Thanks." She pushed some of the flowers around to create a more balanced look, blending in the forest blooms the pair had found during their mission. Obviously, that wasn't all they'd found out here. Her grin widened. "Hey, umm, Runway"—she deliberately used Ethan's radio call sign, thinking it would help the guy in the composure realignment department—"you have...some lipstick..."

"Shit." Ethan wiped at his mouth. "Where?"

Rayna looked up to assist with the pinpoint. "Everywhere."

She giggled.

"*Shit.*"

"Don't worry. Cut up the path to the right after you go back through the gate. There's a side door into Sage and Garrett's kitchen."

"I owe you big-time."

She laughed again, but the mirth faded fast as she turned up the path herself. As Ethan headed toward the shortcut, he ducked his head as if panicked. A second later, she saw the reason why. The mist gave up Zeke's distinct form. Ethan had avoided getting caught in his uniform and a face full of smeared lipstick by two seconds.

The close call had nothing to do with her halted heartbeat. Was he even real?

The dark jacket of his dress blues made his shoulders stand out against the fog in broad, perfect relief. His stripes, along with the curved triangle at their bottom denoting his staff sergeant rank, gleamed on his upper arm. His newly short hair turned every bold angle of his face into a proclamation of his power as a warrior and his potency as a man.

You want to repay that favor now, Runway? Make the world go away so I can drag your teammate into the mist and hump him like a naked forest nymph.

They walked toward each other with slow, hesitant steps. Rayna picked nervously at the bouquet as she walked. Hell. Cue the sappy soundtrack, and they'd make for damn great filler footage in a campy cable TV movie.

When he got within a few steps, Z stopped. "Christ." His tone was full of reverence. "You're fucking beautiful, Ray-bird." He grunted at himself. "Shit. Sorry."

"It's all right." Rayna let the corner of her mouth tilt up.

"I'm the one who knows you're human, remember?"

She expected a snarl. She got a self-deprecating laugh instead. "Right. Thanks for the reminder." He lifted a hand toward her but dropped it after a few inches. "You okay?"

She rolled her eyes. "That question's getting redundant, Sergeant."

"I know. But I'm human, remember?" He ducked his head to look through the trees, across the grass at the ceremony site. The string quartet started up, sending the strains of Brahms's Menuetto toward them. "I think it's residual paranoia, too. Garrett's freaking out. Sage probably is now, as well."

"What? Why? I left five minutes ago, and she was only at alert level orange on the spaz scale."

"That was before we realized Franz is a no-show."

"Oh, damn."

"Oh, damn is right. Not often you get to have a CO who's also ordained."

She smiled. "Franzen's a pretty cool guy."

Zeke tucked her arm beneath his as they walked back through the gate. Rayna was tempted to pull away, but he kept his fingers pressed atop hers, a silent order to let him be gallant. It wasn't like he was guiding her back to civilization by the ass. Not that she'd fight him much on that scenario, either.

"Well, right now his 'pretty cool' presence has been missing since he and Hawk traded texts yesterday at lunch. He confirmed he'd meet us for some beers at the Opal last night and never showed. Now this."

"What do you think's going on?" She knew he'd feel better if he could vocalize his strategy. If there was anything she knew categorically about Z by now, it was his allergy to helplessness.

He slowed their pace and lowered his voice. "I think

whatever they're spinning up for us on the mission, it's going to be complicated and dangerous. I think they've sealed Franzen behind closed doors for the briefings on it."

"Crap."

"Pretty much." He glanced to where Tait, Kell, Rhett, and Rebel helped to seat people at either side of the ceremony arch. His mouth became a tight line. "Which is why it's really vital we get our friends married today."

Rayna yearned to refute the inference of his tone. But playing ostrich didn't do anyone good. Garrett needed to put a ring on Sage's finger now. Her future, and the future of their child, might depend on it.

"So what's the plan?" she insisted. "Do we have one?"

"Yep. It's called stalling. Major Boone has a couple of chaplain friends and is sure he can round one up."

"Thank goodness."

They were back at the door to the canopy that covered Garrett and Sage's back patio. Reluctantly, she let her hand slip from Zeke's arm. The next appropriate step would be a cordial goodbye. Z was right. Sage was likely pushing code red in the freak-out department and needing her.

Her brain pounded with what Zeke had just shared with her. *Complicated. Dangerous.*

That meant some of the team could die. That meant Z himself could die. Shit. *Shit.*

When he grabbed her fingers again, she clung just as tight in return.

"Rayna," he murmured. "Listen. When we're out there, I could really use—" He cringed and cleared his throat. "What I mean is—" He stopped again, shaking his head. "Fuck. I know you can't do the Friend Zone. I don't blame you. But it would be cool if—"

She cut him off by pressing her palm to his jaw. "You know where to get me. You know you can call anytime, Z."

The caramel warmth that entered his gaze melted her blood to the same consistency. She wanted to strip right here and take a bath in it—but in her fantasy, she'd only gotten her heels off before Garrett charged up and grabbed them both. His handsome face was alive with a manic combination of emotions.

"Franz is here. I just saw his truck pull up."

"Thank fuck," Zeke answered.

"No shit." Garrett snatched the bouquet from her and passed it off to Heidi, who'd just shown up with a gleeful grin on her face. "Is it okay if we skip your walk down the aisle, Ray? They've bumped up the snow call by two hours, and I want my bride's lips pink, not blue, for that first smack I'm gonna give them."

"Not a problem." She actually blew out a relieved breath. Having to pace down that white runner with Zeke waiting at the end next to Garrett was a pill of heartache she wasn't looking forward to swallowing.

Garrett kissed her cheek. "Good girl."

Did she hear a threatening rumble come from Z's chest at that?

There was no time for the contemplation. After Heidi assured them that the major was ready and she'd personally fuss over Sage's final details, Rayna had no choice but to rush for the altar with Garrett and Zeke. The quartet segued into their processional song, Pachelbel's Canon in D. The ribbons on the altar blew softly. A fine layer of mist still covered the ground. The crowd quietly buzzed with excitement. Rayna waved at many friendly faces from the base, as well as Garrett's Uncle Wyatt and Aunt Josie, whose belly was round with their own child.

As soon as Franzen joined them, everything would be set.

John Franzen appeared, all right.

He was dirty, sweaty, wild-eyed—and wearing nothing but a torn khaki T-shirt, scuffed shorts, and his combat boots.

Rayna joined the crowd in a gasp of shock. She looked over to Zeke, who motioned her to join them on the groom's side of the aisle. As she did, Franz grabbed Garrett by both shoulders, his Maori-tatted biceps bulging with tension.

"Holy fuck. You *are* getting married."

Garrett's jaw worked, but nothing came out for another fifteen seconds. "Uh...yeah. Like we talked about yesterday, Captain? After you texted me the alert about the op?"

Franzen had big eyes, but they bulged even wider. "The *what*?"

"The operation. As in the mission?" Garrett exchanged a look with Z that went beyond perplexed. If Rayna guessed it right, they hovered together in the realm of alarm.

"What mission?"

"Captain." He reached for Franzen's shoulder, but the man shirked him off. "Don't you remember? We pop smoke tomorrow. You told us to prep for heat and bugs. You texted everyone about it, except Zeke—"

"Who I pulled off the AWOL list."

At least the man said that with conviction. But after that, his strong face dissolved once more into confusion and loss. He gazed at the crowd like they were an army of enemy robots he'd have to fight with his bare hands any second.

"Right," Garrett confirmed.

"Which I did an hour ago."

"Which you did over *twenty-four* hours ago."

"Holy shit." Franz scraped a hand over his close-shaved skull. "Th-That's the last thing I remember doing."

Zeke leaned forward. "Before what?"

"Before I woke up this morning." He swallowed hard. "In a room that looked like Shakespeare threw up. In Las Vegas."

"In *Vegas*?" Zeke and Garrett fired it off together.

Franz nodded. "Yeah. *Sheez.* I was buck fucking naked. There was only this shit to wear. My phone, wallet, money, and tags were on the nightstand. I still had exactly ninety-three dollars in cash. Nothing was tampered with—except my phone. When I read the texts that *I* supposedly exchanged with Hawk, I knew some bad wango-tango had gone down."

"What the hell?" Zeke muttered.

"Why didn't you text me then?" Garrett asked.

"After I woke up naked on satin sheets, half expecting some sugar daddy to prance in and call me stud muffin? I had no idea what they might have done to *you*, Hawk. Or if those messages were even from you anymore."

"Valid points," Zeke concurred.

"Christ," Garrett said, shaking his head with obvious disbelief. "How did you get back?"

"In the casino I found a couple of newbs who gave me a lift to Nellis." He fixed Garrett with a dark stare and a tight jaw. "You say I had a whole conversation with you? As in, we talked?"

Garrett nodded. "Franz, it was you."

"How did I sound?"

"Happy for Sage and me." Suddenly, Garrett's eyes narrowed. "But distracted. *Really* distracted."

"Or drugged," Franz growled.

As if someone punched a turbo boost on his focus, Zeke's demeanor zapped from active listener to decisive leader. "Someone needed to completely control your narrative," he asserted at Franz. His shoulders tensed as he adapted the same battle-ready pose as his CO. "Someone who needed you out but not dead, who didn't want the mess of murdering you. Someone who knew you'd be a nonissue as soon as they used you to make us all think a mission was going down."

"But why?" Garrett questioned.

Franzen wheeled around. "They wanted Z back in play."

Zeke didn't return his CO's scrutiny—because his had swung to Rayna. She gulped. His face was full of sharp, glinting fear and a pleading, parted mouth. "No," he uttered. "They weren't after me. They were after Rayna."

"*Garrett!*"

Rayna's body turned to ice as her friend's cry shattered the air. Zeke seized her and dragged her next to him. That didn't stop her from shuddering from head to toe as she forced her stare down the aisle, looking to where Sage now stood—

In Mua's grip.

CHAPTER TWENTY-THREE

Do not let her go. Do not let her go. Do not let her go.

As the self-imposed command thundered in his mind, Z's body shifted into moves his muscles remembered from thousands of repetitions. "Down!" he bellowed. "Everyone down now!"

He did the same but not before wrenching Rayna under him first. Immediately he looked up to locate Garrett, though he could've written the script for what his damn fool friend did. The guy had his gun in his hand and his heart on his fucking sleeve before he took two steps up the aisle. Zeke dropped his face into Rayna's hair, expecting to endure Sage's horrified scream any moment. He was certain Mua hadn't come alone, meaning there was a small army of henchmen ready to drill Hawk full of lead any second.

Sure enough, Sage's cry sprang through the air. It was pitched in pure joy. Zeke gaped as she ran from Mua, sprinted straight up the aisle, and leaped into Garrett's arms. Her shriek was joined by the heavy shouts of his men—Ethan, Tait, Kell, Rhett, Rebel—along with the dozen other soldiers in attendance at the wedding, now with pistols locked on members of Mua's force. Not a single shot had been fired.

Not yet.

"Freeze, asshole!"

Having heard Franz roar those words a few hundred times, Z nearly chuckled at this rendition. The syllables rang with a distinct overtone of glee, especially because Ethan, having tossed his own pistol to Franz, now wielded the M4 he'd pilfered from Garrett's loaded mission pack—right at the middle of Mua's spine.

Yeah, the situation had let's-all-laugh-and-congratulate-ourselves all over it. But nobody did. Zeke glanced around. Everybody was stopped by the same glaring questions that he was.

Why, if Mua's team had the element of surprise, did they all drop and surrender so fast?

Why had Mua simply let Sage go?

Why the fuck was the man even still here in the city...in the *country*?

And most importantly, why did the shiny-suited bastard look more peaceful than the goddamn egrets about it all?

Trying to deduce any answers made his gut writhe and his blood boil.

Because all the answers led back to Rayna.

Mua clucked at Franzen while slowly raising his hands. "My goodness, Captain," he intoned. "Touchy, touchy—especially for a man who's had such a long and pleasant nap."

"Pleasant, my ass," Franz growled.

Mua tilted his head and eyed the captain's shorts. "Hmm. Your ass certainly *does* look nice from here, but do we wish to digress at the present moment?"

Z could feel Franz's blood pressure rocket from where he still crouched over Rayna. She winced and squirmed a little. He pressed a gentle hand on her back. "Bird? Are you hurt?"

"N-No." She used the same whisper he had. "But shit... Zeke..."

"Then don't move a fucking muscle. Do you understand

me?"

She went still beneath him.

"Good girl."

Oh, yeah. That sounded way better coming from his lips instead of Garrett's.

A gust of chilled wind blew in off the lake. Zeke sniffed. There was snow on the air. It was coming soon, and it wasn't going to be light, fluffy, and pretty. It was going to be Seattle snow, soggy and messy—just like this entire confrontation if they didn't soon congeal this walking pond scum into some wrist and ankle cuffs.

Thank God Franz was tuned to the same frequency. Like the pissed-off bronze dragon he sometimes resembled, their CO boomed, "The only place you're digressing is onto the ground, Mua. On your stomach now, unless you want me to do the honors. I haven't dissected a worm since eighth grade. It'll be a lot of fun."

Z snarled with deep approval but didn't dial back an ounce of vigilance, a precaution justified by Mua's reaction to Franz. The dickwad chuckled like a damn game show host.

"While I enjoy your colorful banter, Franzen, the answer is no."

"Is that so?" Franz nodded at Ethan, who loaded the M4's chamber. "I don't think you have a lot of choice here, scumbag."

"Choices are so subjective," Mua drawled, "are they not?"

Zeke grunted, his frustration mounting. "He's stalling!" he yelled. "Get the bastard and his latrine logs out of here!"

His burst caused a noticeable rustle among Mua's men. Though they all still knelt at the ends of his team's guns, they glanced his way with unmistakable interest. Odd behavior from guys who'd just been likened to excrement and were bound for federal prison as accessories to Mua's crimes.

"Ah-ha," Mua called. "Sergeant Hayes. Seattle's newest celebrity. Come out, come out, wherever you are." He concluded with the words that connected him to the motive Z had dreaded behind all this. "And while you're at it, please bring Ms. Chestain along, as well."

"Suck my dick, Mua."

"You both stay put, Zsycho," boomed Franz. Zeke watched him direct the other guys to round up Mua's men and lead them into the reception tent. "These mates will be leaving the party soon." Without taking his eyes off Mua, he called out again, "Ladies and gentlemen, we hope that directive will include you soon, as well. Until we know what mischief our friends are up to, we don't want to endanger anybody. Thank you for your patience."

Surprisingly, that phrase cut loose the opposite effect on Mua. The man released a savage yip, his face twisting tight. "Your presumptions disgust me, Franzen. I'm a businessman, not a fucking savage. Set the peasants free. They mean nothing to me."

"Which is why you'd think nothing of blowing them all up to get what you want."

The accusation made a bunch of women in the crowd whimper. Beneath him, Rayna didn't make a move or a sound. He only knew she was terrified because his hand was flattened beneath her breasts, feeling every terrified thrum of her heart. "It's going to be okay." He pressed every word to her ear in a determined whisper.

"Franzen, you know what I want." Mua's voice was still a lethal drawl. "Let's stop wasting each other's time."

Zeke watched Franz widen his stance and steady his gun.

"Sergeants Weston and Chestain aren't on this bargaining table."

"*Acchh.* Weston isn't my concern anymore." He waved a dismissive hand. "As much as I would relish watching the little bitch scream for the part she played in King's demise, I am, as stated, a businessman. A knocked-up slut is of no use to me." The slick surety slid down to his lips. "There. Now I have sliced your dilemma in half."

"You've changed nothing." Franz took a careful step toward him. "We're done with this bullshit."

"Why don't you let Sergeant Chestain be the arbiter of that?"

"I told you already, asshole. Rayna doesn't come anywhere near this discussion."

"She might disagree with you, Franzen." Though Mua complied with the shove Ethan gave him, driving him down to his knees, his smile didn't waver. Zeke craned his neck, determined to keep watching the bastard even if he had to do it through a sea of folding chairs and a shitload of aisle ribbons. "She might really disagree with you, once she asks Zeke how his little wound is doing."

Z's chest suddenly throbbed. Though the pain was real, it was intensified by the horror that now tiptoed out from the edges of his brain and laughed at him in full, wicked glory. It had been lurking there since yesterday—since the moment Luna had hugged him and *accidentally* bumped his injury. He'd had enough gouges taken out of him over the years to know that a *bump* wasn't supposed to yield the kind of pain he'd experienced after that—but he'd written off his suspicions to the stress of the wedding and the stupidity of being paranoid about everything from hangnails to overly friendly trash collectors.

"Holy shit," he choked.

Rayna threw a stunned stare back at him. "Z? What—What is it?"

He wasn't being paranoid.

It wasn't just a bump.

It hadn't been just an accident.

"It's a chip." He tore off his tie and ripped free the top buttons of his dress shirt. "Holy fuck. It makes sense now." With his shirt loosened, he could finally get at his upper back. He instantly went for Rayna's careful bandage work—and clawed it off. "They got it into me during the bust-up on Saturday night. It was why that round-faced asshole let me go at him with the chain like that. He was using that chance to put it into me." He looked down at Rayna, still so goddamn gorgeous and perfect against the grass, and he struggled to form clear thoughts. Even *one* clear thought.

"*What*?" she demanded. "He put what into you? Damn it, Zeke, what is it?"

He met her gaze directly. "A tracking chip."

"A *what*?"

Her shriek blew their location even if her bolt upright didn't. Zeke grabbed both her wrists, keeping her pinned to the ground at least, but the action didn't help this time. It didn't stop the coil of dread that unfurled now at exponential speed, pulling all his logic from him...all his control.

"They knew we were up at the cabin the whole time." He let her go to claw again at the wound, tearing at his skin, grimacing from the pain but continuing on. "They knew because of me. Every move we made. They were probably watching us the whole time."

Mua's evil was inside him.

Being used against Rayna. *Against Rayna.*

He clawed harder at his back.

"Zeke!" The fear in Rayna's voice drew him back to her. "Stop it! You're tearing yourself up!"

Mua's hearty laugh burst down the aisle as if they'd merely shown up late at a cocktail party. "Ahhh, there she is! Rayna, my dear, how lovely you are. The royal hues suit you well."

"Shut up," Franzen ordered. "Archer, if he so much as sneezes again, fill his ass full of lead and then make your way to his brain. Slowly."

"Roger," Ethan uttered. "Gladly."

"No!"

Before Zeke could move, Rayna squirmed free of him with frantic fury. She threw off her heels and started racing down the aisle. He bellowed her name, making it an unmistakable order to stop, but if the fury in her head matched the wrath of her steps, she was too consumed to hear or care. He stumbled to his feet and went after her. Too late. The little lunatic swept right past Franzen and launched herself at Mua, slapping him hard across the face.

"What the hell have you done to him?" She swung her hand the other way, clipping him with a backhand that made even Z's eyes bug. "I'm here, you giant ball of stinking rat sweat, so spit it out." When Mua didn't make a sound or lift a single finger at her, she seethed, "You think you can get at us with a stupid little tracking chip? Is that your idea of playing rough, Mua? Oooo, I'm really scared now."

Zeke took a stance next to Franz. After his CO assured himself Z was okay, he lurched to pull the plug on the confrontation with Rayna. Zeke backhanded the man's chest.

"Let her run with this." Part of him was proud as hell of her for standing up to the vermin who'd sent his goons after her in the street in front of Bastille. But another part sensed, as deep as the cells of his blood, that Mua had more in this game than tracking them here. The mongrel was obsessed with her. That much was clear now. He wasn't leaving the country unless Rayna was with him. But where was his leverage for making that happen? Rayna had just paraphrased as much, and the confidence of it followed every step she paced in front of Mua now. Z watched every move she made, ready to pounce if the asswipe even swayed her direction.

"Okay, since you won't talk, asshole, I will," she continued. "I've got a scalpel in the basic kit in my car that'll get that ridiculous chip out. Thirty minutes after they haul your sorry, skinny buttocks into the darkest hole they can find for you, I'll have that thing out of Zeke." She stopped and leaned over him. "Whatever your purpose was here—blackmail, fear tactics, I don't know—won't work anymore, Mua. None of it ever did. Your media smear tactic for Z didn't work. Tracking us into the mountains didn't, either. And now, this pathetic attempt at hijacking a wedding is your most stupid idea yet. You're done."

Zeke longed to let out a whoop of triumph before swooping her into his arms and kissing her blind. But he waited. And watched. Something about the subtle quirks at the edges of Mua's lips held him back from unlatching the last chain on his jubilance.

Damn it.

The man's quirks turned into soft chuckles. Then a burst of laughter.

"Oh, little Rayna, how you amuse me," Mua finally sneered. With a teasing bite of his lower lip, he went on. "I thank you for the clever recap of all our recent adventures. But I guarantee this is only the beginning of a colorful journey for us both."

Rayna crossed her arms and smiled. "You're going to prison, Mua. For good this time."

The man released his lip. And returned her smile. "I'm going to walk out of here in fifteen minutes. A car with a full tank will be waiting for my use. And you'll come with me, Rayna. Willingly."

Rayna let out a laugh now. But Franzen didn't join her. Neither did Zeke. The dark snakes in his blood slithered faster, flashing fangs that were set to chomp on him any second. "Fuck," he muttered under his breath. "Fuuuuck. This isn't good."

Rayna cocked a saucy pose and finally quipped, "You going to enlighten me on how that plan will roll for you, Willie Wonka?"

Mua siphoned out a calm breath. "King and I invested some sizable amounts of money into researching new technology for insertable human chip technology."

"Of course you did," she spat.

He let her slur pass with a mild roll of his eyes. "We already knew from the widespread use of chips as tracking devices for pets, cattle, and research animals that the chips worked for basic tracking purposes. Our main concern centered on new attachments for disciplinary uses." At that, his gaze shifted to Zeke. "You, Sergeant Hayes, are the inaugural recipient of such a chip."

Rayna's sass was dynamited by stiff fear. "Wh-What?" Her eyes, darkened by horror and hatred, locked on Mua. "What the hell are you saying?"

The man didn't detract his stare from Zeke. "But you already knew, didn't you?" His inspection went from interested to openly curious. "It feels different, doesn't it?"

Zeke parted his lips, baring his teeth. Did the fucker think he was going to give up an answer that easily? "You used Luna for it," he snarled instead. "Yesterday. Right?"

"Luna?" exclaimed Rayna. "What about Luna?"

"We ran into her yesterday. She hugged me goodbye— in a really weird way. That was what triggered it. It was that goddamn hug."

Mua curved a small smirk. "I admire her, you know. She's a very determined young lady. Willing to do the hard work to get what she wants."

Rayna stumbled forward. Her chin shook. Zeke balled his hands to control himself from hauling her over and crushing her to his side. But he had a feeling, a bad one, even that wasn't going to help this time.

"What the hell does that mean?" she finally demanded.

"Hmm," Mua said. "Let me try to be simple. When your little friend Luna embraced your big lover Zeke yesterday, she officially unveiled the newest phase of our insertable discipline technology. A vial attached to his chip was activated, releasing a dose of concentrated neurotoxins into his bloodstream."

"What?" Franzen barked.

"What?" Rayna gasped.

"Fuck," Zeke muttered. But then weirdly, he laughed. If they were playing on the same side, Mua's ingenuity would actually be impressive. "All right, let me go next," he went on, directing a glare right back at the urbane asshole. "You control the on-and-off button to this thing, right? And as long as Rayna is stateside, the button stays on."

Mua's hands were still raised in front of his shoulders. But with a subtle flick of his right wrist, he got his sleeve lowered to expose a silver contraption that looked like a fancy watch. Embedded into it were a row of buttons that all glowed green, next to a little slider bar. "The slider's position means the chip is set at the lowest secretion right now," he explained, looking at Rayna, "And it shall remain that way, as long as you leave with me right now."

"The fuck she will." Okay, this shit scared him. But it was no worse than a HALO jump behind enemy lines at midnight. Or going home to find out you didn't have a home anymore. Just like those times, he wrapped himself around the defense that saved his ass every time. Pure defiance.

Mua went on as if he hadn't said anything. "If we receive clearance for a flight by the end of the day, Sergeant Hayes will emerge from this escapade with nothing more than treatable dizziness, sleeplessness, and a little muscle pain. If we're delayed or if your friends throw 'snags' at us, the slider gets moved."

Rayna hadn't said a word. Hell, she barely moved. The terrified depths of her eyes spread their misery across her face as she finally looked at him. Her lips shook as she whispered desperately to him. "Oh, God. Oh, Zeke."

He fought for something to say. Nothing emerged but a horrible, haunted growl. Meeting her eyes...he could barely stomach it. She was the monster's property again because of the poison that had been shoved into him. Because of the evil that lived in him.

"No."

It was hardly a word once it tore out of his lips. The letters ceased to be consonant and vowel, more a vehement rebellion that began in his gut and curled into his whole body. "She's not going to do it, you filthy fuckwad." He clutched her close, inhaling her, feeling her, branding her onto the mind he'd likely lose in another second. "She's not yours. She'll *never* be yours!"

With his lips against her neck, he growled, "Because. You're. Mine."

Mua let out a prissy snort. And, as Z had expected, clicked a button on his wrist.

Fuck.

He expected the toxin blast to be like a nuclear drop. A flash of light, blissful nothing. *Kaboom.* Done. He'd either be dead or rocking turnip salad for a brain; either scenario ended Mua's hold over Rayna forever. And Franz and Runway would finally have their legal justification for plowing the bastard full of lead.

Trouble was, the shit was more like napalm. Thick as lava, burning like his blood had turned into the River Styx. He moaned, and it wasn't pretty. It was a messy, shitty hell. He fell away from Rayna, rolled to the ground, and felt a chair go flying from his kick. Inside seconds, he was on his way to a full seizure.

"Zeke!" Rayna's scream tore into his brain like a meat cleaver dipped in battery acid. "Oh my God, no! Noooo! Turn it off! Turn it off now!"

"Rayn-n-n-na." He had no damn idea how his mouth formed the word. "No. *No*, god-d-d-damnit!" Or those, either.

"Who am I listening to, Rayna?" Mua's voice was full of sickening silk.

"Me!" Zeke shouted.

"Me!" she cried. "I swear to God, Mua, if you don't turn it off now, I'm not moving another inch!"

"N-N-N-Not moving anyway." Holy hell, why did he have to have such a high pain threshold? He should be unconscious by now. *No. Stay aware. Stay alive. Keep* her *alive.* "You—not—moving. I—order—it!"

"And I am *not* your sub."

"Rayna!"

"Mua, *turn it off.*"

The bomb was suddenly doused.

His nerves, muscles, and mind danced in gratitude.

His heart crashed in despair. His soul curled up in its own shadows.

"Rayna," he whispered to her from that abyss. It was all he could do. Though the pain was gone, his body rebelled against movement. His mind struggled to remember his own name. Did it even matter now?

It was so fucking cold. Snow fell on his face. Ice, too. No... the ice was his creation. It was formed of his tears, flowing and freezing across his face as well as the lips continuing to plead her name. He was trapped in a glacier of helplessness called his own body. In short, he really was in hell.

For two miraculous seconds, summer returned. It warmed him like an Indian sunset and smelled like cardamom sprinkled on apple tarts. He sighed as he breathed in the bliss of it.

"Zeke. I love you."

Then summer was gone. His sigh turned into a moan. He let it fade to silence as the shadows in his spirit turned to pitch-black midnight.

CHAPTER TWENTY-FOUR

Rayna didn't know who was more eager for the private jet to get here and land, her or Mua. The sooner the damn thing landed, the sooner they'd be on it and airborne—and the sooner Zeke would be safe.

She was certain her fervent glances into the sky outnumbered the man's by now.

Man?

She dropped her head and kicked at the floor of the Spanaway Airport terminal. How had she remotely thought of that word to qualify the creature standing before the plate-glass window? She wasn't sure *monster* filled the bill anymore. Not when she thought about everything that had happened this morning. Not when she remembered everything he'd done to Zeke.

Not when she lifted a hand to the tidy nick at the base of her own neck now.

Her insertion site was small and sterile. No gashes or screwdrivers like they'd used on Zeke. One of Mua's goons had done it in the car on the way here. He'd even used surgical gloves and alcohol.

Just like the woman King had used to put in the piercing between her legs.

She shuddered and sucked in a breath.

Real monsters didn't hack out your humanity in bites. They drilled it out, bit by excruciating bit, with needles.

No, Rayna. This piercing isn't your shame. It's your true medal of honor. Don't forget...

She bit back a sob. She clung to his words, to his voice in her heart, but hated them at the same time. She looked to the sky again, pulled by its numbing gray pallor, longing to drag it over her heart like a giant, dark blanket. *Don't forget?* How the hell did she do anything except remember? How the hell did she take another step, pull in another breath, have another thought without being reminded of what she was—a woman who held the life of the man she loved in every move she made until that plane landed and she made Mua destroy his magic Rolex for good.

The snow turned into a sopping rain. The runway remained bleak and empty.

What the hell was taking so long? Seattle had a hundred private jet charter outfits. It took no more than three computer mouse clicks to order one up.

Exhaustion slammed her. She looked up and headed for the ladies' room. A couple of Mua's men hustled to her side. They were brand-new minions since Mua had allowed Franz to go ahead and arrest the team who'd accompanied him to the wedding.

"Seriously?" she asked them. "I'm going to pee and wash my face, boys. If you want the play-by-play, ask Mua if you can borrow his tracking toy."

The men backed off, though they took up positions on both sides of the bathroom door. She went inside, used the facilities, and then did her best to wash off the stress of the day. Her face and hair were at Broom Hilda status, still streaked and tangled respectively due to her faceplant in the grass beneath Zeke as well as the meltdown she'd had while watching him writhe from the neurotoxin attack. She braced herself against the sink, weathering the violent shivers just from the memory of it. Somebody had propped open the window at the end of the stalls. She stepped beneath it, gratefully sucking in the crisp air, trying to wrap the memory of rain, wind, and pines into her senses. All too soon, her world would be nothing but sweat, heat, mud, and bugs.

She doused that thought by thinking of Zeke. They'd surely gotten him to the base by now, started him on detox from the poison Mua had pumped into his system—and gotten together a contingency in case the monster chose to ram that slider again for the sick fun of it.

The sky roared to life with the engines of a descending plane.

Her chest constricted with a mix of happiness and horror.

"The beginning of the end, Ray," she whispered. "Let's get going."

When she emerged from the bathroom, the henchmen attached themselves to her sides, one at each elbow. Their grips were ironclad, matching the tenacious triumph on Mua's face. He spoke on a throwaway cell but motioned them forward, making it known that he'd watch her board first from the safety of the terminal.

The first goons pushed open the glass door toward the tarmac where a sleek white corporate jet had skidded to a textbook stop. The men tightened their holds and pulled her into the rain.

Despite the icy drops on her skin, her face burned as terror detached her mind from her body. If she consciously thought about her steps being part of Mua's victory procession, she'd crumble in grief. The son of a bitch wasn't getting the satisfaction of watching that.

The boarding door peeled back from the plane. A steward descended the short stairway and locked it down from the bottom.

Just before ten soldiers in full battle gear spilled out from it.

She was too petrified to scream, not that she could have. Both her watchdogs were instantly shot down, their grips taking her down with them. Their deaths saved her skin. She was able to flatten herself as the terminal's big window was shattered from inside. An object had been flung from it.

"Grenade!"

The bellow came in Franzen's distinct baritone. Rayna gasped from the awareness. *Franzen? What the hell?* What was the man doing here, leading a mission that would ensure Zeke's mind was fried from the inside out before they were done?

Now she knew where Z had picked up his big, dumb, and grizzly streak.

She scrambled back toward the terminal as the explosive went off, deafening her as it blew a hole into the pavement and set the service shed on fire. But she didn't stop her frantic crawl back to Mua. She huffed in desperation, begging fate that she wasn't too late to stop the monster from throwing the switch on Zeke.

Past the ringing in her ears, she heard Franzen yell again. "Rayna, no! Goddamnit, Chestain, don't you dare go back—"

She jerked open the door. "I'm not *your* sub, either," she said under her breath.

The second she clambered back inside, Mua jerked her to her feet. His hair tumbled into his face. His nostrils were wide, his teeth were bared. "What the *fuck* is this?"

"You think I have a clue?" She fought to jerk back. Being this close to him nauseated her. "I haven't peed without you knowing about it, Jabba the Hut. Tell me when I've had a chance to coordinate shit like this."

Mua coiled his hand into her hair. "Your sarcasm is not attractive, my dear. You'll soon learn to bite that pretty tongue of yours. We'll start with a lesson right now—and I know just the person to help you learn it. Let's hope Sergeant Hayes is up for the task."

"No." She croaked it. "Please! Mua—"

The rest of it died before it reached her lips. Shock was a damn good mute button. "Huh?" she finally rasped, blinking at the contraption on the man's right wrist. Though it was still silver and still sported all the mechanisms Mua had unveiled this morning on Garrett and Sage's lawn, nothing was lit. The thing was no better than a fancy stage prop.

"What the fuck?" Mua repeated.

"Hey, Mua."

The saucy taunt, issued from the back of the small waiting room, captured Rayna's curiosity as much as the man who held her. She rapidly altered the perception. Mua wasn't curious. He was horrified.

Guess that was how monsters looked when the real version of their favorite play toy was transformed into a twisted piece of expressionist art—and dangled from the fingers of a catsuit-clad woman with a matching feline smirk.

"Looking for this?" Catwoman teased. She tossed her chin with a purring *tsk*. "You boys are so stupid about where you put your gadgets when you shower. Somebody could come along and tamper with them so easily."

"Luna." Both syllables were twists of raw rage. "What the *hell* have you done?"

"No shit," Rayna seconded. Her own reaction to the woman's appearance was an unnervingly mixed bag. She couldn't believe this long-legged hybrid of Lara Croft and fetish fatale was the same meek, spaced-out subbie she'd seen at Bastille less than a week ago—or the woman so desperate to get Zeke for her own, she'd done Mua's dirtiest work for him.

"What I should have done yesterday," Luna declared. "Or for that matter, the day before. It's called the right thing, Mua, and I'm doing it now."

Mua erupted with a snarl. "You fucking fool!" His fingers tightened against Rayna's scalp. "What's done is *done*, Luna."

"No." She threw the chip controller down and then crushed it beneath her boot. "It's not done. I was listening this morning, asshole. At the mansion, when all of you boys were off having your fun at the wedding, I engaged the radio capability on your phone. Yeah, guess what? Dorky little Luna knows a thing or two about all that technical shit, too. I heard it all, Mua. I listened to every second of what you did to Zeke." Her face contorted. "You said it would be simple. You said he'd suffer nothing worse than a Taser hit!"

"You have no idea what you're talking about." His breaths, harsh and desperate, resounded in Rayna's ear. "You weren't there, you little idiot. You have no idea—"

"I have *every* idea." She hooked a heel beneath the mangled machinery and kicked high, sending the thing through the window he'd broken with the grenade. "You tortured him, you goddamn monster. I listened to every disgusting second." Her glare gleamed with brilliant purple fury, though tears glistened when she shifted her focus to Rayna. "And I listened to what it did to you, Rayna." A heavy swallow moved down her throat. "And I heard what you told him."

Rayna gulped, too. She didn't know what to do with that. Was it supposed to encourage her? Scare her? Luna talked about the right thing, but yesterday, the woman's idea of that was the pain-slut's version of a Judas kiss. *Come here, Zeke. This neurotoxin will only hurt for a second, and then we can be together forever.*

"I was wrong." Luna spoke it to her with the conviction of knowing just where Rayna's thoughts had gone. "About all of it. What I did for him—what I did *to* him—wasn't love."

Mua cut in with a biting laugh. "Very sweet, darling. But very late. *Too* late. What you did, despite your charming crisis of integrity, is going to land you in prison."

"I know." Luna gave him another saucy smile just as a handful of soldiers burst through the back entrance of the terminal, filling in behind her. "But unlike you, Mua, I'm going to look damn good doing it." She flipped her ebony hair with the confidence of a rock star before hiking herself onto one of the snack bar tables and thrusting her wrists forward. "Cuff me, guys. And if you want to spank me on the way to the courthouse, I won't mind a bit."

It was done. Game over. Rayna only wished someone in the room would convince Mua of that. As the team advanced on them, he hurled her away. Her head snapped around as she fell to the floor. Sights flew past her vision in a blur. Mua's features, warped with outrage. The sweat running down his neck. The tension of his fingers as he curled them in a fist. The violence in his body, heaving with every word he roared. "You stupid twit! You mindless, witless slut!"

His shrieks tore through the room. They impacted Rayna

like underwater explosions. The whole room suddenly seemed submerged, a frustrating lethargy against the terror of her new realization.

Mua's hand wasn't curled in a fist.

It was curled around another grenade.

"Nooooo!"

She screamed it a second too late. Two soldiers tackled Mua the instant after he pulled the pin and threw the grenade, a fastball that landed the thing beneath the table where Luna was still preening for her soldiers.

She didn't think. She lunged toward Luna and grabbed her with both hands. The two soldiers, who now saw the pineapple themselves, helped continue her momentum out the terminal's back door.

There was a terrible, consuming boom. Searing heat. Biting pain. Noise, so much noise and chaos. She tumbled and hit the ground. The soldiers shouted. *Assets down! Assets down!*

Then the cold came. The chasm loomed, threatening to swallow her. She shuddered, shaking her head, mentally skittering back from the edge of that hole. "Don't want to go," she protested. "Don't make me go. Don't make me—"

"Rayna." The voice was firm, forceful. "Can you hear me? It's Franz. Are you with me, sweets?"

Her head pounded from her chattering lips. "Don't make me go. Don't make me—"

"It's gonna be okay, Rayna. Do you hear me? Hang on, damn it!"

Sirens and horn blares. Shouts and orders. Thunder and the din of pouring rain. None of it made the black pit go away. None of it pulled the icebergs from her blood or the glaciers from her muscles.

"Ray-bird."

A sigh caught in her throat. Escaped her in quaking spurts. She wanted to think she wasn't dreaming. She wanted to think the envelope of his arms was real. She wanted to think he was really whispering against her forehead, kissing her eyelashes, brushing the warmth of his breath across her face.

Maybe if she kept her eyes closed and imagined they were back in that tunnel in the park again and he was chasing away Kier for her again...

No. They were back in the jungle, and he was carrying her to safety again.

No. They were in the middle of an enchanted forest, and he was saving her sanity again.

"Hayes, you have *not* just defied the dozen orders I issued for your ass to stay put in that hospital bed?"

"My ass was all about toeing that line, Captain. But it is regrettably attached to the rebellious rest of me." A mouth, warm and full, dipped to her ear and whispered, "Namely my heart, which really needs to tell you that I love you, too, Rayna Chestain."

A soft sob spilled off her lips. She opened her eyes. He was still here. He was still alive. He was still real.

He slid his lips across her cheek, brushing them across her mouth before going on, "Just to be clear, the fact that I love you doesn't get you out of how I'm going to open you up for that damn fool stunt with the grenade."

He was still her hero.

CHAPTER TWENTY-FIVE

"Eat your JELL-O."

Zeke parked himself on Rayna's hospital bed, grinning at the fact that he weighed down the mattress enough to roll her closer to him, and shoved a spoonful of the wobbling red food at her. He also tried to ignore the fact that her answering pout all but begged him to kiss her instead of feed her.

"*Rayna.*"

"No!"

"Are we going to do this again?"

"I'm sick of the damn JELL-O."

"Eating the damn JELL-O's going to get you out of here."

"You only had three days of this shit. I'm going on day number seven here, Hayes."

"I didn't run to save Luna Lawrence from a fucking grenade, Chestain."

She stuck her tongue out at him and tried to roll away. Zeke caught her by the waist and yanked her back. Frustration was painted across her adorable face, and understandably so. She'd been forced to do most things in this side position because of how the blast had caught her. She and Luna had cleared the terminal's back door before the grenade blew, but that hadn't stopped huge chunks of the wall from getting her. Everything between her nape and tailbone was pretty much a mess.

It could have been worse. Much worse. If she'd tripped or stopped...or been delayed by even another second...

He gulped hard while tightening his hold by a few careful degrees.

"Luna's the reason you're alive and I'm not chained up in some jungle shithole, you dork." She poked him in the chest. He would have growled, but she lingered her touch, using a finger to trace the outline of his dog tags through his T-shirt. "She did the right thing in the end," she went on in a more sober tone. "She went to Franz and worked with him to nail Mua." She turned a hopeful glance up at him. "Did you talk to her guards? Is she okay?"

"She's doing well," he assured her. "She got buried beneath you in the blast. They're actually releasing her to the prison infirmary today."

Her smile made her face dance in new beauty. Z was tempted to go silent and simply stare at her, but he'd come here to say some things to her. Things that couldn't wait any longer.

"You shouldn't have been in that grenade blast with her, Rayna."

"Z–"

"You should have heeded me at Garrett and Sage's."

"Really? And let that bastard deep fry your nervous system?"

He rolled his eyes. "That wasn't going to happen."

She dug a knuckle into his chest now. "The hell it wasn't!"

He yanked aside her hospital gown to seize the skin at her hip. At the same time, he stretched his body down the bed, lying fully next to her. "You disobeyed me, Rayna."

Her lips pursed. The skin-to-skin contact accomplished his intent. He had her full attention. "I wasn't yours to command."

"As you clearly informed me." He flexed his inside hand

against her jaw, nudging her face up. Their gazes locked. He took full, glowering advantage. "I didn't like it."

She didn't respond to that in words. But her eyes returned his penetrating favor, saying so much more. They were perfect and lush and green, reminding him of the oaks in that park the day he'd taken her from Kier...the palms in the forest the night he'd taken her from King...and the pines of the mountains where he'd taken her for himself.

That reflection stirred the next words to his lips. "I didn't like it," he repeated, "and I don't want it to happen ever again."

Her brows lowered, a pair of dark strawberry slashes over her darkened gaze. "Oh? And how do you propose that prevention, Sergeant Hayes?"

His grasp on her jaw intensified. "For starters, you'll stop calling me Sergeant Hayes. And you'll start calling me Sir."

Her brows shot back up. Her jaw popped open, letting her throat release stunned gasps past her cute pink lips. She almost made him snicker with her gorgeous case of shocked shitless. Fortunately, he was preoccupied with pulling out the thin black leather collar he had coiled in his back pocket. He straightened it so the single, delicate flame-shaped drop was centered at the front as he slipped it around her throat.

"This," he explained, "will help you remember, firebird."

Her lips slammed shut as she gulped hard. "F-Firebird?" she stammered.

"Yeah." It resonated with the warmth that suffused his chest as his heart sped up with anticipation. "That's what *I'm* calling *you* from now on." He pulled gently on the red-and-amber gem. "Master Z's subbie needs more than a collar. You'll bear the name I give you, too. It's pretty fucking perfect anyhow, yeah?"

Her jaw opened and shut a bunch more times. "Zeke," she finally blurted, "wait. Are you really—"

He cut her short with a deep growl and a tongue-tangling kiss. "Don't you dare ask me if I'm serious," he issued when they broke apart. He slid his hand beneath her panties, going for an open grope of her warm, firm ass. "That question, that doubt, doesn't belong here. Not between you and me." He lowered his head, biting at her mouth with savage possession. "Rayna Eleanor Chestain, you are *mine*. You have been mine for fifteen years. Fate had to kick me in the fucking teeth to show me, but I'm never ignoring that bastard again." He loved watching her tearful giggle at that. He kissed her softly again before whispering, "I'm going to care for you and cherish you, honey. I'm going to spoil you and pleasure you. I'm going to give you everything you want, but not before you get what you need. And yeah...I'm going to dominate you in every way you'll let me."

She sighed and gave him the gift of her glimmering smile. "Yes, Sir."

Zeke took her lips in a longer, deeper kiss. As he did, he trailed his hand under the cotton that draped her sex, letting his fingers drift into the heated crevice where her thighs joined. "Mmmm," he growled. "Say it again."

"Yes," she offered, so utterly sexy, so completely free...his bird taking flight on the wings of her surrender. "Yes always, Sir." She moaned as he slid in a finger, claiming the most sensitive ridge of her wet, pulsing pussy. As she threaded her fingers into his cropped hair, she exclaimed, "Oh my God... once I'm out of here, I can't wait to get started!"

He dipped his lips to her jawline. "Who says we're waiting until you get out?"

"Whaaat?"

"My collar is on your throat, firebird. You've said yes. Your submission to me *re*starts now."

She stiffened a little with nervousness, though the tissues beneath his fingers turned even more moist and plump. "Y-Yes, Sir."

"Good girl," he crooned. *Shit*, he loved saying that to her. "Now raise your leg and rest it on top of mine. That'll open up your lovely cunt for me." He realigned their mouths so he could give his next command in a murmur only she could hear. "I'm going to fuck you with my fingers, firebird—and you're going to let me. You're going to get slick and wet and hot, and then you're going to come for me right here in this bed, in this room. Do you understand?"

It took her a full ten seconds to reply, since he didn't relent the pressure on her clit at all. "Oh, God! Yes, Sir!"

He tried to start out slow, but once he got inside her, she gripped his fingers with such tight heat and quivering need, it was a Herculean effort not to unzip, free his cock, and push inside her that way instead. They both breathed hard as he pumped into her with two and then three fingers, hooking the tips to get at the secret spot deep inside that made her pull at his hair with wild need.

With a violent keen and a feminine grunt, she broke apart in his arms. Her body clamped on his fingers. She moaned hard against his neck. Her tears soaked his shirt.

Many minutes later, he gently withdrew and used the tissues from her nightstand to clean her up. When he'd finished that and righted her gown and blankets, she tugged him next to her again. He lowered the bed so he could stretch his arm along her pillow and cradle her head in the crook of his elbow. The entire time, the impish intent in her eyes didn't dim.

"All right," he charged with a chuckle, "what the hell are you thinking now?"

Rayna bit her lip and grinned. "It was more a question than a thought."

His lips curled up. He played with the ends of her magnificent, fire-colored hair and stroked the light cream column of her neck. It struck him now why the idiot prince in the ballet had let the firebird fly free. The dumbass was afraid—though in many ways, Z got that now. When a man held magic in his hands, it was rough to feel anything *except* afraid.

But a brave man learned to live with the fear.

He pushed through it every step of the journey, every minute of the day, every moment the ghosts came and tried to tell him how he wasn't brave enough, strong enough, or good enough for the magic.

And he always remembered that the bird had landed in *his* hands.

Trusted *him* with her heart. Given her magic exclusively to *him*.

And that made him the bravest fucking warrior on the face of the planet.

His grin split wider. He traced the outline of her mouth with the pad of his thumb. "Hmmm," he issued, making it half a growl. "Ask away, magic bird."

She giggled softly, snuggling closer. "The next time we do that, will you handcuff me first?"

A laugh filled his chest. He slid his finger off her lips so he could mold his mouth to hers, claiming her with all the passion that filled his soul and the love that consumed his spirit.

"Sure can, honey. We'll just use the ones you've locked forever on my heart."

Continue the Honor Bound Series with Book Three

Seduced

Available Now!

ALSO BY ANGEL PAYNE

The Misadventures Series:
Misadventures with a Super Hero
Misadventures of a Time Traveler

Honor Bound:
Saved
Cuffed
Seduced
Wild (January 2018)
Wet (February 2018)
Hot (February 2018)
Masked (February 2018)
Mastered (Coming Soon)
Conquered (Coming Soon)
Ruled (Coming Soon)

**For a full list of Angel's other titles,
visit her at www.angelpayne.com**

ACKNOWLEDGMENTS

As you all know, Zeke and Rayna's story holds a special place in my heart. It's really the story that busted me beyond so many comfort levels, but what an epic and awesome ride it was for both the first edition as well as this new Waterhouse release.

On that note, I cannot let a chance go by to thank the entire team at Waterhouse Press for believing in "The Boys" enough to give them a shiny new burst into the world. It's an amazing feeling to have your support and belief in each wild ride of this world!

So many hugs and love for the incredible people who have loved this story from the start and have taken countless hours out of their lives to give the feedback that made the story shine. Shannon Poole and Tracy Roelle, your loving honesty has *always* meant—and continues to mean—the world to me. So much love and thanks to the original editing team on the book too: Jacy Mackin and Meredith Bowery, you both rock! A huge note of thanks to Scott Saunders, who gave this version the extra sheen it needed!

Most of all, thanks to every reader who has believed in the wild, passionate Honor Bound men from the beginning—and to those of you taking a chance on a new series and joining us now, too! You all are so special, and I appreciate you beyond measure.

Thank you!

ABOUT ANGEL PAYNE

USA Today bestselling romance author Angel Payne loves to focus on high-heat romance starring memorable alpha men and the women who love them. She has numerous book series to her credit, including the Suited for Sin series, the Cimarron Saga, the Temptation Court series, the Secrets of Stone series, the Lords of Sin historicals, and the popular Honor Bound series, as well as several standalone titles.

Angel is a native Southern Californian, leading to her love of being in the outdoors, where she often reads and writes. She still lives in Southern California with her soul-mate husband and beautiful daughter, to whom she is a proud cosplay/culture con mom. Her passions also include whisky tasting, shoe shopping, and travel.

Visit her here:
www.angelpayne.com